-winning author **Jennifer Faye** pens fun, heart-
ng, contemporary romances, filled with rugged
ys, sexy billionaires and enchanting royalty.
tionally published, with books translated into
ni nguages, she is a two-times winner of the
RT ok Reviews Reviewers' Choice Award. She has
also n the CataRomance Reviewers' Choice Award,
been amed a TOP PICK author, and has been nomi-
nated or numerous other awards.

a Senate has written many novels for Mills &
nd other publishers, including her debut, See *Jane*
vhich was made into a TV movie. She also wrote
books for Mills & Boon True Love line under the
ame Meg Maxwell. Her novels have been
hed in over twenty-five countries. Melissa lives on
ast of Maine with her teenage son; their rescue
erd mix, Flash; and a lap cat named Cleo. For more
nation, please visit her website, melissasenate.com

HER CHRISTMAS PREGNANCY SURPRISE

JENNIFER FAYE

A WYOMING CHRISTMAS TO REMEMBER

MELISSA SENATE

MILLS & BOON

First Published in Great Britain 2019
by Mills & Boon, an imprint of HarperCollinsPublishers,
1 London Bridge Street, London, SE1 9GF

Her Christmas Pregnancy Surprise © 2019 Jennifer F. Stroka
A Wyoming Christmas to Remember © 2019 Melissa Senate

ISBN: 978-0-263-27268-0

1119

Printed and bound in Spain
by CPI, Barcelona

HER CHRISTMAS PREGNANCY SURPRISE

JENNIFER FAYE

PROLOGUE

October...
Ross Tower, New York City

Was this really happening?

An invitation to one of the most exclusive parties in New York City. It didn't get much better than this.

Okay, it wasn't quite an invitation. Still, she was here among the crème de la crème of New York society—actresses, models, politicians, and the list went on. How she got here shouldn't matter, right?

And, okay, she just happened to be one of the waitstaff. Not an actual guest. But still, this wasn't just any party. This was Simon Ross's party at the top of the tower. She stifled a squeal of delight as she considered pinching herself just to make sure this was real.

Pepper M. Kane resisted the urge, but barely. After all, she had landed—correction, her bakery had landed—this prime opportunity, and she wasn't going to do anything to ruin it or her reputation. If she could make a good impression here, the connections and possibilities were endless.

By the end of the party, she'd handed out countless business cards. Her cheeks were sore from smiling so much. And her feet ached from the heels she'd decided to wear instead of her usual flats. She couldn't wait to get home, curl up on the couch and put on an old black-and-white movie from her ever-growing collection.

There were still a few lingering guests, not to mention the host—the very sexy host. Her gaze moved across the

spacious conference hall. There stood the man himself.
More than six feet of tall dark sexy goodness.

She clearly remembered their first meeting this past
summer. It had been very early one morning when Simon
had strolled into the Polka Dotted Bakery. It had been just
like any other day when her life started to change. There
had been no lightning strikes and no earthquakes, but his
entrance into her life had caused ripples through her heart.

At the time, she'd thought he was just another customer.
Well, not just any customer—he'd been the only customer
at that early hour. Even the sun hadn't risen yet.

Pepper remembered quite clearly that particular morning. She'd been working the front counter when he'd
stepped up to the glass display case to peruse the baked
goods, from croissants to donuts to cookies and everything else in between. He'd chatted with her about her
selection of donuts. And then he'd ordered two coffees,
plus two cherry turnovers. After he paid for them, he'd
handed her the second coffee and the extra turnover. No
one had ever done something like that for her before. She
was truly touched.

He had a billion-dollar smile that could melt the frosting right off Pepper's triple-chocolate cupcakes. And he
had these dreamy espresso brown eyes that she could stare
into the entire day. With his short-styled hair and designer
suit, he could easily grace the cover of any magazine or
romance book.

The longer she talked to him, the more she'd noticed
that he had something weighing on his mind. Pain flared
in his eyes. It touched her, and though they were strangers,
with her staff handling things in the kitchen, she'd invited
him to sit and drink his coffee with her.

He hadn't said much at first, but as one thing led to another, their conversation deepened. And then he'd revealed
that he'd just received news that a childhood friend had
died. Pepper never thought anything good would come

from losing her mother and grandmother, but she was able to draw upon that experience to give some sort of comfort to Simon. It was as though that morning they'd formed a bond—a bond forged in loss and wrapped in hope.

And so for the past five months, Simon had been stopping by the bakery at least once a week early in the morning for two large black coffees and two cherry turnovers. Pepper looked forward to those mornings as they chatted about current events, the bakery or whatever was on their minds. She had made a new friend—a good friend.

And then out of the blue, he'd offered her the opportunity to cater for the Ross Toys expansion party. At first, he'd caught her off guard, as they hadn't exchanged last names. But when she found out he was Simon Ross of Ross Toys she was left speechless. For Pepper, it was a crowning achievement. Ross Toys was one of the biggest businesses in the country.

Today Mr. Ross, as she insisted on calling him at the party, was the host and she was the baker. Today they were not coffee mates or friends. They each had a job to do—expectations to be met. The announcement of a new chain of stores had been made to the world—Ross Pet Playground. Speeches had been made. Thank-you's had been issued. And predictions were bandied about while Pepper and her staff kept the trays on the buffet table filled.

Pepper had just returned from helping her staff load the empty trays into the delivery van. With both employees and the carts, the van was full. She'd sent her staff back to the bakery to unload and then head home. She'd driven separately, but before leaving, she had to finish cleaning up.

She rushed in the back door and came to an abrupt halt. There stood Simon Ross not more than ten feet from her. He wasn't just another New York City businessman. He had been voted the city's sexiest bachelor, as well as Business Person of the Year, in addition to being CEO and founder of Ross Toys. He was quite a package for some lucky lady.

At the moment, he was deep in conversation with another man in a similar dark suit and tie. Before she could discreetly make it past the men, Simon's gaze met hers. It was only for the briefest of moments, but it was long enough for her heart to start racing. Heat rushed to her face. What was wrong with her? Why couldn't she treat him like any other client?

A mocking voice inside her head said it was because he wasn't like any other client. He'd started off as her friend. And then there was the part about him being smoking hot. She didn't know a man could look that good in a suit.

She moved to the buffet tables, finding them still covered with fine white table linens and a cake platter. She lifted the end of a long white linen—

"Would you like a hand?"

She didn't have to turn around to know that deep, smooth voice belonged to none other than Simon. Her stomach shivered with nerves. She glanced over her shoulder as he moved next to her. "Thanks. But I've got this. Don't you have to tell your guests good-night?"

He frowned.

"I'm sorry." That hadn't come out like she'd intended. "I didn't mean to sound dismissive. I just don't want to take you away from your guests."

"They've all gone now." A smile returned to his very handsome face, making her heart beat faster. "So tell me, what needs to be done?"

Pepper could fold the cloth herself. She'd done it countless times in the past, but she'd been hoping all evening to have a little of his time.

"You could help me fold the tablecloth."

He moved to the other end of the table and lifted the corners of the cloth. They approached each other. Her gaze caught and held his. Her pulse raced and her knees felt as though they'd turned to gelatin. With concerted effort, she kept putting one foot in front of the other. All the while, she wondered if he could hear the pounding of her heart.

And when they brought the material together, their fingers brushed. A jolt of awareness had her gaze dipping to his mouth—his very kissable mouth. The tip of her tongue moistened her lips.

For the longest second of her life, neither of them pulled away. In fact, it was as if time had slowed down. A rush of energy pulsated through her body.

This was ridiculous. It wasn't like this wealthy, extremely handsome, very eligible CEO would be interested in her. She was just a baker with a polka-dotted apron and her hair pulled up. And she was his friend. Nothing more. Just someone to occasionally start the day with over a cup of hot coffee—even if those were the days she most looked forward to.

She moved her hands to lift the fold. "Mr. Ross, I think you had a very successful event."

He arched a brow. "Since when do you call me anything but Simon?"

She glanced around to make sure no one overheard them. "It's different here. Someone might overhear."

"And that would be a problem?"

He was right. She was getting too worked up about protocol and appearances. Still, she couldn't resist glancing around again just to make sure no one was watching or listening to them. Satisfied they had some privacy, she began to relax.

"Congratulations on the new store chain." She took the tablecloth from him, in order to make the final folds. "Your guests all seemed excited about the plan."

"Thanks. It won't be long now. The first store opens just before Christmas."

"Can I ask you a question?"

He shrugged. "Sure."

"If you like animals enough to start up a chain of pet stores, why don't you own one?"

Simon didn't want to think about the past and how he'd wanted a puppy so badly. Yet the door to the past had been cracked open and now the memories slithered through, filling his mind.

He remembered the little black puppy he'd fallen in love with. The neighbor's dog had given birth. And his best friend, Clay, had offered him a puppy. He'd snuck it home, not wanting anyone to know—if they didn't know, they couldn't ruin this for him.

Except two days later, his father found out and there'd been a high price to pay. Simon absently rubbed his right arm. He slammed the door on the memories. He wasn't going to open up about his horrific past, not even for the amazing woman standing next to him.

"It's not a chain of pet stores. It's a toy store for pets."

"There's a difference?"

He nodded. "We won't be selling food and basics. We'll tailor our supplies to keeping the consumers' four-footed friends entertained." A frown came over his face. "As for me not owning a pet, it's the way I like it."

"Sorry. I didn't mean to overstep."

He cleared his throat. "I think we both had a successful evening. Are all of your business cards gone?"

"Almost." She pulled a dozen or so out of her pocket.

"I predict you're going to be very busy in the near future."

"I hope so."

"Trust me. I see a brilliant future for you." He smiled at her.

Her stomach dipped. No one had a right to have such a sexy smile. What were they talking about? It took her a second, but then she got her mind back on track.

Her gaze met his and held, much, much longer than

was necessary. Her heart started to beat faster. "I... I want to thank you for hiring me—for hiring the bakery—my bakery."

Oh, why am I tripping all over my words? It's not like this is a date or anything.

He smiled. "There's no need to thank me. I wanted the best. And you are the best."

Pepper felt as though her feet had just left the floor. He thought she was the best? Her lips pulled up into a big, broad smile as her heart continued its erratic *tap-tap-tap-tap*. It was like it was beating some Morse code signal or something.

"Yes, there is. It means a lot that you think enough of my baked goods to want me to serve a party."

He continued to stare deeply into her eyes. "Of course, I think your food is amazing. But I didn't hire you."

"You didn't?" She studied him, not sure what to think.

He shook his head again. "I have staff that take care of things like that."

"Of course you do," she mumbled under her breath. The blaze of heat singed her cheeks as she glanced away. What made her think he would be bothered hiring a caterer?

"Not that I wouldn't have hired you." His gaze met hers yet again. "It appears I'm not the only one to think you have the best bakery in the city."

Once again the heat flamed in her cheeks. She glanced up. "Thank you. I should be going." When he didn't make any move to leave, she said, "I'm sure you have other plans."

She wanted to ask if he had a girlfriend, but it was absolutely none of her business. And she didn't want him thinking she was hitting on him—that would be the end of their easy friendship. Besides, a friendship was as much as she was willing to offer anyone. The thought of caring for someone—of losing another person in her life—scared her.

"For once, I don't have plans."

And so he lingered while she placed the tablecloth in a box with some other items. "You must always be so busy. I can't even imagine what it would be like to run a company this size. I know that my little bakery keeps me busy from morning until night." She was running out of things to say, but he still didn't make any movement to leave.

"Usually, I spend my evenings in the office."

"So you like to stay on top of everything?"

He nodded. "I do." He started helping her pick up things. "Just like you do by being here for the party."

Heat rushed to her cheeks. He was referring to the fact that she was here in person instead of sending someone from her staff. "The truth is I like to handle these events."

He arched a dark brow. "You like to make connections and expand your business. And your staff can't do that as well as you do. I totally understand. You and I, we aren't so different. If you ever want to discuss your business model or plans, let me know."

Pepper couldn't believe what she was hearing. Simon Ross, *the* Simon Ross, was offering to help her with her business. Like he didn't already have his hands full with a Fortune 500 company that kept rising in people's estimations. If anyone could help her, it would be him. She'd love to hear what he had to say.

"Thank you," she said, carefully placing a stray cake server in the box. "I'd really appreciate it. Right now, I could take all of the help I can get."

"Do you have any plans for tonight?"

"No. I don't." The words slipped past her lips before her mind had a chance to catch up. Some helpful business advice would be just what she needed. But she sensed he had more than business on his mind.

As though he was reading her thoughts, his gaze dipped to her lips. Could this really be happening? The girl voted most likely to run away with the circus because of her strawberry blond hair and her colorful clothes. The girl who had never fitted in until she opened her bakery. Within those walls, she could unwind and be herself.

He picked up her box from the floor. "Are you ready to go? We can grab a late dinner."

She had to make sure this thing arcing between them was real—that it flowed both ways. And it wasn't some sort of misunderstanding. Staring into his eyes, her heart pounding, she asked, "It isn't business you have on your mind, is it?"

He stepped closer to her. His voice lowered to a sexy, hushed tone. "No. Is that a problem?"

He was giving her an out. Knowing they came from totally different worlds, she would be smart to back away. But she was drawn to him unlike any other man in her life.

Simon didn't see her as the awkward girl in school that never could manage to be just one of the crowd. Those days were in the past—or so she wanted to believe.

When concern touched Simon's eyes, she realized the brief memories of her past had her frowning. She turned that frown upside down and sent him one of her brightest smiles. She was no longer the girl kids would point at and whisper about. Now, she was a confident business owner.

With Simon standing so close to her, she had to tilt her chin upward for their gazes to meet. As she stared into his dark eyes, she felt as though she could get lost in them. She couldn't think of anything she'd rather do than spend the evening with him.

"I'd like to go to dinner with you."

His voice lowered even more. "You don't know how long I've wanted to ask you out."

"Really?"

He nodded. "You intrigue me."

A flutter of excitement filled her chest. "So why didn't you ask me?"

He placed the box on the table next to them. "It was

never the right time. I was busy with plans for this new venture. And you were busy with the bakery."

It was true. They were busy people, but she would have made time for him, just as she had in the mornings for coffee over the last several months. It was during those mornings that they'd slowly let their guards down—revealing parts of their lives. But how had she missed that he was interested in her?

He reached out to her. His thumb gently caressed her cheek. "You are so beautiful."

She leaned into his touch. His gaze held hers, as though he needed the connection more than oxygen. And then his gaze lowered just a bit. Her racing heart jolted with anticipation. He was going to kiss her.

The breath caught in her lungs. As his head lowered, she gave herself over to the moment. Her eyes fluttered shut. And then she melted into his very capable arms. Her hands landed against his muscular chest and moved slowly up to his shoulders.

The kiss, though gentle at first, picked up its pace. His mouth moving over hers, his tongue probing her mouth and her giving in to the ecstasy.

Crash!

Pepper jumped back. Her heart careened into her throat. She pressed a hand to her sensitive lips. All the while, her gaze moved about the conference room, searching for the source of the noise. And then she spotted the box on the floor. They must have bumped into it while they'd been kissing.

She scanned the room again. There had been no one else around. Their kiss was still their secret. She liked the thought of sharing a moment of passion with Simon— something only the two of them knew about.

Her gaze returned to the upturned carton. "Oh, what a mess."

"Don't worry. I'll help clean it up."

Together they knelt down, Pepper righting the box and the few things that remained inside it. Simon handed her the scattered contents. In no time, the mess was cleaned up.

When they'd both straightened, Simon leaned in and pressed a kiss to her lips. It was short, but it left no doubt in her mind that there was chemistry between them—as in the sizzling, smoking, combustible kind.

She swallowed hard as her heart pounded in her chest. All the while, her gaze followed him as he shifted. She should say something. Yes, she should not let on that his touch had rocked her to her very core.

Summoning her wits, she smiled at him. She just couldn't let him see how much he got to her. "What was that for?"

He smiled at her. It was one of those lazy smiles that showed just a bit of his straight, white teeth. Her stomach dipped. No man had a right to be that handsome.

When he spoke, his voice held a rich timbre. "I wanted something to tide me over until dessert."

He was back to flirting with her and she liked it—she liked him. And the way he looked at her, it was like he was making love to her with his eyes. No longer the social misfit, she'd blossomed into Cinderella.

Her gaze strayed across the sharp contours of Simon's face, down to his broad shoulders and muscled chest. Oh, yes, he was definitely her Prince Charming.

CHAPTER ONE

Seven weeks later...

The Polka Dotted Bakery

THERE'S ONE THING about fairy tales...

They don't always have a happily-ever-after.

Not even a happy-for-now.

Pepper glanced out the decorated storefront window and didn't see any paparazzi. She took an easy breath. It was the first time in weeks. Seven whole weeks plus one day of being hounded for photos and comments.

And she was tired. Tired of it all.

But at last, there was peace.

In the end, she'd done nothing wrong. Nothing, except for letting her defenses down with a man that she'd thought— Well, it didn't matter what she thought because she'd been wrong about him, about the evening together, about them. And now, the paparazzi wanted a comment.

She'd been counting off the days since their night of passion turned into a morning of regrets. It had been fifty days since she'd found herself in the arms of Simon Ross. Forty-nine evenings since she'd spent the most glorious night with him. And seven long weeks since her life had felt like her own.

And a lifetime since she'd last seen him.

Not that she missed Simon...at all. Not a bit.

The very next morning after her fairy tale had begun, her life had spun into some sort of soap opera. One photographer had spotted her leaving Simon's building in the wee hours of the morning. How he'd known she'd come from Simon's place, out of all the condos in the high-rise, was beyond her. Perhaps it was the doorman, or maybe it'd been a nosy neighbor anxious for a quick payoff, or possibly someone had spotted them kissing after Simon's big announcement.

Then Simon had phoned. The first words out of his mouth had been an apology.

Her heart sank down to the tips of her cotton-candy-pink painted toes. It was obvious he regretted their night together, and everything that she'd thought was happening between them had been nothing more than a figment of her imagination. But then he'd sent her a link to a website with a picture of them kissing after the party, and it became clear what he was apologizing for.

Billionaire Bachelor Interviewing New Love Interest!

The headline was outrageous. How had their brief relationship been leaked to the press?

It was then that she knew she had to end things before he did. She told him that they'd just gotten caught up in the moment and it should end right here and now. He hadn't said a word. He obviously agreed. That was it. No discussion. No nothing. The night before, they'd made love, and the next morning, it was over.

Until that moment, she'd never appreciated her freedom to move about the city basically anonymously. For the most part, no one knew her and didn't pay attention to what she did. From that day forward, it was like everything she did had to be analyzed for the world to read and to figure out what, if anything, it had to do with Simon.

A single photographer had quickly turned into a gaggle of them. Keeping them out of the bakery had become a full-time job for her staff. With her apartment above the bakery, there was no getting away from them.

One morning, she'd glanced out her apartment window to find a photographer hanging from the tree. Seriously. He'd just been hanging there like he was part monkey, with a camera in hand. She'd closed her mini blinds and then drawn her curtains. She'd never felt more invaded in her entire life.

But then they'd started dissecting her life, from her mother's death to her life with her grandmother. She'd felt naked and exposed for the whole world to see. She didn't know how Simon lived in the spotlight. And then they'd sought out people who had known her in school. Every insecurity she'd ever had in her youth came rolling back.

Little did the paparazzi know that it'd been nothing more than a brief fling with Simon. She thought of telling the photographers that they were wasting their time, but her wounded pride and the prick to her heart kept the words locked deep inside her.

From One Night to Wedding Bells!

Honestly, who came up with these outrageous and totally false headlines?

Her friends commiserated with her. And told her to look on the bright side—business at the bakery had never been better. They were right. She was doing a booming business.

And then the next headline came quite unexpectedly.

Billionaire Bachelor Moves On...

One minute the paparazzi had them picking out wedding venues, with a photo of two people who were quite obviously not them, and the next they had him moving on. Although this time the photo was most certainly Simon. He'd been spotted the following week with his arm around a leggy blonde as they attended a Broadway show opening. As Pepper stared at the photo, she resisted admitting to the sharp piercing pain.

So much for their special evening meaning anything to him. Her back teeth clenched together. Lucky for him, he hadn't been back for his weekly order. He might have ended up wearing his coffee.

And the part of her that missed his bright smile and his flirty ways that made her feel like the most beautiful woman in the world? Well, she shushed it right up. He wasn't worth missing. Simon Ross lived up to his reputation as the uncatchable bachelor.

It didn't help that she hadn't felt great for the past few days. She had a slight headache and she blamed that for her queasy stomach. It wasn't enough to stop her though. Whatever it was, it would pass.

It was no wonder she didn't feel good, aside from the mess with Simon. She had competition. A new bakery had just moved in on the next block. And her business took an immediate hit. Customers strayed to the new place, eager to see what they had to offer.

To that extent, she supposed her friends were right and the coverage about her and Simon wasn't all bad. People had visited the bakery to meet her, but she made sure to stay busy in the back. Still, while they were there, they bought her products. They bought a lot of products. If things had ended better with Simon, she might be inclined to thank him. But as it was, she didn't think she'd ever speak to him again.

The new bakery was pulling out all the stops with big ads, radio spots and every other promotion they could think of. The bakery was part of a national chain that could afford to undercut their prices to drive the competition out of business. Then once the competitors were out of business, they'd jack up their prices. The nerve of some people. But Pepper refused to let them drive her out of business—not without a big fight. She'd sunk everything she had into making this bakery a success. It was a dream of hers—a dream that she refused to let die, even if it meant doing things that she wouldn't otherwise have done, like working round the clock if she had to. The chain couldn't keep up their deep discounts forever. At least, she hoped not.

In the meantime, she was taking every Christmas party she could cram onto her calendar. It was exhausting, but her grandmother had always told her that nothing worth having came easily. This bakery definitely wasn't going to be easy.

She worked from the time she woke up, which was hours before the sun decided to rise, until she fell into bed early in the evening utterly exhausted, sometimes still in her work clothes. And so far, it was working. She was keeping her existing clients and gaining new ones. Things at last were looking up. Her clients recognized true quality and not frozen mass product.

Now that Christmastime was here, it was time to sparkle. Pepper loved Christmas above all other holidays. And that was saying something because they all had a special place in her heart. But she not only loved Christmas, she really *loved* it. It was magical and it brought out the best in people. People were a little nicer to others, holding doors, sharing a smile or a nod. If it was possible, she'd have Christmas all year round.

It was almost time to open up for the day. She loved this early morning hour. In her mind, each day was a new beginning with new possibilities. And she had a feeling something big was going to happen. Maybe they'd be hired for the wedding of the year. Or perhaps she'd meet a big client at the holiday party she was catering that evening. A smile pulled at her lips as anticipation put some pep in her step.

She moved to the stereo system and turned it on. Over

the speakers came the deep timbre of Michael Bublé's voice as he sang "It's beginning to look a lot like Christmas." She glanced out the window as the flurries swirled through the air. This really was her favorite time of the year.

Yesterday had been Sunday, the only day of the week the shop was closed. She'd taken advantage of the downtime to get out the holiday decorations. It took all day to exchange the Thanksgiving fanfare for the homey Christmas look, but that was because she'd baked and crafted a lot of the decorations herself.

She paused next to the glass display cases and glanced around at her handiwork. On the brick wall where floating shelves normally displayed an array of antique dishes, she'd replaced them with gingerbread figures, from a giant gingerbread man to a gingerbread train. There were also red ribbons, greenery, pinecones and a poinsettia bloom here and there.

She loved gingerbread. Not only did it taste delicious, but there were so many things to do with it. And so she might have gone a little overboard this year with gingerbread. It was even in the store window.

Looking around at all she'd accomplished, she realized she'd done it all alone. As much as she loved this bakery, she'd give it up to have her family once more. The joy the bakery brought to her life just wasn't the same as having her family by her side, especially during this festive holiday season.

Walking through life alone was not how she'd envisioned her future. And yet that's exactly what she was doing. Because each and every person who meant something to her had been torn from her life.

She'd learned to close her feelings to others little by little, and her grandmother's death had been the last straw. That was it. The protective walls had fully encased her heart. She was done with loving and losing.

Pepper moved to the front door and turned the lock. She smiled as the first rays of sun lightened up the inky sky. Beneath the streetlights, a light coating of snow was detectable. It had fallen last night, coating the grass but leaving the street clear.

"It's going to be a good day. A very good day indeed." If only wishes came true.

"What did you say?" Charlotte asked from behind the counter.

Pepper shook her head. "Nothing important."

Charlotte arched a brow. "Talking to yourself again?" When Pepper shrugged, Charlotte continued, "You keep that up and I'm going to start worrying about you."

Pepper moved behind the counter. Her gaze strayed across the little stuffed dog she'd had since she was a girl. When she was young, they'd lived in an apartment—a small apartment—that didn't allow pets. And she'd wanted a dog in the worst way. Every birthday and Christmas, when anyone asked her what she wanted, she would tell them a puppy.

Her mother felt so bad that she gave Pepper this designer stuffed beagle and a promise that someday when they moved to a bigger place that allowed pets, she would get her a dog. But that day never came.

She'd lost her mother at the tender age of eight, after a car had run a red light and struck her mother as she'd crossed the street. Pepper had gone to live with her grandmother, who was allergic to animals. Bugles McBeagle had come with her.

She sighed as she ran a finger over the dog's plush fur, promising herself that someday she would have her puppy. Just not today.

The business phone rang. Pepper rushed over to answer it. "Hello. This is the Polka Dotted Bakery. How may I help you?"

"Pepper, this is Mike. I'm sorry to do this, but I quit."

"Quit?" Not again.

"I just couldn't say no."

"No? To what? To whom?" She had a sinking feeling she knew who he was talking about, but she had to hear him say it. She needed the confirmation.

"The other bakery. They approached me when I was leaving work yesterday. They offered me a lot more money. And with the baby on the way, we need all of the money I can make. Pepper, if it wasn't for that, I swear, I wouldn't be leaving. Honest."

She liked Mike. He'd been with her since she'd opened the shop. And even though she didn't want to, she understood he had to put the needs of his family before his loyalty to her and the business.

She wished him well and hung up. So now she was short a baker and she had a party to prepare for...alone.

Not wasting any more time, she got to work.

CHAPTER TWO

THIS COULDN'T BE HAPPENING.

How had he let this slip through the cracks?

With the tinted rear windows of the car, no one could make him out. Simon was free to stare at the passing buildings and people hustling along the crowded sidewalk. The Polka Dotted Bakery was a place he'd thought of often in the past several weeks. He tried to tell himself that it was the fragrant and rich coffee that he missed, but it was something more than that. An image of Pepper laughing flashed in his mind. He recalled how her lush lips would part, lifting up at the corners, and her pinkened cheeks would puff up. But more than that, her eyes would twinkle and the green of her eyes reminded him of gemstones.

And then a much more somber memory rushed to the forefront—his last conversation with Pepper. There had been no smiles, no friendliness. She'd dumped him, dismissed him, had no use for him. That was something he was not used to, at all. He was the one who always ended relationships. Not the other way around.

"Pull over here," he said to his driver.

He didn't normally have a driver, but seeing as he was headed for the bakery and parking could be quite limited at this time of the day, he'd decided it would be prudent. He'd considered calling her on the phone, but he didn't feel right about it.

Simon opened the car door and immediately the distinct nip in the air assailed him. The holidays were here and so was the winter season. He tugged at the collar of his black wool overcoat and pulled it close to his neck to keep out the chilling breeze. Not even the midafternoon sun was enough to warm him.

There had been so many times over the past several weeks when he'd wanted to swing by the bakery. He told himself that it was the cherry turnovers that he craved—not staring into the green eyes of the very beautiful baker.

And it didn't help that when he suddenly stopped bringing the mouthwateringly good baked goods to the office it was noticed by his employees. When he got questioned enough about the lack of treats, he started going to the new bakery, though the service wasn't nearly as friendly and the turnovers—well, they were dry and overly sweet. And though his staff didn't say much, the number of leftover pastries at the end of the day said it all.

Though everything in his body wanted to turn around, he kept putting one foot in front of the other. The streets were decorated with garland and on each lamp post was a large wreath with a great big red bow. Shop windows had holiday displays. Some had Santa figurines and others Christmas trees. Everything to put the passerby in the holiday spirit—except for Simon.

However, when he reached the large picture window of the Polka Dotted Bakery, he slowed down. How could he not? The holiday-themed display was literally a work of art—all made out of baked goods.

It was a wintery scene, with a white tree with gingerbread ornaments trimmed with white frosting suspended from it. And beneath the tree was a gingerbread house. Not just four walls and a roof of gumdrops. Someone had gone all out, detailing not a one, not a two, not even a three, but a four-story house decorated with white and pale pink frosting. He didn't have to guess. He knew it was Pepper's work. She was quite talented, making the window shutters out of white frosting, and there was even a chimney.

He drew in a deep breath, straightened his shoulders and opened the glass door of the bakery. When he stepped inside, he found it empty. Not one single customer. Sure, it was a little past three in the afternoon, but from what Pepper had told him, there were usually customers streaming in and out of the bakery all day long.

He stepped further into the shop to find the display cases completely full, as though none of the goods had sold that day. How could this be? Pepper, by far, had the best pastries in the city.

"I'll be right with you." Her voice was light and friendly, just the way he remembered it before things had spun out of control.

He turned to her, bracing for Pepper's onslaught of angry words. She knelt down, placing something in the glass display case. When she straightened—when she saw that it was him and when she heard what he'd come here to tell her—he was certain her tone would change drastically.

And then she straightened with a smile on her face. Her beautiful long auburn hair was pulled back in a twist, pinned to the back of her head. When the lights hit her hair, the deep red highlights shone. Her bangs fell to the side of her face and a few wispy curls fell around the nape of her neck. Was this the real reason he'd come here? To have one more look at her—to drink in her beauty?

As recognition flashed in her eyes, her friendly demeanor vanished in a heartbeat, replaced with a distinct frown. "You." Her green eyes widened with surprise. "What are you doing here?" Then she held up a hand as though stopping him from speaking. "Never mind. I don't want to know. Just leave before someone sees you here."

"Pepper, we need to talk."

She shook her head. "If anyone spots you here, the press with be back. I can't deal with them. Just go."

He knew how bad the paparazzi could be when they were chasing what they thought was a story. "I've taken precautions so no one knows I'm here."

She didn't say anything for a moment. "They'll still

find out. They even dug into my past. My past! People I never thought I'd speak to again were giving interviews about me. Do you know how that invasion of privacy felt?"

"I do. And I'm sorry." His whole life had been aired in the papers since his business took off. It had been hard, but he was somewhat used to it now. "Just hear what I have to say and then I'll go."

She placed her hands on her waist. If looks could vaporize a person, he would be nothing more than mist. Wait. How did she get to be so angry with him? She was the one who had dumped him.

Not that the night would have led anywhere. He didn't do relationships—not even with the very sweet, very tempting Polka Dotted Baker. He wasn't cut out to be someone's boyfriend, much less someone's husband or worse yet, a father.

Still, she glowered at him. He didn't move an inch. If this was a struggle of wills, he would win. He'd come here for a purpose. He thought he was doing a nice thing. Now, he was having second thoughts. Still, he was here. And he wasn't leaving until he'd had his say.

She stared deep into his eyes. "Make it fast."

"Where are all of your customers?" He sensed something was very wrong. "And why does it look like you haven't sold anything?"

"Things have changed. I don't have time to chat. I have work to do." She moved past him, leaving plenty of room between them so their bodies didn't touch.

She stepped up to the front door and flipped the sign to Closed. He couldn't help but notice her craning her neck to gaze up and down the walk, as though checking to see if anyone had spotted him in her shop. As far as he could tell, his ball cap and dark sunglasses had kept his identity under wraps.

"There's something important I need to tell you."

She shook her head. "How about we just go back to

pretending we don't know each other? Life was so much easier back then."

He wished he could rewind time. "It's too late for that."

She didn't say anything as she moved past him and kept going toward the back of the bakery. What he didn't understand was her hostility. If he'd dumped her, he'd get it. But she'd been the one to end things. Sure, he'd been getting ready to do it, but she'd beaten him to the punch.

He followed her because he still hadn't told her the reason for his visit. She led him to a small office. The room had vacant white walls, which surprised him after getting to know Pepper's lively personality and her penchant for decorating. A solitary desk in the room was buried beneath a mountain of paperwork. She grabbed a small quilted backpack with a red-and-white pattern, as well as a digital notebook.

When she turned to the door, she practically ran into him. She glanced up as though she'd gotten lost in her thoughts and had forgotten him. His ego was taking hits left and right. He still wasn't sure why she was so steamed with him.

She glanced at her wristwatch. "If you came here to talk about the past, don't. It was a stupid mistake. It won't happen again."

If he'd had any doubt about her sincerity, he had his answer. She wanted nothing to do with him. That was a first for him. She certainly was different than everyone else in his life.

And this was why he'd been drawn to Pepper in the first place. She wasn't a pushover. She wasn't out to see what he could do for her. She was her own woman, who took life on her own terms.

She placed her things on the counter. After washing her hands, she set to work. Pepper continued to move about the kitchen as though he weren't even standing there.

"Why are you so mad at me?" He stood at the edge of

the large kitchen with all its gleaming stainless surfaces. "As I recall, you're the one that dumped me."

Her cheeks filled with color. "I didn't dump you."

She added sugar into a saucepan and placed it on the gas stove. She kept her back to him as she adjusted the temperature. He was in absolutely no mood to be ignored.

"I'm pretty sure you did." His bruised ego could attest to it. "So why all of the hostility?"

She spun around. Her gaze clashed with his. "I'm not hostile."

He arched a disbelieving brow and waited for her to explain herself. He didn't mind taking the heat when he deserved it. But in this case, he didn't do anything wrong. Thoughts of nipping the relationship in the bud didn't count. Pepper might be good at figuring out people, but even she wasn't a mind reader.

She sighed. "You're right. I'm taking my frustrations out on you." She paused as though choosing her words carefully. "I… I'm sorry." Her gaze met his briefly, but she turned away before he could read her thoughts. "Things at the bakery haven't been going well." She took the saucepan and stirred as the sugar began melting. "But you didn't come here to hear about my troubles."

At last, she was beginning to sound like the Pepper he'd gotten to know and trust. "Would you believe I missed your cherry turnovers so much I couldn't stay away?"

She tilted the pan, letting the melted sugar roll across the bottom. She didn't say anything, concentrating on what she was doing.

And that was why what he had to say next was that much harder. He wasn't so sure he wanted to have this conversation while she was distracted, but she wasn't leaving him much choice. She took a spoon with a long round handle and began to drizzle the caramel onto it. All the while, she turned the handle so the caramel would make a corkscrew shape.

He never knew there was so much more to baking than mixing up some delicious-tasting batter and pouring it into a pan. But Pepper was showing him another side of the business and he was enthralled with it. She made it look so easy—like anyone could do it. Even him.

She moved the corkscrew to a piece of waxed paper and then started to make a new one. They were beautiful. They were like little pieces of art.

And the guilt he'd been carrying around with him most of the day mounted.

"Pepper—"

"Just give me one more minute." Her full attention was on her work and he couldn't blame her. What she did here was like magic. If he tried to do the same thing, he'd end up with burnt sugar.

He knew he should hurry. He didn't have that much time to get out of the city and to his country estate, where the big Christmas celebration was taking place. But he didn't move a muscle as he stood there watching Pepper do her thing. Each golden caramel corkscrew was then placed atop a cupcake. They looked too good to eat.

When Pepper had finished with all the cupcakes, she straightened, glanced at him and blinked, as though she'd forgotten that he was still there waiting to talk to her. And then her gaze moved to the clock above his head.

"I have to hurry." Her beautiful face creased with worry lines.

"What happens if you don't finish these?" He knew the stakes were high, but he wondered how high they were.

Pepper shook her head as she boxed up the cupcakes. "That can't happen."

He moved next to her, placing a lid on the full box. "Pepper, stop for just a moment."

She turned to him. "Simon, I'm sorry. I just don't have time to talk. I have a very important party."

"That's the thing."

"What's the thing?"

His gaze met hers. "The party. It's mine."

"Yours?" She shook her head. "I spoke with a woman. Elaine something or other. I have her full name written on the order. And this party is in Connecticut."

He nodded. "Elaine Haskins is my assistant and the party is at my country home."

Pepper's face creased with lines of frustration. She didn't say a word as she digested the information.

"I'm sorry," he said. "This is my fault. Everyone was so impressed with you at the office party that Elaine added you to our catering list. After what happened between us, I forgot to say anything to her. I totally understand you wanting to cancel—"

"Cancel?" Her shoulders straightened and she lifted her chin slightly. "I'm not canceling."

"You're not?" He was so confused.

"We have a contract. I expect you to keep your end of it."

"But why? I mean, why would you want to cater a party for me?"

"Because this is business. It's not personal. I can't believe I have to explain this to you."

And then he thought of the empty bakery and the overabundance of unsold goods. Something had happened to her business, and he wondered if it had anything to do with the paparazzi fuss when they'd caught on to their night together. His jaw tightened. He was so used to it that he hadn't stopped to consider how it might affect Pepper.

"And you don't mind working this party, even though it's for me."

She straightened her shoulders and there was a slight tilt to her chin. "I'm a professional. I can do this job. There won't be any problems."

"I know you are and I didn't mean to imply otherwise." He couldn't shake the thought of the baked goods going to waste in her display cases. "I'll throw in extra if you include everything in your cases."

Her mouth gaped. She quickly regained her composure. "Why would you do that? If you want a cherry turnover that bad, all you have to do is ask."

He would make sure and set those aside for himself. "I have some extra guests," he said, which was the truth, but just part of it. "I want to make sure there's enough for everyone."

"Oh. Okay. I'll get them boxed up."

He glanced around. "Are you the only one here?"

She nodded. "Don't worry. I have a couple employees meeting me at your estate."

"Let me give you a hand." He slipped off his coat.

"You don't have to do that."

"Sure I do. I'm the one who insisted on the extra items. The least I can do is give you a hand boxing them up." He didn't mention that he'd noticed the dark smudges under her eyes. She was working too hard and not getting enough sleep. At least he hoped that's all it was.

They worked together, packing up all the delicious treats. Simon snagged one of the cherry turnovers. He couldn't wait until later. His palate had been in withdrawal for weeks now. He was only so strong.

"Look at the time." There was mild panic in Pepper's voice. "With the traffic, I'm going to be late."

"Not if you leave now."

"But there's still all of this to load in the van."

"I'll help you."

This time she didn't argue. They moved the baked goods on carts out to the delivery van painted in white with big black polka dots all over it and the logo for the Polka Dotted Bakery painted in bubblegum pink and lime green. He couldn't help but smile. It was unique, just like its owner.

The truck was quite full when they were done and

Simon wasn't sure what he was going to do with all the extra food, but he would deal with that problem later.

He climbed out of the back of the van. "You're good to go."

She stood frowning.

"What's the matter?"

"I forgot something." And then her eyes widened. "My backpack. It's on the counter."

When she went to turn and rush back inside, he reached out to her. "You stay here. Close up the van and I'll grab your stuff."

She nodded.

He ran back inside the bakery. The only problem was that there were a lot of counters. His gaze moved around the kitchen in a counter clockwise manner. And then he spotted her red and white backpack as well as the digital tablet next to the stove. He rushed over and grabbed them.

He moved too quickly and the backpack knocked over a tall stack of business cards, as well as some papers. A frustrated groan formed deep in his throat. He rushed to clean up the mess. He guessed that Pepper meant to take the business cards with her to hand out at the party. He took most of them and her backpack. He flipped off the lights, exited the building and, using the keys Pepper had placed in the door earlier, locked it.

She was in the back of the van, doing something with one of the boxes.

"I've got it," he called out.

"Okay. This is all set." She climbed out, closed the door and turned to him. "I just have to set the alarm system."

She rushed back inside. He checked the time. It was most definitely late, and it was his fault for insisting on taking her extra pastries. He owed it to Pepper to make sure she arrived on time. He called his driver to tell him to head to Connecticut without him. Simon had just hung up when she returned.

"I'm never going to make it on time," she said.

"You will if you take a couple of shortcuts I've learned."

She shook her head. "I'll just get lost. I'm going whatever way my phone app tells me."

"Trust me. I'll show you the way."

"You?" She shook her head. "I don't think so."

"Think of it this way. The longer you stand here arguing with me, the later you'll be."

Her lips pressed together in a firm line. And unhappiness was written all over her face. "Fine. Let's go."

He hadn't imagined the day taking this most unexpected twist. What would they talk about? On second thought, it was probably best to remain quiet. This was going to be a very interesting ride indeed.

CHAPTER THREE

WHAT WAS SHE THINKING?

The last time she'd been alone with this man, her world had come undone. Pepper kept her gaze focused on the busy roadway. But she couldn't ignore Simon's presence. With him next to her, it felt as though the interior of the van had shrunk.

He was so close that she could reach out and touch him—like they'd done after his party to announce the launch of his Pet Playground stores. They'd been hand in hand as Simon drove them back to his place. They'd laughed. They'd talked. The exact opposite of now.

She quietly followed Simon's instructions as she weaved her way through traffic. Even with Simon's input, it still wasn't a quick journey.

And with hustling out the door, she couldn't help but wonder if she'd turned everything off. She hated rushing. It left room for error and she always strived for perfection, though she never reached it. But she'd grabbed everything for the party and she'd set the alarm.

Still, worry niggled at her.

"What's the matter?" Simon asked.

"Did I turn off the lights?"

"You did."

"Did I lock the front door?"

"You did."

"Did I get everything?"

"Pepper, what's the matter?"

She sighed. "I just have the feeling I'm forgetting something."

"I don't think you have to worry. Everything is under control."

She hoped he was right.

Other than some instructions on where to turn, silence fell back over the van. It wasn't a comfortable silence. In place of conversation was a strained void. She should have refused his offer to ride with her. But then she would most definitely be late and that would be very bad, especially if this guest list was anything like his last party.

She couldn't help glancing around in traffic just to make sure the paparazzi weren't following them. Thankfully, they weren't. She glanced over at Simon as he lounged back in his seat, checking messages on his phone.

The silence in the van was deafening. She reached over and turned on the radio. She adjusted the tuner to a station that played nothing but Christmas tunes. Andy Williams's "Sleigh Ride" was playing. At least it was upbeat, unlike her passenger. She turned it up.

She chanced a quick glance at him. The frown on his face had deepened, marring his handsome face with deep lines. What was up with him? Did he regret offering to ride with her?

"Is something bothering you?" The question popped out of her mouth before her brain had a chance to restrain her tongue.

"What?"

At the same time, they reached for the radio. Their fingers touched. A tingle pulsed up her arm. She glanced at him. His gaze met hers, making her heart pound.

She yanked her hand away as she turned her attention back to the road. Simon lowered the volume on the radio. She swallowed hard, gripping the steering wheel with both hands as she tried to put a lid on whatever it was that just happened between them.

"That's better," Simon said. "Now what did you ask?"

She felt really weird asking him now, but she refused

to let on how their contact had unnerved her. "Is something bothering you?"

"You mean besides you being angry at me when it was you who dumped me?"

So they were back to this again. "I didn't see you minding so much when you were out with that tall blonde the next night."

"It wasn't the next night." His tone was gruff. "It was two weeks later."

"A day. A week or two. It's the same difference."

"Turn left right up here." He was quiet for a moment. "And it does matter, because it wasn't the same thing."

She made the turn. She shouldn't care, but her curiosity was eating at her. "Why is that?"

"Because that appearance wasn't a date. It was arranged to draw the paparazzi's attention from you."

It wasn't a date? She caught sight of the serious look in his eyes. Should she believe him? After all, they had looked like a real couple in the photo. "But they said you were both on the rebound."

"Turn left in a mile onto Willow Lane." He shifted in his seat so he could look at her. "Since when do you believe what they print online? Remember, those are the same fools that said we were getting married."

"Like that would ever happen."

"Exactly." His tone softened just a bit.

He didn't have to agree so quickly, like the thought of marrying her would be worse than a death sentence. Maybe it was better if they didn't talk. In fact, that sounded like a really good idea.

The ride had gone far worse than he'd imagined.

Thankfully, the Christmas party was faring much better.

Simon was certain he was losing his touch with women. That or Pepper was immune to his charms. Rekindling their friendship was never going to happen. The realization was a sobering one.

But even though their relationship was broken beyond recognition, he noticed that didn't stop her from putting on the most amazing display of pastries. But it wasn't just sweet treats. She'd mingled in flowers and twinkle lights. The display really drew the eye.

She was attentive to the guests as their hungry gazes meandered over the lengthy selection of sugary temptations. She was kind. She was patient. And she beamed as she talked about the baked goods and her beloved bakery.

As a professional, he had no qualms with her. On a personal note, he wished they'd never taken things to the next level—even if it had been the most amazing night of his life. The price had been too high. It had cost him a friendship that he didn't know how much he valued until it'd ended.

He made his way through the great room, greeting all of his guests. These were important clients who'd helped get his products on the store shelves. And now that he was branching out with his Pet Playground chain, he was talking it up, hoping a groundswell of excitement would carry through to his launch at Christmas.

"Your Christmas tree is gorgeous," the wife of a business associate said.

"Thank you." Simon didn't admit that the tree wasn't his. His assistant had hired a decorator to come in and stage the house with holiday cheer. When the party was over, the tree, the twinkle lights and all of the other decorations would go away. None too soon as far as he was concerned.

But the funny thing was, as much as he tried to talk business, everyone wanted to talk about the baker he'd hired. Forget the heated appetizers; they were all agog over the sweets. Not that he could blame them. They were delicious.

"Isn't she the best?" Elaine stepped up next to him.

His assistant was a few years younger than him, married and the most efficient assistant he'd ever hired. He would be lost without her. She kept him and his calendar on task.

"Yes, Pepper is very good." He only hired the best.

"The guests seem to love her. And everyone seems to be enjoying themselves."

He nodded. "You've done an excellent job coordinating this party."

He made a mental note to speak with Elaine at a later date about removing Pepper from their list of vendors. No matter how good Pepper was, they needed to maintain their distance. He felt bad about having to do it, but it was for the best—for both of their sakes. Because no matter how much they both wanted to deny it, there was still chemistry sizzling between them.

His gaze kept straying to Pepper. He assured himself that it was his job to keep an eye on the staff, to make sure the party was running smoothly. He noticed her on the phone. He couldn't have his employees chatting while they were supposed to be working. She turned her back to him and headed toward the kitchen with the phone pressed to her ear.

His jaw tightened. Surely she had to know how important this party was to him. He set off after her. When he stepped into the kitchen, the door almost bumped Pepper.

"Are you sure?" she said into the phone. "Okay. Okay. I… I'm out of town. I'll be there as soon as I can."

He couldn't see her face, but he could hear the tremor in her voice. "What's the matter?"

She turned to him. Her face was white like the frosted snowflake cookies on the buffet. Her eyes filled with unshed tears, but she didn't speak.

"What's the matter?" He repeated with more urgency.

"I have to go." She rushed to the coat check.

He followed her. "Go where?"

She attempted to shove her hand in the sleeve of her coat, but missed. She tried again and got it. Her movements were quick and jerky. She muttered something under her breath.

"What did you say?"

"My backpack. I need my backpack."

It was hanging right in front of her. He took it down from the hook. "Here you go. Now tell me, what is going on?"

"I don't have time. I have to go."

Concern pumped through his veins. He took her by the shoulders. "Pepper, look at me." When her wide-eyed stare met his, he said, "Tell me what's going on."

"The bakery. It's on fire."

"Fire?" This was the very last thing he was expecting her to say. "Are you sure?"

"It was the alarm company."

"Okay." He rushed to process this information. "Maybe it's a false alarm. Those happen all of the time."

"I have to go." She looked as though she was trying to figure out how to get around him, as he was blocking the doorway.

There was no way she was in any condition to drive. Before he could decide the right and the wrong of it, he said, "I'll take you."

"Fine. Let's go."

The fact that she didn't argue with him let him know how scared she was of losing the most important thing in her life. He texted his driver to meet them in the back. And then he texted Elaine to let her know that she was in charge of the party, as he had an emergency.

Once they were seated in the back of the black sedan, the driver wasted no time heading south to the city. Simon wasn't sure what to do to comfort Pepper. She wrung her hands together as she stared out the window at the passing lights.

He wanted to say something—do something—to lessen her worry. "Everything will be all right."

Her head whipped around and her worried gaze met his. "You don't know that. I was certain I'd forgotten something when we left. What if it was the stove? What if I started the fire?"

He reached out, taking her hand in his and giving it a squeeze. "If that's the case, we'll deal with it."

"Everything I had—everything I dreamed about—is tied up in the bakery. What will I do? How could I be so stupid?"

"Calm down. You don't even know if anything happened."

She left her hand in his. It felt comfortable there, as though they'd been doing it for years. And though it was a small gesture, at least he was able to do something for her.

CHAPTER FOUR

RED LIGHTS FLASHED off the nearby buildings. There were emergency vehicles and people loitering everywhere. A news crew was filming in front of the bakery—or what was left of the bakery.

"This can't be happening," Pepper whispered to herself, willing herself to wake up from this nightmare.

"Pepper?" Simon's voice drew her from her troubled thoughts.

She glanced back out the window. She knew that once she stepped outside the car this horrible scene would become her reality. Her dream had quite literally gone up in smoke.

How had this happened? She'd been so careful, having the place rewired from top to bottom and having a pricey alarm system installed. She'd done everything she could think of, and still it wasn't enough.

"Pepper, if you'd rather remain here, I can go check on things for you," Simon said in the gentlest tone.

She gave a resolute shake of her head. This was her nightmare. She should be the one to face the damage. Pepper drew in a deep breath and released an uneven sigh.

She clutched the door handle. All she could see were the flashing red lights. She had no doubt that for a long while she'd be seeing them every time she closed her eyes. She couldn't stall any longer. She had to go. She would be told what she already knew—her dream had gone up in smoke.

She wasn't sure how she got from the car and past the police officer who was keeping people back from the scene, to stand in front of her bakery. Black soot trailed up the front of the building. The air was heavy with the foul odor of smoke.

The backs of her eyes stung. All she could do was stand there, struggling to take it all in. Just a couple of hours ago she'd had a home, a business. Her heart splintered into a million pieces. Now she had nothing. Only the clothes on her back.

Her throat tightened. Her knees gave way. And then there was an arm around her waist. Simon pulled her back against him. He held them both up.

"Let me take you back to the car," he said gently.

She shook her head, not trusting her voice. She didn't want to go anywhere.

She wasn't sure how much time had passed when a firefighter stepped up to them. "I was told the owner is here." The older man's gaze immediately moved to Simon. "Is that you?"

"Pepper owns the bakery."

She glanced at the man's helmet. It said Captain on it. To her, he was the messenger of bad news. "The bakery—is it completely burned?"

"Afraid so."

In that moment, she was thankful for Simon's support. This was like losing a member of her family…again. She'd lost her eccentric mother and her conservative grandmother. The bakery was all she had left of either of them. And now she didn't have it either.

"But there's some good news," the fire captain said. "Thanks to the fire alarm, we were able to get here fast enough to save the second story. Granted, there will be smoke damage, but it won't need the repairs the first floor will need." The man paused and looked at her as though expecting her to launch endless questions at him. "I'm really sorry, ma'am."

"How…how soon can I get in there?"

He shook his head. "It'll be a while. The fire marshal has been requested."

"The fire marshal?" Simon finally spoke.

The captain nodded. "In cases like this, he's called in to determine if this was a case of arson."

"Arson?" Pepper's eyes widened. "Who would burn down a bakery?"

The captain looked at her, but he didn't say anything. And then she realized she was now considered a suspect—torching her own place for the insurance money. She was certain it wasn't a secret that her bakery was struggling now that the chain store had moved in.

The fire captain seemed to size her up with his gaze. He was trying to figure out if she had it in her to burn down the place.

"Stop looking at me like that. I didn't do this. I would never do this." Her voice was rising and people were starting to turn in their direction. "I'm not an arsonist. Go find who did this! It's not me! It's not me!"

"Let's go," Simon said calmly.

"I don't want to go until he stops looking at me like I'm some criminal."

"Maybe just a little space will help."

She looked at Simon. "Do I look like a criminal to you?"

With his arm still around her waist, Simon directed her away from the bakery. "You look beautiful to me."

Any other time, his compliment would have stirred something within her, but right now there was nothing but torment, angst and grief. There was no room for good feelings. Life as she knew it was over—again.

Why did she keep losing the things and people that meant the most to her?

Her head started to pound and her stomach churned. The rest of it was a blur, until she was once again sitting in the back of Simon's car. They were rushing down the street and she had no idea where they were going. It wasn't like she had anywhere to go.

"Here." Simon pressed a bottle into her hand. "Drink it."

She glanced at the bottle and then at him.

"It's water. Drink it. You look like you're ready to pass out."

Her gaze searched his. "Tell me this is a nightmare. Tell me that when I wake up it will be over."

"I wish I could."

Her bottom lip trembled.

"My beautiful bakery. It's gone." Her voice cracked. "It's all gone."

Was this shock? She'd heard people talk about out-of-body experiences. Was that what was happening to her?

"Do you want me to take you to the hospital?" Simon asked. The concern was evident on his face.

"The hospital? Why? I wasn't in the fire."

"For shock. This can't be easy for you."

She had to pull it together. She'd been doing fine on her own. She couldn't let a fire undo her. She was made of sturdier stuff than that; at least that's what her grandmother used to always tell her when she missed her mother. The Kane women were made of sturdy stuff. They could get through anything.

Pepper glanced at the water. She didn't want it, but she knew if she didn't pull herself together that they would be at the ER posthaste. And that was one more bill she didn't need.

She pressed the bottle to her dry lips. The cool liquid soothed her scratchy throat. She drank half the bottle. After handing it back to him, she leaned back against the black leather upholstery and closed her eyes.

With her eyes still closed, she asked, "Where are we going?"

"Do you have someplace to go? A relative?"

She shook her head. "There's just me."

"A boyfriend?"

Her eyes sprang open and narrowed in on him. "After my last brief but disastrous romantic encounter, I haven't bothered with dating."

Simon's mouth opened, but then he seemed to decide it was best not to say anything at this particular juncture, and his lips pressed together in a firm line.

Good. Because on top of the fire, she didn't have the energy to argue with him.

"Just let me out here." Why was she telling Simon? It wasn't like he was driving the car. She leaned forward, speaking to the driver, "If you could pull over, I'd appreciate it."

The driver didn't say anything. But she could see his gaze in the rearview mirror moving to Simon with a question in his eyes.

Simon shook his head.

Pepper huffed out an indignant breath. "Simon, what are you doing? You can't just kidnap me."

"I'm not. I'm being your friend. You had a huge shock tonight and I'm worried about you. Until I'm sure you're okay and have a safe place to go, I'm going to keep an eye on you."

If he expected her to be grateful, she wasn't. She was... She was full of pent-up anger. It was like the world was out to get her. Every time she found happiness, the rug somehow got ripped out from under her.

And she was taking all her frustration out on Simon. He watched her with concern in his eyes. And rightfully so. She was acting strangely. And she was pretty certain they were nearing the hospital.

Get it together, Pepper.

"I have to go back. I have to look after the bakery," her voice wavered, "My home."

"I'll take care of it." He withdrew his phone from his

pocket and made a brief phone call. "Your building will be secured."

She wondered what it was like to make problems disappear with a mere phone call. If only that's all it took to right all that had gone wrong in her life.

She took a moment to steady her rising emotions. "Where are we going?"

"To my place."

She shook her head. "I can't go back there with all of your guests. I couldn't possibly face them."

"Don't worry. We're not going back to Connecticut. We're going to stay right here in the city. Home, James."

The car slowed at the next intersection and turned away from the hospital that was now only a block away. Thank goodness. If it came down to facing a bunch of doctors or facing her ex, if she could call him that, she would pick Simon. She wasn't sure it was the smartest choice, but it seemed like the simplest at that moment.

The fight had gone out of her, to the point where he feared she might very well collapse. On the ride up in the elevator, he kept a steady arm around her waist, pulling her weight against him.

Once inside his penthouse, he thought of getting her a drink. Something strong to take the edge off. But he didn't know what sort of alcohol she drank or even if she drank at all. And then a thought came to him. It was something his mother used to do for him when he was very young and too worked up to sleep after a run-in with his father.

He led Pepper toward the kitchen. She didn't question where they were going. She simply let him lead the way. If this kept up much longer, he was following through with his initial instinct to take her to the ER.

"Here." He guided her to one of the stools at the center island. "Sit down."

She did it without a fuss.

He hesitated to move from her side, afraid without him next to her that she would collapse. But she held her own and sat there, staring blindly ahead.

"I'm just going to get you something warm to drink." For all intents and purposes, he was talking to himself.

There were just a couple of things he did well in the kitchen. And this happened to be one of them. He set to work.

A couple minutes later, with a warm mug in hand, he turned to Pepper. She looked dazed and lost. Deciding she'd be much more comfortable in one of his guest rooms, he moved to her side.

"How about we make you comfortable?" When she finally looked at him, he asked, "Can you stand?"

She did so without a word.

Together, they made their way to the guest room with the king-size bed. He guided her to it. She sat down on the edge.

He held out the mug. "Here. Have a drink."

She shook her head. Still no words.

He knelt down in front of her and gazed up at her. Her eyes shimmered with unshed tears. That had to be a good sign. Right? Something was going on inside of her. Now if he could just get her to talk.

He lifted the mug. "Go ahead. Have some."

Her gaze moved from him to the mug. "What is it?"

He let out his first full breath since her meltdown back at the bakery. "It's hot chocolate. It's what I used to drink when I was little and had a hard time going to sleep. This is good, but it isn't my secret recipe. I didn't have time to make it tonight, but I promise to make it for you some other time."

She reached for the cup. When her fingers brushed his, he noticed how cold she was. While she drank the hot chocolate, he grabbed a fluffy white throw blanket from the bottom of the bed. He draped it around her shoulders.

She set the cup on the nightstand and leaned back against the headboard. He slipped off her shoes, setting them at the foot of the bed. When he glanced up at her, he noticed her swiping away the tears.

He sat on the edge of the bed. He hated this feeling of helplessness. It was a position he wasn't used to being in. Pepper looked so fragile, as though a breeze could scatter the pieces that made her whole.

He swallowed hard. "Can I get you anything?"

Silence was the only answer.

There had to be something—anything that he could do to help her. He assured himself that it was nothing more than he would feel for a stranger in a similar situation.

"I was thinking—" her soft voice broke through his thoughts "—that I can't remember what we talked about the last time…the last time we had coffee together at the bakery."

He didn't say a word for a moment. This was what she wanted to talk about? With her world crumbling around her, she wanted to talk about them?

He knew it wasn't a good idea to go strolling down memory lane. In fact, it was a very dangerous path laced with emotional bombs that could go off at any time. But at least she was communicating with him. He just wasn't sure how to respond to her.

"I know we talked about a lot of things over the months," she said. "Those early morning coffees were so cozy because no customers ventured in quite that early. It was my favorite time of the day. It was my chance to enjoy the bakery instead of worrying about producing all of the orders for the day. In those early morning hours before the sunrise, everything held such promise. And the bakery was filled with the most amazing aromas from the fresh baked goods." She inhaled deeply as though in her mind she could still smell them instead of the lingering scent of smoke that seemed to follow them around.

He should probably say something here. But these were Pepper's precious memories and he didn't want to say anything to sully them. So he sat by quietly as she took them both back in time to that very special bakery.

She fidgeted with a loose thread on the throw blanket while averting her gaze. "I looked forward to your Wednesday morning visits. I'd tuck away in my mind all of the interesting things that had happened since we last met, just so I'd have something to talk to you about. Each time we parted, it was just until the next time. I never thought there wouldn't be a next time. And now I've been trying to remember the last time we shared coffee at the bakery..." Her voice cracked.

His mind rewound back in time. He remembered everything about her, from the way she fidgeted with the silver necklace when she was nervous to the way her smiles would light up her emerald green eyes. He'd quickly learned that Pepper was someone he would never forget. No matter how much he tried.

"I was late that morning." His gaze met hers, hoping he was doing the right thing. "You were wearing an orange, green and red polka-dotted apron. You called it your autumn apron. And you were all excited because you'd just perfected a new recipe."

As he spoke, she relaxed against the pillows. He longed to reach out and smooth away the strawberry blond curls that rested against her pale cheek. But he didn't want to frighten her off. She'd had enough turmoil for one evening. And so he kept his hands to himself while doing his best to comfort her with his words.

Still, his chest ached for her and all she'd lost that night. That bakery had been so much more than her job. It had been her life. And he ached for the very special friendship that he'd ruined with one night of passion. By letting go of his common sense and following his desires, he'd lost a dear friend. Pepper had been someone who was so easy to be around. She wasn't pushy and she wasn't needy. She was warm and understanding. Sometimes they'd just sit quietly, drinking their coffees and watching as the first morning rays filled the sky.

He clearly recalled the softness of her laughter. Oh, how he missed how her eyes would light up. And he missed how she would tease him about being a workaholic, which he'd often turn around on her, as she worked as many hours as him, if not more.

As her gaze prodded him for more details, he said, "I remember not having time to sit and talk that morning because I was running late. I'd been up most of the night before brainstorming an idea for the Pet Playground. I had a meeting to get to and you had a special order to bake. But we paused at the counter long enough to agree to go out and celebrate after I launched my chain of stores and you added a new line of cakes."

Her eyes lit up as though the memories were starting to come back to her. "The new recipe was a carrot caramel cake. It was going to be a signature cake."

He nodded. "It was moist and delicious. When I went to leave, you stepped out from behind the counter and handed me a box of pastries for the office. I caught a whiff of your perfume." He inhaled deeply, as he had that day. "It was a soft floral fragrance."

"Lavender." She settled further down on the pillows. Her eyes looked heavy.

He thought about it for a moment and then nodded. "The scent works for you."

He couldn't help but wonder if he were to lean forward, if she would smell of lavender. Instead, he remained perfectly still.

"Those were good times." Her voice grew softer as utter exhaustion hit her.

"They were the best." He stood.

"I don't know what I'm going to do." Though her voice was barely above a whisper, he could still hear the raw pain.

Sympathy welled up in him. This shouldn't have happened to her. Pepper was the sweetest, kindest soul. She deserved only the best in life. It was probably the reason she'd dumped him as soon as he'd let down his guard with her. Beneath the stylish haircut and the expensive clothes, he was a damaged soul.

He gave himself a mental shake. This wasn't the time to consider himself. Right now, Pepper needed all his attention.

As a tear trickled down her cheek, he gently swiped it away. "Shh… Just rest for tonight."

"Tomorrow…" Her eyes closed.

Tomorrow would come too soon for both of them. Tomorrow she would have to relive the pain of loss all over again. And he would once again experience that helpless feeling. But that was then and this was now.

He retrieved another blanket from the closet and laid it over her. She was still fully dressed and that couldn't be comfortable to sleep in, but he wasn't going to disturb her. The fact she was sleeping was miracle enough. He hoped in her sleep she was able to escape the nasty reality of her life. He wished for her the sweetest dreams.

He stopped next to her. A strand of hair lay across her face. He reached out, moving it to the side. She didn't stir.

It was then that he noticed the tear tracks on her pale cheeks. Sympathy welled up in his chest. He bent over and placed a gentle kiss to her forehead. If only he knew how to make this better for her…

He reached for the switch on the bedside light. His hand paused in midair. If she were to suddenly wake up, she would most likely be disoriented. But the constant glare of the light might stir her from some much-needed rest. In the end, he turned it off, hoping she would sleep through the night. He walked softly to the doorway. He paused and glanced back. She hadn't moved at all. She was out cold.

As he moved toward the master suite, he couldn't help but recall their early morning chats. If he didn't know better, he'd have sworn she'd taken him down memory lane just to torture him. But he knew she wasn't a vengeful person. Tonight, she'd just needed the comfort she found in those memories.

When the sun rose and reality settled in for both of them, it would be quite apparent that too much had happened for them to go back in time and rekindle that friendship. She could stay until other reasonable arrangements could be made, which should be as soon as the insurance company released funds for temporary lodging.

Until that time, he would keep his distance. It was best for both of them.

But just in case Pepper awoke during the night and needed anything, he left his bedroom door ajar. After changing out of his clothes, he lay in the dark. He stared at the ceiling because he knew sleep would be illusive. Sure enough, his thoughts of Pepper kept him awake long into the night.

CHAPTER FIVE

HE WAS WORRIED.

Maybe they should have gone to the hospital last night.

The following morning, Simon was sitting in the living room at ten o'clock. He'd had his first, second and third cup of coffee. He'd skipped his routine of going to the gym because he wanted to be around in case Pepper needed anything. And she still hadn't roused.

Should he go check on her? After all, he did say he was going to keep an eye on her. Wasn't it his responsibility to make sure she was fine?

He folded the morning paper that he'd skimmed without really noticing anything on the page. He kept thinking of Pepper and remembering her look of utter devastation. He'd never seen anyone look so distraught. He couldn't blame her. He knew how much she cared about the bakery. She was handling the loss far better than he would have should he ever lose Ross Toys.

He moved silently along the hallway toward the guest room. He paused. There were no sounds coming from inside. Maybe she was still sleeping. He glanced at his wristwatch. He doubted it. She was an early riser just like him.

It's one of the reasons they'd become friends over this past year. And since the paparazzi debacle, he had really missed their friendship. He hadn't realized just how much he looked forward to their early morning chats over coffee and a pastry in the wee hours before the bakery filled with people.

Because he'd let his guard down—because he'd allowed himself to get caught up in the moment—he'd lost someone who treated him like a normal person instead of like a boss or a rich man or an eligible bachelor. To Pepper, he'd just been a friendly face. And maybe it was selfish of him, but he wanted that friendship back. Would she be willing to give him another chance?

He raised his knuckles to the door.

Tap. Tap.

He waited. No response.

Tap. Tap. Tap.

"Pepper?"

Still no response.

He was really starting to worry.

His hand moved toward the door handle. He hesitated. Something could be wrong with her. Or perhaps she'd left during the night and was meandering the streets. The thought twisted his gut with worry.

Or maybe she was in the shower. Or perhaps she hadn't slept well and was finally dozing. And it wasn't like they hadn't spent the night together and he hadn't seen her in bed. Still, a lot had changed since that night. In fact, everything had changed.

"I'm coming in," he called out. He eased the door open slowly. "Pepper?"

Silence.

He stuck his head inside the room. He immediately spotted the empty bed and disheveled covers. At least she had gotten some rest.

Just then the door to the en suite opened. Pepper's surprised gaze met his. But it wasn't her reaction to him being in her room that bothered him, it was her pale face.

"Simon, what are you doing in here?"

"Sorry. I knocked. I knocked a lot. And when you didn't respond, I started to worry that you might not feel well."

"I… I'm fine."

He searched her face. He could tell she was lying, but he didn't dare accuse her. Instead, he would pretend everything was fine, which clearly it wasn't. But until he figured out what he could do to help her, it was best to play it safe.

"Can I get you something to eat? Eggs? Toast? Waffles? Or pancakes?"

At that, Pepper's face turned about three shades of green. She held up a finger indicating he should wait. Then the bathroom door slammed shut. What in the world?

As he approached the door, he knew what was the matter. Pepper didn't feel well. It was the shock from last night. He couldn't blame her. If his business was to suddenly go up in flames, he would be utterly devastated too. But she just had to realize that this was just a temporary setback, not the end.

Unless…unless she didn't have insurance. He couldn't imagine not having insurance, but he also knew when money was tight, corners were cut. If that was the case, it just might be the end. No wonder she felt so poorly.

He wasn't sure what to do. He didn't want to make matters worse, so he moved to the doorway and waited. A few minutes later, the bathroom door opened. Pepper stood there. Even her lips were pale this time.

He rushed over to her. "Maybe you should sit down."

She didn't say anything or put up a fight as he guided her to the side of the bed. She must feel as bad as she looked.

"Stay here. I'll be right back."

He rushed to the kitchen. He knew his housekeeper/ cook kept it well stocked. He was about to find out just how well stocked. The pantry was not a place he ventured very often, but when he opened the door, he was quite pleased with the selection.

He quickly located a can of ginger ale. And then he moved to the fridge. Recalling what his mother used to give him when his stomach was upset, he toasted some bread and served it plain.

He returned to the room to find Pepper had made the

bed and was straightening the place. He was shocked she was up and about. She hadn't looked well enough to do any of this. And she was still looking ill.

"You don't have to do that," he said.

"Of course I do." Then she frowned. "You're right. I should strip the bed in order to wash the linens."

He was horrified that she thought she had to come here and do the laundry. "Pepper, come over here." He gestured to a small table in front of the window. When she didn't move, he said, "I pay people to take care of things like changing the bed and washing the laundry. You are my guest. And you don't feel good. You need to take it easy. You had quite a shock last night."

She sighed and moved to the table. She sat down and looked at the things he'd brought her, but she didn't make any motion to eat or drink.

"It's ginger ale and some plain toast," he said, sitting across from her. "My, uh, mother used to give it to me when I didn't feel good. I thought it might help you. But if you prefer something else—"

"No. This is fine." And then her gaze met his. "Thank you for being so thoughtful. And I'm sorry about everything, from tearing you away from your party to making a scene last night and then putting you out—"

"Stop. You don't have to be sorry about anything. To be honest, that party was boring. It was a bunch of people who wanted to be seen."

"Then why did you host it?"

"Because it was expected."

She studied him. "So you did it because people expected you to do it, even though you, personally, didn't enjoy it."

"Something like that. But enough about me. What can I do to help you?"

"You were helping me."

"I was?" He didn't follow her meaning.

She nodded. "By talking about yourself and your party for just a few brief seconds, I was able to think about something besides the nightmare that is now my life."

"Oh." He wasn't used to talking about himself. In fact, he made it a point to share as little as possible, because whatever he told people eventually ended up on some tabloid site.

But Pepper was different. He'd told her a lot about himself and none of it had ended up on any gossip sites. All their morning chat sessions had been kept private.

And even after their night together, when things had gone terribly wrong, she still hadn't turned to the tabloids and vented. Was it wrong that he'd braced himself for that exact eventuality? How could he have doubted Pepper's character? She was exactly what she seemed—a wonderful, caring person.

The events of last night felt like a nightmare.

The problem was, when she woke up this morning, it was all real.

With her stomach now settled, Pepper was on the subway headed toward her bakery. Wearing the same clothes she'd had on yesterday, she sat on the bench as her stop quickly approached.

Soon she would be back at the bakery—or what was left of it. She wrung her hands together. She was hoping in the light of day that the damage would be less than she imagined. Maybe it was just a small stove fire that could be quickly and easily remedied. Could she be that lucky?

She didn't consider herself a lucky person. Everything she'd gained in life she'd worked for, or it had come with a very dear price. Her thoughts turned to the loss of her grandmother and the modest inheritance she'd received. At first, she hadn't wanted to take the money. It just felt wrong to take her grandmother's money and roll it into her dream of a bakery.

And then she'd received a letter from her grandmother's attorney. Her grandmother had written her a short but pointed letter, basically ordering Pepper to follow her dreams. It was so like her grandmother to propel her forward into the unknown, because nothing was gained without taking chances.

But now it had all gone up in smoke. The thought weighed heavy on her heart. She had no idea where to go from here. She definitely needed a plan ASAP.

She couldn't believe Simon had cared for her. She must have been a pathetic mess, for him to take her home last night. She knew the only reason he would take her in would be pity. Because she knew without a doubt that he had absolutely no feelings for her.

It was nice that he'd lingered around the penthouse that morning to make sure she was feeling better and over the shock of the fire. He'd left before her, but she didn't waste much time. She had to find somewhere to live besides Simon's place. She hoped that it would be back in her apartment.

She exited the subway and made her way toward Mulberry Street. It wasn't far from here. Light flurries fell from the sky, melting as the snow hit the sidewalk. Normally, she'd enjoy the wintery scene, but today she was too distraught to find the beauty in anything.

Her feet felt heavy as she walked. Her steps weren't as quick as they'd normally be. All the while, she tried to prepare herself for what she might see, but how did one prepare for the end of a dream?

As she turned the corner, she caught her first glimpse of the bakery. There was yellow caution tape up around it. Pepper barely noticed the people she passed on the sidewalk or the cars rushing up the road. Her sole focus was on the bakery.

And then she stopped across the street from it. Her heart clenched. Her beautiful bakery was a broken, sooty mess. Tears stung the back of her eyes. She blinked them away. She'd fallen apart last night, but today she had to keep it together. She had to formulate a plan.

She hesitated. She stood there taking in the boarded-up display window and the stripes of soot running up the white painted brick. The black awning seemed to have fared okay. She crossed the street, finding it was only an illusion. Upon closer inspection, she could see the toll the fire had taken on the material. It would need replacing.

It might be a mess, but the bakery was still standing. That had to be a good sign. A glimmer of hope flickered within her. Was it possible to rebuild her beloved bakery?

She moved to the door. There was a sign on it, but she didn't pause to read it. She was anxious to get inside and see what needed to be done.

Her hand touched the door handle just as it was pulled open. A tall man in a firefighter's jacket stood there. His expression was serious as he frowned at her.

"You can't be here. Didn't you read the sign?"

"But I own the bakery."

He nodded. "You still can't be here."

"But I live here." All she had were the clothes on her back. "I need to get to my things."

"That's not going to happen. The fire marshal hasn't been here to do his report yet."

"What report?"

He didn't answer her as he stepped outside, forcing her to back up on the sidewalk. The man was so tall that she couldn't see around him to get a glimpse of the inside.

The man eyed her as though making up his mind about her. "There's a suspicion of arson."

"Arson?"

In the back of her mind, she vaguely remembered arson being mentioned the night before. The memories were blurry. But by the way this man was looking at her, he thought she was guilty.

* * *

The bakery was as bad as he remembered.

Simon had just had a look at the back of the building, since no one would allow him inside. He'd been hoping the fire was minor and Pepper could return home today, but it wasn't going to happen. That much was evident from the outside. He could only imagine the damage to the inside.

He thought of Pepper and another wave of sympathy came over him. The fire last night had hit her so hard that he wasn't sure how she was going to take the sight of her bakery all charred. It didn't even slightly resemble the trendy bakery that it'd been a mere twenty-four hours ago.

He rounded the building and stopped on the sidewalk in front of the bakery as he spotted Pepper. The short-tempered fire captain that he'd had the misfortune of running into was now walking away from her. That man was definitely not the friendliest guy. His words were short and blunt.

When Simon had tried to get inside to eyeball the damage, he'd been told no. There was no room for discussion. The captain didn't care who Simon was, and that was fair enough, but the man provided absolutely no information that would help Pepper. None whatsoever. And so Simon had to wonder what the man was holding back.

He focused his attention on Pepper. His jaw tightened when he saw the distressed look on her face. He was certain the captain had done nothing to help matters.

Simon approached her. "Are you okay?"

She shook her head. "Have you seen this place?" And then she moved her distraught gaze to him. "What are you doing here? Shouldn't you be at the office?"

"I wanted to see where things stood."

"Don't worry." Her eyes reflected her pain. "I'll be out of your penthouse as soon as I contact the insurance company."

"There's no rush." He instinctively reached out to her,

drawing her near. Initially, she resisted, but then she let herself be drawn into a hug.

There on the sidewalk, with flurries swirling around them, they stood wrapped in each other's arms. Holding her close drove home how much he'd truly missed her—missed everything about her.

He murmured against her hair, "You can stay as long as you need."

She pulled away, and with great reluctance, he let her go. "I'll make other arrangements. You've done too much already."

Perhaps it was best to change the subject. "What did the fire captain say to you?"

"That I couldn't get inside." Her fine brows drew together. "Did he let you inside?"

Simon shook his head. "He's a very unfriendly guy."

"That's what I thought. I tried to tell him that I live here and I needed to get to my stuff—especially my clothes. He didn't care."

"Hopefully, you'll be able to get inside soon. Can I give you a lift back to the penthouse?"

She shook her head. "I have some shopping I need to do."

"Can I drop you anywhere?"

Again, she shook her head. "It isn't far and I feel like walking."

He watched her walk away, wondering if he should go with her. Something told him if he tried, she'd refuse his company. At least she had his phone number. If she needed anything, she could call him. But would she?

CHAPTER SIX

AND THE HITS kept coming.

The insurance company refused to release the funds until arson was ruled out.

Pepper couldn't believe she was suspected of arson. Her. A person who loved her little bakery with all her heart. A person who was lost without her warm kitchen filled with scents of cinnamon, apples, cherries and a bunch of buttery goodness.

Not sure what to tell Simon, she took advantage of his invitation to make herself at home in his penthouse. So after a quick stop at the grocery store, she made her way to Simon's massive kitchen. She lost herself in her baking. It was cathartic for her.

And then it was time to head to the animal shelter where she volunteered at least once a week, sometimes it was more. Next to her bakery, it was where she was most comfortable. And until the renovations were complete, Pepper looked forward to her visits to the Helping Paw Shelter each weekend. She carried in the boxes of cookies, cupcakes and Danishes for the adopt-a-pet event.

"Pepper, I didn't think you'd be able to make it." Stephanie, the assistant director of the shelter, rushed over and gave her a hug. "We heard about the fire, and I'm so sorry. Is there anything I can do?"

"Thank you. I appreciate the offer, but there's nothing to do right now but wait for all of the paperwork to get done." She didn't want to discuss the arson investigation.

"How bad was it?"

Images of the scorched front of the bakery flashed through her mind. "It looks bad from the outside."

"What about the inside? What about your apartment?"

Pepper shook her head. "I don't know. They won't let me inside yet."

"Oh, Pepper, that's awful. Where are you staying?"

"With a friend." Heat rushed to her face when she thought of Simon. She didn't know if he still qualified as a friend, but she didn't know what else to call him.

A smile eased the worried look on Stephanie's face. "Must be a guy friend."

Her body grew increasingly warm. "Why would you say that?"

"Because you're blushing. Tell me it's Simon Ross."

"Shh…" Pepper glanced around to make sure they weren't overheard.

"It is." Stephanie grinned and quietly clapped her hands. "How did this happen?"

Pepper needed someone to talk to about the events of her life and Stephanie had become a good friend. She gave her a brief overview of the events of the last twenty-four hours.

"Wow. I can't believe all of that happened to you."

"Me either." Her thoughts turned to the problems with the insurance company. "I don't know what I'm going to do."

"I'd offer to let you stay with me, but all I have is a lumpy couch. It's yours if you want it though."

"Thanks. I'll keep it in mind."

Stephanie checked the time. "Let's get a table set up for all of your goodies."

Pepper glanced around and noticed that nothing for the event was set out. They must have thought she wasn't coming. "I should have called to let you know I could still make it. And I have some goodies for the four-footed little ones." Lately, she'd started baking doggie biscuits and experimenting with kitty treats.

"You know, they like them so much that you should consider starting your own pet line." Stephanie's gaze moved to all the baked goods. "I can't believe you baked all of this, considering everything that just happened to you."

"It felt good to bake. I might have made a little too much."

"Never. It'll all be gone by the end of the evening."

Pepper set up the table with the pastries she'd brought with her. "You really think so?"

"I do." She glanced up at the clock. "We have a little time before the adoption party. Come with me."

Pepper glanced back at the table that wasn't totally set up. She really should stay here. She needed it to look its best. Even though her bakery was temporarily out of business, she was not giving up. She intended to use the insurance money to fix everything and then life would go back to normal. In the meantime, she was passing out her business cards in hopes that people would call her for cakes and remember the name of her bakery and come to visit when she had her grand reopening.

"You can do that later," Stephanie said. "I have someone for you to meet."

Meet? Pepper wondered who it could be. She'd been coming to the shelter for so long that she knew all the volunteers by name. Maybe they'd taken on someone new.

Pepper followed Stephanie to the back of the shelter where they housed the puppies. Each doggie looked so sweet to Pepper. They all had their sad stories that pulled at Pepper's heart strings. If it were up to her, she'd adopt them all. If only she had a big enough house and all of the hours necessary to care for them.

She did take care of foster dogs from time to time. They were usually very special cases. However, with the opening of the bakery, she hadn't had the free time that she used to.

Stephanie led her to the last kennel and stopped. "Pepper, I'd like you to meet Daisy."

Inside the kennel was a beagle puppy. She was timid and smashed herself against the back corner. She was the most adorable fur baby with her brown, floppy ears. Pepper's heart immediately melted.

"What happened?" she asked.

"We don't know the details. Only that someone found the puppies in a box in the freezing cold. Daisy was the only one to make it. However, she isn't ready for adoption yet. She has a lot of recovery to do. And as you can tell, she needs to be socialized. She doesn't trust people, and with her history, I can't blame her."

"Can I try?" Pepper was drawn to the puppy.

"Go ahead. I don't have to tell you to take it slow."

No, she didn't. Pepper had done this countless times. She opened the kennel door. "Hey, Daisy. My name's Pepper." She wanted the puppy to get used to her voice. "I was hoping we could be friends."

Daisy silently stared at her with those big brown eyes. Her whole body, from her nose to the tip of her tail, quivered with fear. She was going to be a tough case, but Pepper was eager to work with her. Immediately, Pepper felt a bond forming between them.

In one breath, she knew she wanted to take Daisy home. In the next breath, she remembered the sobering fact that she didn't have a home. And Pepper was quite certain that Simon would not appreciate having a puppy on his gleaming floors or near his priceless pieces of art. To Pepper, it was like the man lived in a museum rather than a home.

"I'll just let you two get acquainted," Stephanie said with a knowing smile.

A while ago, Pepper had mentioned that she would love to have a beagle. Leave it to Stephanie to remember. But she was not adopting Daisy. She was in absolutely no position to even consider it.

Pepper reached into her pocket and pulled out the doggie biscuits she'd made. They were all too big for the little girl. "I'm sorry," Pepper said, "I don't have any treats for puppies. We don't have too many puppies your size that pass through here. But I promise to make you some for our next visit."

Pepper stayed there visiting with Daisy for as long as she dared before going to finish setting up the table. And then she took a seat at the information desk, where she was assigned to work for the next few hours.

She was tired. Absolutely exhausted.

It felt as though she hadn't slept in days.

Pepper used the spare key Simon had given her to let herself into the penthouse. All she wanted now was to curl up with a black-and-white classic movie—

"You're home."

Pepper jumped at the sound of Simon's voice. She dropped her things near the door, then followed the voice to the living room. Simon stood next to the wall of windows overlooking Central Park.

"Did you need something?" she asked.

"I didn't know where you were, and when I couldn't reach you on the phone, I, uh, didn't know what to think, with you not feeling well this morning."

She pulled her phone out of her back pocket. The missed calls appeared on the screen. He hadn't called once. He'd called twice.

Was he worried about her? Really? Simon Ross had been worried that something had happened to her?

For the briefest moment, she toyed with the idea that he still cared—that they were still good friends. And then she dismissed the ridiculous notion. He was most likely hoping she'd found other accommodations.

She had a tiny amount in her savings. It wouldn't tide her over for long, but she didn't have much choice.

"Sorry. I had my phone on Mute. I'm feeling better now. Nothing to worry about." She thought about telling him that she'd been at the animal shelter, but she decided they weren't back at the stage where they were sharing things with each other. "Before I go, can I get you something to eat?" It seemed like such a small way to repay him for all he'd done for her, but at the moment it was all she had to offer.

He shook his head. "I'm not hungry."

"Then I'll get my things and leave."

He pressed his hands to his sides. "Where will you be staying? You know, in case something comes up and I need to reach you."

What would come up that he'd need to reach her? She refrained from posing the question. Instead, she mentioned checking into a small motel in New Jersey.

He frowned. "Surely your insurance can do better than that."

"They aren't paying. I should get going before it gets late." She turned to walk away, hoping he wouldn't ask more questions—questions she didn't want to answer.

"Why aren't they paying? You do have insurance, don't you?"

She turned back to him and shrugged her shoulders. "I do. But there's a suspicion of arson. And until it's resolved, they've put a hold on the money."

"That's not right. If they knew you, they'd know you would never do such a thing."

It felt good to know that he was in her corner, believing in her innocence. "But that's the thing—they don't know me." She worried her bottom lip. "What if it was arson? How will I ever prove that it wasn't me?"

Sympathy glinted in his eyes as he approached her.

"Don't worry. It'll all work out. And soon you'll have your bakery back."

"But not in time."

"In time?" His brows drew together.

"For all of the holiday events I had scheduled."

"I'm sure you'll get plenty of orders once you've re-opened."

She wished she felt as confident as he sounded. "Only time will tell."

She turned and headed for her room. It wouldn't take long to pack her things. She had a bag of clothes she'd just purchased and that was it.

Tomorrow she'd have to start canceling her remaining list of events that she had scheduled. No matter what happened with the arson investigation, there was no way the bakery would be open and ready for operation.

Knock. Knock.

She hadn't closed her door. She turned to find Simon standing there. His forehead was creased as though he had something on his mind.

When he didn't say anything, she asked, "Did you want something?"

He nodded. "I want you to stay."

Her heart leapt into her throat. What was he saying? Had she heard him correctly? Surely not. It had been a really long day.

"What did you say?"

He stepped further into the room. With each step he took, her heart beat faster. For just a moment, she imagined him sweeping her into his arms and passionately kissing her like he'd done on that not-so-long-ago night. She missed him, his embrace, his mouth against hers—

"I'd like you to stay." His voice startled her from her wayward thoughts. "You know, until your apartment is ready. You can use the kitchen to bake. It's not like I ever use it."

She struggled not to stare at his inviting mouth—to remember the delicious things he could do to her with it. What was wrong with her? They came from very different worlds. They obviously wanted different things in life. So why was she still drawn to him? Why did she long for him in her dreams?

Oblivious to her inner turmoil, Simon said, "I'll go order dinner while you unpack."

"Wait," she called out. "Why would you do that? Why would you want me here?" And then another more troublesome thought came to mind—troublesome from the standpoint that she didn't trust herself around him. "We aren't going to share a bed."

"No. That was a one-time thing."

His brush-off stung. It put an immediate end to her heated thoughts. Not that she wanted to pick things up where they'd left off. Still, she'd thought that night had been special for not just her. Obviously, she'd been wrong.

She told herself it was for the best; everyone and everything she cared for was eventually lost to her. She couldn't lose anyone or anything else. She was better off on her own.

"Won't my staying here be awkward?"

"I work long hours. I'm not seeing anyone. So you'll have the place to yourself most of the time. Now, I'll go order dinner."

And with that he turned and walked away like it was all settled because he said so. Part of her wanted to stay. Though this place was a bit on the cold, minimalist side, it was clean. She knew on her budget the cleanliness of the motels she could afford would be iffy at best. But why would any of that matter to Simon?

She followed him into the kitchen, where he'd just disconnected a phone call. His motives shouldn't matter to her, but they did. She tried to tell herself it was idle curiosity, nothing more.

"I hope you don't mind pepperoni pizza," he said.

"It's fine. But I can't accept your offer to stay here. It's too much. I could never repay you. You've already done so much."

He sighed. "The food is ordered. You have to eat. And it's getting late. Stay the night and think about it."

What would one more night hurt? It would certainly help stretch her funds. But she had to do something for him in return.

"I could bake you something to take to the office. Perhaps some cherry turnovers."

He didn't say anything at first, but a spark of interest shone in his eyes. "It's a deal."

Not exactly an even exchange—far from it—but at least she could hold her head up.

CHAPTER SEVEN

HE HAD A very important meeting.

It was about his company's expansion.

Simon bounded out of bed, ready to take on the world. The plan was to kick off the new line of stores right before Christmas with a shop here in New York, and then after Christmas, they would start unveiling the chain in various large cities throughout the country. But something just wasn't right.

As he grabbed a quick shower, he mulled over his uneasiness with the project. It had been bothering Simon for months. There was something lacking from their plans, that extra oomph to take their Pet Playground from okay to amazing. They didn't want to be just another pet store. They needed it to be a destination. They needed to offer something shoppers couldn't get anywhere else.

He'd had his team working on it for months. And so far, they'd come up with some good ideas, but nothing to wow him. And now their first store was about to be revealed without the wow factor. If he didn't do something fast, the new chain would sink before it even launched.

And he wouldn't let that happen.

But in the back of his mind, his father's harsh words echoed. *"You're a loser. You'll always be a loser."*

It wasn't the only time his father had spewed such hurtful words, but those were the final words his father had ever said as he was led in handcuffs from the courtroom. Ever since, Simon had strived to prove the man wrong—to prove to himself that he wasn't anything like the man with whom he shared DNA.

Simon sighed, closed his eyes and shook his head, chasing away the troubling thoughts. The ghosts of the past weren't worth dwelling on. He had more important things to do—lots of things that required his full attention.

He opened his eyes, focusing on the here and now. He dressed and headed for the kitchen. When he stepped through the doorway, he expected to find Pepper already busy baking up some wonderful smelling creations. Or decorating something she'd baked the evening before. But when he stepped into the room, there weren't any lights on. The kitchen was empty.

Where was Pepper? She'd told him the night before how much work she had to do today for the party this evening. She'd even asked how early she could start in the kitchen without disturbing him. So where was she?

He headed for her room.

Tap. Tap.

"Pepper?"

"Come in." Her voice sounded weak. It definitely lacked her usual pep.

He opened the door to find her in bed. He didn't have to ask her to know that she didn't feel well, again. This was the second day in a row. And she didn't seem to be getting any better.

He could understand the first day, with the shock of the fire. But two days due to shock with no improvement? He wasn't buying it. There was something more afoot.

"Get dressed," he said, pulling his phone from his pocket. "You're going to the doctor."

"What? No. I'll be fine. Just give me a bit. I promised to bake the items for the office—"

"Forget the baking." He shook his head. "You're not well. And this has been going on too long. I want a doctor to have a look at you and make sure it's nothing serious."

Pepper jumped out of bed. "See? I'm—"

Her face grew pale and she rushed to the bathroom. She sent the door slamming shut behind her.

Fine. Right. And I'm Santa Claus.

He pulled up the number of his family doctor. The man may be old now, but he'd been treating Simon his whole life. He wouldn't trust anyone else with Pepper.

By the time he got off the phone, having arranged an appointment right away, Pepper had returned from the bathroom. "I'm fine. I just got out of bed too fast, is all."

As though she hadn't just made the flimsiest excuse, he said, "You have a doctor's appointment this morning. Get dressed and we'll be off."

She perched on the edge of the bed. "I told you. I'm fine."

"Actually, you got to *I'm* and then you rushed out of the room. So I don't believe you're fine. I think you need to see a doctor, because this could be something serious."

She shook her head. "You're making too much of this."

"And you're not making enough of it."

She crossed her arms and stared at him. "I can't go."

He pressed his hands to his waist. He could be just as stubborn as her. "Why not?"

She didn't speak at first. When she did, her voice was soft, as though the admission was hard for her. "Because bad things always happen to my family when it comes to doctors and hospitals." She shook her head as though chasing away bad memories. Softly but firmly she said, "I can't."

His arms lowered. "I had no idea." He sat beside her. "What happened?"

She glanced away, keeping him from seeing into her expressive eyes. "It started when I was eight." Her voice was rough with emotion. "My mother was walking home from her baking job at the local grocery store. A car came out of nowhere." Pepper drew in a deep breath. "It hit her, sending her tumbling over the roof—" Her voice caught.

"The driver kept going. My mother…she was taken to the hospital. I—I remember being allowed to see her before surgery. Her hand was so cold. Her face was a pasty white…" Pepper shook her head as though chasing away the painful images. "She died in surgery."

He reached out to her, hesitated and withdrew his hand. "I'm sorry."

"My grandmother took me in. And then one day she went from being healthy and bossy to being a victim of breast cancer. She went through months of chemo before the doctors declared nothing more could be done." Pepper turned to him. "So you see why I keep my distance from doctors."

"But this is different. You'll be fine."

"Exactly." She stood. "That's why I don't need to go."

He got to his feet. His gaze met hers. They stood there staring at each other for the longest time.

He sighed. "Has anyone told you that you're particularly stubborn?"

"I believe my mother had mentioned it on occasion. So, are you going to stand there all day?"

He rubbed the back of his neck. How was he going to get through to her that she really needed a doctor to examine her?

As though in answer to his thoughts, her face grew pale. She pressed a hand to her stomach before rushing out of the room once more. His concern for her health intensified.

When she returned a little bit later, she was still pale. "Well, don't just stand there. I have to get ready."

At last he was making progress. "Don't take long. I had to call in a favor to get this appointment."

"I won't. I have work to do. And so do you."

He was already reaching for his phone again as he headed for the door. Once the bedroom door was closed, he started texting his assistant. He told her to cancel any meetings that didn't have to do with the new store launch. And then he had her push back his remaining meetings.

She asked him if anything was wrong. It wasn't like him not to come into the office first thing in the morning, much less cancel important meetings. He assured her that everything was fine. At least, he hoped so.

He was making a big deal of nothing.

And that's exactly what Pepper told the doctor a short time later. The man was older, with silver hair and observant eyes behind his gold-rimmed glasses. He was a quiet man who only spoke when he needed to, but he appeared to listen to everything Pepper nervously said.

It wasn't that she was worried there was something wrong with her. She knew it was just stress—lots of stress. Who wouldn't feel the pressure in her situation? And that's exactly what she told the doctor.

"So you see," she told the doctor. "I'm just stressed out. Simon is worrying about nothing. If you could just tell him that, we can get out of your way."

"We'll just wait for your test results. It won't be much longer."

Simon was out in the waiting room. She could just imagine him pacing a hole in the carpet. Who'd have guessed Simon was such a worrier?

The doctor started for the door.

"Could you have someone show Simon back here?" she asked.

The doctor nodded in his quiet way.

Besides, it would help to have someone distract her. Otherwise, she would soon be climbing the walls, wanting to get out of here. Her grandmother had come to the doctor for one thing and walked out with orders to have tests done for something else entirely.

Was that what was going to happen to her? Surely not.

She was just letting her imagination get the best of her. It was this place. It gave her the creeps…

The door opened and Simon poked his head inside. "The nurse said I could come back."

Pepper sat on the edge of the paper-lined examination table. Her legs dangled over the edge. "I'm almost ready to go."

Simon stepped into the room and closed the door. "Everything okay?"

She nodded. "I told you. It's just stress."

He let out a sigh. "That's good. You had me worried."

"You should have listened to me."

"So what are we waiting for?"

"Your doctor. He's the kind that likes to dot all his i's and cross his t's. I noticed he even has all his charts on paper still."

"He's older. He's set in his ways. But don't worry, he knows what he's doing."

She nodded in understanding. "He just has a couple of tests that he's waiting on."

Simon rested his hands on his waist as he rocked from side to side. He looked about as comfortable as she did. They both just needed a distraction.

"What would you be doing if you were at work today?"

He glanced up with a surprised look. "You're interested in my work?"

She shrugged. "Sure. Why not?"

He sighed. "I'd be working on the new chain of stores we're prepared to open in the coming year."

"That sounds so exciting. I'll just be happy to reopen the bakery by Valentine's Day, if I'm really lucky."

"Don't worry. I'm sure you'll be up and running in no time."

If only he was right. But she didn't want to talk about the bakery. Not right now.

She noticed he wasn't smiling. In fact, he'd frowned when he mentioned the new stores.

"What's bothering you about the new stores?"

He glanced at her. "Why do you think something is wrong?"

"Just a feeling I get. Talk to me. Sometimes it helps to vocalize your concerns." So long as the topic wasn't about those test results.

"Because there's nothing to make the chain stand out."

"Won't you have Ross Toys designed for pets?"

"Yes."

"Well, there you go. Ross Toys is world renowned. Pet owners will want only the best for their four-legged babies."

"Agreed. But I feel that we're missing something. I just can't put my finger on it. But I'll know it when I see it."

"Wish I could be of more help—"

Tap. Tap.

The door opened and the doctor stepped inside. The moment of truth had arrived. And Pepper was pretty certain the doctor was going to confirm her self-diagnosis of too much stress.

In fact, she was so certain that she said, "There's nothing wrong with me, right?"

The doctor smiled and gazed at her from behind his bifocals. "Not exactly."

"What is it?" Simon asked. "And when is she going to get better?"

"I'd say in seven or so months."

"What?" Simon asked.

Realization was dawning on Pepper. She'd been so stressed over the bakery and the messy breakup with Simon, not to mention the paparazzi, that she'd missed what was right in front of her face. All the pieces fell into place.

"You're pregnant," the doctor said.

He continued to talk and handed her information, but all she could think about was that she was pregnant with

Simon Ross's baby. When she finally gathered her wits, she glanced at Simon. He looked like his whole world had just blown up. She supposed in a way it had.

As with the fire, she had no idea how to deal with this latest surprise.

CHAPTER EIGHT

COULD THIS REALLY be happening?

He was going to be a father?

No words were spoken on the ride home, but it was a far from quiet ride. Rapid chaotic thoughts ricocheted in Simon's mind. Pregnant? They were pregnant? He was going to be a father?

How could this be? Well, he knew exactly how it had happened. In fact, he could replay the night of conception scene by vivid scene in his mind. And that's how he knew it was possible.

And here he touted himself as such a cautious man. A man who planned for things and didn't take unnecessary risks. Long ago, he'd sworn to himself that he was never going to have kids. He couldn't take a chance that he would mess them up as badly as his father had with him.

And what had he done? Broken that promise to himself.

He didn't even remember the elevator ride from the underground garage up to the penthouse. He unlocked the front door and stepped aside to allow Pepper to enter.

"Pepper?" When she turned to him with a stunned look still in her eyes, he said, "We need to talk."

She nodded before heading into the living room. She perched on the edge of the couch for a few seconds. Then she stood and moved to the window. She didn't say anything, leaving it up to him to start this difficult conversation.

"Did you know?" He wanted to think she hadn't purposely been keeping him in the dark, but he had to know for sure.

"Is that what you think? That I was keeping this great big secret from you?"

"You kept refusing to go to the doctor. If you already knew you were pregnant that would explain it."

"No." Her voice was adamant. "I didn't know until the doctor told both of us. If I was trying to keep it a secret, do you think I would have asked you back to the exam room?"

She did have a good point. But he wasn't ready to accept that he was going to be a father. Not yet. "And the baby... You're positive it's mine?"

Her gaze narrowed into a glare. "Unlike you, I don't immediately jump from one relationship to the next."

He supposed he might deserve that comment. Until now, he'd never had a reason to remain in a relationship. But everything was changing rapidly and he was struggling to keep up.

He raked his fingers through his hair, not caring what it looked like. "What are we going to do?"

"We? When did you and I become a *we*?"

"When your pregnancy test came up positive."

She crossed her arms. "I can do this myself."

He restrained a sigh of relief. On the ride home, he'd thought about their circumstances and he'd come to one conclusion. He was not under any circumstances following in his family's misguided steps and getting married out of some misguided sense of obligation.

His mother had been pregnant with him when she'd married his father. It had been the single biggest mistake of both their lives—at least that's the way he saw it. His mother might have a different opinion. But no matter what, a baby would not change his stance on marriage—it wasn't for him.

"You don't have to do it alone," he said. "But I'm not getting married."

"Neither am I. Not a chance."

He had to admit that he was shocked at her adamant

response. "I didn't know you were opposed to marriage. Or is it me that you object to?"

"Why does it matter? It's not like you're offering."

It was true. He shouldn't care. He took off his suit coat and tossed it over the back of the couch. He paced back and forth. This bickering wasn't getting them anywhere. They had to make a plan.

He may not be into marriage, but that didn't mean he was walking away from his obligation. He definitely wouldn't do that. He wasn't sure he was father material. In fact, he was quite certain he was a less-than-ideal candidate. But he could and would support both Pepper and the baby. It was more than his father ever did for him and his mother.

The memories came flooding back. His father was a man with two faces. The smiling, charming man for friends and acquaintances. But behind closed doors, his father was a totally different man. Nothing was ever good enough for him. And if something was wrong, it was always Simon's mother's fault.

Simon squeezed his eyes closed, blocking out the painful images. But there was one thing he couldn't escape—his fear that lurking within him were the same traits his father had. What if he ended up hurting Pepper and, indirectly, their child? Not physically. He'd never ever raise a hand to a woman or a child. But emotionally, he had scars that he couldn't move beyond.

His blood ran cold. That couldn't happen.

He didn't know what to do about his DNA. There was no way to run from it—to hide from the genes that made him. And then there were the things he'd seen and heard growing up. The yelling, the fighting—it was all he'd known. Could a person really change what had been practically stamped upon his DNA? He highly doubted it.

The key to his child having a happy, loving home was Pepper. She was so full of goodness that it radiated from her. She loved life. She loved baking. She loved tending to her customers—including him.

He'd never forget the morning when he'd gotten word that his childhood friend had unexpectedly died. He'd felt lower than low because he'd let distance grow in the relationship. His friend, Clay, had tried over the years to rekindle the relationship, but Simon had let his drive for business and his need to become someone totally different from his father be his sole focus. That gray drizzly morning, after hearing of his friend's unexpected death, he'd strolled into the Polka Dotted Bakery. He'd been out walking aimlessly, as sleep had evaded him.

And there had been Pepper. She'd been like a ray of sunshine in a dark, stormy sky. And he'd clung to that bright light. She'd never known how much her company had meant to him.

Instead, they'd just sat there talking about the bakery and a bunch of trivial things. And yet that conversation was what he'd needed to survive his guilt—to keep putting one foot in front of the other as he'd attended the funeral, as he'd faced his own mortality.

And then the next week, when he just couldn't stay away, he'd made his way back to the bakery. He didn't know if she'd be there. At the time, he didn't know that she owned the bakery. Still, he'd had to go back if there was a chance that he'd see her again—talk to her again.

If she could do that for a perfect stranger—make that much of a positive impact—he was quite certain she would make the perfect mother for his son or daughter.

Pepper turned her back to Simon.

He wasn't the only one caught off guard by this news.

A baby changed everything. It meant opening her heart to another person for the first time in a long time. The thought stilled the breath in her lungs.

She wasn't ready for this. She'd lost so much already.

The thought of caring for someone else, a little human counting on her for everything, was daunting. But the baby didn't have a choice in these matters.

And neither did she. Pepper moved her hand over her abdomen, imagining the little baby inside her. She loved it already. How could she not?

With a baby to support, she'd need the bakery. If only the fire marshal would complete his report so she could get the repairs started.

She glanced over her shoulder at Simon as he yanked his tie loose and unbuttoned the collar of his white dress shirt. For a man known for his coolness in some of the toughest business negotiations, he had certainly lost his cool when he'd found out he was going to be a father.

But she had to wonder if he was planning to be in the baby's life. After all, a baby wouldn't actually fit into his glass-and-modern-art decor. But could he really turn his back on his own child?

She sensed Simon stopping behind her. She turned to him and their gazes met. They couldn't leave things like this. She had to know if she was in this all alone.

He cleared his throat. "I'm sorry I'm not handling this better. I never thought I'd be in this position."

"I know you don't want to get married. And neither do I. But I need to know if you're planning to be in our child's life?"

"I'll pay child support."

"What about partial custody or visitation?"

He didn't say anything.

Pepper went on, because she had strong feelings about the subject. "I know fatherhood might not have been something you planned for your future, but now that it's a reality, I hope you'll be a part of the baby's life."

His troubled gaze met hers. "You don't know what you're asking."

"I do know. I grew up never knowing my father. I always thought someday my mother would tell me about him. But then she was killed and my chance to learn about him died with her. I don't want our child to wonder about you."

His gaze searched hers. "You want me to be a regular part of the child's life?"

She nodded. "It's important not only for our child, but for you too. I know you, Simon. You'd never forgive yourself if you weren't a part of our son or daughter's life."

He shook his head. "There's so much you don't know about me." He glanced away. "I'm not this great guy you think I am. I have skeletons in my closet."

"Everyone does. It's what you do about them that decides what sort of person you are."

His gaze returned to hers. "You do know that you'll never have to worry about money. I'll make sure the baby has everything they could possibly want—"

"Except you?"

He shrugged. "I… I don't know. I need to think."

It wasn't a yes, but it wasn't a no either. So she'd take it.

"We were both caught off guard today," she said. "It'll take time to figure this out. But I hope you'll keep an open mind where the baby is concerned."

He nodded. "I will."

"You should probably go to the office and deal with the upcoming store opening. I have a party to finish preparing for." And then, realizing that the news of the baby might have changed their arrangement, she asked, "Is it all right if I still use the kitchen?"

His eyes widened with surprise. "Of course. You'll be here when I get home?"

"I will."

He left for the office looking a bit disheveled compared to his normal clean-cut appearance. She couldn't blame him. It had been quite a day and it wasn't even lunchtime yet.

Where did they go from here?

CHAPTER NINE

HE'D THOUGHT AND thought and then thought some more.

The answers about the baby still eluded him.

How was he going to be a good father when he'd never had one?

The next morning, Simon sleepwalked through his usual routine. He'd been up most of the night tossing and turning. His thoughts halted as he opened his bedroom door. He inhaled the most delicious aroma. He followed it to the kitchen, where he heard Christmas carols playing and the sweet sound of Pepper's voice.

He placed his hand on the swinging door and pushed. He entered the kitchen to find Pepper in a black apron, pulling a tray out of the oven. She turned and placed it on the enormous island. Her gaze strayed across him and she pressed her lips together, silencing her beautiful voice. She didn't smile, but she didn't frown either. That was something at least.

She moved to her phone and silenced the music. "Sorry. I didn't mean to bother you. Sometimes I get to baking and totally forget about everything else."

"It's not a problem. In fact, I like hearing you sing. You have a beautiful voice." He didn't come in here to flatter her, but he'd been moved by her voice. "Are you feeling better this morning?"

She shrugged. "It comes and goes."

He glanced around at all the finished baked goods. "You must have been up for hours."

"I didn't sleep well."

"Me either." He walked over to take a closer look at the

gingerbread men on the kitchen island. "I'm glad to see you're making yourself at home."

She arched a brow at him. "Are you?"

She doubted him? But then again, he hadn't been the most congenial host after they got the news about the baby. "I wasn't myself yesterday."

Pepper placed another tray of cupcakes in the oven and set the timer. Then she turned back to him. "I want you to know that this pregnancy wasn't planned."

"I didn't think it was."

Pepper was the most honest person he'd ever known. And whether he wanted to admit it or not, she was good for him. She made him want to be a better person—to know that if he kept trying, he could overcome whatever stood before him. And his life was noticeably dimmer without her in it.

Her gaze met his. "Do you mean that?"

He nodded. "I do. And I'd like you to stay here, until your apartment is repaired."

She shook her head. "I don't think that's a good idea."

"You're better off here than in some motel. If you need anything, I'll be here for you." This was more important to him than he'd ever imagined. "And you can use the kitchen to continue doing as much of your work as you feel up to."

Before she could say anything, the doorbell rang.

A frown pulled at his face. He wasn't expecting anyone. He rarely entertained guests in his penthouse. He preferred to keep it as his private domain.

"I'll be right back." He turned for the door.

With a doorman, unannounced guests were limited to those who were preapproved. The list was quite short. But it could be a delivery for Pepper.

He swung the door open and found his mother standing there, every dark strand of her pixie cut in place and her makeup perfectly done. She did not look like a woman on the verge of her sixtieth birthday.

"Mother, what are you doing here?" He didn't know whether to be more shocked that she was at his place or that she'd arrived at such an early hour.

She swept past him into the foyer. "Is it true?"

"Is what true?" As he closed the door, he realized he had absolutely no idea what she was talking about.

Her eyes widened. "You haven't heard the news?"

"Obviously not." He worried that something had gone terribly wrong with his new expansion. He knew his competitors were not happy about the launch, but he'd been able to overcome every roadblock they'd thrown in his way.

His mother pulled out her phone and quickly pulled up an article. He was curious to see what had her so worked up that she'd left home before the time she normally had her second cup of coffee. She held her phone out to him.

He took it from her and stared at the photo. It was of him and Pepper leaving the doctor's office. His gut twisted in an uncomfortable knot.

Billionaire Bachelor to Billionaire Daddy!

An unnamed source said the happy couple had reunited and were now expecting their first child. His hand tightened around the phone. A frustrated growl grew deep in his throat. There was more to the story, but his anger kept him from comprehending the rest of the article. This couldn't be happening.

The last time the paparazzi got involved, Pepper had ended things with him. The thing he didn't know was how big of a part the press had played in her decision. If the paparazzi had left them alone, would things have gone differently?

"So, is it true? Are you finally making me a grandmother?" There was a hopeful glint in his mother's eyes that surprised him.

"Simon?" Pepper stepped into the foyer and came to a stop upon noticing his mother. "Sorry. I didn't mean to interrupt."

"Is this her?" his mother asked.

Pepper's puzzled gaze moved between him and his mother. He'd been really hoping to avoid this for a while, but it looked like he had no other choice.

"Mother, this is Pepper Kane. Pepper, meet my mother, Sandra."

Pepper stepped forward, shook hands and exchanged pleasantries.

Simon opened the door. "Mother, we'll have to visit later. Pepper and I have some things to discuss."

His mother's eyes lit up as she moved toward the door. "So it's true."

It wasn't a question; it was a statement. And he wasn't in any position to correct her. "We'll talk later."

"Yes, we will." His mother glanced over at Pepper. "It was so nice to meet you, dear."

"Um, nice to meet you too." Pepper looked utterly confused and he couldn't blame her.

His mother gave him a butterfly kiss on the cheek and then left with a trail of Chanel No. 5 in her wake. His mother wasn't born into money, in fact, she was born far from it. Still, when he'd established himself in the business world and was able to care for her, she'd taken to the elevation in her lifestyle like a duck to water. After what his father had put her through for years, Simon was glad she'd found some happiness—even if the uneasiness between them still existed.

He closed the door. He wanted to shield Pepper from the headlines, but he knew the reporters would flock to the building, if they weren't here already. There was no hiding from this story.

"That was nice of your mother to stop by. You should

have invited her to stay. I have your coffee started and there are plenty of pastries in the kitchen."

He shook his head. "Now isn't the time for visitors. You and I have something to discuss."

Although coffee did sound good. He made his way to the kitchen and poured himself a cup. He nearly moaned in delight when he took his first sip.

His gaze moved to Pepper. "It tastes just like the coffee at the bakery."

She smiled and nodded. "I take it you like it."

"I love it."

"Drink as much as you want. Now that I'm pregnant, I can't have it."

He hadn't thought of that. There were a lot of things he hadn't thought of yet. And he didn't want to ruin this easy moment between them. But it was better she heard it from him than to be blindsided by the paparazzi.

"My mother stopped by for a reason."

"Is something wrong?"

"In a way." How did he tell her this gently? He didn't think there was any way to do it. "She knows about the baby."

"What? But how? I didn't think we were to the point of telling people."

"We aren't. I—I didn't," he stammered. "I wouldn't do that without talking to you first. She read it online."

"What?" Pepper's voice rose.

"Apparently, someone inside the doctor's office spotted us and sold the story. I don't know if it was staff, which I highly doubt, or if it was another patient."

Pepper worried her bottom lip as though she was replaying the events. "There were a few people around when the nurse rushed into the waiting room to give me the prenatal vitamins that I'd forgotten in the exam room." She looked crestfallen. "This is all my fault. If I hadn't forgotten them—"

"It's not your fault." He stepped up to her and gazed deep into her eyes. "None of this is your fault."

She pressed a hand to her abdomen. "I can't do this."

Worry gripped him. "Do what?"

She moved her hand between the two of them. "This. Everything you do is headline news. I don't want our baby caught up in a media frenzy—"

"Don't worry. We'll work things out."

Her eyes filled with fear. "You can't promise me that."

He sighed. "You're right. I can't promise the media will leave us alone, but there has to be a way to minimize their interference. We have a lot to figure out." And then before he analyzed the right and wrong of it, he pulled her into his arms, attempting to will away her inner turmoil.

He wanted to make this better for her, but the problem with success was that everything you did made headlines.

He continued to hold her close. "Together, we'll do what is best for the baby."

CHAPTER TEN

AND SO SHE'D STAYED.

Pepper hadn't been sure in the beginning of their living arrangement if it was a good idea. But with the paparazzi hunting for a story, she didn't have much choice. Trying to stay in a motel with the press hounding her would have been a disaster. At least when she was in Simon's penthouse, they couldn't photograph her.

And she was able to leave through the garage in a private car with tinted windows that Simon had put at her disposal. She didn't like having to rely on him, but with the baby's safety to take into consideration, she'd decided to take him up on his offer.

But one day had turned into two days. And two days had turned into a week. At last, the paparazzi had moved on to a new scandal. Pepper felt sorry for the young woman at the center of it. She knew what it was to be hounded day and night.

Friday afternoon, she had no baking scheduled. It wasn't her day at the shelter. And she had no idea what to do with all the time on her hands.

With Simon going out of his way for her, she wanted to repay him. It had to be more than his morning coffee and daily supply of cherry turnovers. She wanted to do more. But what? She frowned as her mind drew a blank.

Her gaze moved around the stark, monochrome penthouse. Pepper sighed. This place exuded money, but it was so cold. Not temperature-wise, as she had the fireplace lit, but in a personal way. She noticed there weren't any photos, not of him, not of his family, not of anyone. She found that strange.

She would be lost without her photos. Her heart clutched. What if they'd been lost in the fire?

Immediately, tears pricked the back of her eyes. She told herself to calm down. Though they hadn't let her into the apartment yet, they'd said the damage on the second floor was limited to water and smoke. She just had to hope the pictures had survived.

Instead of sitting around worrying, she knew she had to get busy. Her grandmother used to say that idle hands were the devil's workshop. In Pepper's case, it was an idle mind.

If she was going to continue to stay here, something had to be done with the place. There wasn't one thing around the penthouse that resembled Christmas. Not even a red or green anything. The color scheme was limited to black, white and gray.

The penthouse exuded a high-powered executive life-style. But it didn't look like anyone actually lived there. She turned in a circle, taking in the two long couches forming a right angle near the black marble fireplace. A large smoked-glass coffee table was devoid of everything, not even a houseplant or magazine was on it. How did this man live like this?

And then she realized the answer: he lived at his office. If it wasn't for her presence, he wouldn't be home nearly as much. Maybe she needed to give him a reason to come home—a place to unwind. Since the Polka Dotted Bakery, where he used to let down his guard, was currently out of commission, she'd have to create a homey atmosphere here. Or as close to it as she could get.

She grabbed her purse, coat and knit cap. Out the door she went. She was a lady on a mission.

What in the world…?

Simon came to a stop at the edge of the living room.

He blinked, making sure he wasn't seeing things. He hadn't been sleeping well, with all the latest developments in his life and a big launch ahead of him. He blinked again—but there was still a ginormous pine tree leaning against the wall. What in the world?

How did it get in here?

He glanced around for Pepper. It was too big for her to carry, but he'd bet his business that she had something to do with its presence.

"Pepper!"

He wasn't a man who normally raised his voice, but these obviously weren't normal times. And all he'd wanted to do was come home, yank off his tie, undo the top buttons on his dress shirt, have a drink and unwind.

"Pepper!"

"Why are you yelling?" The voice came from behind him.

He spun around to find Pepper standing in the doorway with shopping bags in her hands. He rushed forward and took the bags from her so she could take off her coat and hat.

He returned to the living room and his gaze settled on the Christmas tree—the source of his agitation. He set the bags on the couch and turned to her. "What is this doing here?"

She pulled off her cap and smoothed her hands down over her hair. When her gaze landed on the tree, a big smile lit up her pretty face. Instantly, his agitation started to fade.

"It looks perfect in here. I was afraid it would be too small, but I also worried about getting something too big, you know, with the elevator and everything."

He didn't do holidays. The only ones he endured were those for employees or business acquaintants. But he certainly didn't have a tree and decorations for his own benefit.

"It has to go." His tone was firm. His mind was made up.

"What?" Pepper's eyes widened in astonishment. "But why?"

"I don't want it here." He rubbed the back of his neck. He shouldn't be so brusque with her. It wasn't like he'd told her about his "no Christmas" policy. "I don't celebrate Christmas."

"You don't believe in Santa?"

There was such sincerity and awe in her voice that for a minute, he thought she was being serious. When his gaze caught hers, he couldn't read her thoughts. "Please don't tell me you believe in Santa."

She shrugged. "I don't believe there's a man who lives at the North Pole who delivers Christmas presents around the world in one night, but I believe in the spirit of Christmas. I believe it lives in each of us."

He shook his head. "Not me."

She frowned at him. "Even you."

He shook his head again. "There's nothing good about Christmas."

Her mouth gaped open. "How can you say that?"

"Because Christmas was always the worst time in our house." It didn't bring their family together. Instead the holiday drove a bigger wedge between him, his mother and his father.

"Really?" Sympathy shone clearly in her big green eyes. "I'm sorry."

He shrugged off her sympathy. He didn't want her to feel sorry for him. He just wanted her to make this Christmas tree go away.

He went to sit on the couch and bumped into her packages, which spilled onto the floor. There were all sorts of Christmas decorations—things for trimming the tree. He inwardly groaned.

He knelt down and began stuffing the shiny red balls back in the bag. The next thing he knew, Pepper was kneeling beside him. Together, they worked to clean up the mess of decorations.

As the time went by, the shock of finding a Christmas tree in his place wore off and he realized Pepper could never understand the horrific memories he had attached to the holiday. He was quite certain they were much different than her experience with the holiday.

Simon settled on the floor and leaned back against the couch. He needed to smooth things over with Pepper. They'd come a long way this week toward being friendly with each other again and he didn't want to ruin their progress. "I'm sorry for grouching at you. I was caught off guard when I came through the door and found a tree in the living room."

"I understand. I should have asked you first. I… I wanted to surprise you. Obviously, I did that, but not in a good way like I'd been hoping."

He sighed. "I'm not like other people."

He was broken. But he couldn't admit that to Pepper. He couldn't have her look at him like he was less of a man. Or worse, with sympathy in her eyes. He'd spent his whole life proving he was no longer that scared, helpless child.

"You're definitely unlike anyone I've ever known." She sent him a hesitant smile. "Have you noticed this amazing Manhattan penthouse you live in? Most people could only imagine living in a place like this."

"It wasn't always that way. I didn't grow up with a silver spoon in my mouth." He was very proud of the empire he'd built, one toy, one store, at a time.

"What was Christmas like when you were young?"

This was not the direction he wanted the conversation to go. "It was fine."

"Fine? That's an odd description." Pepper placed the bag on the floor and then sat on the couch near him. "We never had much when I was little, but my mother made the most of the holiday. We went caroling and sledding. We baked cookies and watched Christmas movies. She emphasized the time we spent together instead of the lack of presents under the tree."

"Your mother sounds like she was great."

"She was, but…"

He moved so he could look at her. "But what?"

"She was eccentric and definitely flamboyant. That's hard to deal with as a kid, when all you want in the world is to fit in and be just like everyone else." Pepper pulled a strand of lights out of another bag. "I bet you had the perfect Christmases—the kind in those holiday movies."

"Far from it. My mother tried to have a fun Christmas, but my father always ruined it. He would be furious and accuse her of wasting money—money that belonged to him." He could still hear the echo of his father's booming voice. Every word he bellowed was laced with anger. "My Christmases were more *Die Hard* than *National Lampoon's Christmas Vacation.*"

"I'm sorry. I never imagined."

"Most people don't. It's the way I like to keep it."

"Is that why your place is so…so impersonal?"

It didn't surprise him that she didn't care for his ultramodern, minimalist style. It was the complete opposite of her warm, cozy bakery. "It's not to your liking?"

She glanced away. "It…it just needs some personality."

He glanced around the room, trying to see it through Pepper's eyes. Whereas Pepper's bakery had photos on the walls, his penthouse only had a large skyline photo of the city at night. At the bakery, there were knickknacks, including a stuffed dog that he'd meant to ask her about but never had the chance. He didn't have knickknacks. He'd never even thought of getting any.

The Polka Dotted Bakery oozed charm and hominess that made it unique. His penthouse was cool and detached. He realized that if he were to pack up his clothes, he could move out and it would be ready for the next occupant. It was more a hotel room than home.

Simon was stunned. He'd never seen his penthouse like this before. It was quite eye-opening. And not in a good way.

"Don't worry," Pepper said. "I'll have the tree taken away."

He shook his head. What would it hurt to let her keep it? After all, it must be important to her or she wouldn't have gone to the trouble of buying it or the decorations. When she moved back to her apartment, he'd have it delivered to her.

"The tree—it can stay."

Pepper's eyes lit up. "Are you sure? I mean, you didn't seem all that happy it was here."

"Are you trying to talk me out of this?"

"No. No. I just wanted to make sure you're truly okay with it. After all, this is your place."

"And for the moment, it's yours too." He didn't know why he'd said that. Maybe he just wanted her to feel at home. Because he certainly didn't mean to imply that this situation would be anything other than temporary.

He got to his feet and turned to head to his study. He had some work to do. In fact, he had a lot of it to do. Normally, he'd have stayed at the office until late, trying to catch up, which never happened. But knowing Pepper was here had lured him home. He told himself it was the right thing to do, as he was the host and she was his guest. But deep down, he knew it was more than that. He just wasn't ready to admit it to himself.

"Simon?"

He paused at the entrance to the hallway and turned around. "Did you need something?"

"Yes. You."

"Me?"

She nodded. "Don't you want to help?"

"Help?"

She gave him a funny look. "With trimming the tree?"

"No."

Her beautiful face morphed into a frown. "Oh."

She turned away and began rifling through the bags on the couch. He'd hurt her feelings. He hadn't meant to. The fact of the matter was that outside of the office, he kept to himself as much as possible. Sure, he had the occasional obligatory dates to social functions, but he never invited those dates back here—back to his domain.

Pepper was the first woman in his penthouse. And he had to admit that his interaction with her was a lot different than dealing with his employees at the office.

At the office, he told people what to do and they did it. They didn't ask for his company. They didn't want to have personal conversations. They all had one goal—to make Ross Toys the biggest and the best.

But here with Pepper, he'd lost his footing. He couldn't boss her around. He subdued a laugh at the thought. If he did try telling Pepper what to do, she'd probably knock some sense into him with her rolling pin.

And yet they did have a common goal—their baby. If they were going to raise a normal, well-adjusted child, they were going to have to learn to make compromises. Lots of them. He supposed this was one of those compromises.

And though it went against every grain in his body, he returned to the couch. He suppressed the memories of his past and the horrid Christmases that his family had shared. He would do it for Pepper and the baby.

"How can I help?" he asked.

She shook her head, not looking at him. "It's fine. I've got this. I'm sure you have more important things to do."

"This is important to you, so it's important to me."

That got her attention. She turned to him. Her green gaze studied him. "Why?"

"Why what? Why am I helping?" When she nodded, he said, "Honestly, because you want me to."

"Why do you still hate Christmas after all these years?"

Her question poked at him in the most sensitive spot. He didn't talk about his past with anyone, including his own mother—especially his mother. If it were up to him, he'd just as soon forget about the past—about Christmas, about family.

But Pepper and soon the baby weren't going to make that possible. Instead, he would have to figure out a way to deal with it. He just wasn't sure how to do that except to push through and do what needed to be done as quickly as possible.

He reached for a box of ornaments. "Shall I put these on the tree?"

"You aren't going to answer my question?"

"It doesn't matter." It did matter. It mattered a lot.

But he didn't want to scare Pepper away for good. And so he kept quiet about the other skeletons in his closet. It was just the way it needed to be.

CHAPTER ELEVEN

TALK ABOUT YOUR MYSTERIES.

Simon Ross was one walking puzzle.

And Pepper wanted so badly to sort out the pieces that made him whole. But she had to be careful how hard she pushed him for answers. Or he'd totally shut down on her.

Pepper picked up the string of twinkle lights. They were assorted colors. She loved colors. It was a part of her mother that had rubbed off on her. The older she got, the less she cared about what people thought of her and just let herself enjoy her differences.

Except Simon.

She did care what he thought of her. She knew she shouldn't, but she couldn't help herself. It wasn't that she was going to change herself to suit him, but now that they were living together, she hoped he'd continue to accept her with her sometimes out-of-control hair and her eccentric tendencies. Perhaps she was more like her mother than she'd ever considered.

"Something on your mind?" Simon's voice drew her from her thoughts.

"Ah, yes. I was wondering if I got enough lights." Her gaze moved to the two bundles of lights and then moved to the tree. "The tree looks a lot bigger than I remembered."

His gaze moved to the bundles of lights. "Did you get those from your apartment?"

"Um, no. They still haven't let me inside."

The truth was she'd purchased them from a thrift store. It was where she made a lot of purchases. Paying for the bakery took most of her income. What was left, she had to budget carefully. Still, she just couldn't imagine telling this man, who could afford to buy anything his heart desired, that she was decorating his place with second-hand decorations.

"Let's see about getting the lights on the tree." And just like that he let the subject of the lights' origins drop. Either he knew or it wasn't important to him. Either way, she was relieved.

And so they worked together for the next couple of hours placing the decorations on the tree. She'd greatly underestimated its size. The decorations were sparse. She felt terrible.

Ding, dong.

"I'll get that," Simon said. "It's about time the pizza got here."

Pepper continued to study the tree, trying to figure out how to improve it. If it were in her apartment, she wouldn't have bought one nearly so large, because her ceilings weren't nearly as high. And the decorations wouldn't look so sparse. But here in the luxury penthouse, it looked all wrong.

She moved to the tree and started taking off the ornaments. What had she been thinking? People like Simon, they hired people to decorate their trees with the finest decorations that probably cost more than her annual salary.

"I hope you're hungry..." Simon's words faded away as he spotted her dismantling the decorations. He set the pizza box on the coffee table and moved next to her. "Hey, what are you doing? Rearranging the ornaments? I wasn't sure where to put them."

"I'm taking it down."

"Down?"

She nodded. Her emotions were rising. She remembered what it was like back in school when she'd tried to fit in with the other girls. Her mother had found her some stylish clothes at the thrift store. In the end, it turned out they had been donated by one of the rich girls. The blouse had tiny initials on the cuff—the girl's initials. Pepper had never been so devastated.

This was another of those moments when she was trying to fit in. And there was absolutely nothing she could do to fit into Simon's world. He might as well live on Mars, that's how far apart their realities were.

Her fingers trembled as emotions both new and old coursed through her. Simon placed a hand over hers, stopping her from removing yet another ornament.

"Pepper, talk to me. What's wrong? I know I was hesitant about the tree in the beginning, but I thought we had a good time decorating it."

She concentrated her gaze on his long fingers draped over hers. "I shouldn't have done this. I shouldn't have forced this tree on you. You don't want it."

He clasped his hand with hers. She relaxed her hand within his. It felt natural for them to be holding hands. When did that happen?

His fingers tightened as he led her to the couch. She didn't want to sit down. She knew he was going to want to talk things out, and then she was going to appear even sillier than she already felt.

"Pepper." He paused as though waiting for her to look at him.

She didn't want to face him. The heat of embarrassment was already lapping at her cheeks. Still, she wasn't a wimp. Even when the other kids had made fun of her, she'd stood her ground. As badly as their words had hurt, she'd stood there and faced them down. Why should she do any different now?

And so with all the willpower she could muster, she turned her head until her gaze met Simon's. "We don't need to talk about this. I'll just get rid of the tree and things can go back to the way they were."

"What if that's not what I want?"

"What?" Surely she hadn't heard him correctly. "You can't mean you want the tree."

"Actually, I think I do."

He did? Wait. She was missing something.

"Just a few hours ago, you were telling me it had to go. Now you're telling me it has to stay?" Her gaze searched his as she tried to figure out his abrupt change of mind. "Simon, what's going on?"

He shrugged. "I don't know. Maybe I've been holding on to my resentment of the past for too long."

"You resented Christmas?" Who resents Christmas? It's the best time of the year.

He rubbed the back of his neck. "What can I say? I'm unusual." His gaze turned back to the tree. "So what do you say? Can we keep the tree?"

She didn't know when this had all gotten so turned around, but somewhere along the way their roles had gotten mixed up. She followed his gaze to the tree. Maybe it wasn't so bad, after all.

"I suppose I could get some more ornaments for it," she said.

"You know, I just might be able to help you with that."

"What? How?"

He headed out of the living room. She followed, having no idea what he was up to now. He headed down the hallway. He stopped outside a closed door. He opened it and flipped on the light.

She glanced inside, finding stacks of cardboard boxes. "What is all of this?"

"Things that were given to me—mostly by my mother. I didn't know what to do with all of the stuff so I put it in here to deal with later." He started opening boxes. "When I first moved in, I remember her bringing over Christmas decorations."

"Did you ever use them?"

"No."

Pepper nodded, though she didn't quite understand. "Can I help you?"

"If you want."

Together, they went through the boxes until they uncovered two boxes of assorted ornaments. They carried them to the living room, where Pepper turned on some Christmas carols.

The longer they worked, the more he loosened up. The more he let down his guard, the more she remembered what drew her to him in the beginning—his deep, warm laughter that filled her with joy, his big smile that filled her with warmth—

"Pepper?" His voice startled her from her thoughts.

She lifted her gaze to meet his. "What did you say?"

He smiled, sending her heart tumbling in her chest. "Something on your mind?"

"No." Heat rushed to her cheeks. Did he know where her thoughts had strayed? Of course not. "What do you need?"

"Some more silver balls. I think I saw some in the box. Never mind, I'll get them." He climbed off the ladder next to the tree.

"I've got it." Pepper rushed to the box.

There were a lot of decorations in it. It'd be nice to find a place for all of them. After all, this penthouse was huge. Plenty of room to use all the decorations.

She reached in the box, moving items around. She didn't see any silver ornaments. She placed items outside the box as she sorted them.

"Found them," she said gleefully.

"I found something too." He held up a ball of greenery with red berries and a gold bow.

"It's pretty. What is it?"

His eyes twinkled with mischief. He raised his arm, dangling the ball over her head. Suddenly she knew it was a mistletoe kissing ball. Her heart raced.

Her gaze moved to Simon. He wasn't going to...

Simon leaned toward her, pressing a kiss to her lips. His mouth was warm and oh-so-tempting. It was as though time stopped. And she didn't want it to start again.

So many nights she'd dreamed about this moment, longed for this moment. And now it was so hard to believe that it was happening—that Simon's mouth was moving over hers.

Was it wrong to give in to the moment? To let herself savor this moment? Her heart and mind were at odds.

Something that felt this good couldn't possibly be wrong. She leaned into him. Her hands landed on his chest—his very firm, very muscular chest. She stifled a moan as common sense got lost in a haze of desire.

Her mouth moved beneath his. A soft moan of pure pleasure formed at the base of her throat. Simon's tongue delved into her mouth. He tasted sweet, like the peppermint candy he'd enjoyed earlier.

Buzz. Buzz.

The sound of the phone brought her feet back to earth. She pulled away from him and pressed her fingers to her sensitive lips.

She backed away from him. Moving out of his gravitational pull, she felt her common sense start to return. She walked to the big window overlooking the city. The millions of lights sparkled like diamonds.

Simon stepped up behind her. "Pepper, I'm sorry. It seemed like a good idea at the time."

"It's okay." Her insides shivered with a rush of emotions. She wasn't okay. Far from it.

"Pepper—"

Buzz. Buzz.

"You should get that." She turned and moved past him.

She picked up the silver ornaments and moved to the tree. She forced her thoughts to the work before her, because every time she recalled the way his lips had moved seductively over hers, her stomach dipped and her face flamed with heat. She couldn't let him see how he'd gotten to her.

By the time Simon finished his call, she'd placed all of the silver ornaments strategically on the tree. Truth be told, she might have put more thought into their placement than was necessary.

"Pepper?" Simon's voice came from behind her.

Her breath hitched in her throat.

Just pretend like the kiss didn't happen. Because it was a mistake. One not to be repeated.

She turned to him. "Do you need something?"

He approached her and then, as though he realized that wasn't a good idea, he stopped. "I'm sorry about that."

"No problem. I know you're an important businessman."

He shook his head. "I meant the kiss. I shouldn't have done it."

"Don't worry. It's already forgotten."

Liar. Liar.

For a moment, neither spoke. It was as though each of them was trying to find their footing once more.

This whole situation was a lot for them to deal with. They didn't need to complicate matters more than they already were. Her hand moved to her still-flat abdomen. It was best for all of them.

CHAPTER TWELVE

SHE'D MADE IT.

The next morning, Pepper stepped through the doorway of Helping Paw. She glanced at the clock, finding she still had some time before lunch. Not as early as she would like, but considering she was beginning to think she'd have to forgo her impromptu visit, she was pleased.

This day had not started as she'd hoped.

Pepper sighed as she ran a hand over her hair, which was pulled back in a messy ponytail—very messy indeed. The day began with her sleeping in and then being hit with a serious bout of morning sickness. She'd hoped it was just a one- or two-time thing, but it appeared it was going to hit her every morning of her first trimester.

But it'd be worth it in the end. She resisted the urge to place a hand on her still-flat abdomen. With every day that passed, her excitement about the baby was growing.

After telling herself that she was done caring for people because the price was too high, she couldn't imagine not loving this baby. It was such a powerful attachment. And though at times it scared her to think how precarious life could be, her love for the baby trumped her fear.

Life right now was challenging enough with the aftermath of a fire to deal with, a very sexy roommate who was off-limits and a penthouse that seemed to grow smaller with each passing day. She supposed she could have given up on volunteering at the shelter—even temporarily. But she knew the shelter was hard-pressed to find people willing to give up their time to help out. And there were so many animals that needed love and support. She couldn't turn her back on them. Not even if it meant her life wouldn't be quite so hectic.

And then there was Daisy. Pepper looked forward to seeing her as much as possible, even on days when she wasn't scheduled to volunteer. They still hadn't been able to put the pup up for adoption, but shy little Daisy was making progress.

"Hey, is everything okay?" Stephanie gazed at her with a worried look on her face.

Pepper forced a smile, hoping it would alleviate her friend's concern. "Yeah, I'm fine."

"You don't look fine." Stephanie gestured to a stool. "Maybe you should sit down."

Did she really look as bad as she felt? Maybe she should have paused and fixed her makeup before rushing over here. She hadn't even thought of stopping for a second look in the mirror before rushing out the door, and that wasn't like her. Not at all.

"Now that you're expecting, you're going to have to slow down," Stephanie said.

It was no secret that she was pregnant. Every single person she knew had read it all over the internet. Even total strangers who recognized her from her picture would offer their congratulations. But at least the paparazzi wasn't following her every minute of the day.

Pepper sat down on the stool. "I can't stay long. I just wanted to check in on Daisy."

Stephanie's brow rose as she nodded. "You two are becoming quite close."

"She trusts me now. That's a big step. The trick is getting Daisy to trust others. I don't know what was done to her in the past, but it was bad. The poor thing. She just needs lots of time and love."

Buzz. Buzz.

Pepper looked at her friend. "You can go ahead and get that."

"It's not my phone."

It rang again. That's when Pepper realized the sound was coming from her coat pocket. "That's strange. It's not my normal ring tone."

She pulled the phone from her pocket and glanced at the screen. Her name and number were displayed. She was calling herself?

Pressing the phone to her ear, Pepper said, "Hello?"

"Pepper. Oh, good." It was Simon's voice. "We mixed up our phones this morning in the kitchen."

"Oh. Sorry."

"If you can let me know where you are, I'll swing by and we can exchange them. I'm really lost without mine. I didn't realize how much information I store on it."

She didn't want him to have to go out of his way. "I can stop by your office."

"No need. I'm still in the car."

She gave him the address. He promised to be there in a few minutes.

"Did I hear correctly?" Stephanie asked. "Simon is coming here?"

Pepper nodded. She wasn't sure how she felt about having him here at the shelter. She knew it shouldn't be a big deal, but with every day that passed, it was like another part of her life was revealed to him. Soon he would know everything about her.

"I'm going to go visit Daisy while I wait." Pepper got to her feet and moved to the back of the building.

Daisy was isolated from the other adoptable dogs, but wouldn't be for much longer. When the puppy saw her, her tail started to wag. Pepper wanted to believe it was her the dog was excited about and not the little dog biscuits she'd started baking and kept in her pocket.

"Hey, girl. You look happy today." Pepper opened the crate. "Let's go stretch your legs."

Daisy wiggled around excitedly while Pepper tried to attach the leash. "You are a wiggle tail."

The leash attached, Pepper placed Daisy on the floor and off they went, strolling along the back of the building. It was taking Daisy a while to be leash trained, but she was finally taking to it.

"Pepper?" It was Simon's voice.

Daisy stopped in her tracks. And the teeny tiny puppy let out a really big howl. Pepper didn't know such a large sound could come from something so little.

Pepper knelt down and picked Daisy up. She ran a hand over Daisy's short fur. "It's okay, girl." When Daisy continued to howl, Pepper decided to distract her with a biscuit. It worked.

And then to Simon, she said, "We're over here."

When Simon stopped in front of her, his gaze moved from her to Daisy and then back again. "I didn't know you worked here."

"She doesn't." Greta stepped up to Simon and extended her hand, with her long, polished deep red nails. "I run this shelter. And you would be Simon Ross."

He turned a blank expression to the woman. He hesitated for a brief moment before shaking her hand.

"So what brings you here?" Greta's dark eyes glinted with interest.

Pepper stepped forward. "I think he's here for—"

Greta stepped between Pepper and Simon. "I've got this." The woman never took her eyes off Simon. "Pepper, don't you have something to do?"

Pepper gaped at the back of the woman's head. Had Greta really just dismissed her from speaking to the father of her baby? How dare she?

Just as Pepper was prepared to set Greta straight, Daisy started barking. While Greta was distracted, Simon signaled for her to let this woman dig her own hole.

"Pepper, take that little monster back to her cage."

She was tempted to ask the woman if she was referring to herself. Instead, she quietly walked away.

Had that really happened?

Simon was so relieved to have disentangled himself from Greta. For some reason, he thought people that headed up animal shelters would be kind and generous. Obviously, that wasn't always the case. But since the shelter meant so much to Pepper, he'd minded his manners and not told the woman exactly what he thought of her rude and pushy tactics.

Simon caught up with Pepper and Daisy. "Does that woman really run the shelter?"

Pepper nodded. "No one can figure out how she got the job."

"She certainly doesn't like animals."

"Not at all."

"But she does like money. She hit me up for a very large donation."

Pepper's cheeks grew pink. "I'm so sorry."

"Don't be. I wasn't giving that woman anything." When he realized that might have come out wrong, he added, "But if you were to ask, that would be a totally different matter."

"I might take you up on the offer. The shelter is hurting for money so badly that they're starting to turn away animals." Worry reflected in her eyes. "We've tried everything we can think of to raise money, but it never seems to be enough. But that isn't the reason you're here."

He made a mental note to have the shelter looked into. He was more than willing to make regular donations, but first he wanted to make sure where his money would be going. And he didn't want Greta to take credit for the shelter's turnaround.

"I have your phone." He held out the phone to her, and with her free hand she removed his from her pocket.

"And here's yours."

Daisy started to wiggle, so Pepper put her back on the ground. "Would you like another treat?"

Arff! Arff! Arff!

"I'd swear she knows what the word *treat* means."

Daisy barked again.

Pepper pulled another treat from her pocket. She held the biscuit out to Simon. "Would you like to give it to her?"

He shook his head. "I don't think so. I don't know anything about dogs."

"Well, then you and Daisy will get along fine. She doesn't know much about people, but she's learning." Pepper placed the little biscuit in his hand. "Place it on the flat of your hand and hold it out to her. She'll do the rest."

Simon crouched down and did as Pepper said. Daisy was hesitant, but couldn't resist the treat. He couldn't help but smile at the eager look on the puppy's face or the thumping of her tail. She was really cute—not that he was a dog person.

When he straightened, she said, "Maybe you want to look around and adopt a dog. Or perhaps you're more of a cat person. Or maybe one of each."

He shook his head. "Not me. I'm not good with animals."

"Daisy might disagree. Huh, girl?"

Simon glanced down as the little dog crunched on the biscuit. "She really likes that treat."

"She does. I've been working on perfecting them."

Simon glanced at her. "Perfecting?"

Pepper nodded. "I've started making treats for the dogs. At first I was just playing around, trying something different. But with the shelter hurting for money, they can't afford extras for the animals. So I've been making as many treats as I can and bringing them into the shelter. The dogs seem to really like them."

He paused as a thought came him. "These treats... You've developed your own recipes?"

She nodded. "I figure if I can make cake recipes, it can't be much harder to make pet-friendly recipes."

This was what his Pet Playground stores were missing—the personal touch. They needed something that wasn't mass produced. They needed Pepper's treats. But how would he make it possible to have fresh baked treats in each store of a chain that eventually would extend from coast to coast?

"Simon?" Pepper looked at him with a look of concern.

"Sorry. I just had a thought about work." He thought back to their conversation. "Is there anything you can't do?"

Her cheeks pinkened. "Lots of things. I don't know how to fly a plane or create the hottest toy of the year. I heard on the radio that your company has one of the most sought-after toys for Christmas. Your miniature robo ball is wildly popular."

A smile pulled at the corners of his mouth. "It's sold out. We're checking to see if we can get more produced and shipped before Christmas, but it's going to be close."

"Then it sounds like you're a hit."

"Not me. The toy." He glanced down at the phone in his hand as it buzzed. "I should be going."

He leaned forward to kiss her goodbye. It seemed so natural. So right. And then he spied the wide-eyed surprise on her beautiful face.

He pulled back. "I'll, uh, see you at home."

"See you there."

And with that he walked away. He couldn't believe he'd almost kissed her. It hadn't been anything he'd planned. It just seemed like the right thing to do in the moment.

Things were changing between them. Quickly. But he wasn't ready to examine the implications.

He was a man on a mission. He pulled out his phone to contact his assistant. He wanted meetings set up for the rest of the day with various departments. There was no time to waste.

He knew it was far too late to implement the homemade biscuits and treats in the grand opening, but he wanted to be able to announce it at the grand opening. It was the perfect time to grow a swell of interest. And it would be the perfect thing to help Pepper now and in the future. But would she agree to sell him her recipes?

CHAPTER THIRTEEN

HOW HAD THINGS gotten so comfortable?

Three days later, Pepper moved around Simon's enormous kitchen in her bare feet as though she'd lived there for years. The gleaming white tiles were cold to the touch, but with the dual ovens going, the air was quite warm and the coolness of the floor felt good to her.

She glanced up to find Simon in the doorway, staring at her with a smile on his face.

"What?" she asked, feeling self-conscious. "Do I have batter on my face?"

He shook his head. "No. You just look cute in your jeans and apron. Maybe instead of being called the polka-dotted baker, we should call you the barefoot baker."

She glanced down at her holly berry dazzle nail polish. She wiggled her toes, letting the recessed lights catch the sparkles and make her toes twinkle.

She lifted her head and smiled at him. "You like them?"

"Actually, I do. And with that red ribbon around your ponytail, you look like you're ready for a Christmas party."

"Hardly. I'm a mess."

He stepped up to her. He stopped just inches from her. "If this is you looking a mess, I like it."

He was flirting with her? Heat swirled in her chest and rushed to her face. She wasn't sure what to say. When he was looking at her like she was a cherry that he was eating up with his eyes, her thoughts scattered and her ability to make quick comebacks utterly and completely left her.

But knowing that she had to get this order done in the

very near future, she said, "You know, instead of standing around talking silliness, you could be helping."

"It's not silliness." His voice lowered as his gaze caressed her face. She could feel the way his gaze moved over her just as surely as if he'd reached out and touched her. "You are beautiful. Don't ever doubt it. Both inside and out."

"Thank you." Now her face felt as though it were pressed against the hot oven. A trickle of perspiration ran down her cleavage. She resisted the urge to fan herself, but if Simon didn't move away soon, she was afraid her entire body would go up in flames.

"No need to thank me. I'm just stating a fact." And still he stared at her with a smile on his face.

He had no idea how much she just wanted to toss aside the bowl of batter and melt into his embrace as her mouth sought out his. But that wasn't part of their arrangement. They'd agreed to this living arrangement just until she completed her Christmas commitments. By then, her apartment over the bakery should be deemed safe to move back into.

Until then, she had so much to do. And then she realized that Simon was home early—earlier than normal on a Monday. "Why are you here?"

His dark brows rose. "Am I not allowed to leave work early without suspicion?"

She shook her head, swishing her ponytail over her shoulder. "Sorry. That's not what I meant."

"It's okay. I was just giving you a hard time." He stepped away from her and suddenly she missed having him so close to her.

"I thought you had some important meetings today."

He rubbed the back of his neck. "I did. But I rearranged them and got them done earlier than I had originally planned." He glanced around the kitchen. "Looks like I wasn't the only one busy."

She followed his gaze, taking in the sight of bowls, pans, spoons and numerous other kitchen items dirty and in need of cleaning. "Sorry. I just had so much to do today that I couldn't keep up with the cleaning, baking and decorating." She glanced at the timer. She didn't have long until the current batch of cupcakes came out and the new batch went in, if she wanted to get all of this delivered in time for the party. "I'm sorry. But I have to get back to work."

"Don't let me hold you up."

She turned to the kitchen island and continued to fill each cupcake liner three-quarters full. She struggled to keep her attention on the task at hand and not on the way Simon had been looking at her. Things were definitely changing between them. The thought sent a shiver of excitement through her.

In the background, she heard water running. She wondered what Simon was up to. She desperately wanted to turn and check him out, but she denied herself that privilege. She had a deadline and she needed to keep her attention focused on her work.

Yeah. Like that was going to happen.

She tilted the bowl up and moved to the next empty cupcake liner. She reminded herself that just because there was obvious chemistry crackling between them, it didn't mean they should forget what they'd agreed to. Roommates. Nothing more. Because soon she'd be going back to her apartment—if the fire marshal would release the scene so she could start the repairs—and she had to keep her attention on the bakery.

When the tray of cupcake liners was filled and the dribbles wiped clean, it was ready for the oven. Pepper turned and placed the bowl on the counter. It was then that she spotted Simon. He had his sleeves rolled up as he worked in a sink full of soapy water. With the top buttons of his dress shirt undone, he looked totally adorable as he hand-washed a pan for her. What in the world had gotten into him? Whatever it was, she liked it.

Still, she should tell him to stop. This wasn't his responsibility. Part of their agreement was that she would see to the upkeep of the kitchen. But with the soapsuds on his arms, he looked utterly irresistible. Some woman was going to be very lucky when she landed him.

Pepper didn't know where the thought had come from, but it totally dampened her mood. The thought of him cooking and cleaning in the kitchen with another woman made her stomach sour. She dismissed the thought, shoving it to the far recesses of her mind.

Now more than ever, she needed to get him out of the kitchen. As sweet as he was to help her without her even asking, he was that much of a distraction. And tonight's party was very important. She couldn't mess things up.

The apartment phone rang, which usually meant it was the doorman. Simon dried his hands before answering it. She couldn't make out what he was saying.

Pepper looked up from where she was pouring batter into the cupcake pans. "Are you expecting guests?"

He shook his head. "It's the fire marshal."

Immediately, concern coursed through her. "What do you think he wants?"

"I guess we'll find out."

She still hadn't gotten past the part where the fire captain had mentioned arson and then looked at her like she was guilty. If this was going to be more false accusations, she wasn't going to stand by and take it.

Just then the timer for the other oven went off. She sighed.

Simon glanced over his shoulder at her. "It's okay. You take care of things in here and I'll get the door."

She didn't have any choice but to nod in agreement. The last thing she needed was to ruin a batch of cupcakes, or worse, fill Simon's penthouse with smoke while the fire marshal was there.

Pepper swapped the finished cupcakes for the unbaked ones. She'd just set the timer when she heard Simon call out her name. She slipped the timer in her pocket, as she didn't have time to make another batch should these ones accidentally stay in the oven too long.

She headed for the door, all the while preparing herself for more false accusations. When Pepper approached the foyer, she found the two men having a relaxed conversation. She wasn't sure how to react.

When the fire marshal's gaze caught hers, he said, "Ms. Kane?"

She nodded. He stuck out his hand, giving hers a brief but firm shake.

"I'm Inspector Hayes. I've just completed a total review of the fire at your bakery. I know you and Mr. Ross have been very interested in the results."

Interested? That was an understatement. When you're accused of arson, you want your good name cleared as soon as possible.

A denial of any wrongdoing hovered at the back of her mouth, but deciding that it would just make her look guiltier, she held back. Instead, she said, "What have you found?"

He lifted a black leather binder and flipped it open. His gaze scanned the page. "I noticed that you've recently had the bakery remodeled. Is that correct?"

"Sort of." She wondered if everything she said to him was about to be used against her.

As though Simon was reading her thoughts, he asked, "Is this something she should have an attorney for?"

The fire marshal's head lifted and surprise filled his eyes. "Oh, no. I'm sorry. I should have started with the fact that the fire has been ruled an accident. There was some faulty wiring in the kitchen."

"Oh." It was all Pepper could muster as the relief hit her.

The fire marshal flipped back to the top sheet. "I just have a few questions that I need answered before I can finalize the report."

He asked Pepper about the remodel, the date of the remodel and a few other questions. And then he said, "And that should be it. I'll make sure the insurance company gets a copy."

"Am I free to get into the building?" Pepper asked.

"Yes. But I'll caution you to be careful. You're going to want a clean-up crew in there before you try to do anything."

They thanked the fire marshal for stopping by and completing the report so quickly. As the man exited the penthouse, Pepper felt like the end of this chapter of her life was looming in the near future. Because once the apartment was cleaned up, there would be no need for her to stay with Simon. Was it wrong that the thought of going home no longer thrilled her? Had the short time she'd spent with Simon made that much of a difference?

Because the longer she was here—the longer they were together—the more she wondered what might have been. And she just couldn't afford to give her heart to someone else that would leave her. She'd been left behind by everyone she'd loved in her life. She couldn't do it again.

CHAPTER FOURTEEN

At last the day had come…

A frigid Tuesday morning made even the snowmen dotting the sides of the streets, dressed in colorful scarves and assorted hats, shiver. A fresh layer of snow blanketed all of New York City.

As Pepper stood on the sidewalk outside her bakery, she didn't notice the cold or the flakes landing on her hair and coat. A gust of wind rushed past them. Pepper stood like a statue staring forward at the place she'd once called home—still called home, even in its total state of devastation.

The outside of the bakery was still stained with soot trailing up the front of the white painted bricks. Plywood covered all the windows.

The back of her eyes stung with unshed tears. Her stomach made a nauseous lurch. She struggled to maintain her composure.

She blinked. The nightmare was still there, playing out in a slow, excruciating sequence. Would the interior be better than she was imagining? Or worse? Her palms grew clammy. She didn't want to see the inside of the bakery— yet she had to see it.

A hand touched her back. "You don't have to do this."

She turned to Simon. "Yes, I do."

Concern flooded his eyes. "I'm here for you."

"I know. Thank you."

She squared her shoulders. She was stronger than this. She'd buried her mother. She'd buried her grandmother.

In the grand scheme of things, this was a setback, not the end of the world. So then why did it feel like it?

She forced herself to take one step and then another.

She lifted the caution tape and then stepped beneath it. With shaky hands, she opened the door. Taking a deep, calming breath, she stepped into the darkened room. Even in the shadows, she could make out enough to know that everything she'd worked for—everything she'd loved— was charred and ruined.

She switched on the flashlight app on her phone. The stream of light highlighted one slice of the room at a time. Everything was layered with dark soot. The glass display cases were covered in debris and the fronts were cracked or broken.

This is bad. So very bad.

The light landed on the shelves behind the counter. There was Bugles McBeagle. Her heart ached. She rushed forward, tripping over the debris on the floor.

Simon's hand reached out, catching her arm. He held on until she'd regained her balance. "Be careful. There's a lot of mess on the floor."

She nodded because she didn't trust her voice. Emotions had clogged her throat. She continued moving toward the stuffed animal that she'd owned most of her life. It had so many memories attached to it, from her mother giving it to her to holding it when she'd packed her bags and moved in with her grandmother. It had seen her through all the tumultuous times in her life—including this one.

She knew it was silly to be so attached to an inanimate object, but she couldn't help it. Losing Bugles was like losing an important piece of herself. She reached up to the shelf and wrapped her fingers around the stuffed dog, surprised to find it was still in one piece. She pulled it down. It had soot on it, but other than that there didn't seem to be any other damage. How was that possible when it looked like a war had been waged within these walls?

"Pepper?" Simon's voice drew her out of her thoughts.

For a moment, she'd forgotten he was here with her. He was being so quiet and letting her walk through the bakery at her own pace.

Holding Bugles close, she said, "I… I'm okay."

What else was she supposed to say? That she was utterly devastated? That she felt as though her life had been ripped out from under her? That she didn't know where she would find the strength to start her life over once more?

They moved toward the kitchen. This was where the real devastation had taken place. Things in here were charred. Her beautiful stainless-steel appliances were black now. Her utensils were melted unrecognizable blobs. Her heart cracked a little more.

Simon stepped in front of her. He reached out and gently swiped a tear from her cheek. She didn't even know she'd been crying.

"Pepper, look at me." His soft voice coaxed her.

She didn't want to. Taking her gaze off the devastation took effort. When she did stare into his eyes, she saw sympathy in his eyes.

His hands gripped her shoulders. "You'll get your bakery back. It'll be better than ever. And I promise to do whatever I can to help."

She shook her head. "It's my problem. Not yours."

"But I want to help. Please let me."

She didn't say a word. Right now, the fight had gone out of her. She just needed a moment to wrap her mind around the fact that the bakery of her dreams was gone. Sure, she could build a new one, maybe even a better one, but it would never be the same.

He felt terrible.

Simon had some inkling of an idea what Pepper was feeling. And it wasn't good.

They'd both created their own happiness. His happiness had been in creating toys—toys he'd wanted so much as a kid but couldn't have because his father lost one job after another. Her happiness had been found in the kitchen creating the most amazing treats—treats that he surmised reminded her of the family she'd lost. In that they had a special bond.

But if his company were to be ripped out from beneath him, he couldn't even imagine the devastation he would feel. He glanced over at Pepper, who was doing her best to maintain her composure. He admired her strength. He wasn't sure he would be able to stand tall in similar circumstances.

Now, as they toured her apartment above the bakery, he could see a glimmer of hope in her eyes. It was much better than the downstairs, as the fire hadn't reached this floor. Still, the heavy odor of smoke clung to everything. When Pepper went to pack some clothes, her nose curled up. Still, she kept grabbing things as though she worried she'd never see any of it again—photos, binders and some kitchen items.

He carried her things out to the car and placed them in the trunk. He'd never seen such a look of utter despair on a person's face. His heart ached for her. If it was within his power to rectify this nightmare, he would in a heartbeat. But this was a project that was going to take time to make right.

Certain Pepper had had more than enough for one day, he coaxed her out of the building. She walked ahead while he secured the building. He turned to find she'd made her way down the walk. He rushed to catch up to her.

When she passed by his car, he didn't say anything. After the lingering scent of smoke, the fresh air was a welcome relief. As they continued walking, he noticed the snow had lightened up. Getting through the city would be slow going but it was still doable.

It wasn't until they were at the end of the next block that Pepper stopped. She turned to him. "Where's the car?"

He pointed over his shoulder.

"Oh. Sorry. I was lost in my thoughts."

"No problem."

"But you have to get to the office."

"The office can wait."

She arched a fine brow at him as though she was trying to figure out if he was being serious. "We better go."

When he didn't move, she made her way past him. Tracking through the inch of new snow, she led the way back to the car. He followed her, knowing he needed to say something encouraging. Yet he struggled to find the right words.

At the car, he opened her door. She paused in front of him. She lifted her wounded gaze to meet his. "Thank you for being so understanding."

"I wish I could make this all better for you."

"I know." Her voice cracked with emotion.

He stepped toward her and pulled her into his embrace. He didn't have any other words to offer her. He only had his shoulder to offer. Her whole body leaned into him. They fitted together as though they'd been made for each other. Her gentle breath fanned over his neck and warmed his blood.

He turned his head just slightly and inhaled her lavender scent. He would never smell lavender again without thinking of her. He pressed a kiss to her head.

When she pulled back, his gaze moved to her rosy lips. He wanted to kiss her again. He wanted to wash away her worries and sweep her up in a moment of passion.

He hesitated. She'd been through so much, inspecting the damaged bakery. He wasn't sure she would welcome his advance. And he wouldn't do anything to make this day more stressful for her. Kissing her would have to wait for another time.

With great reluctance, he stepped back. She climbed in the car and then he closed the door. He crossed in front of the car and then climbed in. Once the engine was started and the heat turned up, he paused.

He hadn't been planning to have this conversation with Pepper just yet, but after seeing her turmoil today, maybe now was best. It wasn't like him to rush into anything. He liked to take a slow and cautious approach. But what he was about to propose he knew was the right thing—for both of them.

"Simon, what's wrong? Is it the snow?" Concern rang out in her voice.

He leaned back in his seat. His gaze caught hers. "It's not the weather. I want to talk to you."

"About what?"

"There is something that I've given a lot of thought. I wasn't planning to bring it up just yet, but there's an urgency to it. I have a proposal for you—"

"No, Simon. We already talked about this. A marriage for the baby's sake would never work—"

"Whoa. Slow down. My apologies for giving you the wrong impression. My proposal isn't one of marriage. It's a business proposal."

Her perfectly plucked brows drew together. "Business proposal? But I don't have a business—at least, not right now."

He drew in a deep breath, figuring out the best way to explain his vision. "Do you remember when I visited you at the shelter?" When she nodded, he continued. "That's when I got the beginning of an idea. Remember those snacks you baked for the animals?" When she nodded, he continued. "Well, I'd like to buy the rights to the recipes."

"What?" Her mouth gaped.

"I promise to make it a lucrative deal with you receiving a percent of future sales." Normally, he wasn't a generous businessman, but this wasn't just any business deal.

He was dealing with the mother of his child—the woman who'd given Christmas back to him.

"But why?"

He smiled. "I guess I skipped right over that part." He cleared his throat. "I've mentioned the Pet Playground store chain that we're opening." When she nodded once again, he continued. "I knew there was something missing from it—something that would take it from being just another pet store to something exceptional. I'd been racking my brain for that special element and then you presented it to me. A gourmet bakery in each store. It will cater to the pet owner that wants something special for the four-legged friend." When Pepper didn't immediately respond, he started to worry. "What do you think?"

"I think it's a wonderful idea."

"Would you consider being my partner? You know, with the recipes, making sure the bakeries are set up properly and approving the staff?"

She didn't say anything for a moment. "I've never been involved in something like this. It sounds enormous."

"It would be, but it won't work without you."

"I like the idea. Really, I do. But I have my hands full getting the bakery back up and running."

"I thought you might say that so…" He reached in his coat pocket and pulled out a business card. "I took some liberties and contacted my best contractor. This is his card." He handed it over to her. "He's waiting for your call. His men have been on standby, waiting for the building to be given the green light."

She accepted the card and read it. "You mean these men are being paid to stand around, doing nothing, while waiting for my call?"

He nodded. "I hope you're not upset, but I wanted to help."

She didn't say anything and he worried that perhaps he'd gone too far. He knew waiting times for contractors could be quite long—especially in the city. He'd only wanted to help.

She pulled out her phone.

"What are you doing?" he asked.

"I'm calling your contractor—who is now my contractor. I'm giving them the go-ahead to clear the debris. And those binders you were so nice to carry to the car have my original notes and plans for the bakery. I'd like to make it look as close to the original plan as possible."

"I like that idea. The bakery was perfect." And there was one more thing he needed to know. "And the idea for the gourmet pet bakery?"

"I love it. But I have one condition."

He'd thought that he'd proposed a very generous offer, but it wouldn't hurt to hear what she had in mind. "Let's hear it."

"I'd like a portion of sales to be donated to animal shelters."

He smiled. "That's a fabulous idea. It's a deal."

They shook on it.

He had a feeling that both of their futures were going to benefit greatly from this union. Now Pepper would be in his personal life as they raised their child, and in his business world too. The thought of her always being around brought him a happiness he'd never known before.

CHAPTER FIFTEEN

"We have a problem."

The next afternoon, Pepper gripped the phone tighter. "What sort of problem?"

Stephanie sighed. "I don't think we should discuss it on the phone. Can you come to the shelter right away?"

"Actually, I'm on my way to meet with my insurance agent—"

"I wouldn't ask if it wasn't urgent." There was a desperate tone to Stephanie's voice that Pepper had never heard before.

She'd just been at the shelter yesterday afternoon. Everything had been all right then. What could have gone so wrong so fast?

"You're worrying me. Please tell me there's nothing wrong with Daisy."

Silence was the only response.

Pepper's heart lurched. Daisy was so sweet and had so much love to give if she would just learn how to trust people again.

And then a worrisome thought came to her. What if someone had seen Daisy, even though she wasn't ready for adoption yet? What if they'd bonded with Daisy and wanted to take her home?

Pepper's heart sank. She knew that was the danger of volunteering at the animal shelter. Each and every stray that came through that door just wanted to be loved. And Pepper loved them all. If she could, she'd take them all home. But there was something about Daisy that truly tugged at her heartstrings.

Stephanie knew how she and Daisy were starting to bond. Of course, Pepper would drop everything to be there for the beagle pup. Besides, she doubted that a face-to-face meeting with her insurance agent was going to produce any faster results than her daily phone conversations.

"I'll be right there."

After a quick, apologetic phone call to her agent, Pepper rushed to the shelter, not sure what sort of problem she would find. She prayed Daisy was all right.

She stepped inside the shelter and didn't notice anything amiss. She moved toward Stephanie's office. "What's going on?"

"It's Daisy. She has to go."

"Go? Go where?"

"Daisy can't stay here any longer." She looked as though she had the weight of the world upon her shoulders. "Greta has demanded the dog be gone."

Pepper immediately frowned. Nothing good could follow the mention of Greta. In fact, she was quite certain that woman lacked a heart. If ever there was a Grinch, it was Greta. And sadly, the woman was in charge of the shelter. Pepper never did understand how that had happened.

Stephanie stood, moved around her desk and stepped to the doorway. She glanced up and down the hall before closing the door ever so gently, as though not to make a sound.

Pepper's worries increased. She'd never seen her friend act so oddly. She couldn't imagine what was wrong, but if Greta was involved, she knew it had to be bad. That woman was a menace.

Stephanie spoke in whispered tones. "Greta is claiming that Daisy bit her."

"What?" Pepper couldn't believe what she was hearing. "Sweet Daisy wouldn't hurt a fly. Sure, she growls, but that's just because she's scared. She doesn't mean it."

"I know that. And you know that. But Greta doesn't like her."

"She doesn't like her because I like Daisy."

"I don't know. I just know Greta is claiming the dog is dangerous."

"Daisy is a puppy." With every passing moment, Pepper was growing more and more defensive about the puppy. "And she's not dangerous."

"The thing is, Greta says Daisy has to go. Today."

"But this is a shelter. This is where homeless dogs are supposed to go." This couldn't be happening. She was finally making headway with Daisy. The puppy was learning to trust her. "She isn't ready to be adopted."

"That's the thing. With Greta claiming she was bit— which I checked and I couldn't even see a scratch on her—I can't adopt out Daisy."

"What…what will happen to her?"

"I told Greta I would make sure Daisy is gone before tomorrow. Otherwise, she says she's taking matters into her own hands. And you know that won't be good."

Chills ran down Pepper's arms. "I don't know why that woman even works here, much less is in charge."

"You know and I know that it's for the money. And the fact she pulled strings to get the job."

"It's not fair to the people who work here and certainly not the animals. She doesn't even like animals."

Stephanie held up her hands helplessly. "At the moment we're stuck with her."

"And Daisy?"

"That's what I'm hoping you can help me with."

"Me? How?" She would do anything to save Daisy.

"I need you to take her home." Before Pepper could say anything, Stephanie held up a finger to pause Pepper's rebuttal. "Listen, you and I both know that's what you were working toward. Maybe you weren't willing to admit it to yourself just yet, but Daisy belongs with you."

She was willing to do anything for Daisy...but take her home. "I don't have a home to take her to. Remember? The fire."

Stephanie's gaze pleaded with her. "But you said you were staying in Simon's great big apartment."

"It's a penthouse. And the man who's letting me stay there doesn't like dogs. Or cats. Or anything that can make a mess, makes noise or needs taking care of." She thought she remembered all his reasons not to have a pet. How exactly was he going to deal with a baby?

Stephanie's mouth gaped. "And he let you stay with him?"

Pepper shrugged. "I clean up after myself."

Stephanie shook her head. "Surely there has to be a place you can keep Daisy until your apartment is ready."

Pepper thought of everyone she knew, including her second-in-charge at the bakery, but her daughter had asthma and was allergic to most pets. And there wasn't anyone else she would feel right about imposing on.

And then her gaze landed on Stephanie. "What about you?"

"You know I would if I could. But I've already taken in three dogs. One more and my landlord has threatened to kick me to the curb. Besides, I don't think Daisy will go with anyone but you."

"But Simon is going to throw a fit."

"Better him than Greta."

"True. But still... He might toss me to the curb."

Stephanie sent her a knowing smile. "You forget I saw him when he came to the shelter. I saw how he hung on your every word. I don't think you have a thing to worry about."

Was she serious? Pepper was never quite sure where she stood with Simon. Some days she thought he liked her just fine and other days she felt like she was nothing but in the way—another problem for him to deal with.

And now with Daisy, well, she was certain he wasn't going to take it well at all. But she couldn't let Greta do away with the puppy. Chills rushed over her skin. That woman was just pure evil. The shelter would be so much better off without her. If only there was a way to get rid of Grinchy Greta.

"Pepper, you have to decide now."

"Fine. I'll take her." She forcefully blocked out what this would mean to her relationship with Simon.

She probably should ask him before taking the puppy home, but this way she was saving him from having to say no and from her having to ignore his wishes. It still didn't leave her in a great position, but perhaps she could move back into her own apartment, even though it wasn't finished.

And so Stephanie set her up with everything she'd need to care for Daisy, including a crate. One of the volunteers offered to give her a lift back to the penthouse. Pepper could only hope it was early enough that Simon wouldn't be home yet.

She took the private elevator from the underground garage to the top floor. Pepper caught herself holding her breath as she entered the penthouse and looked around. Today was the housekeeper's day off, so that definitely helped things. To her great relief, Simon wasn't home.

She placed Daisy on the marble floor of the foyer. Immediately, the puppy had an accident. Oh, boy, they were not getting off to a good start.

"Don't worry," she said. "I'll get you in the bedroom and then I'll come back to clean it up."

Pepper led Daisy down the hallway to her bedroom. Along the way, Daisy took the time to investigate her surroundings. Her nose was going a mile a minute as she inspected everything in the wide hallway.

Daisy was like a new dog now that she was out of the shelter—much more relaxed. "I'm so sorry you've had a rough start in life. But don't worry, you'll be safe and hopefully happy from now on."

Pepper wasn't sure what the future held for the two of them. She was starting to wonder if there were any motels in the area that she could afford and that took pets.

She knelt down in front of Daisy. The puppy sat down and looked at her with those big brown eyes that instantly melted her heart.

Pepper moved slowly so as not to scare Daisy with any sudden movements. In the great big bag that Stephanie had packed, she found Daisy's stuffed blue bear. At the sight of it, Daisy's tail started to wag.

Pepper held it out to her, but Daisy didn't move. "It's okay. You can have it."

Still Daisy didn't move. Pepper placed the bear on the floor in front of Daisy. Immediately, Daisy gripped the bear with her mouth. The bear was almost the same size as Daisy. But that didn't keep Daisy from dragging the stuffed animal over to the fuzzy white rug next to Pepper's bed. There the dog lay down and put her head on the stuffed animal.

Pepper watched Daisy for a moment to make sure everything would be all right. Daisy's eyes started to grow heavy. She'd had a really big day. Pepper cringed at the thought of Grinchy Greta yelling at the puppy. That woman. Pepper's back teeth ground together as she held back a string of heated words. Daisy didn't need to hear Pepper vent. The pup needed some peace and quiet to get used to her temporary lodgings.

When Simon found out about Daisy, Pepper wasn't so sure they'd have a roof over their—

"Pepper!"

Oh, no. Simon is home.

And by the tone of his voice, he was not happy.

Daisy's head immediately lifted. And in a second or

two both she and the teddy bear scooted under the bed.
Poor baby.

"Pepper!"

"Daisy, it's okay. His bark is worse than his bite. I'll be
back." She wasn't so sure about letting the puppy lose in
a room with expensive decorations, but Simon obviously
wasn't in the mood to wait.

She rushed out of her bedroom and down the hallway.
She skidded to a halt when she noticed the angry look on
his face.

"Are you all right?" he asked.

She nodded.

"No accidents or anything that I should be aware of?"

Heat rushed to her face. Did he know about Daisy already? Had someone spotted them coming into the building and told him?

She shook her head. All the while she tried to figure
out how to break the news gently to him. Was there any
way to tell a man who didn't have pets, who didn't want
pets, that there was now one living in his house?

"Mind explaining this?"

She followed the gaze to the floor—and his stocking
feet. "You took your shoes off?"

He shook his head and pointed. His new-looking black
dress shoe was sitting in the dog pee. Ugh! She'd hoped
to clean that up before he got home. Daisy's homecom-
ing was getting off to an even worse start than Pepper had
imagined possible.

"I can explain."

Simon pressed his hands to his trim waist. "I'm listening."

"I was going to clean up the mess."

"Why is there a mess in my otherwise immaculate
foyer?"

By the stormy look on his face, nothing she said was

going to make this better. She might as well just go pack her stuff—not that she had much to pack.

This couldn't be happening.

His neat, formerly clean, quiet life was being upended.

Simon moved to the living room in his stocking feet. All the while, Pepper followed him, telling him about the drama of her day. And this person named Daisy.

He held up his hands. "Who is Daisy?"

"Didn't you hear me?"

The truth was, he'd been wondering how one five-foot-five woman could take his otherwise routine life and spin it on its head. Not only was she living with him, she was having his baby and now Daisy was staying with them.

He cleared his throat. "I have a lot on my mind."

Pepper looked uncertain of what to say.

Arff! Arff! Ooh-whoo!

"What in the world?" His gaze narrowed in on Pepper, whose face filled with color. "Do you have a dog in here?"

Arff! Arff! Ooh-whoo!

"I'll explain in a second."

"You'll explain now." He frowned at her. "You know I don't want pets."

"But if you just give me a chance to explain, you'll see that there really wasn't any other alternative."

Arff!

"I'll be back." Pepper turned and rushed out of the room.

She couldn't just walk away. They weren't finished with this discussion. He followed her down the hallway to her room.

Pepper opened her bedroom door and out rushed a puppy.

"Daisy," Pepper called.

But the dog didn't listen. Simon should have known it wouldn't even be trained. The puppy rushed right up to him and then stopped to sniff his pants and then his feet. He recognized the puppy from the shelter.

He wanted to be angry. He'd told her point-blank when she'd tried to talk him into adopting a dog that it wasn't for him. He was better off alone. But this dog was still a puppy. He knelt down to pet it. And it was sort of cute.

"Be careful," Pepper said.

He glanced up at her. "You brought home a vicious puppy?"

"Well, no. But…but she doesn't really know you. And she's not sure where she is."

He turned his attention back to the puppy. He let her sniff his hand and then he ran his hand over her smooth coat. She certainly didn't seem vicious.

Simon scooped up the puppy and straightened. He arched a brow at his flustered houseguest. "I think you should come with me and explain why this puppy is running around the house."

"Just a second." Pepper ducked into her room and returned with a blue teddy bear.

He wasn't quite sure about the necessity of the stuffed animal, but maybe it was a new baby toy that she'd picked up.

Simon turned with Daisy in his arms. He continued to pet the dog and she remained contentedly in his arms. In the living room, once he sat down, Daisy wiggled to get off his lap. He set her down.

Pepper joined the puppy on the floor and waved the teddy bear in front of Daisy. The puppy took hold of the teddy bear and moved beneath the coffee table.

"The stuffed animal is for the dog?" he asked.

Pepper finally smiled. "Yes. Daisy loves her stuffed animal. She always sleeps with it."

"Interesting." He continued to watch the dog as it left the teddy bear on the rug as it began to explore the room.

"I'll get her," Pepper said.

"Leave her. She isn't hurting anything." And then under his breath he said, "At least not yet." He cleared his throat. "Tell me more about this puppy."

And then Pepper went back to the beginning and told him everything, about the puppy, from its tragic past to the Greta woman accusing Daisy of being a vicious dog.

"I take it you don't like this Greta?"

"Like her? I can't stand her. Neither can anyone else at the shelter. My friend Stephanie could run the shelter if given a chance. Instead she's Greta's assistant, aka the person who does all of the grunt work but gets none of the credit."

He recalled how the pushy woman had hit him up for a donation. His gut told him the animals wouldn't benefit from the money. His investigators still hadn't come up with any concrete evidence against her. Perhaps it was time for him to contact Greta about a five-figure donation.

The more he thought about it, the more he liked the idea. All he had to do was provide the bait and he was certain Greta's greed would do the rest.

He made a mental note of this. He may not want a pet, but that didn't mean he didn't care. And whatever upset Pepper upset him—

Hold it.

When had that happened?

"Simon, what's wrong?" Pepper looked at him with concern in her eyes. "If it's Daisy, I'll go stay at the apartment."

"You can't."

Her fine brows drew together. "How do you know?"

"Because I stopped by at lunchtime. The apartment still isn't ready for anyone to live there. But don't worry, I put more men on the job. They'll be working round the clock."

"But how? I don't even have the insurance straightened out."

He shrugged. "It doesn't matter."

"It does matter. How am I ever going to pay you back?"

"Pepper, stop worrying. If I didn't want to do it, I wouldn't have. Everything is fine."

She opened her mouth and then closed it. For a moment, they both watched as Daisy nosed her way around the room. And then Pepper turned back to him. "I'll get my stuff. Daisy and I will find a motel."

"No." He couldn't believe he was saying this. "You and Daisy will stay here."

"But you don't want her here."

"Are you trying to talk me out of it?"

She shook her head. "I'll try to keep her out of sight."

Just then Daisy meandered over to him and sat on his foot. "Don't make promises you can't keep."

Pepper rushed over, scooped up the puppy and grabbed the teddy bear. She started toward her room. She paused and turned back to him. "Thank you. I just couldn't let anything bad happen to Daisy. She's already gone through so much as a puppy."

And then both Pepper and the puppy were gone. He sat there for a few minutes, thinking Pepper would return so they could finish their talk. But as the seconds turned to minutes, he realized the puppy was going to change things between him and Pepper—similar to the way the baby would change everything.

Maybe he should rethink things. Maybe Daisy could be a trial run for them—learning to share responsibilities. The more he thought of it, the more he realized he needed all the practice he could get—even if it was with a puppy.

CHAPTER SIXTEEN

IT WAS GETTING LATE.

And he still wasn't home.

Thursday evening, Pepper ate her dinner on the couch with Daisy next to her. The pup had become her shadow. If Pepper ever had any thoughts of rehoming Daisy, they'd been quickly forgotten.

Still, this was the first time Simon had said he would be home for dinner and then was a no-show. She never thought this arrangement would work out. In fact, she'd been downright certain it was a huge mistake, from the press hounding them, to the unexpected news of the baby—her hand pressed to her slight baby bump—to the fact she couldn't let herself fall for him.

Simon didn't do commitments. He'd told her that.

He also normally didn't work nine-to-five. So then why until now did he make such an effort for them to share their breakfasts and most dinners—even sometimes slipping home for lunch?

He was going out of his way to make her comfortable. Again, she came back to the question: *Why?* She told herself it was because he was just being a good host. Nothing more. But then why did it feel like more? Why did it feel like they'd become some sort of an insta-family? And if that was the case, where did they go from here?

Daisy lay in the corner of the kitchen, where she could keep an eye on Pepper. Talk about your loyal companion. Pepper smiled. "You're a good girl."

Daisy lifted her head and wagged her tail, understanding what Pepper had said.

And then because she couldn't resist such cuteness, Pepper grabbed a dog biscuit from the plastic bag on the counter and gave it to Daisy, who readily accepted it.

With the dirty dishes rinsed and loaded in the dishwasher, the countertops wiped down and nothing left to do for the day, she glanced at the clock. It was well past six. Where was he?

Don't worry. It's none of your business. He's only your host. Nothing more. Except the father of your baby.

Did that make a difference? Enough for her to butt into his life and make sure he was okay? Their situation was so complicated. She wasn't sure what was right. And what was inappropriate.

She glanced at her purse on the bar stool at the giant island. Sticking out of the top was the mail she'd picked up on her way back from the animal shelter. A padded manila envelope snagged her attention. She was pretty certain what was inside—a new-to-her DVD.

She didn't care if some people called her old-fashioned. She loved black-and-white movies. She collected them. Though some were available for streaming, a vast number were not. She had a huge collection of VHS tapes she'd inherited from her mother, and slowly over time she was replacing them with DVDs.

She pulled out the package. Maybe she should sit down and get lost in a movie. After all, she was caught up with everything she had to prep for tomorrow.

Her gaze strayed to the clock on the wall. It really was late for Simon. Worry settled over her, dampening her mood. Where could he be?

Silly question. She assured herself he probably got wrapped up in a project at work and forgot the time. She knew how that could be. When she was developing a new recipe, she could be at it for hours until she got just the right match of ingredients.

Maybe she should call him, just to make sure that was

the case. She moved to get her phone from the counter next to the fridge. She picked it up and pulled up Simon's number.

Her finger hovered over the call button. Should she? Or would it be overstepping? What would Simon think—

She heard the sound of the front door opening. She set her phone aside and rushed out of the kitchen, with Daisy right behind her. There stood Simon in the foyer. His black wool overcoat glistened with quickly melting snow.

He slipped off his coat and hung it up to dry. He glanced up. "Sorry I'm late. It's getting nasty out there."

"You're late?" She tried to act like it was no big deal— like she hadn't been worried about him. "I hadn't noticed."

He arched a disbelieving brow at her. "Are you trying to tell me that you haven't eaten yet?"

Heat rushed to her cheeks. She'd been busted. "I tried to wait. Honest."

He smiled. "So, you did notice my absence?"

Heat licked at her face as she shrugged. "I guess I got used to our routine. I started to worry when you didn't show up." Now what in the world had she gone and said that for? "I mean, I know you have a lot of work to do and sometimes you have to stay at the office late."

"Actually, I didn't work late."

"You didn't?"

He shook his head. "I stopped by the bakery. I wanted to see the progress."

"The bakery?" Was he getting anxious for her to move out?

He nodded. "I was curious how things were going. But no one was there."

"I was there earlier. They're waiting on the city inspector. He should be there tomorrow morning. I intend to be there when he arrives."

Simon's gaze met hers. "Are you sure you're up for everything you have going on?"

Her chin jutted out just slightly, as she didn't like the thought of being judged differently because she was carrying a little human inside her. "I'm managing just fine—at least until the baby arrives."

"Okay then. I will leave it to you to handle. But if you need anything—anything at all—tell me." He bent down to greet Daisy.

"I will." There was something more she'd been meaning to tell him. "Thank you."

"You don't need to thank me—"

"I do. You helped me through one of the most difficult times in my life." She took a deep breath. This admission wasn't easy for her. "My life has a lot of difficult twists and turns. I felt as though I'd finally got my footing and then the fire happened." She blinked back the sudden rush of tears. "But you helped me through it. I don't know what I'd have done without you."

"You didn't need me. You are amazingly strong—stronger than you give yourself credit." His eyes reflected his sincerity. "But I'm glad you think I was able to help you in some manner."

"They say the bakery will be up and running by the end of January. But I don't know. There's so much damage."

"If it takes more men, I'll make sure you have them."

He really was in a rush to get rid of her. She lowered her gaze to Daisy, who was sitting next to her. Pepper had definitely overstayed her welcome. But he was too much of a gentleman to tell her that he was tired of having her here in his space. Now that the situation with the insurance had been cleared up, there were funds for temporary housing.

"Hey," he said, "stop looking so worried. I was going to say that my selfish reason is because I miss your coffee and cherry turnovers."

"Really?" When he nodded, she took her first easy breath. "I was worried that you were tired of having me around."

He frowned at her. "It never crossed my mind. Besides, when you leave, I'll probably go back to takeout instead of the home-cooked healthy options you make."

She couldn't help but notice how he said "when," not "if." Her heart sank.

"Are you up for a little more business this evening?" he asked.

She shoved aside her worries about the future. "Sure. What do you need?"

"I have the contract for your recipes for the gourmet bakeries. Can we go over them?"

She nodded.

And so for the next hour or so, she read the contract. They discussed various points. And he took notes of her idea for the bakeries. The fact that he took her and her ideas seriously touched her.

Ting. Ting. Ting.

Pepper turned to the darkened windows. "Do you hear that?"

Simon nodded. "Sounds like an ice storm. Don't worry. It'll blow over quickly."

She somehow doubted that a winter storm would blow over quickly. For some reason, winter storms seemed to linger, unlike summer storms that would roll in and out in a very short amount of time. Or maybe it was the short days in the winter that made the bad weather feel like it lingered.

The lights flickered.

"That's definitely not a good sign." Her gaze moved to him.

"I'm sure it's nothing big."

Pepper's gaze again moved to the window. Deciding that Simon was right and there was no point worrying about it, she asked, "Have you eaten yet?"

He shook his head. "I didn't have a chance."

"Well then, you're in luck. I made spaghetti and home-made meatballs. I had a craving."

He arched a dark brow. "Isn't it early for those?"

She shrugged. "I've been known to have cravings without being pregnant. I'm guessing it's going to be a full seven months of continuous cravings."

"That should be interesting. Any desire for pickles and ice cream?"

Her nose scrunched up. "That sounds utterly revolting."

"I agree. I was just checking to see what I was in for."

She walked to the kitchen, pulled the plate of spaghetti from the fridge and placed it in the microwave. Her gaze moved to the window above the kitchen sink. The ice was continuing to hit the window. A shiver raced over her skin. She'd never liked winter storms. She didn't like the feeling of being cut off from everyone else; that's why she'd always lived in the city.

Simon stepped up to her. "What's got you rattled?"

"It's just the weather."

"It's more than the weather. Talk to me."

She shook her head. "It's nothing."

"It's something and I'd like to know, if you'll tell me."

Pepper gave herself a firm mental shake, chasing away the bad memory. Retrieving the warmed plate from the microwave, she turned to Simon. "Where would you like to eat?"

He shrugged. "The living room is fine."

Pepper handed him the plate and then retrieved a fork and napkin. She led the way. She settled on the couch and then lifted Daisy to her lap.

He glanced at the movie on the coffee table. "Is that what you were planning to watch?"

Simon, as she was quickly learning, wasn't a television-type person. He'd rather bury himself in reports or read a book, which was fine by her. To each his own. But she didn't want to bore him with her passion.

"It's nothing I can't watch another time," she said, settling back on the couch.

He set aside his untouched dinner. He picked up the DVD case and read the front before turning it over to read the back. "Interesting."

"Really?" She was totally caught off guard. "I didn't think you were into movies."

"I take it you enjoy them."

"I love them. I have an entire collection of old movies." And then she was reminded of the fire. "That is, unless they were destroyed."

"How many movies do you have in your collection?"

"Over three hundred."

"That's a lot of movies."

"I guess I inherited the interest from my mother. She was quite eclectic, which is obvious by the name she chose for me because I was born on Christmas Eve."

"I don't think Pepper is all that rare."

"No. My full name." When he looked at her as though he didn't get what she was trying to tell him, she said, "Pepper Mint Kane."

His mouth opened and his lips formed an O. "I didn't know. That is a bit unique."

"No. It's horrible. Do you have any idea what the kids did to me in school?"

"I'm guessing you wanted to change your name."

She nodded. "My name. My school. My life."

"So why didn't you when you got older?"

She shrugged. "What was the point? The worst of it was over and by then I'd lost my mother." Not wanting to go further down this path, she said, "Anyway, I've been working on replacing my mother's collection of VHS tapes with DVDs. I'm guessing not too far in the future I'll be replacing the DVDs with newer technology."

"Are they all older movies?"

She nodded. "This Cary Grant movie..." she gestured

to *An Affair to Remember*, which was in Simon's hand "…is one of my all-time favorites."

"Isn't it a bit depressing?"

She shrugged. "I guess it depends on how you look at it."

"And how do you look at it?"

"That true love can conquer anything—sometimes it just takes a little bit of effort. But never give up."

Simon looked at her strangely.

"What?" She felt a bit self-conscious under his direct stare. "Simon, stop looking at me like that."

"It's just in all the time I've known you, I never knew that you were a romantic."

"I'm not a romantic." Was she? She'd never really thought about it. "I just like romantic movies."

"Then put it on and let's watch it."

"Seriously?"

"Of course."

He didn't have to tell her twice. She started the DVD, turned off the lights and settled on the couch, leaving a respectable distance between her and Simon. Daisy decided the empty space was just perfect for her and her teddy. And so by the glow of the fireplace, they watched the movie. Even when Simon finished his dinner, he remained.

And then without warning, the power went out midway through the movie.

They both waited quietly for the power to flicker back on, but as the seconds ticked away, the darkness persisted.

Simon moved toward the window and looked out. "Seems we're not alone in the dark. Hopefully, it won't be off for long, but at least the fireplace still works." He turned to her. "Maybe we'll be camping in the living room tonight."

Pepper wrapped her arms about her. She didn't say anything as she was drawn back in time to another place—another time.

"I'll get us some blankets." Using the flashlight app on his phone, he headed toward the bedrooms.

In the short amount of time he was gone, Pepper told herself to quit acting like this power outage was such a big deal. The fireplace would keep them warm and the power company would surely have the lights on in no time. This wasn't the past.

"Pepper?"

She didn't say anything. She didn't trust her voice. And she didn't want to make a fool of herself. After all, it was a power outage. No big deal. But during a winter storm, the chances of the power returning soon weren't very good.

He moved to her side, opposite the dog. "Pepper, talk to me."

"I don't like power outages."

"I don't think anyone likes them, but they seem to bother you more than most. So tell me about your childhood. It might help pass the time."

Her mind flew to all the embarrassing, hurtful things in her past.

Her palms grew damp as her stomach churned. She just couldn't imagine peeling back the layers and exposing herself to him in that way. And that made her a bad person for not wanting to share. She knew it.

But what Simon didn't know was how hard it had been for her to let him this close to her. She knew that people could show the world one face and then in a blink pull off their smiley mask and reveal another, more sinister face.

She turned to Simon. She studied his very handsome face with its strong lines and mesmerizing eyes. Did he wear a mask? Her heart told her that he didn't, but her mind told her to beware.

Perhaps she'd start with why she didn't like bad winter storms. It wasn't like it was a big secret or anything. "It was a long time ago, when I was just a little girl. I remember it being a particularly cold and snowy winter. There was just me and my mom. I never knew my father."

Simon reached across the couch cushion, placing his hand over hers. She found warmth and comfort in his touch. "That's why it's so important to you that I have a close relationship with our baby?"

Pepper nodded as she gazed down at their hands. "My mother was working two or three jobs to make ends meet, but then she lost a job and we had to go without electricity for a couple of very long days and nights. I'd never been so cold in my life. It had been horrible. We'd huddle around a kerosene heater."

"I'm sorry. That must have been scary for you."

"I'm sure you never had to worry about anything like that."

"Pepper, I didn't grow up rich. For the most part, my mother raised me as a single mom too."

"Really?" When he nodded, she added, "It's just that you fit so well in this lifestyle. It's like you've been doing it all of your life."

He shook his head. "I didn't start to make any real money until I was in college. I liked to tinker with things. I always did. But then I started creating things and getting patents."

"That must have been so exciting."

"It was, but I had to overcome a lot of obstacles to make it that far."

"What was your childhood like?"

He shrugged. "Sometimes it was awesome. It was like having the perfect family. But the illusion only lasted for moments at a time. The other times, it was a nightmare."

Pepper felt guilty for thinking her childhood was so difficult. They might have been short on money, but the house had been full of love. It sounded like Simon's childhood home was anything but loving.

"Okay. So I told you my story. Now it's my turn to ask you a serious question. Why don't you like Christmas?"

The doors to the past once again creaked open.

Maybe if he opened up to Pepper, she would understand why they didn't belong together as a couple. She would know how damaged he was and want to keep a respectable distance instead of looking at him with need and desire that was so hard for him to resist.

If they were going to be a family, he didn't want there to be any secrets. He needed Pepper to make sure he didn't turn into his father—that could never happen.

Simon cleared his throat. "My father was an angry man and when he drank, he hurt everyone in his path." He paused as though to gather his thoughts. "There were some days when he was fine, almost human. But most days…most days you just wanted to stay out of his way. And holidays, well, those were the worst."

The memories came rushing back to him in sharp, jagged pieces. Each of them slicing into his scarred heart. And then the long-buried anger and resentment came roaring forth.

"I was nine that Christmas. I was long past the Santa stuff, but my mother shooed me to bed early anyway. She told me I couldn't see my presents until the morning. My father was out, so the house was quiet—almost peaceful—except the silence was more ominous than relaxing."

His mind rewound time until he was back there. He remembered vividly his nine-year-old self, so sure he was no longer a child.

"I'd fallen asleep, anxious for Christmas. I never got a lot of presents, but my mother worked hard to make sure I got one special toy and some clothes. I don't know how long I'd been asleep when I was wakened by the sound of my parents fighting. It wasn't uncommon, but this time it was so much worse than the others. Things were crashing against the wall. My mother was screaming. And my father was out for blood."

Simon glanced over at Pepper. She was quiet and her eyes showed sympathy. But she didn't stop him. So he kept going, leaving the grisly details out for both of their sakes.

"With my mother bleeding, I tried to stop my father—reason with my father. But he'd had too much to drink and he was too full of rage." His voice cracked with emotion. He couldn't stop here or he'd never get the rest out. "I was too small to stand up to a man who did manual labor all day long, but I gave it my all—giving my mother a chance to defend herself. And when I just couldn't anymore, I dragged myself to the phone and called for help."

Pepper leaned into him, wrapping her arms about him. "I'm so sorry."

"The police arrested him. My mother and I spent the rest of the night at the hospital getting stitches, and our broken bones treated."

He could feel the dampness of Pepper's tears seeping into his dress shirt. He wrapped an arm around her shoulders. She fitted there against him as though they'd been made for each other.

"When we got home on Christmas, we saw how the tree had been destroyed, the ornaments shattered. The whole place looked like a bomb had blown up in it. I told my mother I never ever wanted to celebrate Christmas again. She didn't argue. I knew she didn't want to relive that night."

"I'm sorry. I had no idea when I brought home the tree what you'd been through."

"Actually, it was good for me. You helped me see that I was stronger than those memories. So thank you for helping me see Christmas Present instead of Christmas Past."

"Your father... Do you ever see him?"

"No." That was another story of its own. "My mother

refused to testify against him. But I refused to let him hurt us again. I got up on the stand and I sent my father to jail."

Pepper pulled back. "You are the strongest person I've ever known."

"My mother didn't think so. I don't think she ever forgave me for sending him to jail. And then when he died during a riot, it was my fault he died. My mother and I had a very strained relationship after all of that."

She might have been there physically for the milestone moments of his life, but she hadn't been there emotionally. They didn't speak to each other about the important things in life. He never wanted to be like that with his child.

But with his parental role models, he felt doomed. Except there was Pepper. She was filled with sunshine and rainbows. With her to help him, maybe he could be the type of father he'd always wanted—patient, understanding and loving.

"Your mother seemed happy about the baby." Pepper's voice drew him from his thoughts.

He nodded. "She did, which surprised me."

"Maybe it's a chance for you two to reconnect."

"I wouldn't get your hopes up. I've been taking care of her financially and I thought it would make a difference, but there's still this chasm between us."

"Have you tried talking to her about it?"

He shook his head. "The past is best left alone."

"What about just opening up to her about what's going on in your life now? Maybe she isn't sure what to say to you. Maybe if you took the first step…"

He'd never tried because he didn't think his mother cared. But could Pepper be right? Was his mother waiting for him to make the first move?

"I don't know," he said. "I think she still blames me for his death."

"The woman I saw, who got so excited about her future grandchild, didn't look at you with anything but love in her eyes."

"Really?"

"Really. Give her a chance. You might be surprised."

He turned so he could look directly at Pepper. "And what about you? Do you regret getting involved with me now that you know just how damaged I am?"

She reached out and cupped his cheek, her fingertips brushing over his face. "I think you are strong, kind and resilient. You are not damaged. You are the perfect man to be a father to our baby…"

"But what if I turn out like my father?"

"You won't."

"How can you be so sure?"

"Because of the way you've cared for your mother, even though you think she blames you. And for the way you've cared for me, even before you knew about the baby. You have a good and honest heart. This baby will be all the better for having you in his or her life."

Her words were a balm upon his scars.

He leaned forward and pressed his lips to hers. How had he been so lucky to have Pepper in his life? She didn't see him as a rich man with connections; she saw him as he really was, warts and all. And still she was here in his arms.

Her mouth moved beneath his with a hunger of her own. Why exactly had he been holding her at arm's length? The reason totally eluded him now.

And so with the heavy snow falling outside and the puppy cuddled with her teddy on the couch, Simon and Pepper moved to the nest of blankets and pillows in front of the fire. It was there that he held her in his arms and made tender love to her, showing her just how much she meant to him.

CHAPTER SEVENTEEN

This was a bad idea.

A very bad idea.

And yet Simon let Pepper talk him into inviting his mother to the grand opening of the first Ross Pet Playground. He'd tried to tell her that his dysfunctional relationship with his mother was better left in private, but Pepper had looked at him with that pleading look in her eyes.

What was it about her that got to him? If it had been anyone else, he would have shut them down immediately. But Pepper, she was so optimistic, so caring. Except for the woman she called Grinchy Greta.

His people were uncovering every shady thing in her past. They were also tracking the generous donation he'd made to the shelter. It sounded like the Grinch would be dealt with in time for Christmas. He knew keeping the animals safe from that woman would be the best Christmas gift for Pepper.

Simon waited inside the new store as invited guests lined up on the sidewalk just on the other side of the giant red ribbon. A hired car pulled to a stop. His mother stepped out of the back seat of the black sedan with tinted windows.

She looked particularly pleased, especially when the press recognized her. They took her photo, which she posed for, smiling brilliantly.

Simon inwardly sighed. His mother was no shrinking violet. Once she'd got out from under his father's thumb, she'd shown a surprising amount of spunk. Over the years, she'd made a point of putting herself out there, trying new experiences and meeting new people.

Simon glanced at his watch. Only two more minutes until the ribbon cutting. Even the news crews had arrived. But there was no sign of the one person who he really wanted to be here. Pepper.

She was the one who'd helped him take this pet shop to a new level with its gourmet bakery. With her recipes, it was going to be a huge success. He'd really wanted her to stand up here and cut the ribbon with him, but she'd refused.

But later, they'd share a private celebration with a glass of sparkling grape juice and a kiss beneath the mistletoe. He couldn't wait. He had an early birthday surprise for Pepper.

Ninety seconds to go.

"Are you ready?" his assistant, Elaine, asked.

He nodded.

Another car pulled up. It was a business associate. Simon restrained a frustrated sigh. Behind that car was another. Would it be Pepper?

No.

He shoved aside his thoughts of Pepper, who would be here soon, just like she'd said she'd be. Instead, he needed to focus on this moment. Today was about... What was it about? It was more than a new store opening—much more. And it was no longer about conquering yet another challenge. His thoughts came full circle.

Today was more about Pepper. As she was the one who had given him the drive to make this a success—for more than himself. And Pepper would see that, if she would just show up.

"It's time," his assistant said.

He forced a smile to his lips as he kept checking to see if she'd arrived. He was so disappointed that she was going to miss this, because he had a surprise for her. One he was certain she would approve of.

But with the cameras rolling, he couldn't stall. The show, as they said must go on. He stepped outside. A round of applause rolled over the crowd.

"Thank you all for coming." All the while, his gaze scanned the crowd, searching for Pepper. "It seems like forever since we did something special like this for Ross Toys. And thanks to all of you, it's going to be a huge success."

Again, there was applause.

"But this moment is even more special for me because this accomplishment isn't just for me." Simon paused. He'd thought he saw Pepper. He scanned the faces again. Yes, there was she was, toward the back.

Simon placed his hand over the microphone in order to speak to Elaine, who was standing off to the side. "Pepper arrived. She's in the back. Please escort her here."

Elaine didn't say a word but instead nodded and set off to take care of the task.

Simon turned back to the crowd. "Sorry about that. A special guest has just arrived. This person has helped me take Ross Pet Playground from just another pet store to something extra special. I have a surprise announcement that hasn't been released to the public."

A hush fell over the crowd as they waited to hear the news.

"Within each and every Ross Pet Playground there's going to be a gourmet bakery." An excited murmur moved through the crowd. "We will be starting out with dog and cat treats that are not only tasty and cute, but also baked right in the store with top-of-the-line ingredients."

Pepper appeared off to the side of the stage with Daisy in her arms. He gestured for her to join him. She hesitated and shook her head. He gestured again.

"And you have this wonderful baker to thank for the tasty treats." When Pepper stepped forward, he said, "I would like to introduce the Polka Dotted Baker, Pepper Kane."

Another round of applause. Questions were shouted

from the press, but Simon ignored them. He wasn't answering any questions until the ribbon cutting was complete. And he still had a surprise for Pepper.

"Pepper has a bakery right here in Manhattan." And then he gave the address. "It is going to reopen in the New Year. I hope you'll stop by and give her your support. Just wait until you try her coffee and pastries. They are out of this world." He glanced over at Pepper, who was now blushing. She looked so adorable.

His assistant handed him a giant pair of scissors. When Pepper started to move away, he reached out to her. "Stay. You're really going to want to hear this next part." He turned back to the microphone. "Before I cut the ribbon, I have one more thing to say. With every purchase that's made at Ross Pet Playgrounds, a portion of the profits will be donated to Daisy's Friends. And if you're wondering who Daisy is—" he moved next to Pepper and gestured to the puppy "—this is Daisy. She's a rescue from a local animal shelter. She left behind lots of cuddly friends who need our help. Funds are limited and Ross Pet Playgrounds want to help by supporting local animal shelters."

The loudest applause of all filled the air.

He gestured for his assistant to come forward. "Can Elaine hold Daisy for just a moment?"

Pepper's brows drew together. "Simon, what are you doing?"

"You'll see." He helped transfer Daisy from Pepper's protective arms to his assistant's, who appeared to instantly fall in love with Daisy. He couldn't blame her. That little dog had a way of worming into the most resistant heart.

He spoke into the microphone again. "Pepper, you've been so instrumental in making this opening a success that I'd like you to cut the ribbon with me. What do you say?"

Her cheeks were rosy as she nodded her head. He

gripped one side of the scissor handle and she gripped the other. Together they snipped the ribbon.

And then they moved to the side as the doors swept open and all the guests were ushered inside the store, with its shelves filled with dog and cat toys and Christmas stockings stuffed with pet toys. The shop was decorated with Christmas decorations. In the center was an area for dog training, and along with the bakery expansion there was going to be an adoption center.

"You did a really great job," Pepper said.

Elaine moved up to them and handed the docile Daisy back to Pepper. "I agree, boss. You really outdid yourself."

"But it wasn't me." He was uncomfortable with taking the praise when it was Pepper and Daisy that had inspired the additions to the store.

Elaine turned to Pepper. "I don't know how you did it, but I definitely like the change."

His assistant walked away and Pepper wore a smile.

He was confused. "What did she mean?"

Pepper looked amused. "I think she was referring to you."

"Me? I haven't changed." Had he?

"That was marvelous, darling." His mother stepped forward and gave him a feathery kiss near his cheek. "I must say that I was surprised by the invitation."

"You can thank Pepper. It was her idea. She thought you might enjoy it."

"And I did." Her gaze met his. "Thank you both for including me."

For the first time in forever, he truly believed his mother. She wasn't saying this to impress anyone. Maybe Pepper was right that his mother wanted a chance to mend their relationship.

Pepper elbowed him. He cleared his throat. "I'm glad you could make it on short notice."

"I'll always make time for my family." His mother

turned to Pepper. "I'll be seeing you again soon, at the wedding."

"Wedding?" Pepper sent him a distressed look. She was just as appalled at the thought of marriage as he was, which made him all the more certain that what he had planned for that evening was for the best.

"Mother—"

Before he could say more, a reporter made a beeline for them.

"Gotta go, darling." His mother blew him a kiss and then conveniently slipped out to the waiting car and rode away.

He was jealous of his mother. He wanted to slip away from this crowd with Pepper, but he couldn't do that. This was his brainchild and now he had to see that it was a success. And so he put on his best smile and did his best to dodge any personal questions, while attempting to keep the interview focused on the new store.

By the time he finished with the one reporter, there was another lined up. With the temperatures dipping, they moved inside. Simon looked around for Pepper but didn't see her anywhere. He wondered where she'd gone off to. They had things to discuss.

What had just happened?

Pepper entered the penthouse with Daisy in her arms. "Did you hear that, Daisy? You have a charity named after you! That's pretty cool, right?"

Arff!

Pepper smiled. She loved how Daisy tried to have a conversation with her.

"This means other puppies and kitties that are still looking for their '*fur-ever*' homes will have funds for food, blankets and stuffed animals."

Daisy appeared to be done with the chat, squirming in Pepper's arms, wanting to be put down. She released the leash from Daisy's collar and then placed the puppy on the floor. Daisy took off toward the bedroom as though on a mission.

Pepper headed for the kitchen. Her thoughts were all about Simon and how he hadn't acted any different since they'd made love the other night. She thought it would have changed things between them. It'd changed everything for her. She couldn't hide from the truth any longer.

I love Simon.

The breath hitched in her throat as she acknowledged this truth. If it wasn't for the baby opening up her heart again to love, she didn't know if she'd ever have had the courage to admit her feelings for Simon to herself or anyone else.

And she wanted him to love her too. But as more time passed and he acted like they were nothing more than roommates, she worried that he didn't feel the same way. Or maybe she was just letting her nerves get to her.

She moved around the kitchen, placing the sponge cake layers on the island to frost with mascarpone frosting. She wasn't sure when Simon would make it home, but when he did, she'd planned a small celebration. She just hoped it wouldn't be too small.

She whipped the mascarpone cheese and then added the powdered sugar a little at a time. This was one of her favorite frostings, as it was so light and delicate. It was sweet without being overpowering. It enhanced the cake without taking over.

Daisy, dragging her teddy bear, entered the kitchen. Placing the teddy bear next to Pepper's feet, she lay down. In just a few moments, Daisy's eyes drifted closed. It'd been a big day for all of them.

As Pepper added the frosting to the top of each of the four layers, she thought about how things had changed between her and Simon. He'd come to accept Daisy, in fact, she'd caught them having a conversation the other morning when Simon thought she was still in bed.

He got up early and took Daisy for her morning walk. He even fed her breakfast so Pepper could sleep in. For a man who didn't like dogs, he was wrapped around Daisy's tail.

Was this the beginning of the family that she'd always wanted? Her heart swelled with hope. After losing her family one by one, she was finally ready to build a new family. Her hand pressed to her slowly growing midsection.

With the cake completed, she positioned it on the kitchen island. And then she retrieved the card she'd picked up. It was a Christmas card, but she'd written him a note on the inside. And then to make the scene complete, she added two champagne flutes and an ice bucket with some sparkling grape juice.

She moved to the living room. Pepper turned on the tree lights and that was all. She loved the soft glow that filled the room. It'd grown dark even earlier than normal.

She moved to the tall window that gave an amazing view of downtown. The overcast sky led her to believe that there was more snow on the way. As if in acknowledgment, a lone snowflake fluttered past the window. She hoped Simon made it home before it got bad out.

She'd just curled up on the couch and turned on the remainder of *An Affair to Remember* when the front door opened.

"Simon, in here," she called out.

He walked in and joined her on the couch. He glanced at the large screen television. "You didn't get enough of this the other night?"

"Well, it is one of my favorite movies." She arched a brow. "And we didn't get to see the end. Remember?"

"Hmm… I might remember getting distracted." His eyes sparkled with merriment. He was having fun with her.

With the way he was looking at her, with her own desire reflected in his eyes, her face filled with so much heat that she thought her hair would spontaneously catch fire. She remembered every single last delicious detail of what had happened the other night. The thing she didn't know was where it left them. They'd been so busy and so distracted that they hadn't had time to talk—until now.

As she turned off the television, she had the distinct feeling she wouldn't see the end of it tonight either. Though she couldn't complain. This distraction was definitely so much better than the movie.

Still, she was nervous. They had to talk about the future—their future. And though she had a really good feeling about where they were headed, saying the words would make it real. Her insides shivered with nerves. Not a bad kind of nervous. It was an excited kind of nervous.

She hadn't told him yet, but she loved him. It hadn't happened suddenly, but rather she figured it must have happened slowly over time. Somewhere along the way, as they'd shared their morning coffee and discussed current events, or she'd regaled him with a story about what happened at the bakery the day before, she'd fallen in love with Simon.

Those mornings had seemed so innocent—so laid-back—that she hadn't realized what was happening until now. She was madly, crazily in love with Simon. And now she was having his baby.

And soon they would be one big happy family. Her heart swelled with love. Her happiness overflowed into a big smile that lifted her lips and puffed up her cheeks. They were going to be so—

"I think we should live together," he said.

"What?" She swallowed hard. Was it possible her dreams were coming true? It was time she made her own confession. Her heart hammered so loudly in her chest that it echoed in her ears. It'd be so easy to back out—to keep her feelings to herself.

After all, everyone she'd loved had vanished from her life. What if the same thing happened to Simon?

But she had the baby now. And she loved it dearly. She

had faith that the baby would always be a part of her life, now and in the future. If she could believe that, then she could open her heart to Simon. She could believe they'd have a future.

"Simon." She waited until his gaze met hers. "I love you."

He took a step back as though in shock. Was her admission that much of a surprise? Was she the only one who felt that way?

She couldn't drop the subject. When he didn't say anything, she said, "Simon, do you love me?"

"I… I'm sorry. This was a mistake. I didn't mean to get your hopes up that—that we would be more than we are."

Her heart sank all the way down to her bare feet with her pink shimmery nail polish. His invitation to move in wasn't about love. It was about convenience—Simon's convenience.

She thought lots of things, like falling for him was the biggest mistake of her life. She was thinking it was time to pack her bags and get back to reality. Staying here would only allow her to wonder what if, and that was dangerous.

She turned away.

"Pepper?"

"Leave me alone."

With Daisy right behind her, Pepper moved toward the hallway that led to her bedroom as fast as her legs would carry her. Her knees felt like jelly as she moved. She just needed to keep it together until she reached her room and was able to close the door. It was just down at the end of the hall.

"Pepper."

Unshed tears stung the backs of her eyes. She blinked repeatedly, refusing to give in to them. It wasn't much further now.

And then she was there. She slipped inside and closed the door. The weight of reality pushed down on her. She sank down on the edge of the bed. She knew what needed to be done—she needed to pack.

It was time to go, to get her life back on track. The apartment wasn't finished, but it was close enough. The things that were left to do could be completed with her living there. She didn't have any other choice. As it was, she'd stayed at the penthouse too long.

Once she was back in her own home around her own things, she would feel better. Right?

What choice did she have? She couldn't stay here and take the crumbs of affection that Simon was willing to toss her way. And in the end, he would leave too—just like the other people she'd loved so dearly.

Sheer determination was the only thing that drove her body from the edge of the bed to the closet, where she had some shopping bags and her clothes. She made sure to only take the ones that she'd paid for. She didn't do charity and she didn't want to feel any more obligated to Simon than she already did.

Knock. Knock.

"Pepper, can we talk some more?"

She glanced down at the bed, where her clothes were scattered, awaiting their turn to be folded and placed in the shopping bags. "Now isn't a good time."

"Pepper, this is important."

She knew she was delaying the inevitable. The best thing to do was to get this over as quickly as possible. As her grandmother used to say, it was like ripping off the bandage—quick was the best.

Pepper moved to the door on wooden legs. Dread filled her. She didn't know how Simon was going to react to the news. But it isn't like he should mind all that much. She was just beating him to the punch.

She opened the door and stood there. "I don't think you need to say anything else. The fact is—"

"You're leaving?" He gazed over her shoulder to the bed.

She nodded. "Yes."

A distinct frown marred his handsome face. "And what about the baby?"

"I won't keep you from him or her. I'm sure we can work out a reasonable schedule."

She returned to the bed and continued placing her belongings in the shopping bag. And then she realized what he was waiting to hear. Her thoughts were a chaotic mess or she would have thought of it sooner.

She placed a pair of jeans in the bag and then turned to Simon. "Thank you for everything. You've gone above and beyond for me. I will pay you back. It might take some time, but I will do it."

"And that's it?"

"Yes."

With a grunt, he turned and strode away.

That was the last she saw of him. When she went to leave that evening, he was not in the kitchen nor was he in the living room. She had no idea if he was even in the penthouse. She dropped her keys next to the door. With Daisy in one arm and her meager belongings in the other, she walked out.

Her heart ached for the love that was not reciprocated. How could she have been so foolish? They might have had their special moments in the mornings over coffee and a cherry turnover, but that didn't translate into a life together.

Still, they did have this little one. Her hand cradled her tiny baby bump.

"Don't worry little one. We'll work this out. Somehow."

She hoped.

CHAPTER EIGHTEEN

He'd called off work Monday.

And Tuesday.

Simon found himself utterly alone in his great big penthouse. It was Christmas Eve. And the office was slated to work a half day followed by a catered lunch and the distribution of Christmas bonuses. Handing out the much-anticipated envelopes was a job he took on every year—but not this one.

Today was Pepper's birthday. He wondered if she had any special plans. He had presents for her—kitchen items he'd heard her mention, some brightly colored nail polish because he knew she liked painting her nails, and a diamond necklace because it was beautiful just like her. But with her gone, he didn't know what to do with the packages.

Simon moved from room to room. He'd never felt more alone in his life. He even missed Daisy running around, practically tripping him because she was so excited to be taken outside in the morning.

As he ambled into the kitchen to get some coffee, he paused at the kitchen counter, lacking its usual clutter of recipes, Pepper's phone and the dog leash. He rubbed his hand over the heavy stubble along his jaw. The kitchen was back to its spiffy cleanliness. It felt strange and foreign somehow. It also lacked the homey, delicious scents of Pepper's baking. He missed seeing her move barefoot through the kitchen with a touch of flour on her face and clothes.

Most of all, he missed her smile. It wasn't just any smile. It was a smile that could light up the darkest day.

It would warm him from the inside out. It filled him with happiness and the feeling that if he believed enough, everything would work out.

He backed away from the counter without his coffee. He'd lost his interest in it. As he walked out of the kitchen, his thoughts centered on his last conversation with Pepper. Where exactly had it all gone so wrong?

They'd been getting along so well. Laughing, talking, sharing. For the first time in his life, he'd started leaving the office at a reasonable hour. Not because he felt required to do it, but rather because he wanted to go home. He wanted to find out what Pepper had done that day. He wanted to share his day with her. Was that the way happy, committed couples felt?

He moved into the living room. Without Pepper in his life, he felt aimless. He was going through the motions, not caring about anything but figuring out how he had lost the most important woman in his life—a woman who'd brought the joy of Christmas back to him.

He bent over and turned on the tree lights. Memories of the evening they'd decorated it flashed through his mind. Things shouldn't have ended like this.

The doorbell rang. His heart launched into his throat. Was this it? Was this his second chance? Had Pepper changed her mind?

He nearly tripped over his own feet trying to get to the door quickly. He swung it open, expecting to find Pepper, but instead his mother stood there. Her smile quickly morphed into a look of concern.

"I stopped by because I found the cutest toy for the baby." All the while, his mother continued to take in his disheveled appearance. "Is Pepper around?"

He turned and walked away. "She's not here."

The door shut with a soft thud. He hoped that meant his mother had decided to go away and leave him alone with his misery. But then he heard the distinct click-click of her heels on the marble floor.

"Simon?"

He sat on a chair in the living room. He leaned forward, resting his elbows on his knees while he stared at the floor. He couldn't meet his mother's gaze.

"Simon, what is going on? You're worrying me."

"Nothing is going on."

"I know that we aren't close. A fact I would like to change. But even I know you should be at the office. Instead, you are here wearing...are those your clothes from yesterday?"

He glanced at his wrinkled pants and his partially unbuttoned shirt. He hadn't gone to bed last night, so he hadn't seen the point in changing. Actually, his attire was the very last thing on his mind.

"If you don't like my appearance, you can leave." He knew he was being unduly grouchy, but he wasn't up for his mother's penchant for putting on a good show.

She moved to the couch and sat down. "That isn't what I meant. I... I'm worried about you."

"Don't be. I've been getting along by myself all of this time. I'll be fine." Even he didn't believe his proclamation.

"You aren't fine. Anyone can see that." Her voice cracked. "And I blame myself."

He lifted his head, surprised to find unshed tears shimmering in his mother's perfectly made up eyes. "This has nothing to do with you."

"Actually, I think it has everything to do with me."

"You?" He shook his head. "Why would my relationship with Pepper have anything to do with you? She barely even knows you."

"Because I wasn't a good mother to you."

His gaze met hers. He was supposed to argue with her, but words failed him. Instead, he quietly waited to hear what she had to say.

"You were the sweetest little boy." She smiled as she moved her gaze toward the window. "You were so full of love, but your father—"

"Stop." His self-defensive nature reared itself. "We're not going to talk about him. I know that you've always blamed me for his death."

"What?" His mother's face took on a pained look. "No. I never blamed you."

"Sure you did. You barely spoke to me after he was arrested and I testified against him. We've never been the same since."

"And that's because I was ashamed of myself. How could I not be when my nine-year-old son was stronger and braver than me?"

He studied her face, a face which appeared to have aged in just a matter of minutes. His mother suddenly looked so much older.

She licked her lips and clasped her hands in her lap. "I should have been there for you. I… I should have protected you. Instead, you protected me." Her voice cracked with emotion. "You made sure that horrible man paid for his sins."

Was this for real? All these years he'd kept his distance from his mother because he thought she hated him, blamed him, had been a huge misunderstanding. He continued to study her face, searching for the truth.

"You don't blame me?"

"No. Never." Her eyes pleaded with him. "I've blamed myself. I grew deeply depressed for many years. It is only in recent years that I've gotten treatment."

And he would have known all of this, if only they'd talked to each other. That's what he was doing with Pepper. Letting her walk away without talking to her.

"I'm sorry," his mother said. "Please forgive me."

He hadn't known how much those words would move him. He took her in his arms as she wept.

When he at last pulled back, he looked into her eyes, so much like his own. "I love you, Mom."

"I love you too." His mother stood. "I should be going. But please don't let things end with Pepper. She's good for you."

"Why do you say that?"

"Because I've seen you with her. You smile when you're around her. And look!" She gestured to the Christmas tree, "I never thought you'd celebrate Christmas again."

"But she's the one who ended things."

"Did she? Or did you give her no other choice?"

"I asked her to stay here with me—to continue this life we'd started."

"But did you tell her you love her?"

His head lowered. He hadn't done that. He'd been so busy worrying about protecting her from him—from him hurting her—that he hadn't allowed himself to say so. He'd held himself back and in the process he'd hurt Pepper.

He knew how to fix this. But first he had to grab a shower. He scratched at the unfamiliar stubble on his chin. In the shower, he'd formulate a plan.

"Thank you, Mom." He kissed her cheek. "I have to hurry. Can you let yourself out?"

"Certainly. Good luck."

He was already rushing down the hallway, working on the most important proposal of his life.

"Happy birthday!"

Stephanie handed Pepper a pink cupcake and a coffee. "Thank you."

"I know with you being a baker that it's strange to give you a cupcake, but I didn't want you baking your own birthday cake. It's not as good as yours, but I baked it from scratch. And I ate one just to make sure they were edible."

Pepper smiled. "Thank you. It looks delicious."

"I also come bearing news. You're not going to believe this."

Stephanie stood in Pepper's messy apartment with a mix of glee and awe on her face. Pepper, wearing yoga pants and a big T-shirt, moved back to her spot on the new couch. She placed the cupcake on the end table to eat later when her appetite returned.

The last thing she wanted to do at the moment was entertain guests. But Stephanie was too good of a friend to just turn away. No matter how bad Pepper might feel, she wasn't capable of hurting her friend's feelings.

Stephanie joined her on the couch, as it was the only cleaned-off area to sit. The new chairs were stacked with boxes. Everything was in such disarray that it made Pepper's head hurt.

"Won't believe what?"

Stephanie's eyes lit up. "They hauled away Grinchy Greta."

This got Pepper's full attention. "What? Who did?"

"I don't know all of the details. Most of it was all hush-hush. But I was able to hear them tell her that she was under arrest for embezzling. Can you believe it?"

Pepper's mouth gaped open. "Really?"

Stephanie smiled. "And I'm temporarily in charge. I'm not really sure if that's a good thing, considering there will be audits and changes, but at least the animals will be safe from that woman."

"And this means if she was embezzling the donations, there will be more funds for the animals." Pepper's voice lacked the enthusiasm that this occasion deserved.

"How do you think this happened?"

"I'm not sure." Her mind rewound to her conversation with Simon. He'd been asking a lot of questions about the woman. "But I have an idea."

"Did you turn her in?"

"I would have if I'd known. But Simon was asking a lot of questions about Greta."

"Really? Why would he care?"

Pepper shrugged. "He met her when he stopped by the shelter, and I might have mentioned how horrible she is. And then when I brought home Daisy, I think he understood how miserable that woman is and how she shouldn't be allowed around such sweet, adorable animals."

Daisy came scampering into the room as though she'd heard her name called. Pepper leaned over and picked her up. The puppy wiggled around, so full of energy while Pepper could barely move herself from the couch. She missed Simon—missed the life they'd started to create together. Had she made the biggest mistake by walking away? Would he have eventually come to love her?

"Something tells me that we have Simon to thank for ridding us of the Grinch," Stephanie said.

"I think you're right."

"You should call him."

Pepper shook her head. "I don't think he wants to hear from me."

Stephanie's perfectly plucked brows rose high on her forehead. "Trouble in paradise?"

"I... I left."

"As in you and Simon are over?"

Pepper nodded. "It was never going to work out for us. We wanted different things."

"Really? Because you two seemed so perfect together at the shelter and when I saw you on television together for the grand opening of his store."

"I thought so too. But..."

"But what?"

Pepper drew in a deep breath and let it out. "He doesn't love me."

"Oh." Stephanie frowned. "He told you that?"

"No. But when he asked me to stay—"

"He asked you to stay and still you left."

"Didn't you hear me? He doesn't love me. I can't stay with someone who doesn't love me."

"But you love him?"

Pepper nodded. "When I asked him if he felt the same way, he didn't say anything."

"But you're having his baby. And he wanted you to stay. Wouldn't it be worth giving him a second chance?"

"I don't know if he wants one."

"How would you know unless you ask him?"

Stephanie did have a point. Pepper reached for her phone on the end table. She hadn't paid any attention to it since she'd left the penthouse. There were a number of missed calls. None of them were from Simon. Her heart sank.

And then she stumbled over a text message from him:

Can we meet and talk?

Sure. When?

Top of the Empire State Building? Tonight? Seven?

What an odd choice for a meeting spot.

See you there.

CHAPTER NINETEEN

SIMON STOOD ATOP the Empire State Building.

Alone.

He hunched deeper into his coat with the collar turned up to keep out the frigid breeze. Pepper was late. And if she didn't hurry up, he feared he'd soon turn into a snowman. He'd already gotten some strange looks from other couples as he paced back and forth.

The evening was growing colder with each passing moment. Or perhaps it was he that was growing cold after waiting—for forty-five minutes.

To be fair, he'd been early. She was only...nineteen minutes late. She probably wasn't going to come. This was the second time she'd ended things with him.

He should leave.

What had made him think this was a good idea? Just because they'd watched *An Affair to Remember* and he'd wanted to do something romantic for her—to prove just how much he loved her.

And now the first snowflakes had begun to fall from the inky-black sky. How much longer should he wait? How much longer until he accepted that he'd lost the best thing that had ever happened to him?

There was the elevator. He should go get on it. He must look pathetic, standing here all alone, waiting for a woman who wasn't coming. But his feet refused to move. It was as though if he willed it hard enough, long enough, she would come. Which he knew was totally ridiculous. But the doors to the elevator closed and he remained atop the Empire State Building.

If only she'd give him one more chance, he'd show her just how much she meant to him. But he was also a businessman. He knew when to cut his losses. And so with the greatest reluctance, he told himself that he would get on the next elevator.

He moved inside and waited. While he waited, he replayed the lifetime of memories that they'd shared in just a matter of weeks, from the horrible fire to finding out they were going to be parents. And then there was Daisy. He'd never known that he was a dog person until she came along and stole his slippers. He'd gladly go buy another pair of slippers for her to chew on if his family would just come back home.

His head lowered and he stared blindly at the ground. His heart was heavy. And the weight of misery pressed down on his shoulders.

The elevator doors swung open. He didn't move. It took a concentrated effort to move his feet. There was still a part of him that wanted to cling to hope—

"Simon?"

His heart reacted before the rest of him. It leaped with joy. It took his mind a few seconds to catch up. He lifted his head, needing to see that Pepper was in fact standing there before he let himself believe there was hope for them.

His gaze connected with hers and held. Was she really standing there? Surely he hadn't just imagined her, right?

"Simon, are you all right?" She stepped closer. "You look like you've just seen a ghost."

He didn't dare blink or for one moment take his eyes off her. He didn't want her to disappear. If this was a dream then he never wanted it to end.

"You came."

Her brows drew together. "You said it was important."

"It is. But when it got late, I thought—"

"That I wasn't coming. I'm sorry. There was some

sort of traffic jam and it held up everyone." She glanced around. "Are we the only ones up here?"

He nodded. "There were other people here, but they've gone now. I was just about to leave."

"Oh." Her gaze lowered. "Listen, I know we have to talk sometime and work out arrangements for the baby—"

"I'm sorry that things ended the way they did. I wanted to call, but I didn't think you'd want to talk to me."

"I needed some time to cool off—to think straight."

"I hope it helped."

"It did."

This being distant and cordial was killing him. All he wanted to do was pull her into his arms, look into her eyes and tell her how much he loved her.

But he worried that if he did, she would pull away. That what little progress they'd made would end. And he couldn't go back to the utter silence on her part. His world was so much darker without the brightness of her smile.

What had he wanted?

Why was he acting so reserved?

And what was up with meeting here at the Empire State Building?

For a moment, Pepper felt as though she'd stepped onto a movie stage and she was playing a part. But the question was what sort of movie was this to be? A romance? Or a tragedy?

Maybe it was selfish of her, but she wanted more from life. If she didn't take the chance—if she didn't put herself out there—she knew she would regret it for the rest of her life. And if it wasn't possible, she knew raising a child alone wouldn't be easy, but she could do it. It was the thought of not having anyone to share the day-to-day struggles and joys with that made her sad.

Living in the penthouse with Simon had given her a glimpse of what it'd be like to share her life with him.

And now that she knew what it would be like, it was so hard to accept less.

She couldn't let this drag out. With each passing moment, her heart grew heavier with sadness and loss. "Did you have some papers for me to sign?"

"Papers?" He looked at her with confusion in his eyes.

She nodded. "Isn't that what you called me here for? To sign some custody agreement papers?"

"Um, no." He shifted his weight from one foot to the other. "I wanted to meet you here so we could talk without being interrupted."

What was he leading up to? She had no clue, but there definitely wouldn't be any interruptions up here. At least until the next elevator arrived.

She quietly waited for him to have his say. With each passing second, her heart pounded harder with anticipation.

"Pepper, I'm sorry. I wish… I wish that things hadn't ended like they did. If I could take it back, I would."

She shook her head. "It wasn't all your fault. It was mine too. I wanted things from you that you couldn't give me. I shouldn't have pushed so hard."

"But that's the thing." He stared deep into her eyes. It was as though he could see through all her defenses and straight into her heart that was beating out his name. "I want to give you those things."

"You do?" Please let her have heard him correctly.

He nodded. "I do. But you know about my dysfunctional family and how I had the worst role model for a father ever. I'm afraid that I'll end up like him."

"That could never happen."

His eyes widened. "You really believe that?"

"With all of my heart. You are a good man, whether you believe it or not. Your nature is to protect those you love, not to hurt them."

He paused. "I never thought of it that way." His gaze searched hers. "I love you."

Those three little words knocked the breath from her lungs. She hadn't been expecting them. In fact, she never thought he would ever say them to her.

And then a sneaky voice in the back of her mind wondered if he was just saying what she wanted him to say. Was this his way of getting her and the baby back under his roof?

If so, she couldn't do it. She needed him to love her one hundred percent, for herself, and it not have anything to do with the baby. Because when she gave her heart away, she wanted it to be forever.

She shook her head, refusing to believe he was saying the words that she'd longed for him to say. "You're just saying that because you think it's what I want to hear."

"I mean them." His gaze pleaded with her. "I love you."

This couldn't be happening. It was too good to be true.

"You just want me to move back so you'll be closer to the baby."

"I love you and I don't want you to do anything you don't want to do. Whether you live at the penthouse or live above the bakery, it won't change how I feel about you. I love you. It has nothing to do with the baby. I love *you*. And I'll keep telling you that I love you until you believe me. Pepper, I love you with all of my heart."

He reached out and swiped a tear from her cheek. She didn't even know she was crying tears of joy. She desperately wanted to believe him. So what was holding her back?

"Do you still love me?" he asked.

She hesitated. She knew putting her heart on the line could be dangerous. But she also knew that without taking a risk, she could be missing the best parts of life.

She nodded.

"Then trust me." He held his hand out to her.

Her gaze moved to his outstretched hand. What was he up to now? Curiosity had her putting her hand in his. He led her to the outlook.

With the gentle snow falling upon the city, it looked like pure magic. She was definitely in the middle of a movie—a movie of her life. Her heart thump-thumped. And dare she believe that it was going to be a romance? With its very own happy ending?

As though reading her mind, Simon got down on one knee. And then he slipped a box from his coat pocket, opened it and held it up to her.

Her mouth gaped. She couldn't believe her eyes. In just a matter of a few moments all her wishes were coming true.

"Pepper, you are the most amazing woman in the world. You taught me how to open my heart again. You've shown me that love comes in all shapes and sizes. And I would love to spend the rest of my life with you. Will you be my wife?"

He was full of all sorts of surprises. "Simon, are...are you sure?"

"I've never been more certain about anything in my life."

She pressed a hand to her mouth, holding back a squeal of delight. Her wide-eyed gaze moved from him to the diamond solitaire ring nestled in black velvet. "Simon, it's beautiful. I'd be honored to be your wife."

He removed the ring from the box. He took her trembling hand into his own and placed the ring on her finger.

In the background there were cheers and clapping from the onlookers that must have exited the elevator somewhere in the middle of the proposal. And there were flashes from cameras. And this time, Pepper didn't care. She didn't care if the whole world knew she loved Simon Ross.

Inside, her heart wasn't just thumping, it was pounding. Her palms were damp. And all she could think about was what that ring on her hand meant—they were going to get their happily-ever-after.

"Kiss! Kiss! Kiss!"

The familiar chant filled the air. How could they have forgotten the best part of this—the kiss? Simon straightened and swept her into his arms.

"I love you. Never ever doubt it," he said.

"I will always love you too." Her voice was soft as it floated through the air. "Merry Christmas."

"Happy birthday."

He remembered! "Thank you. This is the best birthday ever."

He lowered his head and claimed her lips. She knew she'd never tire of his kisses. In fact, she was quite certain she would remember this movie-like moment for the rest of her life. When she was a little old lady, she would tell her great-grandchildren about this moment—this very romantic moment. And she would end the story with *"They lived very, very happily ever after."*

EPILOGUE

Valentine's Day, the Polka Dotted Bakery

HER SECOND MOST favorite holiday had just moved to first on her list.

And it certainly helped that the Polka Dotted Bakery was back in business and busier than ever. Old employees and customers had found that the mass-produced cupcakes weren't better than Pepper's homemade ones. As busy as they were, on Valentine's Day they closed the shop a little early—for a private engagement.

Pepper and Simon were now officially married.

How was this possible?

Pepper stood in her apartment no longer Pepper Mint Kane, but Mrs. Pepper Ross. She loved the sound of it. But she loved her new husband so much more.

She stared down at the diamond band on her finger and smiled. The truth was that she hadn't stopped smiling since they were declared husband and wife. Mrs. Simon Ross, Mrs. Pepper Ross, or just plain old Pepper Ross. The smile on her lips grew.

"And what has you smiling so brightly?"

She glanced up at her very handsome husband. "I was just thinking that you're never going to be able to top this Valentine's. Ever."

His brows rose. "Is that a challenge?"

Oh, no. He had that look in his eyes that said she was about to lose. But somehow, she didn't think it was possible to lose this particular challenge. "Yes. It's a challenge."

An *I got you* smile lifted his lips. "I know next Valentine's will be even better. Want to know how I know this?"

"How's that?"

"There will be three of us next year."

Daisy barked her disagreement and they both laughed.

"Okay. There will be four of us. It doesn't get any better than that."

"Why did I ever doubt you?" Her hand smoothed down over her growing baby bump. At four months along, her pregnancy was finally showing.

"You'll learn to trust me. My family will always be my first priority."

She reached up, running her fingers gently down his cheek. "I already trust you with my heart."

He caught her hand and pressed a kiss to her palm. "How did I ever get so lucky?"

"I guess it's true what they say, you know, about the way to a man's heart is through his stomach." She smiled lovingly into her husband's eyes. To think she would get to do this for the rest of her life. Her heart fluttered with joy. "We should head out, if we're going to make it to the country house by dinner."

"Are you sure that's where you want our honeymoon? I could call up the jet and have it fly us anywhere in the world."

She moved toward the kitchen, stopping in the archway to place her wedding bouquet of red roses on the counter. She worried her bottom lip. Was he going to be upset if they didn't fly away to a warmer climate?

Her heart raced as she worried. This marriage stuff might have a bit of a learning curve.

She turned to him. "But it's going to snow this weekend. And I thought we could get snowed in together, next to a roaring fire."

He stepped closer to her. "The image is quite compelling. Whatever my bride wants, my bride shall get."

Daisy barked in agreement.

"You aren't upset, are you?"

He wrapped his arms around her waist and drew her close. "Not a chance. If we're really lucky, we'll get snowed in for weeks."

"Weeks?"

"You're right. That's not long enough. Maybe the rest of winter. Because I couldn't think of any other place I'd rather be than holding you close as the snow falls. I love you, Mrs. Ross."

"I love you, Mr. Ross."

Okay, so maybe the learning curve wasn't as steep as she'd originally feared. She lifted up on her tiptoes and pressed her lips to his. In fact, learning just might be half the fun.

* * * * *

A WYOMING CHRISTMAS TO REMEMBER

MELISSA SENATE

As always, for Max, with love.

Chapter One

"You're my *husband*?" Maddie Wolfe asked.

She tried to latch on to the word, for something, anything, to associate *husband* with the total stranger sitting at her bedside. The stranger holding her hand in both of his and looking at her with worried green eyes.

"My name is Sawyer Wolfe," he said. "We've been married for seven years."

"Sawyer Wolfe. Seven years," she repeated. "And I'm Maddie Wolfe?" She hadn't even known that until he'd told her when she'd woken up just a couple minutes ago with no idea who she was, where she was or who *he* was. Her mind, where her identity and memories should be, was a big blank nothing.

She glanced from him to what was beside her bed—quietly beeping hospital machines, an IV pole. A television mounted on the beige-yellow wall. A long, wide window. A miniature Christmas tree decorated with garland and ornaments on the windowsill and so many poinsettia plants—pink, red, white—she couldn't even count them. There were even more bouquets of flowers.

I'm in a hospital, she realized, reaching up to the goose egg on her forehead and the deep scratch beside it. That would explain why her head felt so woozy and achy. And maybe why her mind was so blank. *I'm…* she thought, trying to come up with her name on her own. *Maddie Wolfe?* Didn't ring a bell. She tried for her age. Nothing. Where she lived. But there was just that nothingness again.

Sawyer Wolfe nodded, his eyes shimmering with tears, relief, concern. When her own eyes had fluttered open, the first thing she saw was him. He'd jumped up, shouted, "Maddie's awake! My wife is awake!" and then grabbed a white call button attached to her bed and pressed it three times before sitting back down and taking her hand, kissing the back of it over and over.

"Your wife?" she'd asked.

He'd glanced up from the kissing of her hand, clearly confused. "Maddie?"

"Maddie?" she'd repeated, more confused.

He'd sat up very straight. "Maddie, do you know who you are? Who I am?"

She'd looked at him long and hard, and believe you me, he was something to behold. But nothing about this man was familiar.

She'd shaken her head, which had her reaching up to the goose egg, the deep scratch beside it.

"Your name is Maddie Wolfe," he'd told her. "I'm

Sawyer Wolfe, your husband. You were in a car crash—it was snowing hard and you hit a guardrail."

Now, before she could ask him anything else, two women came rushing in, one in blue scrubs, the other in a white lab coat with a name tag: Dr. Louisa Addison.

The nurse began taking her vitals: temperature, blood pressure.

"Maddie doesn't seem to know her name or who I am," Sawyer said to the doctor.

Dr. Addison asked her a bunch of questions she didn't know the answers to. *What is your name? What year is it? Who is the president of the United States?*

As the doctor jotted things down on her chart, Maddie wondered how she knew what a chart was if she didn't know what year it was. She glanced at the four pink poinsettias on the windowsill, clearly knowing what those were. Her gaze moved to the little Christmas tree. There were two Woodstock ornaments—the little yellow bird from *Peanuts*, Snoopy's buddy. Why would she know that but not even know it was Christmastime if the tree hadn't clued her in?

Ow, my head, she thought, letting the questions, the confusing buzz go. The blankness came back, and she instantly felt better.

She glanced at the man—six-two, maybe six-three, dark hair, a scar above his left eyebrow. If she thought he looked worried before, it didn't come close to the concern on his face now.

"My mind is blank," she said to both of them. "Why is my mind blank?" She tried to think what day it was, but as she ran through the days of the week, none registered as the right one. She bolted upright. "Why don't I know my name? Sawyer said I was in a car crash?"

Dr. Addison nodded. "You've sustained a head injury that seems to have affected your memory. But rest assured, you're in good hands. You are Maddie Wolfe, thirty-two years old. Your husband, Sawyer Wolfe, is right here—he's the chief of police in Wedlock Creek. You're in Brewer County Hospital in Wyoming, transferred here from the Wedlock Creek Clinic."

No memory: amnesia. She knew what that was. It explained why her mind was full of holes. She grasped on to what she was told. *My name is Maddie Wolfe. My husband is Sawyer Wolfe. Police chief. Wedlock Creek.*

Nothing. Her own name was unfamiliar. Her husband was a stranger.

She swallowed, glancing over at the Woodstock ornament. She kept her focus on the little yellow bird, and for some reason, it comforted her.

"Maddie," Dr. Addison said, "Sawyer hasn't left your side in the two days since you were brought in." The doctor offered an encouraging smile to both Maddie and the man. "Your parents and sister were here this morning and said they'd be back this afternoon."

Parents and a sister! She couldn't even remember her own family.

"I'll go text them that you're awake," Sawyer said, leaping up and heading near the door, where he pulled out his phone.

As the doctor typed instructions into a computer monitor against the wall and the nurse checked her IV, Maddie stared at Sawyer. Surely if he were her husband, she would remember something. A familiarity.

A flash of their wedding day. The two of them at home. Something, anything.

"Will my memory return?" Maddie asked the doctor.

Dr. Addison turned to her. "Amnesia is a tricky thing. There are a few different kinds, and yours is likely caused by trauma. We'll have to wait and see. I did have a patient a few years ago who'd suffered temporary amnesia from a bad fall. His memory returned to full function within three weeks."

"Three weeks?" she repeated. "I might not remember anything about myself for three weeks?"

Dr. Addison gave her a reassuring smile. "Could be sooner. But we'll run some tests, and based on how well you're doing now, I don't see any reason why you can't be discharged later today."

Discharged where? Where did she live?

With your husband, she reminded herself.

She bolted upright again, her gaze moving to Sawyer, who pocketed his phone and came back over, sitting down and taking her hand in both of his. "Do I—do we—have children?" she asked him. She couldn't forget her own children. She couldn't.

"No," he said, glancing away for a moment. "Your parents and Jenna will be here in fifteen minutes," he said. "They're ecstatic you're awake. I let them know you might not remember them straightaway."

"Jenna?" she asked.

"Your twin sister. You're very close. To your parents too. Your family is incredible—very warm and loving."

That was good.

She took a deep breath and looked at her hand in his.

Her left hand. She wasn't wearing a wedding ring. He wore one, though—a gold band. So where was hers?

"Why aren't I wearing a wedding ring?" she asked.

His expression changed on a dime. He looked at her, then down at his feet. Dark brown cowboy boots.

Uh oh, she thought. *He doesn't want to tell me. What is* that *about?*

Two orderlies came in just then, and Dr. Addison let Maddie know it was time for her CT scan, and that by the time she was done, her family would probably be here.

"I'll be waiting right here," Sawyer said, gently cupping his hand to her cheek.

As the orderlies wheeled her toward the door, she realized she missed Sawyer—looking at him, talking to him, her hand in his, his hand on her face. That had to be a good sign, right?

Even if she wasn't wearing her ring.

Almost exactly the same time that the orderlies wheeled Maddie back into her hospital room, her family arrived. Sawyer had been hoping for some time alone with Maddie, but he'd get that later at home. Right now, her family needed to see her.

The MacLeods—pronounced *MacLoud*—all hovered around her bed. They lived up to their name and then some.

"Maddie!" April MacLeod shouted, throwing her arms around her daughter. "Oh goodness, I'm not squeezing any sore spots, am I? Let me look at you. Oh my, that's some goose egg. But that'll go down, lickety-split. We brought you chicken noodle soup from that fancy gourmet place you like in Brewer. You love chicken noodle." She stared at Maddie, then waved her hand in the air. "Did I even tell you who I am? I'm your beloved mother, that's who. You and your sister here are my world. And this guy—" she slung an arm around her tall, gray-haired husband's shoulder "—married thirty-four years next Saturday."

"Glad you're awake, Maddie-girl," Ace MacLeod said, giving his daughter a gentle hug. Tears shone in his blue eyes and he blinked them back. "You scared us half to death."

Jenna MacLeod Spinner leaned down to hug her twin as best she could—her sixth-months-pregnant belly didn't let her get as close as she clearly wanted. "So word is that you don't remember anything. Trust me, we're unforgettable. It'll come back to you."

Maddie gave a shy smile. "I hope so. You definitely seem like people I'd like to know."

April laughed her huge, throaty, I-used-to-smoke laugh. "You adore us. Can't get enough of us. But you take it easy until the doctor says otherwise. I know you'll try to come back to work, and I won't hear of it. Not until you're cleared."

Maddie tilted her head. "Work? What do I do?"

"You manage the family business—MacLeod's Multiples Emporium."

"A multiples emporium?" Maddie repeated. She couldn't even guess what that was.

"Wedlock Creek, our hometown, is famous for its multiples," April explained. "The Wedlock Creek Wedding Chapel has a legend attached to it—for a hundred years now. Those who marry there will have multiples in some way, whether through luck, a little help from science or through marriage."

"Which one are Jenna and me?" Maddie asked with a grin.

"Pure luck," her mom said. "Multiples run on both sides of the family. And since there are so many multiples in town, we started a business devoted to twins and triplets and quads and quints twenty-five years ago. Gift baskets, layettes, baby shower accoutrements, personalized gifts, anything anyone could want to celebrate all things multiples." She glanced at Sawyer, then smiled down at Maddie. "Well, Maddie-girl, we're going to let you get out of here. Sawyer will take you home, and we'll call later to see how you are."

Maddie gave a quick smile and nod, and it was strange how Sawyer couldn't read her expressions anymore. He knew her so well. But now that she didn't even know how she felt about anything or anyone, all her reactions were new to him.

An hour later, after eating a light lunch and having her vitals checked again, Dr. Addison ran through some instructions, handed over the discharge papers and Maddie was free to leave.

"Earlier I asked your mom to stop by the house and bring you clothes to change into," Sawyer said. "And your favorite boots." He handed her an overnight bag.

"Ah, thank you. I'll just be a bit." She headed into the bathroom with the bag.

Why aren't I wearing my wedding ring?

He hadn't answered that question, and he was sure she was going to ask again. But he didn't want to tell her. He didn't want to talk about any of that.

He shouldn't be almost glad that she'd forgotten what had made her drive away from him the morning she'd crashed her car. He couldn't take back what he'd said, even if he hadn't meant it, even if he'd said it in anger and frustration. He *had* said it—and Maddie couldn't remember.

He was going to have to tell her the truth.

His phone pinged with a text. His rookie, Justin Mobley.

Hey, Chief. Annie Potterowski's beagle swiped a hot pretzel out of a kid's hand by the chapel earlier, and the parents want to file a formal complaint. Apparently, it's the second time in a month. I'll handle it.

Sawyer texted back.

Just what I like to hear.

Welcome to Wedlock Creek, where food-snatching beagles accounted for half the crime. The other half was the usual—expired car registration, vandalism, the odd burglary, car accidents, teenagers up to old tricks, fights and occasionally more serious issues. Sawyer had lived in Wedlock Creek his entire life, and very little surprised him. Except what had come out of his mouth the morning of Maddie's crash. And the crash itself. And the memory loss.

His wife didn't remember any of it. The past few months and how hard things had been. Maddie grabbing her cool-gel pillow and stomping from their bedroom to the living room to sleep on the sofa. The conversations that always ended in arguments and then stalemates. She didn't remember any of that.

It's like we can have a fresh start, he thought. Unfairly. Because Maddie was who she was and wanted what she wanted. And she would regain her memory—within a few weeks, if that long. And then what? They would be in exactly the place they were before she'd driven off—and hit the guardrail.

She came out of the bathroom looking more like herself—her beautiful long light brown hair was out if its ponytail, and she'd exchanged the hospital gown for an off-white sweater and jeans. And her favorite footwear, red cowboy boots.

"I stared at myself in the mirror for quite a while," she said with a smile. "I look a lot like my twin. Except for the pregnant belly."

For a moment, a hot surge of panic hit him. He thought she'd regained her memory—and that she'd tell him she wasn't going *anywhere* with him. But he could tell by her warm, open expression that she had no memory of how she and Jenna had always talked of being pregnant at the same time, new mothers together, new aunts to each other's babies together.

She didn't remember any of that.

He slung her bag over his shoulder. "Ready to go?"

"Ready," she said.

This had to be so strange for her. Following him blindly, not recognizing a thing about him or her past or anyone.

He put the bag down and looked directly at her. "Maddie, I want you to know that I love you very much. I've loved you since we were both five years old, and

I'll love you when I'm ninety-two. Anything I can do to make you more comfortable, you just say the word, okay?"

He'd caught them both by surprise with that. She stared at him for a moment, then her expression softened. "I appreciate that. And did you say since we were *five* years old?"

"That's how long we've known each other. My family moved next door to yours."

"That's some history we have," she said. "I wish I could remember it, Sawyer."

"In due time, you will."

Inside his SUV, they buckled up, and he headed for Wedlock Creek, a half hour from Brewer. Maddie asked some questions on the way—if they went to Brewer, a bigger town, often (no); did they have favorite restaurants (yes—Mexican in Brewer and several in Wedlock Creek); what kind of music they liked (Maddie liked her top-forty hits and '70s music, and Sawyer had long been all about the Beatles and had a fondness for country).

Finally, they pulled into town, Maddie staring out the window.

"Wow, this town is so pretty," she said. "All the shops and restaurants decked out for Christmas. Wedlock Creek looks like a postcard. Ooh, look at that," she said, pointing.

Sawyer glanced up at the Wedlock Creek Wedding Chapel, built a hundred years ago. Even on a weekday at 5:17 p.m., there were tourists walking around the grounds, several brides in white gowns, the food trucks and carts at this end of Main Street doing brisk business even on a cold December day. Annie Potterowski, the

elderly officiant and caretaker of the chapel along with
her husband, was walking the pretzel-stealing beagle,
who had a rap sheet for that kind of behavior. Wedlock Creek residents loved the chapel's mascot dog, but
his habit of jumping up and swiping food out of people's hands was cute only the first time it happened to
someone, then they were less inclined to laugh about
it. The beagle was wearing a red-and-green Christmas
sweater, and Sawyer had to admit it added to his mis-
chievous charm.

"That's the chapel your mom was telling you about,"
he said, "with the legend of the multiples." A big green
wreath with a red bow was on the arched door, which
was dotted with white Christmas lights.

"Did we marry there?"

He nodded. *Please don't ask what I know you're
going to ask next*, he thought.

"But no little multiples of our own?"

There it was. "No. Ah, this is us," he rushed to add,
turning onto Woods Road. He pulled into the driveway
of the last house on the dead-end street, an antique-
white arts-and-crafts-style bungalow—or at least that
was what she'd called it. To him it was just home.

She stepped out of the car, stopping to stare up at
the house. "Wow, we live here? It's gorgeous. And the
sparkling Christmas lights around the front trees make
it look like an enchanted cottage."

They day he'd hung the lights, they hadn't been
speaking. He'd needed something to do, something for
her, something for *them*, so he'd spent an hour wrapping
the strands around the trees and the porch. Maddie had
broken their mutual silent treatment by thanking him.

It's Christmastime, she'd said. *We've got to get through this so we can have a good Christmas.* But they'd done exactly that for a few Christmases now, and Maddie had sounded so unsure of herself.

"You fell in love with this house when you were a kid," he said now, handing Maddie her set of keys. "It was built in the early 1900s. You saw it on your paper route and said, 'Sawyer, one day, I'm gonna live in this dream house.' And you do."

She smiled, seeming lost in thought for a moment. "How long have we lived here?"

"I bought it for us as a surprise the day I proposed to you," he said. "My offer was accepted on the house, and I raced over to your condo to ask you to marry me. That offer was accepted too." He smiled, remembering how she'd flung herself into his arms, kissing him all over his face, completely forgetting to say yes. In fact, it wasn't until he'd told her he had another surprise for her and driven her over to the house with the Sale Pending sign in front that he reminded her she hadn't. She'd been sobbing happily over the house and unable to speak for ten minutes and finally took his face in her hands and said, "Sawyer, yes. Always yes."

Always yes. Except recently, when there had been so much *no* between them that their history together hadn't been able to protect them.

She took all that in, then glanced at the key chain. "I'm seeing a pattern here. There's a little ceramic Woodstock on here, and there were two ornaments on the little Christmas tree in my hospital room."

"You like birds. And you love Woodstock. Always have. For your birthday every year when we were kids, I would get you something Woodstock. Woodstock erasers, Woodstock socks, Woodstock key chain. In fact, the one in your hand I gave you on your fourteenth birthday."

She smiled. "Really?"

He nodded. "It's freezing out here. Let's head in." He gestured for her to lead the way because he wanted her to feel that this was her house, even if she didn't remember it.

She used her key and opened the door, slowly stepping inside. "I like it!" she exclaimed, nodding at the colorful round area rug in the entryway and vintage Le Chat Noir poster with the black cat on the wall.

"Oh my, who's this?" she asked as a German shepherd hurried up to her with mournful whines. The dog sat at her feet.

"That's Moose, retired K-9. We worked together for years when I was a detective, but for the last three years he's been enjoying a life of leisure. He's eleven years old and adores you."

"Aw," she said, kneeling down to pet him. "Hi, Moose."

"He missed you the past couple of days." *And so did I. Praying you'd wake up. That'd you'd be okay. Bargaining.*

"I'll take your coat," he said, removing his and hanging it up in the hall closet. She unzipped her down jacket and handed it to him, and he hung it up with her red-and-pink scarf, a gift from her knitting-crazy twin.

He watched her walk around the living room, looking at objects and peering at photos. She picked up their wedding photo off the mantel, one of her favorites because that devilish chapel beagle had photobombed him dipping Maddie in a kiss near the steps.

Her shoulders slumped, and she put the photo back. "I can't remember my life." She shook her head. "And it's clearly a wonderful one. Loving family. Handsome, devoted husband. Lovely home all decked out for Christmas. A sweet dog named Moose." Tears shone in her eyes, and she dropped down onto the sofa, Moose padding over and putting his head on her lap. She leaned over and buried her face in, hugging the dog.

Well, if it makes you feel any better, things weren't all sunshine and roses.

Badumpa. Not.

He sat down beside her, hands on his knees. And before he could even think about it, he blurted out, "It's my fault you got into the accident, Maddie. I said something that upset you, and you got in your car and peeled out fast to get away from me."

She turned to him. "What did you say?"

"That maybe we *should* separate." He closed his eyes for a second and let out a breath. He'd hated saying that. The first time and now.

"The emphasis on *should* makes me think someone else suggested it first. Me?"

He shook his head. "Right before the accident, we'd had our weekly appointment with a mediator slash marriage counselor. We'd been going to her to help us deal with a stalemate. She said it seemed to her that neither of us was willing to budge and that maybe we should think about separating. I got so upset, I stalked out. You followed and we argued outside. And then I said it— maybe we *should* separate."

"What could have possibly come between us to that degree?" she asked.

He took a breath. "Starting a family."

"Ah," she said, looking at her left hand. Her *bare* left hand. "Now things are making sense. Before I got in my car and huffed away, did I yank off my wedding ring because I was angry about that and about you saying maybe we should separate?"

"That's exactly right. You took it off and handed it to me. I have it in my wallet." He'd never forget how that had made him feel, like his entire world was crumbling and he couldn't catch the pieces.

"So I assume it's me who wants kids?" she asked.

He nodded.

"And you're content with things as they are. Wife, dog, job."

He nodded again.

"Married seven years, thirty-two years old, seems like a reasonable time—past reasonable time—to start a family," she said, a prompting lilt in her voice.

Acid churned in his gut. "I never wanted kids. You always did. And you counted on me changing my mind. You had no doubt I would, even though I cautioned you about that. You never really believed deep down that I wouldn't want a 'little Wolfe, a little us'—as you used to say."

She tilted her head. "And you still don't?"

He got up and walked over to the windows, looking out at the snow still clinging to the bare tree limbs. "The past two days, while you were lying in that hospital bed…and I had no idea if you'd wake up…I made so many bargains. If only you'd wake up, I'd agree to ten kids. As many as you wanted."

"So we're going to have ten kids?"

He turned around to face her. "If that's what you want."

"Because you bargained?"

He nodded. "The most important thing to me was having you back. I have that. So yes. Ten kids." He'd almost lost her. He'd said, *prayed*, that he'd give anything to have her back. And he'd meant it.

She stared at him, lifting her chin, and he had no idea what she was thinking. Her expressions, the way her mind worked now—all that was new to him. "Well, the only thing I want right now is my memory back. Maybe just being here, in my home, with you, will jog something, trigger something."

He hoped so. Until then, they had this rare chance to be together without the past stomping on their marriage. He had the unfair advantage of knowing everything about them while she knew nothing, and there was no way he'd take it. He'd always be honest with Maddie. And what was most true this minute was that he loved her more than anything, would do anything for her. Ten children. Twenty.

All that mattered was that she'd survived, that she'd be all right, that she was home.

Chapter Two

Maddie needed to take a big step back, let everything she'd learned settle in her mind, her bones, so she suggested a tour of the house. Sawyer seemed relieved. She followed him upstairs, admiring the photos lining the wall. Pictures of the two of them—together—at so many different ages, from early childhood to what looked like recently. She and Sawyer, age five or six, holding kiddie fishing rods at a riverbank, a bucket between them. She and Sawyer, middle school years, arms linked for a semiformal, Maddie liking her pale pink dress. She and Sawyer, early twenties, Sawyer in a Wedlock Creek Police Department T-shirt, giving Maddie a piggyback ride. A couple with a long history together.

Upstairs was a wide landing with a sitting area. Off it were four rooms. Sawyer opened doors. The first was a guest room. Next to it a large bathroom. And the next room was completely empty.

"Couldn't figure out what to do with the space?" she asked, raising an eyebrow.

"You earmarked it as the nursery," he said, glancing away.

"Ah." She peered into the room—pale gray walls, wood floor, closet, four big windows. It would make a nice nursery—with furnishings in it. She imagined herself walking past this room every day, well aware it was empty. *That must have burned*, she thought. For both of them. A constant reminder of their stalemate.

"And this is our bedroom," he said, opening the door to a big, cozy room, a four-poster bed with a fluffy white down comforter between two windows. There were plump pillows and a table on either side, matching lamps and a book on each—a history of Wyoming and a mystery. She wondered which was her side, her book. *And* what it would be like to slip under that soft, warm comforter beside a man she knew was her husband—and yet didn't know at all. As if he could read her mind, he added, "I can sleep in the guest room or take the couch until your memory returns. I don't want you to feel uncomfortable."

"Well, we don't know what will make my memory return, and since routine might help, I say we do what we always do. You're my husband, and intellectually, I know that, so I'm going with it."

He nodded and, if she wasn't mistaken, looked kind of relieved.

So she would be sleeping beside him tonight. The thought had her taking him in on a purely physical level, and he was so attractive to her that a little burst of excitement and some butterflies let loose in her belly. She liked the way he looked at her with his serious green eyes—as if she were someone very special to him, and despite the issues in their marriage, that did seem clear to her. Plus, her family obviously liked him. And he was tall and strong and the top cop here in Wedlock Creek. Good looks aside, there was something very trustworthy about Sawyer Wolfe.

Of course, Maddie had little to go on in that department. Amnesiac Maddie had known him all of a few hours.

She walked over to a huge closet and opened it. His and hers. Hers on the left. She was very organized. Two piles of sweaters sat next to a row of hung jeans. She had lots of those. She also had a lot of shoes. She moved over to the dresser and opened the top drawer. *Ooh.* Many lacy bras and underwear. Some sexy nighties. A flutter swept her belly again, and she found herself very aware of him sitting on the edge of the bed, watching her.

On top of the dresser was a round mirrored tray holding perfume and a red velvet box. Inside she found jewelry. Earrings, bangle bracelets. A diamond tennis bracelet. Necklaces. A stunning diamond ring, square and surrounded by little baguettes in a gold setting. She thought about her wedding ring inside his wallet. Interesting that he kept it there instead of having put it in here.

She bit her lip and turned around to face him. "I assume asking you why you don't want children, never wanted children, isn't a simple one."

"It is and isn't," he said.

"But after seven years of marriage? A strong marriage?"

"I've always had a lot on my plate," he said, standing up and moving over to the window. He shoved his hands into his pockets. "I've been chief at the WCPD for only almost a year now, and since I got that promotion on the young side, I felt I had to really prove myself. And before that, I *wanted* to be chief and worked double time to earn the job, so the timing just never seemed right to even think about starting a family. I have so much responsibility at work—for the town, for my staff—that I guess I couldn't see having that kind of responsibility at home too. A baby needing more than I could give."

A lot on his plate. A baby needing more than he could give. Both of those sounded like excuses, and she had a feeling the Maddie she'd been before the *thonk* on the head knew the real reasons he didn't want children. The reasons he wasn't mentioning.

"Hungry?" he asked with a tight smile. "I could heat up your mom's chili and corn bread—she brought over a ton of food for me the day of the accident. I could barely choke down coffee, though."

Quite a change of subject. He clearly didn't want to talk about the state of their marriage anymore. "I had the hospital's cream of something soup," she said. "And some stale crackers. So I'm good for a few hours." She glanced outside. "It's a pretty nice day—I wouldn't mind walking into town and visiting my family's store."

He raised an eyebrow. "You feel up to it? Dr. Addison said you shouldn't go overboard trying to get back up to speed or even acclimated."

"I don't feel woozy at all. And my curiosity has the better of me right now." Plus, she wanted to pepper him with questions—about everything—and despite not knowing him at all, she knew from his expression that *he* wasn't up to *that*. "MacLeod's Multiples Emporium isn't far from here, is it?" Their house was just two blocks off the main street with all its charming-looking shops and restaurants.

He shook his head. "Walking distance—it's right on Main Street, a couple minutes' walk from the wedding chapel. You can't miss MacLeod's—there's a painted wood sign with baby stuff on it—crib, baby shoes, baby bottles. And the windows are decorated to the nines for Christmas."

I love Christmas. The thought startled her until she realized it was new knowledge from her response to that adorable miniature tree on her hospital windowsill and the shops decked out and the way their house was decorated for the holidays. She had no doubt she'd always loved Christmas. "I'd like to go check it out. Since I worked there, maybe it'll ring a bell."

"You'll call me or text me if you feel overwhelmed or want to go home?" he asked. "I'll come get you right away."

She nodded, scrolling through her contacts on her phone. "Yup, there you are. Sawyer—cell and work." Her family was in there too. And a bunch of other people whose names she didn't recognize.

"I'll drop you there, then go check in at the station for a bit," he said. "We can meet up when you're ready to go home."

"Sounds good," she said.

They headed back downstairs, and he handed Maddie her down jacket and scarf and put on a heavy brown leather jacket. He stood in front of the door, and Maddie had the feeling he almost didn't want to let her go, that he liked having her in the house, their house. She wondered if he was worried about their marriage, if their impasse had gotten even bigger than their shared history, their love.

And *she* wondered if, when her memory did return, they'd be right back in that snowy moment outside the mediator's office.

According to Sawyer, thirty-eight degrees in Wyoming in December was practically springlike, so they decided to walk the couple of blocks into town. He'd mentioned that the police station was just another half mile down. Wedlock Creek was bustling, people going in and out of stores, carrying bright bags with wrapped gifts poking out. The moment they arrived on the corner of Main Street, they were mobbed by well-wishers.

"It's so wonderful to see you out and about!" one woman said, reaching for Maddie's mittened hand. "We were all so worried. No one more than Sawyer, of course. And maybe your mom and dad."

Sawyer smiled. "You're right, Brenna," he said, making a point of her name.

Maddie caught on quickly that, after the third such back-and-forth, Sawyer was covering for her lack of memory, and luckily, acquaintances were giving something of a wide berth since she'd gotten out of the hospital only that afternoon. "Do I know *everyone*?" she asked as they finally headed across the street toward MacLeod's Multiples Emporium.

"Yup. Both of us do. Wedlock Creek is a small town, and we've lived here our entire lives. And I'm the chief of police, so everyone knows me. We knew everyone without that added to the mix."

Maddie looked up at the pastel painted sign atop the length of her family's business. A family walked past— with two red-haired identical twin girls. A woman wheeling a triple stroller was across the street. Multiples everywhere. Including right here—*me*, she thought.

"Your dad made the sign and painted it," Sawyer said. "He's quite a craftsman. He hand makes all the furniture MacLeod's sells, cribs and bassinets and other wood items. He has a big following."

"How wonderful," she said, admiring the sign and the easel out front listing a colorful array of items in someone's excellent handwriting. Everything from personalization to layettes to baby paraphernalia to children's clothing. She watched two women wheeling twin strollers go inside the shop; two more came out carrying big yellow shopping bags with the MacLeod's logo.

"I'll probably be thirty minutes or so," she said to Sawyer. "I'll just visit the store and say hi to my family if they're there. I don't think I'll walk around town just yet on my own in case I run into someone who knows me and I have no idea who they are. Seems so complicated to explain about my memory."

He nodded. "I'll pick you up here in thirty minutes."

She smiled, and he leaned over awkwardly and kissed her on the cheek. He hesitated before pulling back, and she had the feeling he'd wanted to embrace her. More than embrace—hold her, tightly. Frankly, she could use a hug.

"See you in a bit," she said, those flutters in her belly again, and darted into the shop. She turned back to see Sawyer watching her as if to make sure she was okay. She gave a wave and walked in farther. When she looked back, he was finally heading up the street.

The shop was both elegant and folksy at the same time and separated into sections for clothing and furniture and baby paraphernalia. The place was pretty crowded too; Maddie could see two saleswomen with MacLeod's name tags helping shoppers.

"Maddie!"

She turned to find her twin, Jenna, smiling and rushing up to her. She and Jenna really did look a lot alike. They both had the same blue eyes and slightly long nose, wavy light brown hair past their shoulders. Jenna wore a dark purple maternity wrap dress and gray suede knee-high boots, lots of gold bangles on her arm. And a gold wedding band and solitaire diamond ring.

"I'm surprised to see you," Jenna said, straightening a huge stuffed giraffe. "Feeling all right?"

"I feel pretty good. A little weird not knowing anything about myself—okay, a lot weird. I figured I'd come check out the family business. Do you work here too?"

Jenna nodded. "I'm a saleswoman, and let me tell you, the huge belly helps. Five minutes ago, I sold three personalized cribs—the ones our dad famously hand makes—and then the mom and her mom came back a minute later and added the triple bassinets they were waffling on. And then the mom bought three of these," she said, pointing to three big stuffed bear chairs with pink or blue bow ties around their necks.

"Ooh, you are good. Did I work on the floor too?"

"Nah, you're more a back-office type. You're not a pushy schmoozer like me."

Maddie laughed. "Speaking of pushy, can I ask you something?"

"Of course."

She leaned a bit closer to whisper. "Was I pushing Sawyer to have a baby?"

Jenna's smile faltered. "Maddie, I love you. You're my sister, my twin. But you don't remember anything about your life, and I'm not sure I should fill in details that are personal between you and your husband."

Maddie thought about that. "I get it. How about details *about* my husband. He said we grew up next door to each other."

"More like Sawyer grew up in our house. He's been an honorary MacLeod since he was five, when he and his dad moved into the in-law apartment of our neighbors' house. The Wolfe door opened very close to our side porch, so that's how you and Sawyer became such good friends. Apparently I was anti boy, but you adored Sawyer from the get-go."

"He and his dad lived in an in-law apartment? With his dad's in-laws?"

Jenna shook her head. "No. That's just what one- or two-bedroom apartments attached to private homes are called. They were usually meant for parents or in-laws as they aged. The neighbors back then were friendly with Sawyer's mom, so they felt terrible about the situation and gave his dad a big break on rent."

"What situation?" Maddie asked.

A shopper walked up to them. "Excuse me, is it possible to get those adorable little cowboy hats personalized for my impending triplet nephews?"

Jenna nodded at the woman. "Personalization is MacLeod's specialty. I set aside two of those hats for my little babies-to-be—a girl and boy. My husband and I still can't agree on names, so the personalization will have to wait."

The woman laughed. "Names are the one thing my husband and I *do* agree on." She put three impossibly tiny leather cowboy hats in her basket and continued on in the stuffed animal area.

Jenna led Maddie over near the checkout desk away from the shoppers. "Sawyer's mom died from complications after his birth. His dad raised him alone. Well, he tried, I guess. But he really wasn't cut out for fatherhood. I think the landlords let him stay to make sure Sawyer would have a safe place to live next to caring neighbors. They were traveling a lot, but between them and us looking out for Sawyer, he had what he needed."

Maddie frowned. "Sounds rough."

"I'm sure it was. No mom. A father who wasn't really present—and lots of girlfriends in and out. To be honest, if he hadn't lived next door to us and slept over so often, there's a good chance he would have been taken away and put in the foster-care system. His father was that neglectful. But no one wanted to see that happen."

Maddie thought about how Sawyer had said he'd always known he hadn't wanted kids. That made a little more sense to her now.

She imagined a little Sawyer, three, five, eight, ten.

No mother. A father with issues. Alone, hungry, no guidance. Slipping next door to the warm, welcoming MacLeods. She was glad her family had been there for him. That *she'd* been there for him. They'd been best friends their whole lives.

She could *also* imagine wanting to start a family. Being thirty-two and the ole biological clock ticking away. "I must have figured he'd change his mind about wanting kids," Maddie said. "But he never did, huh?"

Jenna bit her lip and seemed unsure if she should say anything. "No. This is all secondhand from you, so I guess it's okay for me to tell you." She shook her head. "How crazy is this situation? Anyway, yes. In fact, he put off proposing because of it. Because he knew you wanted a houseful of kids, and he just wanted you and a good dog."

"But he did propose. He told me he bought my dream house and then proposed."

Jenna smiled. "He asked Mom and Dad what to do. He told them he loved you more than anything, but he didn't want kids and you did, and how could he propose when he couldn't promise the one thing you really wanted. They said he'd change his mind. *I* said he'd change his mind. *You* said he'd change his mind. And finally, Sawyer got to a place where he could *imagine* changing his mind—one day. Maybe. I think because he loved you so much he could imagine it, you know, even if he didn't want it for himself. You told me he made it very clear he couldn't promise he'd ever want kids and that there was a very good chance he wouldn't."

Yikes. "I feel awful," Maddie said, tears stinging

the backs of her eyes. "He was so honest about it. It's not fair to him."

"And it's not fair to you either, Maddie," Jenna said gently. "You were both always honest with each other. But suddenly time stopped being on your side. And let me tell you, having a pregnant twin sister didn't help."

Maddie eyed her twin's big, lovely belly. "I bet." She sucked in a breath. "All I want now is my memory back. My life back. I don't even remember wanting a baby. I don't really know what that would even *feel* like."

"Well, maybe you and Sawyer can use this time to get to know each other all over again without that stalemate pressing on you. It's always been there the past few years, worse this past year. But now the two of you can just be Maddie and Sawyer again. For a time anyway."

Maddie nodded. "Because my memory will come back. Dr. Addison said it could be a week, three weeks, possibly longer, but she thinks just a few weeks."

"It'll all come back. With these new memories you're making every moment now."

"Do you think we were headed for a separation?" Maddie asked.

Jenna frowned. "I can't even imagine it. You were class BFFs every year since first grade. You were MadSaw— your own celebrity nickname. You guys love each other."

"He said he made all kinds of bargains while I was unconscious. That if I woke up, he'd give me ten kids."

"He told you that?" Jenna asked, touching a hand to her heart.

Maddie nodded. "That's not how I want to start my family off. I'd want to have a baby with a man who wanted that baby. Not because of a harrowing bargain he made skyward."

"Oh, Maddie. It's complicated, right? Just get to know your husband during this time. You'll be getting to know yourself too. You're still you."

"Excuse me?" a very pregnant woman said. "Do you make programmable lullaby players? My husband is a budding country singer, and we want a player that has those stars-and-moons lights for the ceiling while playing my husband singing."

"Absolutely," Jenna said. "I just ordered my version of that. Little cows jumping over the moon to the tune of lullabies sung by one of my favorite singers. Let me show you our catalog."

The woman's face lit up. Suddenly Maddie realized that she may have been more a back-office type because all the moms-to-be buying such fun stuff must have made Maddie feel very left out.

The door jangled and there was Sawyer. Maddie wrapped her sister in a hug. "Thank you," she whispered. "You helped a lot."

Jenna hugged her back and waved at Sawyer. "I'm always here for you."

Maddie smiled and left Jenna to her customer. Suddenly she felt a lot better and a little heavyhearted about what was to come.

But as she walked over to Sawyer, the handsome, green-eyed man in the brown leather jacket, she wanted to wrap her arms around him—tight. That much she knew for sure.

Chapter Three

They walked home from town, Maddie linking her arm through his, which buoyed him like nothing else. There was affection in that gesture, a degree of trust, and that meant a great deal to him since he'd lost that over the past several months. Once, for a very long time, she'd believed he'd never hurt her. Then he'd started outwardly denying her what she wanted most. And the bond began fraying.

Now, in the simplest way, he felt her saying yes to him, to *them*.

"How about lasagna for dinner?" he asked. "Your mother really did stock the freezer after your accident. She said all that cooking gave her something to do with her mind and hands or she'd have gone nuts. There are five containers of lasagna alone."

Then again, Sawyer thought he should be doing more

for Maddie than just heating up her very kind mother's
bounty of food. But April MacLeod was a great cook
and he a mediocre one, and she'd made their favorites. Lasagna. Shepherd's pie. Fettuccini carbonara. Her
amazing chili and three pans of corn bread, which Sawyer could polish off in one sitting. He felt like he should
be cooking for her, figuring out how to make some of
her favorite dishes, such as blackened salmon, without
burning it, and risotto.

"Do I love lasagna?" she asked.

"It's only your very favorite food on earth. Mine too.
We used to make it as teenagers. I did a layer, you did
a layer and then we'd stuff our faces."

She smiled. "What else do I love?"

"Blackened everything. Also, fish tacos. Caesar
salad. Cheeseburgers. The Pie Diner's chili potpie. Your
mother's brisket. Coffee chip ice cream."

"What don't I like?" she asked. "In general, I mean."

"That you can't figure out yoga. You don't like corn.
You don't like horror movies."

She smiled. "What did I do when I wasn't working?"

"Well, the past few months you started volunteering
for the town's Holiday Happymakers program. You devoted quite a few hours a day to it."

"Holiday Happymakers? What's that?"

"A group that plans ways the town can help those
who can't afford Christmas or can't do much in the way
of celebrating because of illness or other issues. You
started an adopt-a-family program to provide holiday
decorations and gifts for each family member. Anyone
can leave a letter on the Christmas tree in the community center with a wish list for the family or a relative."

"I sound kind!" she said. "Glad to hear it."

"You are. Very."

"What was Christmas like when you were growing up?" she asked.

He frowned at the thought. "I spent every Christmas at your house. My dad didn't always have his act together, or he disappeared to a girlfriend's. Your parents always hung a stocking for me—stuffed it too. And there were always presents for me under the tree. I got them gifts, too, and always wished I could have afforded better than a scented candle for your parents. But that's what I got them every year."

"Aw," she said. "I'll bet they loved it."

"Your mom always made a show of sniffing it and lighting it and setting it right on the mantel." He'd never forget her mother's kindness. Ever.

"My sister told me the basics of your childhood," she said. "I hope that's all right. She figured because it was something we all knew, it wasn't telling tales or talking about your personal business, which she refused to do."

"I don't mind your family filling in holes," he said. "The truth is the truth. And I'm not interested in hiding anything from you. Our marriage was rocky two days ago when you got into the accident and months before that. Very rocky."

"I'm glad I don't remember," she said, tears poking again. "I guess that's wrong. But all I know is that I'm not unhappy or sad or anxious or wanting anything. I don't know who I am, but I feel safe because of you and the MacLeods. So if I'm in limbo, at least it's a nice limbo. A Christmas limbo, at that."

He smiled. "That's a nice way to look at it."

She tightened her hold on his arm, and again he felt like they had a chance. Even if it was just this limbo chance. This Christmas limbo chance. Right now, she was his again.

At the house, Sawyer let out Moose, who raced around the yard, which still held a good covering of snow. Maddie threw his favorite squeaky ball at least twenty times, and he chased it over and over, dropping it by her foot.

"Sorry, Moose, I think my arm is going to give out," she said, kneeling down to give the German shepherd a rub and a pat.

The phone was ringing, so they headed inside, Moose going over to his big red fluffy dog bed by the fireplace in the living room. They missed the call, and about twenty others, from Maddie's parents and sister, checking in, and friends and fellow volunteers on the Holiday Happymakers committee.

"That's really nice," Maddie said after she listened to all the messages.

Sawyer nodded. "Everyone likes you. Well, I'm gonna go get dinner ready. Want a glass of wine?"

"I have a craving for a little eggnog. Do we have any?"

"Of course. You love eggnog." He was back in half a minute with two glasses of eggnog. He handed her one, then clinked hers.

"Yum," she said. "You don't want help with dinner?"

"My job is reheating," he said. "So no. You relax. It'll be ready in fifteen minutes, per your mother's very specific instructions."

She flashed him a smile and sank onto the couch,

Moose coming over and sitting in front of her, his head on her knee. Sawyer watched her give the dog a warm hug, wanting more than anything to pull her into his arms and hold her. But he was afraid to overwhelm her, and he had a feeling he should let her make any physical moves.

Over dinner they talked more about what they liked and didn't, laughing more in twenty minutes than they had in the past three months. After dinner and cleaning up the kitchen together, they bundled up and took Moose on a long walk around the neighborhood, enjoying the holiday lights. Back home they watched a singing competition on TV, Maddie sitting very close beside him on the couch as she drank a little more eggnog. Then she yawned—twice—and they realized she'd better get to bed. It had been a long day for her, busier than either expected it'd be once she was discharged, and she could probably use the rest.

He followed her up the stairs, Moose trailing them. In their bedroom, she poked around her dresser drawers and pulled out blue flannel pj bottoms with little Woodstocks all over and a long-sleeved pink T-shirt.

"So…I'll change in the bathroom," she said. "Is that weird?"

"Not at all. We just met this morning."

She laughed. "It really does feel that way."

It did feel that way. And not—at the same time. All their history was front and center in his head and heart, weighing heavily. He was taking a T-shirt and pair of sweats from the dresser when she came out of the bathroom. Her hair was pulled back into a low ponytail so her goose egg was even more prominent, the scratch beside it too.

"Which side of the bed is mine?" she asked.

"Window side. I'm the door side."

"Ah," she said, "so the robbers get you first."

He smiled. "Exactly. And so I can roll out of bed and rush out if an emergency call comes in."

She picked up the mystery on her bedside table and looked at the cover. "Am I reading this?"

"I think you just plucked it off the bookcase to pick up whenever I'd come in the bedroom—to avoid talking," he said. "When you weren't pretending to be sleeping."

"Yeesh. That bad, huh?"

He looked at his wife, his beautiful Maddie, wishing he could say otherwise. "Yeah. There were recent moments, though, that even our stalemate couldn't ruin. When I plugged in the Christmas tree for the first time. When Moose ate a stick that required a trip to the vet, and we were both so worried about him that we actually held hands in the vet's office for the first time in forever."

"Was Moose okay?" she asked, sitting on the edge of the bed and turning toward him.

"Yeah."

"But we weren't. We're not," she amended. "I'm not sure I want to remember that, Sawyer."

"Well, like I said, I'm prepared to give you ten kids. So, once your memory is back, we're all set. We'll start a family."

She frowned. "But, Sawyer, you don't want a baby.

You're only agreeing because you made a spiritual pact."

"But I meant it. I'm prepared to have a baby."

"Well, that's not what Maddie-who-I-don't-remember would want. That Maddie would want you to *want* to have a baby, a family of your own."

He let out a breath, exhausted. "I don't know that there should be conditions. A yes is a yes, right?"

"No. The yes was about something else. Having your wife back. Giving her what she wanted so badly because you made a bargain with the heavens. It's not actually about what you want, Sawyer."

"So what you're saying is that I can't win?" That came out sharper than he intended. They weren't supposed to be arguing. Maddie needed her head to settle; she needed rest. Not this. He turned away, barely able to take it—that they were back in this place, arguing.

"I don't know," she said. "I don't really know anything, do I?"

Dammit. He walked over to her side of the bed where she was sitting, and he held out his arms. She bit her lip and looked up at him, then stood and walked right into his embrace. He wrapped his arms around her, resting his head atop hers, and hell if he didn't feel tears stinging his eyes. "I'm just so grateful you're alive, Maddie. That we have a second chance. That's the truest thing I know."

She raised her head and looked at him, then kissed him on the lips, just a peck, but a kiss nonetheless. Then she got into bed and drew the down comforter up to her neck.

He slipped in beside her knowing there was no way he'd get a wink of sleep tonight.

Maddie's eyes fluttered open as she felt Sawyer suddenly bolt up beside her. She heard the doorbell ring—twice. Then a third time.

She sat up and glanced at her phone on her bedside table. It was 12:19 a.m.

"Someone's at the door?" she asked.

His phone pinged, and he grabbed it, reading the screen. "Oh man."

"What?"

"It's my brother. He's the one ringing the bell." He texted something back, then got out of bed. "I'll handle this. Try to go back to bed, Maddie. You need your sleep."

Sawyer had a brother? No one mentioned a brother.

There was no way she was going back to bed. Sawyer's brother was at the door after midnight, pounding on the ringer and texting? Something was definitely up.

She found a terry bathrobe on a hook in the bathroom and put it on, then tiptoed out of the bedroom and down the stairs to the bottom step as Sawyer reached the door. Unless she was mistaken, he took a breath before pulling open the door.

Standing there, hands jammed into the pockets of his jeans, was a younger version of Sawyer, with shaggier and lighter hair. He wore a black leather bomber jacket and a thick black ski hat. He had an overnight bag slung over his shoulder.

Before he could say a word, Sawyer barked, "Cole, it's really late. And Maddie's not feeling well."

"Yeah, hello to you," Cole said.

Sawyer didn't invite him in. "The last time you needed a place to crash and I let you stay a couple days, you robbed us blind and disappeared. If you need a place to stay, I'll front you some money I know I'll never see again, but you can't stay here."

"I'm not looking to stay here," Cole said, his body language all fidgety and nervous. "Um, look, it's not good for the twins to be out in the cold so long, okay?"

"What?" Sawyer asked. "What twins?"

Cole leaned down and picked something up out of view. Sawyer stepped onto the porch and Maddie heard his gasp. She rushed toward the door as Cole came inside carrying two infant car seats, a baby asleep in each one.

Sawyer stared at the babies, shutting the door behind him. "What the hell is going on? Whose babies are these?"

Cole put the car seats down on the foyer rug, then dropped the bag off his shoulder, rubbing his face with both hands. He looked absolutely miserable. And nervous.

Maddie stepped out of the shadows. "Hi."

"Hey, Maddie." Cole nodded at her, his expression warmer, and she had the feeling they'd gotten along at some point or that she'd been kind to him. "Whoa, what happened to you? That's some bump on your forehead."

"Car accident," she said. "I'm okay, though."

He nodded and reached out to squeeze her hand. Yup, she'd been right. They had definitely gotten along—or just better than Cole and his brother did.

"What the hell, Cole?" Sawyer barked. "Whose babies are these?"

"I got an ex pregnant," he answered, his voice shaky. "We got back together, but then I was fired from my job, and she told me forget it and hooked up with someone else, but he said no way is he gonna be a father. So she went into labor yesterday and called me and I rushed over. I witnessed the birth—wow, that was something." He shook his head. "And I thought maybe my ex would say she wanted us to have a second chance, but she told me she wasn't ready for motherhood and didn't want the twins. She even signed away her parental rights. Unless I accepted responsibility for them, the state would have put them up for adoption."

This time Maddie gasped. She looked down at the two infants—newborns—asleep in the carriers.

"Good Lord," Sawyer said, shaking his head.

Cole closed his eyes for a second, his expression pained. "I stood outside the hospital nursery, staring through the glass at their bassinets and holding the forms to give up my rights so they could be placed for adoption. A nurse saw me struggling, I guess. She came over and told me that allowing them to be placed for adoption could be the best thing I could do for them if I couldn't take care of them. She said it was up to me, that I was their father. Damn that word, Sawyer. Father. Father. Father." His eyes brimmed with tears, and he slashed a hand underneath and sucked in a breath.

Sawyer put a hand on his brother's shoulder, his expression full of so many emotions Maddie couldn't begin to pick them out.

"But I couldn't sign, Sawyer," Cole continued. "I

couldn't just abandon them completely like that. I know what it's like to be tossed aside."

Maddie's chest constricted. She had no idea what Cole's story was—and from what she knew, he wasn't raised with Sawyer next door to the MacLeods, or his name would have come up. But whatever his story was, it certainly didn't sound good.

Cole dropped down on the bottom step of the staircase, covering his face with his hands, then stood up and paced. "My name is on the application for the birth certificate that Gigi started filling out—and they look like me, I can see that, even though I thought all babies just looked like babies. They're mine. But I can't take care of them. I can't take care of myself."

"Jesus, Cole," Sawyer said, his gaze moving from his brother to the infants.

"The twins were cleared to leave, and the nurses told me what to buy before I could leave with them—two infant car seats. She also told me to buy some newborn-sized pajamas. When I returned with all that, they gave me a starter pack of diapers and formula and other stuff I'd need. I sat in my car in the hospital parking lot for a half hour with the twins in the back seat and completely panicked, no clue what to do, what to think, how I was gonna do this. Then I drove here."

"Did you name them?" Maddie asked gently.

Cole didn't respond; he just ran a hand through his hair. He looked so frantic. "I'm gonna get their other bag from my car. Be right back."

He dashed out, closing the door behind him. Sawyer stared at Maddie, then looked at the two sleeping infants in the carriers again. They looked so peaceful, blissfully unaware of all that had happened since they came into the world just a day ago. All that was going on now.

Maddie heard a car start and peel away, tires screeching.

Sawyer raced to the door and flung it open, rushing out to the porch. Maddie followed, pulling her bathrobe tighter around her in the cold December night air.

She saw the car's red taillights barely pause at the stop sign up on Main Street before turning right. Maddie recalled the sign for the freeway in that direction. "He's not coming back tonight, is he?" she said. More a statement than a question.

Sawyer took her hand and led her inside, closing and locking the door behind them. He stared at the babies, then at her. "I'm not sure he's *ever* coming back."

Chapter Four

For a moment, Sawyer just stood staring at the two babies on the floor in their blue car seats. But then one of them opened his eyes, and Sawyer almost jumped.

The little slate-blue eyes opened a bit wider, the baby moving slightly, his bow lips quirking.

"That one's awake!" Maddie said, stepping over. She picked up the carrier and looked at Sawyer until he picked up the other carrier. His brain was not quite catching up just yet. As a cop, as the chief of police, he never had time to be shocked. Police work, training, protocol always took over. But right now, where his brother was concerned, where his newborn nephews were concerned, shock had permeated. There were few people in this world who could get to him. Cole was one of them.

He followed Maddie into the living room. She set the

carrier on the rug and began unlatching the harness, the baby staring at her, the bow lips still quirking.

"Oh my goodness, look at you," she said, her voice holding a wonder he hadn't heard in a long time. She moved aside the white-and-blue-striped blanket covering the baby, slid a hand behind the baby's neck and another under his bottom, gently lifting him from the seat. "Aren't you just beautiful," she whispered, rocking the infant slightly in her arms.

Sawyer eyed the baby. He looked healthy, good color in his cheeks, eyes clear. He wore plush green pajamas with feet. Thank heavens for that kind nurse, telling Cole what to buy, giving him a little breathing room to leave and return.

He could imagine Cole driving from the hospital with the twins, no idea where he was going, what he was doing. And then the idea lighting in his mind: Sawyer and Maddie.

The baby in Maddie's arms began to squirm some. *You're my nephew*, Sawyer thought, trying to wrap his mind around that. *I'm someone's uncle. Two someones.*

"Hey, there's what looks like an *M* on his cap—in marker," Maddie said, peering closer. "*M* for *male*?"

Sawyer looked at the other baby's cap. "This one has an *S* on it. Could be their initials." He froze, then looked at Maddie. "*M* and *S*? That's us. Maddie and Sawyer."

Her eyes widened. "Coincidence?"

He shrugged, barely able to take in everything, let alone begin to process and think straight.

"Could you root around the overnight bag and see if the starter kit of bottles and formula are inside?" she asked. "He doesn't feel wet, but he's probably hungry.

Babies eat every few hours the first couple of months, I think."

He picked up the bag Cole had left behind and sat down with it, going through it. Yup, luckily there were the hospital-issued beginner supplies. A small pack of newborn-sized diapers. Two bottles and a few different nipples. Pacifiers. Formula. Two blankets, a few extra baby hats. Enough to get through the night.

And some clipped-together paperwork. The birth certificate applications. Cole *had* named them. One was Shane Wolfe. The other was Max Wolfe. Something told him the nurse had initialed their caps as a just-in-case.

"Their names are Shane and Max," he said, holding up the application. He flipped through the papers. The relinquishment of Gigi Andersen's parental rights, signed by two witnesses, both nurses. He shook his head.

"Shane and Max. Sawyer and Maddie. That *can't* be coincidence."

"I'll go make up a bottle," he said, unable to wrap his mind around that. "At the PD, we've watched training videos on assisting with births and newborn care, so none of this is all that unfamiliar to me."

And honestly, he was grateful for the chance to slip away into the kitchen so that he could catch his breath. *Take* a breath. He scanned the directions on the small canister of formula, then added the powder and water to the bottle, shook it up and put on the correct nipple. He quickly made up the other bottle just in case the little guy's brother woke up.

Cries coming from the living room—two different

voices—indicated he had. Sawyer rushed back in, bottles in hand, and gave one to Maddie.

As he reached in to pick up the other baby, he glanced over at Maddie, leaning back against the sofa, feeding the infant, her expression so serene, so full of marvel. *This is what she always wanted*, he thought. *All she wanted.*

His chest squeezed and he focused on the other baby, gently lifting him out and settling beside Maddie with the other bottle.

Man, was this weird. *You're my nephew*, he thought, watching the baby slurping the bottle quite contentedly, his blue eyes opening and closing as if he couldn't decide whether or not he wanted to be awake or asleep again. The baby was his kin, but nothing about this felt natural. Maybe because he and Cole had been estranged for the past couple of years. There had been times over the years when Sawyer had felt close to Cole no matter the distance between them, physical or emotional. But since that last time, when Sawyer had given Cole a place to crash for a few days and he'd stolen cash and a diamond bracelet that Maddie had inherited from her late grandmother, Sawyer's heart had closed up to his brother. He'd felt done with Cole, the last straw.

And now this.

With the newborn cradled in her arms, Maddie reached into the bag and rooted around and pulled out a folded-up mat. "I think this little one needs a change."

She lay the baby down on the mat and undid his wet diaper. She found a small container of cornstarch and gave his bottom a sprinkle, then found some rubbing alcohol and cotton pads and gently cleaned the umbilical cord area before putting on a fresh diaper. "I have no idea how I know how to do all this. Either instinct or common sense."

Or you wanted to be a mother for so long and did so much research in preparation that it's in your blood and bones and veins if not your memory.

Once the infant in Cole's arms was done with his bottle, Maddie reached over for him as well and got him all changed, then they each sat on the sofa, just holding the twins, unable to even speak for a time.

"I guess we'll hang on to the paperwork for a few days," he said. "See if Cole returns." He looked down at the baby in his arms, *S* for *Shane* and possibly *Sawyer*, then at baby Max in Maddie's arms, *M* for *Maddie*. Their mother had signed away her rights. Their father had taken off. And here were Maddie and Sawyer, caring for them, all of a day old, for God knew how long. "I guess it's fitting they're named after us. *If* they even are."

"Wow—we've got newborn twins to take care of." She stared down at Max, then glanced at Sawyer. She seemed about to say something, but then didn't. "Sawyer?"

He looked at her, shifting Shane in his arms just a bit. The baby didn't even stir.

"Are you okay with this?" she asked. "I mean, taking care of the babies. Given…how you feel about having babies in the first place."

"I do what needs to be done," he said, then regretted it when he noticed the look on her face. A little disappointment, a little surprise, a little *Jeez, really?* "And they're my nephews," he added fast, "so of course I'm okay with it."

The disappointment, surprise and *Jeez, really?* didn't abate with that added pronouncement.

He was striking out here. "Look, Maddie, the most important thing in the world to me fifteen minutes ago was you and only you. You were just in a bad accident. You lost your memory. Taking care of you was my sole priority. Suddenly, we have two newborns added into the mix and no idea what's what."

She took that in, her expression softening a bit. "What's what meaning..."

"Meaning Cole is a wild card. He could come back sobbing in the morning, saying he was just scared and lost his mind and begging us to help him figure out how to do this, be a dad to the babies."

"And of course we'll help."

He nodded. "We will. I'd never turn my back on Cole. I might not invite him to stay here because of what he pulled last time, but I'd never turn my back on him."

"Something about robbing us blind," she said. "Are you and Cole half brothers? You didn't grow up together, from what I can tell."

"We share a father. His mother was a weekend fling, apparently. My dad barely acknowledged Cole—or his mother. If it wasn't for the family resemblance, Hank Wolfe probably wouldn't have accepted him at all."

Maddie shook her head. "Awful. I guess you didn't see him much growing up."

"His mother never brought him around to our place since she didn't trust Hank. I certainly don't blame her. And every now and again, when my dad wanted to get rid of me, he'd drop me off at Cole's apartment two towns over. His mother wasn't thrilled at having another mouth to feed or kid to watch, so she'd always take me back home in a couple hours."

She shook her head again. "I guess you never had the opportunity to get close."

"Nope. And to make matters worse, Cole thought I had it better because at least I got to live with my dad, not that I had a mother ever. He resented that. I tried to tell him our dad wasn't exactly father of the year, but you know how kids can be about that. Grass is always greener."

"But it sounds like you care about Cole," she said, tilting her head.

"Of course I do. I always felt a kinship with him, always wished we could be closer. I tried for a while, but I could never really trust him. He lies too easily. Takes advantage of people. He got into some trouble with petty stuff a couple years ago and suddenly wanted me to make it go away. That caused a rift when I wouldn't. It's one of the reasons I let him stay the last time, even though I wasn't comfortable. To try to get a relationship back. Then he stole five hundred bucks in cash from an envelope in a kitchen drawer that I'd put there for a contractor, and he stole a bracelet your late grandmother gave you." He hung his head back. "I kind of wish I hadn't told you that, since you had the good fortune of not remembering."

"My grandmother's bracelet?"

"A diamond bracelet you always admired. She left it to you. And he took it. I got it back from the pawn shop, but paying for it infuriated me. Man, was I pissed as hell."

"I'll bet. Sorry, Sawyer. All that sounds really hard."

He nodded. "He'll always be my kid brother, though, you know? Despite, despite, despite. And I consider myself a pretty good judge of people and know a liar when I see and hear one, and I have to say, all that angst and pacing and panic from Cole a little while ago seemed authentic to me. This is new—the babies, I mean. Cole has walked away from family, people, jobs—but walking away from his own children, that clearly triggered a lot for him."

"So you think he'll be back," she said. "Before you said you weren't sure he'd ever come back."

He let out a breath, then looked down at the beautiful baby sleeping in his arms. "I guess the more I talk it out for myself, the more I realize I don't know. At first, I thought—Cole is gone. That the babies are just too much. But talking about his upbringing just now, what it meant for him to be ignored by our dad. I don't know. Maybe he'll figure some stuff out and come back for his children."

"Meaning I'd better not get too attached."

He froze, staring at her. "You were thinking this would be permanent?"

She gave a little shrug. "I guess either way, it's okay for me to get attached. Either I'll be raising these guys with you or we'll be aunt and uncle."

"Possibly aunt and uncle from a distance," he said, realizing he had to caution her. "Cole could return tomorrow and disappear with these two. And I'll have no recourse. They're his."

"Well, he brought them here for a reason. Even if he needs a night to get his head together, he knows we'll take good care of them. And if he does come back for them, I can't see him taking them far from a soft place for them to land."

"Maybe so," he said. "Speculation has never been my thing, though, Maddie. I'm more wait and see and operate on facts. Like I said, Cole is a wild card."

So yeah—definitely don't get too attached to these guys, he wanted to say. But he could see she was already bonded, after just an hour.

We'll see what the morning brings, he told himself.

"The extra good news is that MacLeod's Multiples Emporium has everything we could possibly need for these two," she said. "I saw that for myself yesterday."

Something told him they'd be taking a trip over there tomorrow and buying up the place, not that the Mac-Leods would accept a penny.

He *didn't* think Cole would be coming back. Not tomorrow and not next week. And the longer it got, the longer he'd stay away, because that was how it worked. Not so much out sight, out of mind, but out of sight, out of heart, even if Cole had to force it. One day it would feel too late to come back, and he'd convince himself the babies were better off with Sawyer and Maddie.

But here he was, speculating, when he just said he didn't do that. He had no idea what was in Cole's mind, Cole's heart. He just knew his brother *had* a heart. And that was what worried him and made things better at the same time.

At first Sawyer didn't know what he was hearing. Sounded like a baby crying.

He bolted upright. His nephews.

He glanced at the alarm clock. 4:34 a.m. *Ah, babies. Classic.* He looked over at Maddie, fast asleep. *Good.* She needed to rest.

Sawyer gently peeled back the comforter and padded over to where the babies were lying in their car seats on the carpet across from the end of their bed. They'd slept a nice stretch, so the carriers must be comfortable enough. He picked up Max, who was half crying, half squirming, and the baby instantly quieted down.

"What's the matter, guy?" he whispered. "Hungry? Wet? Just need some company?"

The diaper didn't feel particularly wet, but he changed Max anyway on the mat on the carpet, then put him back in the carrier to bring him downstairs to make up a bottle.

Once he had the bottle ready, he settled on the sofa, Max guzzling away. He heard a cry from upstairs and started to get up, but he could see Maddie on the top step, holding Shane.

"I was hoping you'd sleep through the night," he called up to her. "I was about to go get him."

"I like having babies to take care of," she said, coming down the stairs. "The second I woke up when I realized he was crying, I felt a crazy excitement about rushing out of bed to get him. I must have really wanted a baby, huh."

Yeah. You did. "I guess it's a novelty for now," he said. Again, immediately regretting the words coming out of his mouth. "Cole might be back in a few hours."

Was he cautioning her against getting attached again or doing some serious wishful thinking that his brother would return for his children? Did he want Cole Wolfe walking in and then out with these two precious beings? Cole, who couldn't take care of himself? As his brother himself had said?

Sawyer let out a sigh.

Maddie went into the kitchen to fix a bottle, returning and sitting next to him. "And I guess you really didn't want a baby. *Don't*, I should say."

Shane started fussing and kicking his little legs. Maddie held him upright against her, giving his back some gentle taps, and a big burp came out of that tiny body.

"That feels better, huh," she cooed, cradling the infant in her arms as she continued feeding him.

"My sister told me I've wanted to be a mother since I was really young, that I was always asking to play mommy and baby with our dolls and stuffed animals."

He smiled as a memory came over him. "You used to try to get me to play daddy. I remember you had this demonic-looking baby doll you particularly loved, and I'd run and hide whenever I saw you with it."

She laughed. "I'll bet."

"When we were around ten, you used to say you wanted four kids, two sets of twins, because you loved being a twin. And I used to say I only wanted dogs."

"You knew even back then you didn't want a family?" she asked.

"I knew I always wanted *you* in my life. And a dog. That's it. And when you started really pressing me about starting a family a few years ago, I guess I started retreating without even realizing it. I hated disappointing you, hated denying you something so important to you, but the thought of having a child of my own made me go absolutely cold inside. And I couldn't seem to budge from it."

"Even though our marriage was strong?"

He nodded. "It's not about us or the marriage. It's about me."

Even though she didn't remember any of this, he felt terrible for the Maddie she'd been a few days ago. Loving her husband so much, wanting a child so much. And Sawyer not wanting a child with the same vehemence.

Moose came padding down the stairs. He gave Shane a sniff, then Max, and then lay down at Sawyer's feet. "I used to tell you that Moose was our fur baby. You didn't like that one bit."

"No doubt," she said, setting the almost-empty bottle down. She looked at the German shepherd. "No offense, Moose."

The dog eyed her and put his chin on her foot. "He loved you from the very first day he met you."

She smiled, leaning down to give the dog a scratch behind his ear. "So what do we do now? I guess newborns don't play, do they?"

"Well, I'd like to get them checked out by a pediatrician. I know they just came from the hospital and Cole said they were cleared and discharged, but just for my own peace of mind. Then I think we just walk around with them, talk to them and take care of their every need and want."

"That's the life," she said, giving Shane a little rock.

He looked down at the baby in his arms. Once, he'd promised to take care of *Maddie's* every need and want, and he'd denied her so much. He'd denied her *this*.

But as he shifted Max upright to burp him, that same

vague, abstract feeling of terror mixed with *they're not mine, they're not mine* lodged in his gut, as it had when he'd tried to fall asleep last night. Other people always seemed to go to mush around babies, even six-foot-five, two-hundred-twenty-pound Officer Mobley. He'd never heard anyone ooh and aah and then play five rounds of peekaboo like Mobley. But when Sawyer held a baby, all he felt was that dread—and the sure knowledge that the baby belonged to someone else, someone who'd come for him or her.

Except this time.

Chapter Five

Noon came and went, the "deadline" Sawyer had set
for his brother to return. Sawyer had called in a favor
to a pediatrician he knew in town and had the twins
squeezed in for a check-up while Maddie stayed home
just in case Cole came back. The good news was that
the twins were definitely healthy. The bad news: Cole
hadn't called, texted or shown his face at the house.

And so Sawyer and Maddie put the trip to Mac-
Leod's on today's schedule, to buy everything the babies needed. Maddie figured they'd need all the baby
paraphernalia on hand no matter what, whether they
were looking after the babies or if Cole *did* come back
and would bring them by to visit in the typical sce-
nario.

The more she said that kind of thing out loud, the

deeper the frown lines on Sawyer's forehead got. Her way, which she was very slowly getting to know, seemed to be to pounce—to ask about everything, including every raised eyebrow of Sawyer's. She was an asker, and she supposed that was good. You didn't ask, you didn't find out anything.

"Why does that make you…unsettled, Sawyer?" she'd inquired just ten minutes ago as they'd settled the twins back in their carriers after feeding them.

"Well, because either way is not exactly what I had planned. For now or the next eighteen years."

"Life is like that, though. You certainly didn't plan for me to lose my memory. Stuff happens, Sawyer."

"With help," he'd said. "Stuff doesn't just happen. I got you angry and you drove off—boom, accident. Cole is reckless—boom, twin newborns who are now in our custody."

"Is that how you look at it? Like the babies are in your custody? À la police custody?"

The frown lines appeared again. "I just don't know what's going to happen, Maddie. And yes, *that* unsettles me."

When he was like that, when he was sort of vulnerably honest, she would feel herself softening and relenting and wanting to give him a hug. But something also told her that Sawyer Wolfe needed a good push. And boy, was he getting one.

After their conversation, he'd gone to make a pot of coffee, and she'd called MacLeod's to let her family know she and Sawyer would be coming by with their newborn nephews and needed to buy out the joint. Her mother had gasped with joy and said, "Don't you move a muscle! We'll bring everything you need to you! Oh, I can't wait to meet those little MacLeod multiples!"

Forty-five minutes later, the pink-and-blue delivery truck arrived, the MacLeod's Multiples Emporium logo with its six illustrations of infants in diapers unmistakable. As Sawyer went out to thank them profusely and bring everything in with the help of her dad and a delivery guy, Maddie's mother and sister rushed in to see the newest little members of their family.

"They've got Sawyer's eyes!" April MacLeod said, reaching in to gently take Shane out of his carrier. "Yup, those are definitely Sawyer's eyes—look at the almond shape. I'll bet they turn green by the time these two are three months." She sat down on the living room sofa, gazing at the baby with pure love and devotion.

Maddie pictured Cole Wolfe, eyes so similar to his brother's. Last night, his eyes had been full of pain and panic. She wondered where he was right now. Hours across the country? Twenty minutes away in a motel? Or maybe he was just home, wherever that was. She felt for him, she really did, and she was glad that he could rest assured the babies would be well taken care of by their aunt and uncle.

"And there's just something in the expression," Jenna added, reaching in for Max and carefully cradling him in her arms. The infant gazed up at her with curious slate-blue eyes. "Aw, he's precious. They're both so stinkin' cute."

"So what does this make me?" April asked. "Grandmother-in-law?"

Jenna grinned. "I don't think that's a thing. Or maybe it is. Let's make it a thing so I can be the aunt-in-law."

"I didn't even know Sawyer had a brother," Maddie whispered.

"Oh gosh, that's right," Jenna said, leaning back and shifting the baby in her arms. "They've never been close. You tried over the years to invite Cole to holidays and family events. Sometimes he'd show. He'd stick by your side and avoid Sawyer most of the time."

Poor Sawyer. He'd made it clear he'd always wanted a relationship with his half brother. But the more she got to know Sawyer Wolfe, who was truly as brand-new to her as anyone, the more she realized he probably did the pushing away more than he realized. As he and her father and the delivery guy finished unloading the truck and brought mostly everything upstairs, Maddie heard bits and pieces of Sawyer telling her dad about the situation, talking openly. *He trusts my dad*, she realized. Of course he did; the man practically raised him. She could see that Sawyer was comfortable and open with Ace MacLeod, and despite the fact that she couldn't remember her own relationship with her parents, she was deeply touched to see that Sawyer clearly felt very close to them.

Within fifteen minutes, the empty room upstairs had been transformed into a nursery. Two rocking bassinets, a cozy pale yellow glider, a dresser–changing table stocked with everything the twins could need, from diapers to cornstarch to chafing ointment, a lullaby player, a big pile of pajamas and caps, blankets and burp cloths. Shane and Max were now fast asleep in their bassinets.

Maddie watched the twins sleep in the sweet little nursery, but as she looked over at Sawyer, she couldn't help noticing that the frown lines were back.

* * *

With the baby twins surrounded by the MacLeod clan, Sawyer had made an excuse to leave for just a little while, to take the deep breath he'd barely managed all night. He'd needed some time and space to think—to process what had happened overnight, and so he'd let Maddie know he had to go into work for an hour or two. He put on his uniform, stopped at Java Jane's for a strong, hot cup of coffee and then headed to the Wedlock Creek Chapel, to finally have that talk with elderly caretaker Annie Potterowski about her delinquent dog.

"Annie, you've got to keep Champ on a shorter leash," Sawyer told her. "He's swiped food from people six times this month. Twice from the same kid." This morning, he'd gotten an earful on his voice mail from the parent of Danny Peterman, who thought that children should be able to walk down the street in peace with their allowance-purchased hot pretzel without a dog grabbing it and swallowing it in one mouthful. Apparently, Danny had found it hilarious the first time. Not so much the second time. Especially because Annie had flat-out refused to buy the kid another pretzel.

Short, stout, gray-haired Annie threw her hands up in the air and very slowly bent down to faux-admonish the beagle at her side in the small chapel office.

Normally, he'd leave such small potatoes to his rookie, but Annie was a character (as was her husband and fellow officiant-caretaker), and Mobley had tried too hard to be respectful to eighty-three-year-old Annie, an institution herself in Wedlock Creek, and she'd run roughshod all over him. Besides, Sawyer really had needed a little break from home. From the babies. From this crazy situation he found himself in.

His wife didn't remember him or their life.

He was suddenly taking care of two newborns who might or might not be sticking around.

Nothing was sure in this world. He knew that. But such uncertainty left him feeling off balance. He didn't like off balance.

"Chief, I told Champ no more swiping—you heard me tell him. And yes, I'll put him on a shorter leash."

Oh, I'm sure Champ was listening. Not. "Thank you, Annie. And if you see someone coming with food in their hand, you might shorten the leash around your hand even more so Champ can't jump and get it. Also, offering to reimburse what Champ steals from people would be the right thing to do."

"One time I offered, someone actually took me up on it!" she huffed.

"Annie Potterowski," he said in his I'm-the-chief-of-police tone.

"Oh, fine, I will, I will, jeez. So what's this I hear about you and Maddie taking in your baby nephews?"

Word sure spread fast in a small town. "My brother's babies."

"I'm so glad for you and Maddie. Everyone felt so bad," she added on a reverent whisper.

"Bad about what?" he asked. Small town or not, he didn't have the sense Maddie was telling anyone besides her family about their marital troubles.

"You know, your *fertility* issues," she said, whispering the word *fertility*.

Oh, brother. "Why on earth would you think I had fertility issues?"

"You or Maddie. One of you. Otherwise, you'd have three kids by now."

Ah.

"Well, now you have those two little newborns to care for," she said.

"It's not permanent, Annie." It wasn't. It couldn't be.

"Well, for however long. You'll make one heck of a dad, Chief."

He almost choked on his coffee. "What? Me? Why on earth would you say that?"

"You have all the hallmarks of a dad. Dependable. Responsible. Everyone can count on you."

Was that true, though? Maddie hadn't been able to depend on him for the one thing she wanted most out of life: a baby.

"And you're just a good guy," Annie continued. "Kind. Say what you mean and mean what you say. Good sense of humor. Fair-minded. I like you, and I've stopped liking most people. Some of the people I marry in this chapel—I could write a book."

He smiled. "I'm sure."

A knock came at the door. A couple—woman in a wedding gown and veil, man in a tux and a cowboy hat.

"We'd like to get married this minute," the woman said.

"Well, you've come to the right place," Annie said. "Guess you'll need to skedaddle, Chief."

"Got my eye on you, Annie Potterowski," he said, then flashed her a smile. He bent down to give Champ a pat. "You behave yourself, beagle."

As he walked down the long aisle of the beautiful chapel, he easily remembered his own wedding here seven years ago. Maddie had asked him a few times if he was sure he was comfortable marrying at the chapel despite the legend of the multiples. Saying *I do* at the chapel meant not just one baby but two or more. Some might say it was hocus-pocus nonsense, but this town was chock-full of twins and triplets and a few sets of quadruplets. There were even two sets of quints in one family, albeit with quite an age gap.

But Sawyer had known that it meant a lot to Maddie to marry in the century-old chapel, and he'd figured *they* were in control of family planning, not the legend, so the legend itself didn't scare him. Seven years later, no kids, right?

Unless he counted the two in the brand-new nursery of his house.

Those who marry in the chapel will have multiples in some way, shape or form, whether through biology, luck, marriage or happenstance...

He supposed his way was happenstance. Huh.

You'll make one heck of a dad, Chief...

He wasn't too sure about that. He knew he'd do what was needed; that wasn't the problem.

He'd never been able to put the problem into words—that was the real problem, according to Maddie. Or maybe the issue was that he didn't want to put it into words, to dredge up all uncomfortable feelings. His earliest memories included the MacLeods welcoming him at all hours, all holidays, always making a place for him at the table with an "Oh, Sawyer-boy, so glad you're joining us for breakfast—we're having omelets to order." He knew what a good, solid family could be, could mean. He'd grown up witnessing it next door. But his earliest memories also included the ones he'd never been able to shake, the ones that were just there, deep inside him. Times when he couldn't wake up his dad. When he was so hungry for breakfast and the Mac-Leods weren't home and there wasn't any milk for cereal or bread that wasn't half-green. When a strange woman would tell him to scram for a couple of hours, his dad smiling at her while running his fingers through her hair.

When he was a bit older, twelve, thirteen and so on, all that hadn't mattered so much. He'd gotten used to it and had his own money from his paper route. But family, *his* family, those were the memories lodged in his chest, the ones that had the grip on him. He'd explained all this to Maddie many times, but it didn't make sense to her, and it didn't really make sense to him. The feeling where paternal instincts might be was just dead, didn't exist. He'd never wanted to go there. And he'd avoided it as long as he could.

For a long time, their love had won out, had been stronger. Maddie had truly believed he'd change his mind, and though he'd never promised her that or even said there was a real possibility of it, he'd hoped he would change his mind. That was why he'd felt okay about marrying her with such a fundamental issue standing in their way. The hope had been enough, and Maddie had never doubted he would change his mind.

He'd never changed his mind.

He walked the half mile down to the police station, the bright sun helping with the cold temperature. As he passed the community center, an easel out front next to a decorated Christmas tree caught his attention. *Be a Holiday Happymaker! Adopt a family for the holidays!*

That was the program that Maddie had volunteered for. He headed inside and found a few people plucking envelopes off another big Christmas tree. A sign on the wall read: *Pick an envelope and inside you'll find the holiday wish list for an anonymous family in need. Each family member is to receive at least the item noted on the form. Once complete, drop off the unwrapped items in a bag and include the ticket inside your envelope so that we can match the family with the gifts. Thank you for being a Holiday Happymaker!*

Sawyer plucked an envelope off the tree and opened it.

Anonymous Family #7
Thank you for being our Santa. We can barely afford heat this winter, let alone gifts. We sure do appreciate this.

Father: Age 26. Heavyweight wool socks for outdoor work (I'm in construction).

Mother: Age 25. A Christmas Eve ham to serve 4. Thank you.

Son: Age 3. A yellow dump truck.

Son: Age 16 months. Warm pajamas with feet.

Sawyer's heart clenched. The mother's Christmas wish for herself was a ham enough to serve her family? The father wanted socks? To wear at his outdoor job?

Done. All done. And then some. *Family number 7, you'll be getting a lot more than socks and ham and pajamas and a dump truck.*

He was about to pluck another envelope when his cell pinged with a text. Reed Barelli, one of his detectives, wanted to talk over a case. He sent back a quick See you in two minutes, and headed out, turning back to look at the tree. There were so many envelopes that his heart hurt. *Maddie did this*, he thought as he headed into the cold December air. This was her baby, her idea, and she made it happen.

She was such a good person and deserved every bit of happiness. And what she wanted most of all was a family—something he'd denied for so long. He didn't want children; that hadn't changed. But right now, they *had* children—for how long, he didn't know—and while they were here he was going to change his attitude, somehow, someway.

Because hadn't he promised Maddie ten children if that was what she wanted?

Maddie loved the hours she'd spent with the twins and her parents so much that she barely thought about her lack of memory. Her twin had had plans with her husband's family, so she'd had to leave, and the past three hours Maddie and her mom and dad had set up the whole house, stashing "newborn twin survival totes" in all areas so that she—or Sawyer—would never be caught without easy access to a diaper or a burp cloth. April MacLeod had raised twins and was full of tips and tricks for needing more than two hands. By the time her parents had left, Maddie could honestly say she adored the MacLeods, even if she couldn't remember them past yesterday.

She stood in the nursery, admiring the pretty yellow

glider and round shag rug, the mobiles with pastel little stuffed animals that spun around above the matching white spindle bassinets, the beautiful babies asleep inside them, on soft sheets.

"It's way too quiet in this house for newborn twins."

Maddie whirled around. Sawyer was back. She hadn't even heard him come in, likely because he was trying to be quiet for the babies' sake.

"They're asleep?" he asked, peering past her into each bassinet.

She nodded. "They've been asleep for five minutes, but I've just been standing here watching them, their tiny chests going up and down. It's the most beautiful thing I've ever seen."

He stood beside her, looking down at them, Max in his new tiny-monkey-print pajamas, Shane in his green-and-white-striped ones. "No text or call back from Cole. Not even to ask about them or to check in." He shook his head.

"I suppose he knows how they're doing if they're with us," she said, putting a hand on his arm.

He looked at her. "True. It would be nice to be able to count on him the way he can count on us."

Maddie tilted her head, taking that in. With that simple sentence, everything about Sawyer Wolfe made sense to her. He'd never been able to count on his own family. He'd never had a mother. His father had neglected his well-being. His brother never considered Sawyer's feelings or position. Family friends and good neighbors or not, Sawyer had learned from the most tender of ages that family meant sorrow, loss, worry, fear. No wonder it was so ingrained him not to want to create his *own* family.

She was beginning to understand him, to know him. Maddie had a feeling that the wife she'd been, with all her memories intact, understood Sawyer quite well too—so well that she'd waited and waited and waited for the change of mind she believed he'd come around to. And now she also understood why she'd believed. Because Sawyer's not wanting children wasn't so much a choice he'd made but a feeling he'd been saddled with. She'd been trying to show him what love and family commitment was. But seven years later, at thirty-two, watching her twin sister's belly grow every day, working in a shop full of expectant parents, living in a town where many children were its claim to fame, Maddie could see why she had begun to lose patience with her husband.

"Thank you for taking care of them all day," he said. "I'll take the night shift."

"I loved today," she said. "One peep out of them tonight, and I'm there. I won't be able to stop myself."

"Well, I'll beat you to it."

She smiled and put her hand on his arm again, and he turned toward her. She wanted to open her arms to him, hold him, be held, but she suddenly felt shy. *Because you've known him all of two days*, she reminded herself.

She moved behind him and rubbed his shoulders, needing, wanting to touch him. He stiffened for just a second, then relaxed, dropping his head forward and backward. His muscles were amazing. She itched to slip her hands underneath his shirt.

Turn me around. Kiss me.

"I'll go start dinner," he said instead. "I stopped at the market for your favorite kind of fish, and I'll make it with that Spanish rice you love so much. Sound good?"

Oh, Sawyer. You love me. That is not in question. She moved in front of him and stood just an inch from him, her hands on his chest. "That sounds really good."

He stared at her for a few seconds, then covered one of her hands with his. He stepped back with something of an awkward smile, then almost seemed about to step closer toward her. Moose appeared in the doorway, sitting down and watching them. "Someone else wants dinner too. I'll let you know when ours is ready."

He squeezed her hand and then left the room, Moose padding after him.

Thanks, Moose, she thought, shaking her head with a rueful grin. She was pretty sure Sawyer had been about to kiss her.

Wishful thinking—probably. Maddie did think he wanted to kiss her, but something was holding him back. Their pre-accident issues? She'd have to make it clear she wanted him to kiss her. Hey, they were husband and wife.

Three hours later, dinner done—and delicious—the kitchen cleaned up, the babies fed, changed, read to while Sawyer held both cradled along the length of his arms in the glider, and now once again sleeping in the nursery, Maddie let out a big yawn.

"Tired, huh?" he asked, grabbing a water bottle from the refrigerator.

"Very. I'm definitely ready for bed." *Hint. Hint hint.*

"Why don't you head up, then. I've got some paperwork to catch up on. And as I said, I've got the twins tonight. You go get that much-needed sleep."

Humph. She wanted him beside her.

"Sawyer, to be honest, I don't feel like being alone."

He froze for a second. "Well, in that case, the paperwork can wait. I'll just, uh, lock up. See you upstairs in a few."

She smiled. *Ask and you shall receive, right?* Sometimes, but right now, it had worked.

She could wait for him to lock up. But she had a feeling her husband was trying to allow her to once again change for bed in privacy.

In their room, she grabbed yoga pants and a long-sleeved T-shirt and went into the bathroom to change. She washed up, then stared at herself in the mirror. Fresh-scrubbed face, long hair back in ponytail, teeth minty, blue T-shirt. Not exactly sexy.

When she came out of the bathroom, Sawyer was rooting around in his dresser. He turned and kind of froze, staring at her.

"What?" she asked. "Do I have something in my teeth? Underwear hanging out the back of my yoga pants?"

"You just look beautiful," he said. "You always do."

Maddie smiled. "Even with this half bump and scratch down my forehead?"

His face kind of fell, and Maddie realized she was talking from nerves, rambling away. But what she'd done was remind Sawyer of her accident. *Just take a compliment when it's offered*, she yelled at herself.

She got into bed, tucking the comforter under her arms. The bed was king-size but suddenly felt small. Last night she'd been aware of Sawyer getting into bed beside her, but she'd fallen asleep so darn quickly only to be woken up just an hour later by the doorbell ringing, and she'd barely slept since. Her eyes felt heavy now, but she was more interested in Sawyer than sleep.

He stretched out beside her, turning onto his side to face her. *That* was unexpected. She did the same.

"I adopted a family from the Holiday Happymakers tree," he said. "The dad only wants socks. Warm wool socks. The mother asked for a ham big enough to serve four. I'll be tripling everything and adding things."

She smiled. "That's very kind, Sawyer. This is the program I volunteered for?"

"It was your idea last Christmas. And a very good one."

"Tomorrow, I'd like to pick a family or two to adopt."

"I want to adopt another," he said, "so we can head over in the morning."

She reached out her hand and touched his face, soft and slightly stubbled at the same time. Then she wiggled closer and lifted her face.

He cupped her face with his hands and kissed her, a real kiss, but then he moved back a bit. "Maddie, I want you so much. Trust me when I say that sex has never been an issue between us. But the Maddie you were days ago slept on the sofa the previous two nights. You were upset and angry at me." He hesitated for a second. "I was trying to get out of going to the mediation appointment."

"Why?"

"We weren't getting anywhere. And I hated talking about our problems with a stranger. She was good at getting us to open up, me included, and I hated that."

Maddie smiled. "I see."

"I don't want to take advantage of your loss of memory. And touching you when you're not yourself feels wrong."

Her smile faded.

I want *you to touch me. Oh, flip*, she thought—
was she being fair to herself? To the Maddie Wolfe
she couldn't remember? "You want to know what I'm
thinking?"

Surprise lit his face. "Yes."

"I'm thinking I want you to touch me. But you're
right, Sawyer. I want you to touch me because I *don't*
remember. And maybe if I did, I'd be bopping you over
the head with the pillow."

"Oh, I think that's way too playful for how you felt
those last couple of days, Maddie."

"Really?"

Now it was sadness that crossed his features. "Yeah. I
was letting you down. In a very big way. And I couldn't
see a way out of that without saying yes to something
that I couldn't fathom. I'd think of a baby in our house,
and my throat would close up."

"I didn't realize it was that bad."

"I'm not prone to panic, Maddie, but when I would
sit with myself in the dark in the middle of the night,
knowing the wife I loved so much was downstairs, miserable and angry and hurting and that it was my fault,
I'd think, well, maybe we could just do it, have a baby.
And then a rush of cold panic would start in my gut and
threaten to drown me. That's how it felt."

Tears pricked the backs of her eyes. "You *didn't* want
a baby as much as I *did* want one. Oh God, Sawyer."

"It seems like a no-brainer to everyone. A sweet,
darling baby, made of the two of us—what could be
more special, more unifying? It's very hard for people
to understand."

"Did *I* understand? At all?"

He reached out to move a strand of hair from her face. "Yes. But you really did believe the strength of our marriage would show me, change me, and it didn't."

"Is it awful for you to have Shane and Max here?"

"No," he said. "But I think that's because they're not mine. And they're not permanent. At least I think they're not."

"Maybe *they'll* change your mind."

He held her gaze, his green eyes tender now. "Maybe, Maddie." But he didn't sound sure. Not at all.

She, however, *was* sure of something. Why she'd fallen in love with him, despite that big whopper between them. She was falling in love with him now, could feel her heart moving and quaking and leaning toward him.

He was being true to her—the real her—by not touching her. She wondered if she *was* being anti-Maddie by allowing herself to fall in love all over again with a man saying no to what she wanted so badly. Or saying yes just because he'd pleaded for her life and his prayers had been answered.

She could imagine how many nights she'd lain here rationalizing that she loved him more than anything— more than her desire to have children, to be a mother, and that thought, that knowledge had allowed her to sleep and go on to the next day with him. Until she couldn't take it anymore because she thought his reasons for not wanting children were irrational. She figured anyway.

And now she lay here beside her husband, unable to remember any of it. All she felt was a surge of tenderness for Sawyer, a strong physical attraction and a yearning to be closer to him, in all ways.

"We'll figure it out," she said, touching his cheek.

He gave her rueful smile. "That's what *I* used to say."

"Well, we will." She yawned, her eyes getting heavy, and she turned around, curling against him. She felt him freeze for a second and couldn't help smiling at how predictable he was, deeply satisfied when he wrapped a strong arm around her and probably closed his eyes too.

Chapter Six

Another morning arrived with no text or call from Cole. As Sawyer sat at the kitchen table with Maddie, he stared out the window at the snow dotting the trees, then back at his cell phone lying beside his mug of coffee. He kept expecting it to ring or ping with Cole's number. It never did.

"Where do you think he is?" Maddie asked, giving Shane his bottle.

Sawyer adjusted Max in his arms, tilting up the bottle a bit higher. "You reading my mind?"

She smiled. "Just the way you were looking out the window, then down at Max. I just had the feeling you were thinking about your brother."

He eyed her, then put down the almost-empty bottle and took a long drink of his strong coffee. How did she know him so well when she didn't even know herself right now? Which made him realize something else. "I wish I could say I knew him well enough to know where he might be, but I don't. He could be right here in town, hiding out in a motel. He could be clear across Wyoming."

"He looked so upset, though, Sawyer. I can't imagine him just leaving and never coming back. In my current state, I don't know him at all, but from the way he seemed the night he left the twins with us…"

"I know. He was shaken. But people get shaken and they panic and they do crazy things. I see it all the time."

"Is that what happened to your dad?" she asked.

He stared at her. "My dad?" Talking about his dad was his least favorite subject.

"Your mom died right after you were born. That had to have shaken up your father."

He pictured Hank Wolfe. Tall, muscular, tattoos on each arm, working out with the free weights on the padded bench in his bedroom, a bottle of beer on the floor at the ready. He'd inherited his father's wavy dark hair and green eyes, just as Cole had. "I'm sure it did. He didn't talk much about her, and both sets of grandparents died before I was born, so there's no one to ask about their relationship."

"Alone with a baby, grieving. That had to have taken its toll."

He nodded, his chest feeling tight. "Well, these guys are fed. Why don't I get them changed, and we can head out to the community center for the Holiday Happymakers tree."

She set down the bottle, now with just a trickle left,

then brought Shane against her and gently patted his back. "Change of subject. Okay."

"It's not my favorite one, Maddie."

"Well, turns out you're *not* so lucky I don't remember anything because it means I have to ask you questions. Otherwise, I'd be in the dark. And I hate being in the dark."

"Understood," he said. She was absolutely right. But he still didn't want to talk about his father.

In a half hour, the babies were changed and in their heavy winter fleece buntings, ready to go in the double stroller the MacLeods had brought over yesterday. They were all practically out the door when the phone rang— the landline. It was Jenna. Her husband had taken the day off to accompany Jenna to her ultrasound appointment, and they both had baby twins on the brain and wanted to babysit Shane and Max for a few hours as practice, since they'd have their own baby twins in a few months. Sawyer had to admit he liked the idea of having some time alone with his wife; their nephews had arrived that first night she'd come home from the hospital, and their lives hadn't been their own since.

Ten minutes later, the babies and everything that Jenna and her husband could need for a few hours were now in her sister's house. As he and Maddie walked back to his car, he kept feeling like he was missing something.

"I've been without Shane and Max for all of twenty seconds this morning and I keep having these mini panic attacks that I forgot them somewhere."

"I know what you mean," she said. "We had them intensely for over twenty-four hours, and suddenly, we're on our own."

"I'm glad about that, Maddie. I think we could use a little time together."

She took his hand and held it. He was surprised by just how good that felt. "So how about we go to the community center to the Holiday Happymakers tree, and then maybe you can show me around. Places that are important to us, important to me."

"Like a 'This is your life, Maddie Wolfe'?"

"Exactly. Dr. Addison said you never know what might trigger my memory to return. It could happen just like that," she added on a snap of her fingers.

And with it, your burning resentment of me, he thought—unfairly. He loved the way things were between them right now. Light. Happy. All good things shining in her eyes when she looked at him. It had been so damned long since she'd looked at him that way.

He drove to town and parked in the lot near the chapel. As they walked toward the nearby community center, so many people out and about shopping for gifts stopped to ask Maddie how she was doing. That she had temporary amnesia was being kept on the down low, so again Sawyer quietly filled in who was who, allowing Maddie to know how to respond. Maddie did a lot for the town, volunteering to lend a hand in many capacities, and the outpouring of well wishes when word had spread about her accident had touched him. He'd gotten so many calls and texts, and the cards and flowers sent to Maddie at the hospital had meant a lot.

As they entered the community center, the small line for the Holiday Happymakers tree was moving quickly.

Some people plucked and read and put back the envelope if they didn't like what was inside. Others just took an envelope and left with it.

"Not many envelopes left," Maddie noted. "That's great."

He nodded. "I wouldn't be surprised if people took more than one envelope—like I'm about to do."

"Warms my heart," she said.

Finally they reached the tree. He took off another envelope, and Maddie took two, then they headed over to the benches by the door. They sat and opened their envelopes.

"Aw," Maddie said. "Listen to this. 'I'm eight years old, and all I want for Christmas is a stuffed puppy. I want him to be brown and white like the puppy my neighbor has. My parents say we can't have a dog right now. If you get me a stuffed puppy, I promise to take good care of him. From Stevie.' Aww, so much for anonymous. So cute." She put the form back in the envelope and tucked it into her tote bag. "Let's get her a real puppy!" Maddie said.

Sawyer's eyes practically bugged out of his head. "You're kidding, right?"

Maddie laughed. "Yes. Can you imagine?"

"No, definitely not," he said.

As she opened her second envelope, Sawyer opened his.

Here's my list. Tesla Roadster (red). Round-trip tickets for two to Paris the last two week of August. At least $250 in a gift certificate to Lizabett's Italian Ristorante. $500 in cash. Air Jordan Retro sneakers, size 12.5. Hey, you gotta think big, right? Merry Christmas!

Sawyer rolled his eyes, tucked the list back into the envelope and walked over to the tree to clip it back on. It was the only one of two left now, and he had a feeling it would be opened and returned many times till Christmas. He took the other one and opened it.

I'm not getting anything for Christmas because my father only cares about his stupid new wife and always-crying new baby. I could use a bike so I don't have to ask him for rides anywhere. Whatever. This is just fake Santa. I'm sure I won't be getting anything.
—Jake Russtower.

The kid forgot to keep it anonymous. Russtower. He knew that name. He'd have to check his records, but he was pretty sure he'd come across that name. And not in a good way. He had a feeling the tone and the name combined kept the envelope being opened and put back on the tree. He sighed inwardly and slipped the envelope inside his pocket.

"How was your second one?" he asked.

"A teacher at the middle school asking for books for her classroom," Maddie said. "I'm all over that."

He smiled. "Mine's a little heavier. Looks like some family issues. Kid wanting a bike."

"Well, that kid is lucky you're his secret Santa, then." She wrapped her arm around his, and for the moment, all thoughts went out of his head and everything was right with the world.

Even if everything was as upside down as it got.

"Ready for 'This is your life, Maddie Wolfe'?"

"I'm ready," she said.

They headed out, Maddie putting her gloves on and tightening her scarf. He knew just where to start on the Maddie Wolfe life tour. He just hoped it didn't torpedo him.

After a call to Maddie's sister and husband to check on the twins, who were "adorable and a pleasure to babysit," Sawyer drove Maddie to Beacon Road. As he pulled up in front of the white house, his gaze was drawn to the house next door, the side porch that was the entrance to the apartment where he grew up. He wanted to drive away.

"Ooh, what's this?" she asked. "Where we grew up?"

"Yup," he said, getting out. As he came around the SUV, she got out too. "The white house was yours. Your parents sold it about seven years ago. You and Jenna moved out and shared an apartment while you were commuting to Wyoming Western University, and then you both got married, so April and Ace decided to downsize and move closer to town and the store."

Maddie peered up at the house. "I was hoping it would spark something, but nope. Doesn't look the least bit familiar." Her face fell. "I grew up here. I should remember. All my memories are gone. Everything I've been is gone." She turned away, shoving her mittened hands into her coat pockets.

He could kick himself for not realizing she might feel bad about not remembering her own life. Of course she would. Inside, everything might be shiny and new, but she didn't know anyone, didn't recognize anyone, didn't have a single memory beyond the past few days.

"Hey," he said gently, putting an arm around her. "I could fill you in. That was the plan."

She looked up at him. "I guess you'd know. From the very beginning too."

"I do. I've always been there. Well, since we were five."

"Where'd we meet?" she asked.

"I only know this story secondhand. Your mom loves telling us how we met."

"Hi, Chief!" called a voice. Sawyer glanced toward the MacLeods' former front door to find the current owner smiling and waving. Amanda Palermo. He turned to Maddie. "Wait here a minute, will you?"

He jogged over to the woman. "Mind if we pay a visit to your backyard? I was feeling nostalgic and wanted to show Maddie a couple things from the old days. We'll venture down to the creek, too, if you don't mind."

"Go right ahead," Amanda said. "Merry Christmas."

"Merry Christmas," he said.

He headed back to Maddie and took her hand. "Right this way, ma'am."

She slipped her hand into his, and again he loved the way that felt. It had been a while since she'd held his hand before the accident. A while since she'd wanted to be anywhere near him.

"See this spot," he said, pointing beside a bare tree in the backyard not far from the house. "You were making a fort out of a sheet and kiddie chairs, and you had a sandwich and chips on a plate. I came over and told you there was a fat squirrel after your food."

She laughed. "That's how we met?"

"Yup. Then you shouted, 'Let's hide from it!' And

you grabbed the plate into the fort and we sat on the grass under the sheet and you offered me half the sandwich and half the chips. We were best friends ever since."

"Aw. Was that the day you and your dad moved next door?"

He nodded. "I went outside and there you were." He couldn't actually remember being five all that well, but her mother had been sitting on the patio and saw and heard the whole thing and loved to tell the story whenever she got nostalgic.

They walked farther down the yard toward the woods. The property extended a half mile, so they'd played in these woods for hours every day as kids. By the creek, he pointed to a flat-topped rock big enough for two butts. "That's where you told me you had a huge crush on Jonathan Walloway in sixth grade. I wasn't interested in girls then, but I remember feeling all out of sorts about the news. By seventh grade, I knew why. You always had boys chasing you, and I was always the BFF."

Maddie looked surprised. "I must have had a big crush on you too."

"Back then you always used to say, 'Nothing is more important to me than our friendship, and therefore nothing can be allowed to ruin it. So even if I want to kiss you, I'm not going to.' And I said, 'So you want to?' And you said, 'It doesn't matter because we can't.' I was so afraid of something ruining us, too, that I never asked if I could kiss you. We just stayed friends. We did go to a couple dances together but just as friends."

"So we dated other people even though we really loved each other?"

"Well, we didn't know we did in middle school and high school," he explained. "I thought you just liked me as a friend, and you thought I just liked you as a friend. It wasn't until prom night that things got very interesting between us."

"Ooh, what happened?"

"I'll have to take you over to the Wedlock Creek Town Hall for that story." He was glad to be leaving the property. He'd left a lot out.

Such as finding his dad passed out drunk on their tiny portion of patio and being unable to wake him up or move him at age nine. Having to ask Ace MacLeod for help so his dad wouldn't freeze to death. Ace not saying a bad word about his dad, just telling Sawyer outright that anytime, day or night, if Sawyer needed help, needed anything, like now, he was to call Ace or April immediately. He'd made Sawyer promise that he'd always reach out to them for help, no matter what. Sawyer had promised. There were so many memories here that he wasn't sure why he'd hit upon that one. Maybe because he'd never forgotten being unable to help his father, passed out in single-degree temps with just a sweatshirt and jeans.

He never wanted to be in a position where he couldn't help, couldn't do anything.

Lots of unknowns where children are concerned, he thought, catching himself by surprise. He'd never thought about that connection. He'd heard people say that having children was like having your heart walk around outside your body. And he certainly couldn't be there to protect his children 24/7. Hell, he'd been standing fifty feet away from where Maddie had crashed her car; he'd *seen* it happen. Unable to stop her, help her.

Maddie took his hand again, shaking him from the memory, from the unsettling direction of his thoughts. In five minutes they were at the hall, where town residents could hold events and where the Wedlock Creek High School prom was held every year.

"We went to the prom together? Just as friends?" she asked as they walked into the hall. It was empty now, light filtering in from the huge oval windows.

"Nope. You went with a date. The guy you liked finally asked you, and you thought it was going to be the start of something. You slow-danced to three songs, and then he talked you into taking a walk to Legend Point."

Maddie narrowed her gaze at him. "Is this a true story? How do you know how many songs we slow-danced too?"

"Because you told me. Tears streaming down your face."

"Oh. That bad?"

He nodded. "Legend Point is the place where everyone goes to fool around. Or claims to. He got you there and wanted to go further than you were ready for. He got angry and took a wad of dirt and rubbed it on your dress and called you a tease—in a more vulgar way than that—and abandoned you there."

She frowned, wrapping her arms around herself. "Awful."

"Yup. And that's when you called me. To bring you home. But when I found you, sitting with your head down and sobbing between a row of hedges, you couldn't talk or get up, so I just sat and put my arm around your shoulder and you leaned your head against me and cried."

"Poor seventeen-year-old Maddie."

"Yeah. I felt horrible for you. I wanted to kill that jerk. I started telling you how he didn't deserve you, that you were so great, and you said you wished you'd gone to the prom with me, then you popped up and wiped away your tears and said, 'Let's go. We can hang out back and listen to the band and dance if we feel like it.'"

"So in my dirt-smeared dress and…I assume you were in jeans and a T-shirt, we went?"

He nodded. "We stood behind the school, and a slow song came on that you loved, and you put your arms around my neck and your head against my chest and I blurted out, 'Maddie, I love you. I've always loved you.'"

Maddie gasped. "Really? What did I say?"

"You looked up at me with your gorgeous blue eyes and said, 'I've always loved you too.' And then you leaned your head up and kissed me. For the first time on the lips. I almost passed out I was so happy."

She laughed. "Then what happened?"

"We just stayed there and slow-danced through the next five songs. And then I drove us home, and we went down by the creek and sat on that rock and made out and talked about how we'd been so dumb for so many years."

"What about the pact to not ruin the friendship?" she asked.

He smiled just thinking about that moment. "We made a new pact. To never break up."

She threw her arms around him and held on. "I love us. I love Maddie and Sawyer, the seventeen-year-olds."

"Me too. And then suddenly we're talking separation outside a marriage counselor's office with the first snow of the season coming down on our heads." The weight of the world coming down on his, he thought, a jab in his chest.

"I wish we'd been more focused on the first snow, on Christmas, on how much we loved each other."

"You were, until you couldn't take it anymore," he admitted. "You tried—hard."

Snow flurries whipped around them and she looked up. "A sign! A second chance to appreciate what we *do* have."

"That's nice, Maddie, but it's not fair to the woman you were."

"She's not here right now, so it's all I've got," she said with a smile, sticking out her tongue to catch a snowflake.

He laughed, unable to help it. "I don't deserve you, Maddie. How you're able to be so good-humored about any of this is beyond me."

"I probably always was, right? I mean, I *am* me. I'm just not reacting to you based on any kind of history. But the me I am, that has to be the same, right?"

He hadn't really thought about that. But he supposed she was the same old Maddie. Believed in the silver lining. Saw the good. Tried to flip things. She was a nurturer. "Yeah. You're you. The you I fell in love with a long time ago. The you I loved the morning of the accident. The you I love now."

"So no one is separating. No one is getting divorced. We have nephews to take care of."

He was relieved to hear her say that, but again, she

wasn't the Maddie who was sick to death of his stall-ing and "irrational" refusal to take the next step. "What if the twins hadn't been left in our living room in the middle of the night?"

"We'd still have a marriage to save for when I get my memory back," she said, taking his hand. "That's the way I look at it. And anyway, there are too many variables for what-ifs."

He held on tight to her bright pink mittened hand, the flurries dancing around her beautiful face. "With your memory gone, everything is sunshine and roses between us. In the back of my mind, I know that's not fair to you."

"Well, I can't be in a long-term fight that I don't re-member, so I guess we'll just have to get along."

He smiled. "You will get your memory back, Mad-die."

"I wonder what that will be like. The old memories mixing with the new."

"Me too," he said, and they started walking back to-ward the parking lot, Maddie keeping her hand on his. He'd been wondering that a lot. How Maddie would feel about him.

"Know what else I wonder?" she asked as she got inside the car.

He got in and they buckled up. "What?"

"How Maddie-with-the-memories will feel when she finds out you're ready to start a family because of the bargain you made with the universe when she was lying unconscious in the hospital."

He stared at her. "She'll be happy. Having a baby is

the point. The whole point. It's everything that's standing between us."

"So she'll be happy that you're finally saying yes because she's not dead?" She shook her head. "Okay, it's really weird that I'm talking about myself in the third person, but I'm not the woman you've known since age five. That woman's not back yet. All I know for sure is that it's not how *that* Maddie will want to start a family, Sawyer."

He shook his head, confusion flashing in his green eyes. "What matters is that we'll start a family."

"You love your wife, Sawyer. That's not in question. That's never been in question. But trust me when I say the Maddie I'm coming to know will only want a baby with a man who wants a baby too."

He felt a frown pulling at his face. "The baby should be the point, not the why."

"The why is everything. You think you'll have a baby—the ten babies you promised—and suddenly become all excited about fatherhood? Something that terrifies you and sends you in a dark panic?"

Well, when she put it *that* way.

He got it.

"Let's go pick up the twins," he said, his head starting to pound.

Chapter Seven

A few hours later, Maddie was in the nursery, checking on the sleeping Shane and Max and thinking about the conversation she'd had with Sawyer at the prom site, when her sister popped into mind, Jenna telling her she was pregnant and—

Maddie froze. Jenna was six months along. That was quite obvious; her sister certainly hadn't needed to reveal the news of her pregnancy in the past few days. This recollection was just that—a memory! She could see Jenna's nervous smile. Hear the words *I'm pregnant* coming out of her mouth and feel her own combination of pure jealousy and pure joy for her sister.

There was only the snatch of memory. Those few words without context, and she had no sense of where they'd been during the conversation. But she was sure it was a memory.

She sucked in a deep breath. This was good. This meant her cognitive functions were on the way to returning to normal. She sure hoped she hadn't been as jealous with her sister as she'd felt in that memory; the feeling was unmistakable.

Stephen and I waited. Pregnant together. But—

She could hear those bits of words in Jenna's voice. But that was it.

Still, it was more of the memory.

A headache stirred, and Maddie realized she shouldn't push herself too hard to remember. She had to just let it all come in time. As a bit had just now.

Her twin sister had waited? Because of her? That made Maddie feel awful. She could just imagine how gutted she'd been by that realization, how it may have contributed to the strife between her and Sawyer.

Jenna had put off having her first baby out of love and loyalty to Maddie—because Sawyer wasn't ready. And clearly, the writing had been on the wall that Sawyer Wolfe might never be ready. Because Jenna had moved along. Rightfully so.

First a headache, now a stomachache. *Ugh.*

"Everything okay?"

Maddie turned to find Sawyer standing in the doorway. He'd been about make hot chocolate for them when she'd gone up to check on Shane and Max.

"I had a bit of a memory," she said, hearing the cool bite in her tone. "About my sister, telling me she was pregnant. And a moment later, I remembered just a few words of the conversation. I think my memory is coming back."

He clearly heard the frost in her voice too. He hesitated, then said, "That's great, Maddie."

"Is it?" she whispered. "I mean, of course it is. But look, I'm already mad at you." And none of the good humor and levity of earlier was anywhere in her now.

He shoved his hands into the pockets of his jeans. "Because Jenna and Stephen waited because of me and then felt bad about deciding they couldn't wait anymore. I know. I felt horrible about that. *You* felt horrible about that."

"I'll bet. And if I'm mad at you from just a piece of one memory, imagine how I'll feel when I have them all?"

He gave something of a nod. "Ignorance isn't really bliss. Maybe for a few days, yes. But it's not reality. I *want* you to have your memory back. That's the real you, Maddie. And the Maddie who knows everything is the Maddie I love. The Maddie I said I'd have ten kids for."

"You say that like it's a plus." Again.

"I say it because, to me, it tells me loud and clear how much I love you, that having you is more important than anything—including my feelings about having children."

"We had this conversation and got nowhere," she said.

Defeat crossed his face. "You know how many times those exact words came out of our mouths over the past year? A million."

"No doubt," she said. When Sawyer had told her they'd been in mediation with a marriage counselor, she hadn't thought much of it. Now she could barely imagine Sawyer talking about his marriage and the problems between them with a therapist. With anyone. They must have hit rock bottom—the sleeping separately, the stony silences. "I'll call Dr. Addison in the morning and let her know about the memory. I started getting a little bit of a headache, so I think it's my brain's way of telling me not to push it."

He nodded. "You'll be back to yourself in no time, Maddie. And that's what we want. Warts and all."

Except he looked a little nervous about that. As nervous as she felt. She liked the way things were, crazy as that sounded. She felt cherished by this man, by her family. She had an immediate purpose in caring for the newborn twins. She felt cocooned and happy. And as the memories came back, who knew how she'd feel? Angry? Sad? Worried? Unsettled about knowing she'd have her deepest wish fulfilled—to have a baby—only because Sawyer had bargained with the universe and was a man of his word?

Oh yeah, she had a definite feeling Maddie who remembered would not be okay with that.

Sawyer sat at the desk in his home office, Moose lying by his feet, gnawing on a rawhide bone. He'd come in here to check the database connected to the WCPD for the name Russtower, to find out why that surname on his Holiday Happymakers form rang a criminal bell. But he hadn't gotten further than going to the WCPD site. He kept thinking about Maddie and her memory returning.

One small memory had fought its way to the surface of Maddie's mind and the two of them were already in that off-kilter place. Maddie had turned in early, at barely eight thirty, and he wasn't sure if the memory had made her tired or their conversation. Probably both. But her going to bed while he was downstairs felt like old times. In a bad way.

He'd thought telling Maddie about the bargain he'd made when he'd been keeping a bedside vigil would solve the problem. She wanted kids; he'd have ten if only she wasn't taken from him. She'd survived the accident, and now he was making good on his word. But it wasn't enough for Maddie-who-couldn't-remember. According to her, at this point it was less about the agreeing to start a family and more about the wanting to. But wasn't it a compromise? Wasn't that what marriages were based on? Give and take. Finding ways to keep each other happy.

As if he had all the answers. He wasn't getting this right—that was about all he knew for sure.

He heard a cry through the baby monitor next door in the living room and took the stairs two at a time to make sure another shriek didn't wake up Maddie. In the nursery, he found Max waving his arms and scrunching up his face. Sawyer reached in and took him out, checking his diaper, which felt reasonably dry, and then holding the baby against him while he walked around the room, rubbing the tiny back.

A memory of his own popped into his mind. An image of Cole trying to make him a mug of hot tea. Sawyer had been sick with a bad cold and home alone when Cole's mother had uncharacteristically dropped him off at the Wolfe apartment, angry about something and not checking if their dad was home. Sawyer had been using scratchy toilet paper for tissues, his nose red and raw, and Cole had asked if he should go to the drugstore and get Sawyer tissues and medicine, but the store was too far for Cole to walk. Cole had taken it upon himself to make Sawyer tea, and at ten years old had done a semi-decent job, even if he'd put in way too much sugar. Apparently that was how his mother liked her tea.

"Your daddy has a good heart," Sawyer whispered to Max. "Same as I do, even if I don't want kids. No offense," he rushed to say. "If you're staying, I'll take good care of you. I already love you. So no worries, okay? I've got you covered." Saying all that exhausted him, and he sat in the glider chair, staring down at the alert little guy in his arms.

Max stared back.

"You're really quite beautiful," Sawyer whispered. "A perfect little being. You just happen to need every-thing. Love, nurturing, protection, sustenance, shelter." The blue eyes gazed up at him, full of curiosity. His chest felt tight, and he felt a lump in his throat. "How about a story?" He reached for a board book on the table beside the chair, but given his position and the way the baby was nestled, he couldn't quite reach it. "Made-up one by Uncle Sawyer, then."

Max still stared up at him, and Sawyer wondered what the baby was thinking. Could babies think? Be-yond feeling? He'd have to look that up. Or ask Reed Barelli or Theo Stark, the resident baby experts on the WCPD. Reed had toddler triplets and twin one-year-olds. Theo had quadruplet toddlers. Both men knew more about babies than your average bear.

"Okay, so once upon a time there were two brothers named Sawyer and Cole," he said, then hesitated. Had he meant to say that? Guess so, because it had come out of his mouth. "Where's *this* gonna go?" he asked Max, who was clearly getting so bored by the asides that he was now looking nowhere in particular. "Their dad used to tell Sawyer that Cole probably wasn't even his kid, and that anyone could have green eyes and dark hair," he said. "But Sawyer knew Cole was his brother, just *knew*. Even if they'd looked nothing alike, he'd still know, because that was how it was. You just knew some things."

What the hell was he saying? Was it okay that he was being so honest—out loud? He was aware that you were supposed to talk to babies to boost their brain power and language-processing skills. But it wasn't like Max was actually following what Sawyer was saying, so it seemed okay. He'd text Reed or Theo later and make sure.

"I guess there's some stuff I've always needed to get off my chest," he whispered, and Max looked at him and wrapped his little fist around Sawyer's pinky. Sawyer almost gasped. "I'm surprised you like me, but you seem to. I guess I'm doing all right by you and your brother, though." The baby held on, his grip surprisingly tight.

For a moment, Sawyer just stared at this magical little being, wondering if he might be dreaming this all up. He attempted to pinch his arm with his one free hand, and he felt it, so this must have actually been happening. *I'm talking to a newborn. My nephew. Telling him my life story. His father's life story.* Would wonders ever cease?

"Should I continue the story? Yeah? Okay. So the two

brothers, Sawyer and Cole. Cole wanted to be closer to Sawyer, and Cole tried hard to get through for a while, but Sawyer was a stupid preteen and not too interested. Then Sawyer wanted to be closer to Cole, but Cole had no interest. They were never on the same page at the same time. Things get complicated, and people and stupid stuff get in the way."

Such as his dad's girlfriends not wanting another kid around. Cole's mother screaming into the phone at their dad to the point that he'd blocked her calls. And his and Cole's own stupid bravado, not wanting the other to know how much it all hurt. And it had.

He took another long look at the baby in his arms. Seven pounds, five ounces at birth, according to the paperwork. Twenty-one inches long. Healthy. A tiny marvel. "And then you and *your* brother are born, and it looks like your dad named you guys after Maddie and me. Why, you want to know, since we're not exactly close? Since I was so mad at him for stealing from us that I almost pressed charges against him? But didn't. Maybe that answers the question. Maybe your dad knew I wouldn't, that I might hate him or something close to it since I don't think I could ever hate him, but that I would never truly turn my back on him. He knew he could leave you two here and that we'd take good care of you. And we will, you can count on that. No matter what, you can count on that."

Sawyer stared out the dark window at the slight illumination from the porch light. Flurries were coming down again. The baby in his arms let out a funny sigh, his slate-blue eyes drooping a bit. Max seemed to be fighting it, not wanting to miss anything.

Sawyer smiled. "You'll only be missing my story if you fall asleep, and I'm not sure you want to hear it. Your father and I circling each other for years, never landing."

His smile faded and he looked back out the window, wondering where his brother was, what was going through his mind.

He cradled Max a little tighter against him, his heart ready to burst.

Maddie stood outside the nursery, tears stinging as she accidentally on purpose eavesdropped. She felt only slightly guilty about it. About ten minutes ago, she'd heard one of the babies cry, and by the time she'd fully woken up to get out of bed, she'd heard Sawyer's footsteps coming up the stairs and thought she should let him attend to his nephew. Let him spend a little time alone with a baby.

When he started talking about personal stuff, she thought about tiptoeing back to her room, but she couldn't move. She'd been so touched by what Sawyer was saying. And she had a feeling he hadn't said a quarter as much in marriage counseling as he had in the ten minutes he'd been in the nursery.

"Now, Max," she heard Sawyer continue, "I'll only say this because Shane is fast asleep. You were named after your aunt Maddie, at least we think you were, and that's a pretty big name to live up to. Your aunt Maddie is the best thing that ever happened to me."

Maddie put her hand over her mouth to stifle her gasp. She knew Sawyer loved her, loved his wife, but the reverence in his voice was so touching that her knees almost buckled.

"When you find someone like Maddie," he went on, "you give her the world. Everything she wants. Because someone that special deserves everything. I was an idiot for saying no over and over, year after year, to starting a family. I was selfish. Maddie wanted a baby, and I should have said, 'Anything your heart desires.' Because she's that great. And I almost lost her. That's what I meant about agreeing to have ten kids if that's what Maddie wants. Maybe I didn't say it right."

His voice cracked then, and Maddie wrapped her arms around herself and hurriedly tiptoed back to her bedroom. She shouldn't have been listening. He thought she was asleep, not listening to his every word and emotion right outside the nursery.

Sorry, Sawyer, she sent telepathically and got back into bed.

A few moments later, she heard him coming down the hall toward their room. He went downstairs, then came right back up, so he must have just turned off the lights. As she heard him come into the room, she closed her eyes. He kissed the top of her head and then turned around, facing away. Should she leave him with his thoughts? All that heaviosity by himself? If she'd bared her soul to a sleepy baby and *he'd* overheard, she'd want him to hold her, not necessarily to say anything, just to hold her so she wouldn't feel so alone. Yes, as far as she could tell now, she and Sawyer were such different people. She knew that he tended to be a lone wolf, but even a lone wolf needed a pack. She was his pack.

She reached around until she felt his hand, and she held it. He gave it a gentle squeeze but didn't let go.

I love you too, she wanted to say. But she didn't doubt he knew that.

Oh, flip, she thought. *I am who I am, even though I have no memory of myself.* "Sawyer?"

"Yup?"

"I heard everything you said," she blurted out. "I was standing right outside the nursery. I didn't mean to eavesdrop, but then I couldn't stop listening."

He was silent for a moment. Then another. Then he turned around to face her in the dim lighting of the moon. "Who needs a therapist when there are newborns to talk to at all hours?"

She gave him a gentle smile. "I like what you said about me."

"All true," he said, reaching out to touch her face. "Every word."

"I understand a bit better about the ten babies. The bargain and what it meant to you to make it. I might not completely agree, but I understand more now."

"Good," he said. "Because I couldn't explain it well for some reason. Only to a droopy-eyed infant."

She squeezed his hand. "I've been so focused on my memory and the babies and us that I haven't really stopped to think about your relationship with Cole and how all this is affecting you. You really love him, don't you?"

"Of course I do. He's disappointed me a bunch of times, but he's the kid I wanted to protect for so many years that it's ingrained. I always felt so powerless when it came to Cole and my family." He narrowed his eyes as if he'd just realized that this moment. "I still do," he whispered. "He's been headed down the wrong path, and he's either gonna keep going or turn around. I want him to turn around."

"I hope he does."

"Me too."

"I'm going to finish up a little more paperwork," he said, slipping out of bed. "I'll be up in about an hour."

"Okay," she said. She didn't want him to go. But she knew he needed to be alone with his thoughts and the knowledge that she'd heard everything he'd said. She'd been hoping he'd wrap his arms around her and they'd just fall asleep, no need to talk more, but maybe the intimacy was a little too much for him.

One day at a time. Just like Dr. Addison had told her in the hospital when she'd come to. *Don't try to rush it*, the doctor had said. And that went for husbands too.

Chapter Eight

Maddie hadn't gotten much sleep. Sawyer hadn't come up to bed until well after midnight, and she'd been so tired she'd fallen right back to sleep. But before then, she'd tossed and turned, thinking about everything they'd talked about. What she'd overheard. And the memory she'd had of her and her sister talking about Jenna's pregnancy.

She figured it would be helpful to know if she was remembering accurately. In the middle of the night it had occurred to her that she might have imagined the whole thing based on what she'd been told. She doubted that but wanted to check anyway. Plus, maybe talking about the memory would open it up a little inside her head, allow her to remember more.

So after making sure that Sawyer was okay with

being on his own with the twins, Maddie texted Jenna to ask her to breakfast, adding that she remembered something and wanted to talk it over. Jenna had texted back an immediate Ooh! Dee's Diner at 8 sharp. Maddie had headed out through the front door just in time to hear one twin crying in the nursery.

"I could just go see—" she said, coming back inside and taking off her gloves.

"Nope." Sawyer gently turned her around. "I've got this. I need to learn how to take care of them the same as you do. We're an equal opportunity aunt and uncle."

And lucky for him, the crying stopped.

"Ah, see, your mom told me the other day not to rush in at first cry," he said, "but to wait a good ten seconds and they might soothe themselves back to sleep. So go before they both wake up and start bawling. Besides, you need to talk to Jenna. Oh—and you love the blueberry pancakes at Dee's. With bacon."

"Does anyone not love that?"

"I actually don't like blueberry pancakes. I'm an omelet guy. With the bacon and cheddar inside. And a big order of hash browns."

"Did we used to go there for breakfast a lot?"

He nodded. "Lunch too. You love their grilled cheese. With bacon."

"We'll have to go sometime," she said.

The crying started up again. He smiled and kissed her on the cheek. "See you later. Take your time. I'm only expected at the precinct part-time this week, so don't rush back on my account."

I'd rush back because I want to be with you. And the twins.

It was cold but not killer cold, so she put her gloves back on and walked the five minutes to Dee's, which was just a few doors down from MacLeod's Multiples Emporium. She found Jenna waiting at a booth in the back by the window.

Jenna started to slide out, then said, "Oh, who am I kidding?" and slid back in. "I wanted to give you a hug, but my days of getting up and down easily are over."

Maddie laughed. "Hug accepted in spirit from across the table."

"How are you feeling?" Jenna asked, handing Maddie a menu.

"Pretty good. My goose egg is almost gone, and with a little concealer, the scratch is barely noticeable. How are *you* feeling?"

"Not bad. I can't sleep on my stomach anymore or my right side, but Stephen got me this great body pillow, and it's helping me get comfortable."

"I can't wait to meet my new niece and nephew," Maddie said with a smile.

"I love that my twins will have instant cousins. Or cousins-ish."

Maddie laughed. "So let's order, and then I'll tell you about the memory I mentioned."

"I'm so glad to hear you remembered something!" Jenna said. "I hope you don't mind, but I let Mom and Dad know. They're so hopeful for what this means. That you're on the mend."

"I spoke to my doctor this morning, and she said it's a great sign." Dr. Addison had been elated to hear the news but did caution Maddie from trying to think too hard, to remember too much. Maddie was supposed to let the memories come naturally, the way the one had last night.

They spent the next couple of minutes figuring out what they wanted. Maddie wasn't in the mood for blueberry pancakes. But Sawyer's omelet sure sounded good. She ordered that, and Jenna went for what she was craving: French toast drizzled in maple syrup.

Once they had their decaf coffees, Maddie told Jenna about the memory, the snippet of conversation. "So does that sound right? Did I remember an actual conversation?"

Jenna's expression had turned a little…uneasy. "Yes. It was right after I found out I was pregnant. I told you the minute the plus sign appeared on the stick. There was no way I could keep the news from you, Maddie."

"I feel awful that you and Stephen felt like you had to wait until Sawyer came around to start a family. That's not right. Not in the slightest."

Jenna reached out a hand and squeezed Maddie's. "It wasn't really like that. We'd always talked about being pregnant with our first babies at the same time. A twin-palooza. And I wasn't really ready until I hit thirty. I admit that I did start to feel a little antsy the past couple of years. But how could I go ahead without you—especially when Sawyer wasn't budging on the subject?"

"Oh, Jenna. What a cruddy position to be in. I am so sorry."

"It's complicated, Maddie. But Stephen said enough was enough, and so I let you know I was tossing my birth controls in the trash."

"You did? How'd that conversation go?"

"I couldn't not tell you. I tell you everything, Mads. Same for you. We've always been very close."

Maddie felt tears well up and her throat go tight. She barely knew this person sitting across from her, her own twin sister, and she loved her so much at this moment it was as if she hadn't lost all memory of her. "Please tell me I was thrilled for you and excited and didn't burst into tears."

"You were honest. You told me you were very happy for me and hoped I'd get pregnant that night. And then you told me you were jealous as hell and wished your stubborn husband would magically change his mind. Want to know what else you said?"

Maddie grimaced. "Is it bad?"

Jenna laughed. "It's kind of funny. You said maybe he'd get conked on the head by a perp and suddenly want kids."

"Oh my God, I said that?"

"Yup."

"But instead it was me who got conked on the head. And forgot all about wanting a baby so badly I made my own sister feel bad about being pregnant."

"You never made me feel bad, Maddie. I felt bad because of the situation."

The waitress appeared with steaming plates that smelled and looked delicious.

Maddie cut a piece of her bacon and cheese omelet. "Ah, this is good. No wonder it's Sawyer's favorite here."

"I did notice you ordered his favorite. Interesting. Like you want to be closer to him."

Maddie raised an "oh, please" eyebrow. "By eating his favorite breakfast?"

"When you and I went to Cheyenne for a baby expo

for a few days, I ate a lot of Stephen's favorites for that very reason. I missed him."

"I'll bet I didn't order any of Sawyer's favorites," Maddie said.

"Oh, you sure did. You love that man. Tough situation and all."

Maddie pushed around her home fries, thinking of Sawyer at home with the twins. "He's taking care of Shane and Max on his own this morning. Talk about complicated." She thought about all she'd heard last night, and her heart ached for Sawyer.

"Right? Between caring for babies and the fact that they're his brother's… No word from Cole?"

Maddie took a sip of her coffee. "Nope. Sawyer's texted him every day to let him know the babies are fine. I wonder if that will keep him away or make him want to come back."

"What do you mean?"

"If the babies are fine, then Cole may feel they're in better hands and stay away. Or being reminded of his children, that they're fine and not with him, may make him feel unsettled and itchy for them. He could have signed away his parental rights at the hospital. He didn't."

"Do you think he'll come back?" Jenna asked, forking a big piece of French toast and swiping it in syrup.

"I really don't know. If I could remember him, maybe I'd have more of a clue."

"How's Sawyer doing with the babies? Does he hate taking care of them? He seemed fine with them the other day."

"He doesn't seem to hate it at all. I can tell it's weird

for him, to have them in the house. But some of that has to do with his brother, I think. All it's engendering for him. He's good at babysitting. He's so sweet with them."

"Maybe this is exactly what Sawyer needed. A chance to see firsthand what it's like to have babies in the house, to care for them."

"I was thinking that too. My only worry is that there's a brick wall in that chest of his."

"Blocked, huh?"

Maddie nodded. "It's been building since he was a little kid."

"Well, between you and those adorable twins, that wall just might be blasted through." Jenna finished her decaf and insisted on paying for breakfast. She had to get to MacLeod's since a new salesperson was starting today. The Christmas season apparently had the shop packed every day. Maddie was looking forward to getting back to work soon. But she'd be little help managing the store without any knowledge of the place.

After she walked Jenna to the shop and gave her sister a big hug, she headed home, thinking about what Jenna said. About how the wall could be blasted through.

Maddie thought it was a real possibility. Based on the Sawyer she knew now, she saw glimpses of someone struggling to change. Maybe that was more wishful thinking.

What really had her off balance was the realization that when she got her memory back, everything was going to be different.

In the hour Maddie had been gone, he'd had three calls from the MacLeods. Two from April, and one from

Ace. April was checking to make sure he didn't need any help; she'd be happy to come over. Ace had called to say there was no shame in asking for help and that he was all thumbs when he had newborn twins.

I don't have newborn twins. They're not mine, he'd wanted to say.

But were they? Was their father ever coming back?

Sawyer couldn't answer that. So he'd turned down the offers of assistance this morning and said he was doing just fine on his own.

He hadn't been doing all that great, actually. Shane had screamed bloody murder for fifteen minutes before Sawyer had been able to calm him down. Turned out he'd needed to burp and had diaper rash. A good pat on the tiny back and some ointment and cornstarch, and Fussy-pants was good as new. Then his brother started in. No need to burp. No diaper rash. Not wet. Sawyer had finally struck gold when he held cradled Max in his arms and rocked him from side to side while singing a Beatles song. Max clearly liked the Beatles.

Last night, when he'd held Max in the nursery, taking care of a baby seemed so easy. *Sure*, he'd said to Maddie. *Go, no rush, take your time. I've got this.* Ha. He'd been so smug.

I heard everything you said...

He liked how honest she was. Maddie-with-her-memory would have probably come clean, too, but the past few weeks had been so strained that maybe she wouldn't have. It all might have seemed too much.

But once again, he was in his house, a baby in his arms, unsure if this was forever or not. If this was the new normal. Good thing he'd attended one of Reed

Barelli's classes on caring for multiples ages-zero-to-three-months at the community center, because he'd learned—

Wait a minute. Yes. That was it. That was where he'd heard the name Russtower—the surname on the second Holiday Happymakers envelope. A couple months ago, Reed, one of his detectives, had called in a break-in at the community center where he taught his multiples class early in the morning before the traditional workday to make it easier for fathers to attend, since they could bring their babies. Overnight, someone had stolen the props the teachers used for the various baby classes—bottles, burp cloths, diapers, even the curved pad for baby changing. Sawyer had been a couple of doors down and had come over to help with the investigation. He'd asked Maddie if MacLeod's could let the center borrow some items until they were replaced, and of course the MacLeods donated a heap of new baby paraphernalia—all within fifteen minutes so that Reed's class could go on as planned.

Sawyer had stuck around the class, going over the list of registrants, which had included a petty thief named Vince Russtower. Russtower had shown up for class with a one-month-old baby and was struggling; Reed had spent a lot of time with him, repositioning his baby son in his arms, helping him angle the bottle. Reed was sure a few items in Russtower's bag looked like a few of the stolen items, including a blue-and-white baby blanket, but he couldn't be sure, and the case had gone cold.

Sawyer put Shane back in his carrier beside his brother, picked both up and went inside his office. He settled them on the floor, both babies looking at the pastel spinning mobiles attached to the carriers. They seemed happy enough for now.

He reached into the basket on his desk for the envelope from Holiday Happymakers. The one from Jake Russtower. He typed Russtower into the database. Bingo. Vince Russtower had been arrested twice this year for petty theft. He'd stolen a package of steak from the grocery store, and the manager and owner had decided to drop the charges. Then he'd stolen a chocolate heart from the Valentine's Day aisle at the drugstore, and the manager had also declined to follow through with charges, so the case had been dropped. Sawyer had no doubt Vince had been the one to steal the baby items from the community center; it was the guy's MO. A sad MO, at that. A package of steak. A chocolate heart for his wife. Baby bottles and a baby blanket. It was theft all the same, but the kind of theft that made Sawyer think about a person's bank account and desperation.

Sawyer pulled Jake's request out of the envelope and read it again.

> I'm not getting anything for Christmas because my father only cares about his stupid new wife and always-crying new baby. I could use a bike so I don't have to ask him for rides anywhere. Whatever. This is just fake Santa. I'm sure I won't be getting anything.
> —Jake Russtower.

Something in the kid's tone had gotten under his skin, reminded him of himself at that age, he guessed. Sawyer usually volunteered at the community center once a month and knew they had a kids' group there that met after school and on weekends. And now there was a new baby at home—and the new wife. He'd stop by the center tomorrow and see if Jake hung out there. There was strong outreach in the schools to make sure kids who seemed troubled or distracted were aware of the center, so there was a good chance Jake did go there. He'd check on him, make sure the kid was okay.

He heard a key in the front door, and he took the carriers over to say hi to Maddie.

"The bits of conversation I recalled with Jenna really happened," she said, taking off her gloves and hat and putting them in a basket by the door. "My memory is definitely on its way back."

That had never been in any doubt, but he was glad she'd gotten that confirmed for herself.

"I had your favorite at Dee's. Mmm, those home fries were amazing."

He smiled. "I wouldn't mind having some right now."

"Then it's a good thing I got you a bacon and cheese omelet with a side of home fries to go," she said, holding up a white bag.

He was starving and grateful. "That was very thoughtful. Thank you."

"Kiddos give you any trouble?"

"Well, they did scream their heads off for longer than usual, but I managed to get it under control. Look at them now—so curious and alert. You'd never know they'd almost punctured my eardrums a half hour ago."

Maddie laughed. "Well, how about I take these guys into the living room for story time while you eat your breakfast."

He was about to tell her he'd prefer they all joined him in the kitchen, but she'd already picked up the carriers and headed to the living room. Which was interesting because, for a while there, he'd been counting the minutes until she got back so he wasn't solely responsible for the twins. Sometimes they were easy; sometimes they were a heck of a lot of work, and four hands were better than two with two tiny rabble-rousers.

As he went into the kitchen with his takeout and sat down to eat alone, he had to admit he missed Maddie and the babies. He poured himself a mug of coffee, struck by the notion that needing help with them and missing them were two very different things.

Talk about getting under his skin. The newborns had burrowed under the way Maddie had when he was too young to know to keep her out. He'd actually once told the marriage counselor exactly that when she'd asked how he'd managed to get himself married when he'd vowed never to have a family. A wife was family, the counselor had pointed out. Unnecessarily, he might have added.

Because Maddie has always been family, he'd explained. He'd loved her from his earliest memories. The counselor had tried to open up his mind to what that meant, but Sawyer hadn't been having it. Then she'd tried to connect it to his push-pull with his brother, whom he'd also loved from his earliest memories, even if the relationship had rarely been easy, and he hadn't been having that either. Twice, he'd walked out of the room. Maddie had been pissed as hell both times.

So what does it all mean? he asked himself the way the counselor might have. The problem was that Sawyer didn't want to know, didn't want to think about it. That was Maddie's true issue with him. The refusal to dig deep, to "do the work," as she called it. At the time he'd thought, *Lord, save me from Dr. Phil.* But now all he could think was that if he'd "done the work," if he'd dug, Maddie would never have gotten into that car accident. She wouldn't have lost her memory.

He sighed and sat down, his appetite gone, but he opened up the container and ate, since Maddie had been nice enough to bring it home for him. He popped a home fry into his mouth, listening to Maddie tell the boys a story about a striped purple rabbit named Bunnito with long, floppy green ears. Her story was so ridiculous that he found himself smiling, everything forgotten but her melodic voice and the silly antics of Bunnito. He ate his breakfast, enjoying every bite now, finishing up so that he could join them in the living room.

He *wanted* to be with them. His wife and the newborns. He did miss them. Well, they *were* his abandoned nephews—of course they'd gotten under his skin. Of course he wanted to take care of them along with the wife he loved.

He wondered if that bit of introspection counted as "doing the work." He could hear Maddie in his mind saying: *Are you freaking kidding me? You're rationalizing. Abandoned—please. You love them. Just admit it—to yourself if not to me. Same as you'd love your own babies if you'd let yourself have them.*

Wow, did he know his wife well. Himself, not so much.

Sawyer had to go into the PD for several hours that afternoon to guide his rookie through a difficult case, and good old-fashioned police work had taken his mind off home. The precinct, the protocol, his staff—all of it so familiar that he'd relaxed the moment he'd arrived, unaware of how tight his shoulders had been until the muscles actually unbunched and knots came loose.

That he was better as a cop than he'd ever be as a father was not news.

"You're like the dad I never had," Justin Mobley said then, making Sawyer do a double take. Sawyer had been explaining a tricky issue regarding search and seizure when Mobley clapped him on the shoulder and made the pronouncement.

"What?" Sawyer managed on a cough.

"I was raised by a single mom who was great, but whenever I'm mentored by an older gentleman, I feel like I have a dad in those moments."

"Mobley, I appreciate the sentiment, but I'm *thirty-two*. Not fifty-two."

Mobley tilted his head and examined Sawyer's face. "Are you? You seem older. You don't *look* older. You just *seem* older."

"That's because I'm the chief, Mobley. Wise beyond my years. Experience will do that to you."

"What's Barelli's excuse?" Officer Benitez joked, tossing a wad of paper at Reed.

"Hilarious," Reed said, tossing it back.

Ah, Sawyer could stay here all day. And night. Sometimes he had, when the thought of going home had seemed…like an argument waiting for him. That had been wrong. He realized that now. He needed to be more like Maddie—to face things head-on, to blurt out the truth, to ask the questions. Not take cover like a perp. Hide. Hope not to get caught.

That wasn't who he wanted to be.

"Hey, Reed," he said, turning in his swivel chair toward the detective. "Do newborns think? Or do they just feel? It's not like they can follow a conversation."

Reed raised an eyebrow. "They know if they want something, even if they're not sure what that is—food, a dry diaper, a cuddle, a burp, a bottle."

"But if I'm, say, thinking out loud to Max and Shane, I won't be scarring them for life?"

Reed smiled. "Not until they're at least eighteen months."

"Good to know, thanks, Barelli." He swiveled back around, wondering if eighteen months from now the twins would still be in the nursery, Cole nowhere to be found.

He had to get his mind off his brother. He wrapped up the day at the police station, then stopped by the community center to see if Jake Russtower was part of the after-school group. He realized he had no idea what the kid looked like. *Good police work, there, Wolfe.* But then he saw Vince Russtower come through the door, wave at a kid, who jogged over, and Vince put the kid's backpack over his own shoulder and they walked out, chatting. Huh. Not the family scene Sawyer had envisioned based on Jake's anger-tinged Holiday Happymakers form, but looks could be deceiving. So could requests for bikes.

He couldn't get a handle on it, so he figured he'd do a little sussing out of the situation. He told the director he was thinking about volunteering with the kids' group for an hour after work, and the guy was thrilled and said they could use all the support they could get. Sawyer said he'd start tomorrow.

By the time he got home, it was past six. Maddie had let Moose out in the yard, but he owed the German shepherd a walk. Moose didn't love the cold in his older age, but he did like walking on powdery snow, and last night had left a fine couple of inches on the ground. Forty-five minutes later, they returned home. Maddie was in the kitchen, saying she was heating up the last of the lasagna, if that sounded good to him. Lasagna always sounded good.

Dinner was weird. *He* was being weird. And Maddie was reacting to it, tiptoeing around it at first and then doing what she did best: facing the issue head-on.

"You're being weird. Why? Because of last night?"

He almost choked on his bite of gooey, delicious lasagna. "Last night?"

"You know I overheard you say some pretty personal things, Sawyer. Things I didn't know because I don't remember anything."

He put his fork down. "Yeah, I guess. I've been doing a lot of thinking these past several days. Or trying to. I get to one conclusion and then, whammo, something else seems right. Or wrong."

"Yeah, I know what you mean. Well, let's just eat, then, and keep it light. We could both use a break from the big stuff."

He covered her hand with his in appreciation, then they ate and talked about funny things the twins and Moose had done that day. Sawyer insisted on kitchen cleanup and Maddie said she'd luxuriate in a long, hot bubble bath. Which had him thinking about her in the bath. Naked. Some nights over the past year, the heightened emotions between them still led to sex. Other nights, those emotions led to the couch. Alone. He missed sex with Maddie. So much he couldn't take it sometimes.

Once the babies were fed and changed and played with and read to and finally asleep in the nursery, they decided to watch a goofy buddy comedy. Sawyer made popcorn, and they sat on the sofa and watched the movie, Sawyer laughing so hard at a few points that Moose came over to check on him. The comedy had been what they'd both needed. Their moods lightened, they headed upstairs, mimicking lines from the movie, and Maddie was fast asleep by the time he came out of the bathroom. He stood there watching her sleep for a minute, then got in beside her, facing her back, and dared put his arm around her. She stirred but didn't wake up, and he relaxed.

The next thing he knew, Moose was letting out a low growl. Alerting. The room was dark now, moonlight spilling in through the curtains. Sawyer had clearly fallen asleep. He bolted up, grabbing his service weapon from the bedside table.

Then he heard the noise. Someone was on the porch. At—he looked at his phone—2:18 a.m. Gun in hand, he got out of bed and hurried downstairs, moving to the side of the door and ready to announce himself as a police officer to whoever was out there.

He heard a movement. Then footsteps—leaving. At something of a distance, a car peeling out.

Holy hell, he knew *that* sound.

Cole Wolfe's beater car.

Sawyer threw open the door just in time to see the red taillights whip around Main Street. A small shopping bag, with a logo from a baby emporium in nearby Brewer, was on the porch. He took it inside, putting the gun away in the safe in the hallway closet.

So what is this? he wondered, opening the bag. Inside were two baby-sized cowboy hats, yellow straw with brown leather trim.

You and me will be cowboys one day, galloping after outlaws! Cole used to say all the time when he was young, seven, eight, nine, pretending both hands were rifles and making *ka-pow* noises while running in circles. Sawyer had always told him that cowboys rode after cattle, not outlaws; that was what cops did, and Sawyer was planning on becoming a cop. Cole said not him, he was going to be an outlaw-chasing cowboy.

Except now Cole likely felt like the outlaw.

Sawyer looked at the tiny cowboy hats, his heart heavier than he could handle. He shoved the hats back into the bag and went inside, goose bumps on his arms from the cold. And the surprise. The shock.

"What's that?"

Sawyer glanced up to find Maddie coming down the stairs, tying the sash of her robe around her waist.

"Cole." He explained about the noise. And handed her the bag.

She looked inside and gasped. "Do you know what I just heard in my head? Cole saying he was going to be a cowboy one day. Is that a memory?"

Sawyer nodded. "I was just thinking about that myself. I'm just not sure what he's trying to say with this."

She pulled out a mini cowboy hat and turned it in her hand, then glanced at the logo on the shopping bag. "Well, he avoided MacLeod's and went to Brewer to find these."

"He avoided us too. He could have rung the bell and come in. Instead, he chose to drop these off at two in the morning, then rush away. And not just some random gifts. Cowboy hats. That means something to him."

"Is he saying goodbye?" Maddie asked, and he saw tears shining in her eyes.

Hell, now he felt tears stinging his own eyes. He shrugged, unable to speak.

Maddie put down the bag and came over and wrapped her arms around him, and he held her tight, burying his face against the side of her neck.

Don't let go, don't let go, he silently whispered. To her.

She didn't let go. They stood there in the dark hallway, Moose now lying down by the door, his chin on his paw.

"Sawyer," she whispered, "are you worried he's not coming back or that he is coming back?"

"I don't know. That's what has me so off-kilter. Of course I want him to come back. He's their father. You think I want them to grow up knowing their father left him with us and took off, but oh, he did buy you guys little cowboy hats." He let out a harsh laugh and shook his head. "My father was a crappy dad, but he was there. He didn't take off on me." He froze for a second as a sensation like sludge or quicksand flung itself around inside his chest.

My father never took off on me. He was always there.

Not literally every day or night. But never gone for more than a couple of days. I don't recall ever worrying he'd just disappear on me.

Because I knew he loved me deep down? That he did care?

Maybe.

He thought about Vince Russtower picking up Jake from the community center. Carrying his son's backpack as they left. There might have been some tension in the home, but what he saw—and granted, it was only once—it said a lot. Russtower was *there*. That Holiday Happymakers form had lodged in his stomach with the force of a heavyweight's fist, and it eased up some now that he thought about it in this new light.

"Let's go to bed, Sawyer." She took his hand and led him upstairs, and he silently followed her.

She got into bed and so did he, and when she turned onto her side to face him, he did the same. She reached out a hand to touch his face and then kissed him. Gently at first and then not so gently. And then she took off his T-shirt and ran her hands all over his chest, kissing his neck and his pecs, the cool, soft hands everywhere.

By the time she got to his sweats, he was beyond thought and only *felt*.

Chapter Nine

A crying baby woke Maddie at four forty-five, which was almost a reasonable time to wake up. Sawyer was fast asleep beside her, and for a moment she just watched him sleep, marveling at how good-looking he was. The straight, strong profile. The thick dark hair. The five-o'clock shadow.

She wondered if she was a control taker in bed all the time or if she'd simply done what the moment had called for last night. And what an amazing moment it was. Sawyer had responded instantly, and the experience had been so emotional, so intimate, that Maddie had almost cried a time or two until ecstasy had won out. Sex with Sawyer was everything she'd imagined it would be the past several days. She was glad they hadn't waited for her memory to return. She had two tiny memories back now, which meant more would be coming each day. She'd wanted to be with Sawyer as the woman she was now, the one who was getting this rare chance to fall in love with him all over again.

Falling in love without all the history, though, she reminded herself. That wasn't falling in love. That was fantasy.

She frowned, wishing she could stop thinking for just a minute, but *without* a history to call from, her mind wasn't exactly full. She had a lot of space to fill.

The cry came harder, so Maddie reluctantly got out of bed and headed into the nursery.

"What's the matter, little guy?" she said, picking up Shane, whose shrieks instantly stopped as she cradled him against her and rubbed his back. "Let's get you changed."

Once both infants had fresh diapers and pajamas, she brought them downstairs in their carriers to feed them in the living room. She had Shane in her arms when Sawyer came down the stairs, all rumpled and sexy. She blushed thinking about last night, which made her feel silly until she realized it was the first time for her.

"I'll admit I was hoping to wake up next to you and have a repeat of last night," he said.

She grinned. "Me too. But duty called."

"I know I said I didn't think we should be intimate until your memory came back, but to be honest, I've felt so close to you, Maddie. Everything about last night felt so natural."

"I know exactly what you mean," she said, her heart doing somersaults.

A shrill cry came from Max. Translation: *Uh, what about my bottle?*

She smiled. "I made a bottle for Max, too—it's in the kitchen."

He went to get it, then came back, scooped up Max and sat down beside her. She watched him coo at the baby, angling the bottle just so. What was also natural? The way Sawyer was with his nephews.

When Max finished his bottle, Sawyer held him upright and patted his back, then repositioned him in his arms to let him stare out the big sliding glass doors to the deck, the snow still slightly clinging to the trees. "I'm going to look for Cole today," he said.

Maddie stared at him. "Really?"

"I have to talk to him. I imagine him out there, tortured and going crazy, unable to live with himself for dropping off his babies and leaving, but unable to keep them either. That he came to the house to leave gifts tells me he cares—a lot."

Maddie nodded. "It's clear that he cares. I want to come with you to look for him. I'll ask my parents to watch the twins for the day. It's probably better that you talk to him without Shane and Max right there. That might be too much for Cole."

"Agreed. And I'm glad you want to come, Maddie. You might not remember Cole yet, but he always liked you, and having you there will likely relax him. If we even find him."

"Have any ideas about where to look?"

"A few," Sawyer said. "I did a search online a couple days ago actually, but he moved out of the most recent address last Monday—just a few days before he showed up here with the twins."

"Was he evicted? That might help explain him feeling so desperate—alone with newborns, nowhere to live?"

"I spoke to his landlord. Cole hadn't paid rent in two months. He supposedly worked at the rodeo on the outskirts of town, mucking out stalls, that kind of thing, but he was let go. I haven't been able to find a trace of him since, not with a place of employment or home address."

"I hope we find him."

"Me too," Sawyer said, eyeing the bag with the baby cowboy hats on the coffee table.

After two cups of coffee each and eggs and toast, Maddie called her mom, who was excited about babysitting the twins for the day. They were the new store mascots. Within an hour, Maddie and Sawyer had dropped them off, stopped back at the house to take Moose on a walk and were ready to start the search.

"So where to?" Maddie asked as she buckled up. "Think he's still in town?"

"I'm not sure. I didn't even know where he lived. Isn't that crazy?"

"It happens. Families pull apart, relatives get estranged. It's not crazy, just sad that it happens."

"I wish all families could be like yours," he said. "That was the only thing I was ever really envious of as a kid. That my family—if you could call it that—wasn't like yours."

"Of course your family was a family. Even just you and your dad and Cole from afar. That's a family."

"I guess," he said. He started the car and didn't respond, and Maddie got the feeling he needed a break from the conversation. Seemed to her, though, that it was exactly the conversation Sawyer needed to have.

Family meant something sad and scary to him, something he couldn't count on. Seven years of marriage hadn't changed that for him. A solid, happy marriage—until this past year when her biological clock began ticking away.

She was pretty sure that was what had her—the Maddie she'd been—so upset. That their beautiful union hadn't changed his notion of what a family was.

Sawyer pulled onto the freeway, taking the exit for Brewer, which was a half hour from Wedlock Creek. "I'm going to start with the hospital where the twins were born. He might have left his new address when he filled out forms. *If* he filled out forms. Worth a try. He has to be living *somewhere*."

"Sawyer. I just realized something. We were likely in that hospital when Gigi gave birth. When Cole was there, pacing in front of the nursery—you were sitting by my bedside in the hospital, waiting for me to wake up from the car accident. I didn't even think of that till just now."

He almost stopped short. "You're right. That's nuts."

Brewer County Hospital was in a stately old brick building. Maddie recalled leaving there the other day, although she had no memories about being there before.

They followed signs for Labor and Delivery, which was on the fourth floor.

"We were both born here," Sawyer said in the elevator. Four months, three days apart. "I'm the older one."

She smiled. "Was Cole born here too?"

"Yup. And now his children."

And maybe our children. If we have any. She was very sure they would. And not because Sawyer had made a bargain with God or the universe or whomever he'd been praying to when he'd kept his bedside vigil. They'd have a baby because he wanted to have a baby just as she did. Not for any other reason.

She, Maddie-without-her-memory, believed that. Just as Maddie-with-her-memory believed all these years.

Why she had faith in that, in him, she really wasn't sure. The past seven years should have been telling her otherwise. But the man she'd come to know, this Sawyer since she'd come to in this very hospital, the Sawyer who was caring for his newborn nephews, was not the man he'd been before the accident, before the twins arrived. *That* she believed.

As they approached the nurses' station, a nurse came over and gave Maddie a hug. "Hi! Great to see you. Volunteering this week?"

Maddie had volunteered here? She glanced at Sawyer, but he gave her something of a shrug. "I'm recuperating from a car accident so not totally on the mend yet, but give me a couple weeks and I'm sure I'll be back."

"Good, because you're wonderful with the NICU babies." The woman smiled and headed toward a patient's room.

"I volunteered here?" she whispered to Sawyer. "In the neonatal intensive care unit? You didn't mention that."

"I had no idea. But I'm not surprised. You love babies and you love to help. I do wonder why you didn't tell me." He looked toward the nursery window, where they could just see bassinets and a nurse holding a baby. "Actually, I guess I know why you didn't tell me."

Maddie did too. Volunteering in the NICU must

have felt like something she didn't want to share with
Sawyer—the man who was denying her a baby. She
could see herself not thinking that Sawyer would get it
or understand—including how bittersweet it must have
been for her to be around the newborns.

He dropped down onto a bench, and Maddie sat beside him. "I really pushed you away, didn't I? I know
you have no recollection of any of this. But I do. And
I'm sorry." He shook his head, seeming pretty disappointed in himself.

She put a hand on his shoulder. "Hey. Let's go ask
about Cole," she said gently.

He nodded, and they stood and headed back over to
the nurses' station. "I'm Sawyer Wolfe, the chief of police in Wedlock Creek," he said, holding up his identifi-
cation. "This isn't a police matter, but I just wanted you
to know I'm a solid citizen. My brother, Cole Wolfe, is
the father of male twins born here last Thursday. We're
caring for the twins for a while, but I'm wondering if
Cole left behind an address."

The nurse eyed him and his ID again, then clicked
some keys on her computer. "I couldn't give you his
information even if it were here, but I can tell you it's
not. Only the mother's address appears on the intake
forms. I don't see any information for the father, Cole
Wolfe. But I do see him listed as the father and that he
left with the discharged babies last Thursday."

So much for that. Sawyer thanked her, and they left
the hospital, both of them quiet on the way to the car.
They buckled up in silence, and Maddie's gaze was
drawn out the window while Sawyer drove back toward
Wedlock Creek. He must have had a destination in mind.

A glance out the window told her they were on the outskirts of town, heading toward the river, where she and Sawyer used to sneak into one of the abandoned, dilapidated old cabins after school and talk about life—

She went stock-still. Another memory. This one was so vivid, so full. Her and Sawyer as teenagers, sharing the pistachio nuts she was addicted to in those days, sitting cross-legged beside each other, telling secrets. She'd share her crushes, trying to make hers on Sawyer go away. He never talked about his crushes, and she'd thought then that he was private about that stuff. She'd never had a clue he was as in love with her as she'd been with him. She waited for more of the memory, more knowledge of them, to come, but it all faded away.

"Maddie? What's wrong? You truly look like you saw ghost."

"Another memory," she said. "I remember the cabin. Going there to share our secrets."

He gave her a warm smile. "I'm glad you're remembering, Maddie. And so far all good times."

"That's a lucky break," she said. "For both of us. We kept the biggest secret of all from each other at that cabin, though. That we loved each other."

"Yup. I was bursting with it, but I couldn't tell you."

"What's the connection to Cole at the cabins?"

"He's the one who told me about the place. For three or four years when we were kids, the cabins were a mess. The owner abandoned the property, but there were legalities involved, so the bank couldn't foreclose for a long time. I stopped going once the place was sold, but Cole told me he used to sneak there all the time in the off-season. He found comfort in the place and loved the river. I could see him renting a cabin for cheap in the weeks before Christmas when business is slow."

As Sawyer turned onto a dirt road, Maddie saw the sign for RiverView Cabins, 1.5 miles. A clearing came into view, and Maddie could see identical log structures a good distance apart, facing the river. He pulled up in front of the first cabin with a big Rental Office sign on it.

A woman wearing a hunter-green sweatshirt with a RiverView Cabins logo and a name pin that read Joanna Miles stood and smiled at them. "Welcome! Interested in renting a cabin?"

"Actually, we're hoping if you can tell us if Cole Wolfe is staying here. I'm his brother, Chief Sawyer Wolfe of the Wedlock Creek PD."

"I thought you looked familiar," Joanna said. "He was here, the past two nights, actually, but he checked out bright and early, just before eight a.m."

Maddie glanced at the clock on the wall. It was barely eight thirty. They'd just missed him. "Did he, by any chance, mention where he was headed?"

"Only thing he said was that he was starting his new job this morning, and it came with room and board. Nice guy—he left a ten-dollar tip for the housekeeper when most folks leave only a couple bucks."

They thanked the woman and headed back to the car. Once they were inside, Sawyer turned to her, his eyes flashing. "I know where he is. Well, not exactly where. But I have a good idea where to look. One place where you can work for room and board and a small salary is a ranch. Those little cowboy hats meant more than I realized last night. He must have gotten himself a job as a ranch hand. No wonder the guy who skipped out on two months' rent is suddenly leaving tips for the housekeeper—he feels flush right now because he has a job and a place to live."

"That makes total sense," she said. "But there have to be hundreds of ranches in Wedlock Creek and environs. What's the plan to find him? Call and ask if there's a Cole Wolfe there?"

"To start," he said, reaching for his phone.

A half hour later and still in the lot of the RiverView Cabins, they'd learned he wasn't employed at the Triple C or the Dowling Ranch, two of the biggest operations in Wedlock Creek. Sawyer called another large ranch, Great Bear Ranch, forty minutes away—no Cole Wolfe there.

"Maybe he's working a small ranch or farm, one of two or three hands," Sawyer said. "That actually sounds more his speed and more on the down low."

But before Sawyer could even make a list of small ranches, Sergeant Theo Stark called requesting backup with strategy for a string of burglaries, and since Sawyer had been scarce around the department the past several days, he wanted to go in again.

"I'll make a list of possibilities," he said. "And we can check out some ranches tomorrow. If your parents or sister don't mind watching the twins again."

"I'm sure they won't. When we were leaving, I heard my mom say that Jenna was going to be so jealous that they got to babysit the twins."

"Thank God for your family," he said.

Maddie hoped he took his own statement to heart. Sawyer Wolfe might think the MacLeods were outliers in the family dependability department, but all he had to do was look at himself in how he was stepping up with the twins—and looking for his brother now.

She wouldn't point that out just yet. He might just realize it himself.

Sawyer spent a few hours at work, strategizing on the burglary case with Theo Stark and dealing with yet another complaint against Annie Potterowski's food-swiping beagle. It was close to five, so he decided to head over to the community center and see if Jake Russtower was there.

He was.

After a short orientation with the director on volunteering with the kids and introductions to the group and other volunteers, Sawyer headed out into the big main room. There was a section for basketball, a homework-studying station with cubbies and chairs, a lounge area with shelving units stacked with books, games and puzzles, where some kids were stretched out and talking, and a "track" around the perimeter, which no one was making use of at the moment. Sawyer glanced around for Jake. Short for his age and skinny, with auburn hair and dark brown eyes, he was easy to spot. He was sitting by himself on the bleachers, not particularly watching anything. He looked kind of miserable.

Sawyer grabbed a basketball and went to sit next to him. "Hey, I'm Sawyer, one of the new volunteers here. Want a play a game of one-on-one?"

Jake looked over at Sawyer for a moment, his expression bored. "What's the point? I never make a basket."

"Maybe you just need to perfect your shot," Sawyer said.

The kid all but rolled his eyes.

"Come on. I'll go first," Sawyer said, giving the ball a bounce on the bleacher below. "No one misses more shots than I do."

"Well, you just met me."

Sawyer laughed, and the boy actually smiled. Score! Without even shooting.

Jake trailed him to the hoop, and Sawyer bounced the ball a few times, eyeing the basket, hoping he wouldn't make it in on some fluke—he truly stunk. He shot and missed. Sawyer chased after the ball and bounced it to Jake, who aimed and missed.

"Try standing dead center of the hoop and fling it up with a little more gusto," Sawyer said. "And believe that you're gonna make the shot. That's key. *Believe.*"

"You could try that too," Jake clapped back.

Sawyer smiled. "Oh, I will."

Jake repositioned himself, and if Sawyer wasn't mistaken, he closed his eyes for a second to talk himself into scoring the basket. He threw—and it went in! *Thank you, universe.* "Yeah!" Jake shouted.

"Awesome!" Sawyer said. He got the ball and bounced it back to Jake, who threw again and got it in again.

"This is nuts. I never make a basket. Now I made two?"

Sawyer nodded. "You believed you could. I'm telling you, works almost every time."

"Guess it must."

"Have a hoop at home?" Sawyer asked, hoping Jake would open up a little.

"Are you kidding? That would be too loud 'for the baby.'" He scrunched up his face in disgust. "The baby, the baby. I'm so sick of what I can't do because of 'the baby,'" he added in a singsong voice.

"New baby brother or sister?" Sawyer asked.

"Brother. *Half* brother. My dad remarried. And before you ask, let's just get it out of the way because I don't want to talk about it. My mom is dead. She died three years ago in a car accident. Okay?"

"We have a lot in common. My mom died when I was young too. And my dad also had a baby when I was a kid. I was five when my half brother was born."

Jake stared at Sawyer, his mouth slightly hanging open. "Really?"

"Yup," Sawyer said, bouncing the ball and aiming— and missing.

Jake ran down the ball, which meant Sawyer had him on his side. "Try again," he said, bouncing the ball to Sawyer.

Sawyer shot. And missed.

Jake's brown eyes lit up with glee. "Wow, you weren't kidding. I'm kind of amazed you taught me the secrets to getting it in when you can't do it yourself."

"The rules of making the shot apply to most things in life. Center yourself. Believe. Go for it."

Jake shrugged.

"You and your stepmom close?" Sawyer asked, shooting again. And missing.

"I can't stand her even if she's nice most of the time. She's always telling me what to do. So what if I want to eat a bag of Cheetos for dinner? Who cares? And then I argue back why I should be able to, and my dad gets mad. Oh yeah, living in my house is a lot of fun."

His parents seemed to care about him. Jake was

clearly lonely, feeling left out of his family because of the new baby, and didn't seem to have friends. Other kids were in pairs or groups, but Jake had been sitting alone.

"Jake!" a voice called.

"Oh, great," Jake muttered. "It's my dad. We'll have, like, five seconds together on the way to the car where my stepmother and the infant from hell are. And then I'll be yelled at if I breathe too loud."

Sawyer smiled. "Get along with your dad?"

"Sometimes. But all he cares about is stupid dumb Amy and stupid dumb Dylan the brat."

Vince Russtower began walking over, then seemed to recognize Sawyer out of uniform and stopped dead in his tracks. He looked nervous as he approached. "Jake in trouble?"

"Why would I be in trouble?" Jake asked, frowning. "Why do you always think I'm doing something wrong?"

"Because you're standing with the chief of police," Vince told his son. "That's why."

Jake's mouth fully dropped open. "You're a cop? The top cop?"

"I am. Sawyer Wolfe." He extended his hand, and Jake at first didn't seem to know what to do with it, then reached out to shake it. Sawyer turned to Vince. "Vince Russtower, right?"

He caught the slight rise of the man's eyebrow. "Yeah." He had the feeling from Russtower's expression that he didn't want his son to know that his father had had dealings with the police before.

"Nice to meet you," Sawyer said.

Vince's shoulders relaxed. "You too." He turned to Jake. "Ready? Where's your backpack?"

Jake jogged over to the bleachers to get it.

"Nice kid," Sawyer said. "I just started volunteering with the kids."

Vince nodded, and Jake joined them again. Vince took the backpack on his own shoulder and said, "Well, Amy and Dylan are waiting, so let's get going, Jake."

"Thanks for practicing with me," Jake said to Sawyer.

"I'll be here every other weekday from five to six p.m.," Sawyer said. "Catch you next time."

They walked away, and when they reached the door, Jake turned back to look at Sawyer. Sawyer held up a hand and so did Jake, then they were gone.

He let out a breath. That kid reminded him a lot of himself.

Another boy was now sitting by himself on the floor, so Sawyer went over to him and asked if he wanted to shoot. The kid jumped up and said "Sure!" with a big smile.

And put one on Sawyer's face too. Coming here had been a good idea, and he wished he'd done it long ago.

If he hadn't made Maddie feel she couldn't tell him about her own volunteer work with babies, he might have been inspired to offer himself to the community center kids' group years ago. He might have wanted to give back in that way, too, but he'd been so rough with her dream, her fondest wish, that she didn't even want to share with him that she was working with babies at the hospital.

He wished he could change so much about the past. But at least he could work on the future.

And the now.

Chapter Ten

While Max still napped, Maddie held Shane in her arms in his soft green pajamas and showed him the Christmas tree by the window in the living room. "Ooh, look at all the sparkly white lights and the pretty silver star. And these are our ornaments. See the *M* for *Max* and *S* for *Shane*? Okay, fine, it's really *M* for *Maddie* and *S* for *Sawyer*, but now we get to share initials! And there's the Woodstock ornament your uncle Sawyer gave me for Christmas when we were thirteen—"

She remembered that! She waited a beat for more to come, but nothing did. She simply had remembered when she'd gotten the ornament and from whom, but there was no accompanying images in her mind. Too bad. She wanted to remember her childhood, which sounded pretty wonderful.

She was moving around the tree to show Shane

the hand-painted little globe ornament with a photo of Moose on it when she recalled something else. She saw herself sitting in a cozy room on a tan velvet sofa, Sawyer sitting beside her, leaning back while she sat forward. A middle-aged woman she didn't recognize sitting in an ornate chair across from them.

You do have a choice, Maddie, the woman said. *You could accept that Sawyer doesn't want children, something he has always stated and has not wavered on. Or you could not accept it and hope, as you have been, that he will eventually change his mind.*

She must be remembering an appointment with the marriage counselor. Beyond the woman were two arched windows, snow falling gently. It was only December, so this appointment had to be recent.

But both are impossible choices, Maddie said. *I can't bear the former and the latter is killing me.*

The counselor looked at her, then at Sawyer, then back at Maddie. *Another choice is leaving the marriage.*

Maddie gasped. *I don't want to leave Sawyer. I don't want a divorce. I love him!*

Then maybe you need to accept that you're not going to have children, the counselor said.

But why does he get to make that choice for me? If he can make that choice for me, I should be able to make the choice for him—that we're having a baby, end of story.

He's the one saying no, that's why.

So I'm supposed to stay in this marriage and what? Resent him? Watch my sister live my dream?

Sawyer, the counselor said. *Would you like to say something?*

Maddie looked at him. He was tense, his expression grim.

I don't want to lose my wife. But I don't want children.

Broken record! Maddie heard herself scream.

Sawyer dropped his head in his hands.

Maybe you should think about a separation, the counselor said. *To see what it feels like.*

What the hell? Sawyer snapped, bolting up and storming out.

The memory faded to nothing. She wasn't in the counselor's office anymore. She didn't see herself rushing after Sawyer. But he'd told her what happened afterward.

That was clearly right before the accident. She closed her eyes, cradling Shane gently in her arms, grateful to have this precious little being to hold. The memory she'd just had felt so strange out of context, on its own, without the before. She did have the after, though.

She'd felt her frustration on that sofa. Her disappointment and anger. Her helplessness in her own life. She'd hated how she'd felt in that office, like she was jumping out of her skin, unable to direct her own life, unable to make her dream come true because of the roadblock called her husband.

Whom she loved. Maddie knew in that snatch of memory that she'd never considered leaving Sawyer, that she didn't want a baby *more* than she wanted to be with her husband. *Therein lies the damned rub*, she thought, shaking her head.

"I'm glad I don't remember it all," she whispered to Shane. "Sounds really hard. No—it sounds impossible."

Shane gazed up at her with his slate-blue eyes, bow lip

quirking like Billy Idol's, which made her smile. The lip quirked again, and she full-out laughed. *What would we do without you and your brother?* she thought, kissing his sweet little head. The two Wolfe boys had brought joy and purpose and direction to her life since the accident—and hopefully showed Sawyer another side of himself.

She heard Sawyer's key in the lock. She came into the entryway with Shane as Sawyer was taking off his down jacket, his impressive body never failing to catch her off guard and take her attention and breath for a moment.

"Everything okay today?" he asked, closing the closet door. "C'mere you little rascal," he added, reaching for Shane.

He adored the babies. If he didn't, he would give the baby a brief smile and walk right past them into a kitchen for a drink or the living room to relax. But he wanted to hold Shane. Yup, the twins had gotten to him.

Because they're not his? Not here to stay?

Something occurred to her just then. If Cole never came back for his children, and the babies *were* here to stay, was Sawyer able to handle that notion better because they weren't his children? They were his nephews. She frowned, turning that over in her mind.

"Everything was great." She handed the baby to him, her jumble of thoughts obliterated by the loving way Sawyer gently cradled Shane in his arms, careful of his neck, giving him a kiss on his fuzzy head. "Although I did have a vivid memory of that final counseling session. It ended with you storming out. I remembered a very long stretch of the conversation, including the counselor suggesting the separation. Then I was back to being blank."

He looked at her, his smile fading. "That session was brutal. On both of us."

"But necessary, I think," she said. "The counselor laid out the facts."

"And we didn't know what to do with them."

Exactly, Maddie thought. "Which is why the counselor went nuclear with the separation suggestion. To get us to take another step forward instead of remaining stagnant. But I guess time ended up standing still in a different way once I lost my memory."

He nodded and seemed uncomfortable. "Max sleeping?"

Yup. Uncomfortable. Enough to change the subject. "Yeah. He'll probably wake up any minute. Then we can feed them."

"Why don't you go relax," he said. "I've got the twins. You had them alone all day."

I don't want to relax. I want to spend time with you. But Sawyer seemed to want some space between them when they'd had space from each other the past several hours.

Then again, she wouldn't mind a hot soothing bath where she could think. And not about the fact that Sawyer seemed to be trying to avoid her right now.

The doorbell rang, and Maddie turned around on the stairwell and went to answer it, since Sawyer had the baby in his arms.

She opened the door and gasped.

Cole Wolfe stood on the porch.

At Maddie's gasp, Sawyer turned around to find his brother standing in the doorway, his gaze on the baby in Sawyer's arms.

His instinct was to turn and protect Shane, but he fought it. "Cole."

"Can I come in?" Cole asked, digging his hands in his pockets. He wore the black leather jacket he'd had for years, and a thin plaid scarf around his neck. His jeans were worn at the knees and scuffed with dirt. Sawyer would put money on his brother having a job as a ranch hand.

"Of course," Maddie said, gesturing for him to enter and closing the door behind him.

All Sawyer had wanted yesterday and over the past several days was for Cole to call or text, or for him and Maddie to find the guy. Suddenly he was here, in the flesh, and Sawyer wanted him gone.

Why?

Because you don't trust him—and not with the twins, who are reliant on dependable people to have their every need met. That's why. Made sense to Sawyer. So then why had he been trying to find Cole? To talk to him about what? To find out what? There was no way he could imagine Cole walking out of this house with Shane and Max; the guy was completely unprepared to care for them.

Yet you couldn't stop staring at your phone, waiting for him to call or text—and return, he knew.

What exactly did you want to happen? Do *you want to happen?*

Here he was again, off-kilter, unsure of what was going on inside him.

"Which one is that?" Cole asked, and if Sawyer wasn't mistaken, his brother's eyes brimmed with tears. Cole dropped his head and closed his eyes. "I don't even know which baby that is. And he's my son. I'm so pathetic."

"Cole, honey," Maddie said, "if we didn't always put Shane in green and Max in blue, we wouldn't be able to tell them apart so easily either. Old trick my experienced-with-twins mom taught us."

"Shane has slightly sharper features than Max," Sawyer said.

Cole nodded and craned his neck to peer at the baby. *Oh, hell.* Sawyer walked closer to his brother. "He's a good baby. A little more demanding than Max, but a champion napper and snuggler. He likes being held."

"When I held them in the hospital, one at a time," Cole said, "I kept being afraid I'd drop them on their heads."

Sawyer nodded. "I get it. They do seem pretty fragile, but they're hardy little guys." He eyed Cole, suspicion clawing at him. Why was he here? To see the twins? Make sure they were all right, because he cared? To take them?

About that last one: over Sawyer's dead body.

Thing was, as the chief of police, no one knew better than Sawyer that Cole had every right to walk right out of here with the twins.

"Would you like to hold him?" Maddie asked Cole.

"I don't know," Cole said, shifting from foot to foot. "I don't think so. I'm just—I don't know what I am."

"Well, why don't you start by explaining why you're here," Sawyer said.

Maddie shot him a look. *Dial it down.*

Cole stared at Shane in Sawyer's arms. "Because they're here." Again, tears shone in his eyes, and Sawyer felt his guard both go down and back up. Up and down, down and up. Just like his relationship with Cole over the years.

"What do you want to happen, Cole?" Sawyer asked. "Be honest."

Cole dropped down onto the bottom step, scrubbing a hand over his face. "I don't know." He let out a breath, his eyes closed. "I have children. I made children. That baby you're holding is my son. Ever since I left them here, I kept saying that in my head—my sons, my sons. And those words never sounded remotely possible."

Maddie reached out a hand to Cole's shoulder. "I can understand how you feel."

"Who abandons their own kids?" Cole asked, his voice broken. "The worst of the worst. My dad, for example."

Sawyer felt that one straight to the heart. *Cripes, this is complicated.* On so many levels.

"You didn't abandon them," Maddie said, sitting beside him on the step. "You brought them here, where you knew they'd be well taken care of until you got your head together."

Cole looked at her. "You were always way too nice, Maddie."

That was true. And not just where Cole was concerned.

"I got a job as a ranch hand at the Johannsen place. Just me and another guy and the family. I muck out stalls and they're teaching me other stuff, like grooming. Stuff I'm very interested in. When I got that job, I felt like I had a chance, you know? Like I'm where I belong and can make a place."

Sawyer might have congratulated himself for being right about the job on a ranch if he wasn't so stuck on what Cole had just said. "A place for...?" Sawyer prompted. Maddie shot him another look. *Give him some breathing room.* But Sawyer needed to know what his brother was planning. "You can't mean raising infants in a bunkhouse? Who's going to watch them while you're mucking out stalls?"

"I just mean..." Cole's shoulders slumped. "I don't know what I mean."

"Well, how about this, Cole?" Maddie said, sliding a glance at Sawyer before focusing on his brother. "Why don't you visit with Shane and Max right now for a bit, and then you'll head back to the ranch and you'll come here tomorrow for dinner. How does that sound for an immediate plan?"

Cole perked up some. "Sounds good. What time tomorrow?"

"Let's say seven. Good, Sawyer?"

Sawyer nodded. He supposed. A brief visit tonight, dinner tomorrow. Small steps. That actually sounded just right. A cry came from the living room, and they all turned toward the sound.

"There's our cue to go get Max," Sawyer said.

Cole and Maddie stood and they all headed into the living room. Maddie went to the bassinet across from the Christmas tree and scooped out Max, who was flailing his skinny little arm.

"Is he sick?" Cole asked, worry in his eyes.

"Probably just hungry," Sawyer said. "Or wet. Or lonely. Or wants to be vertical."

"Or all the above," Maddie said. "Sawyer, why don't you let Cole hold Shane while you change Max. I'll go make their bottles."

Cole bit his lip and took a step back. "Sure I won't drop him?"

·"Just don't," Sawyer said. "Keep your attention on him and you'll do fine."

Maddie sent him a smile as she went into the kitchen.

"How do I take him?" Cole asked, stepping closer.

"Put your arms out like mine are," Sawyer said. "Make sure you support his neck with your hand or forearm. That's vital until their neck muscles get stronger. You said you held the babies in the hospital, right?"

"Yeah. For almost an hour. I tried to keep it even between them, but I think I held one longer."

Sawyer smiled. "We've been trying to keep things even too. Doesn't always work out, though. Max likes his sleep, so Shane gets more stories and back rubs while I pace the nursery."

Cole eyed him. "You been doing a lot of pacing?"

"What do you think?" Sawyer asked, but this tone was a lot gentler that it had been earlier. He transferred Shane into Cole's arms, and Cole sucked in a breath and then sat down very slowly and carefully on the sofa. His gaze never left his son's face.

Sawyer wasn't sure what he'd expected this evening to be like, but it wasn't this. He'd never seen Cole so… vulnerable. Then again, yes, he had. Many times when Cole was a kid. And even sometimes as an adult—when Sawyer was patient enough to truly pay attention to the underpinnings of what was going on with Cole.

Complicated.

Max let out another wail, and Sawyer grabbed the basket of baby stuff from under the coffee table and set it down beside the carrier on the rug, then took out Max. He laid him down on the mat and changed him, aware that Cole's eyes were on him.

"You make it look so easy," Cole said. "I'm sure I'd put the diaper on upside down or backward."

"I think I did, too, the first time," Sawyer admitted with a smile. He really had, actually. With Max changed, Sawyer scooped him up and sat down on the other side of the sofa.

"I'm sorry for just leaving the way I did," Cole said, staring straight ahead now.

"You talking to me or them?"

Cole glanced at Sawyer. "All of you. I am sorry. I was just freaking out. In a panic."

"I know." But what now? *You're visiting tonight, coming for dinner tomorrow and then what?* Sawyer usually didn't need to have his life mapped out for him, but he didn't like the not knowing, the vague quality about all this. There was a big maybe about a very vital issue. And Sawyer didn't like it.

Maddie came into the living room with two bottles. She sat between the brothers, handing a bottle to Sawyer and then turning toward Cole with the other one. "Here you go. You just hold it angled up, and he'll drink."

Cole took the bottle and hesitated. "What if he drinks too much at once and it pours down his throat too fast?"

"Can't happen," Maddie assured him. "Max controls the flow by sucking on the nipple. Give it a try."

Cole brought the bottle to Max's lips and angled it as Maddie had said.

"A little higher," Maddie said, tipping up the bottle a bit.

"He's drinking!" Cole exclaimed, looking at Maddie and Sawyer for a moment, then back down at his son.

Sawyer sighed inwardly. Something told him Cole

was just too much of a kid, despite being twenty-seven, to be anyone's dad, let alone twin newborns. He might be wrong. And yeah, baby care was brand-new to Cole, and who was to say he wouldn't pick it up and be a master at it. Times two. Could happen.

Except Sawyer didn't see it. Because he was a cynical, world-weary cop? Or because he was realistic and called it as he saw it?

Or because he didn't want it to be true?

"You're doing it just right, Cole," Maddie said with a warm smile.

"How do I know when he's done?" Cole asked. "Will he drink the whole bottle?"

"When he's done or if he needs to burp," Maddie explained, "he'll stop suckling or pause longer between suckles. You'll be able to see it."

"I think he's done," Cole said, removing the bottle and putting it onto the coffee table. Max gazed up at Cole, seemingly satisfied with the world.

"Now slip a hand under his neck and bring him up to your chest, holding him vertically, and gently pat his back so he can burp."

It took Cole a good few minutes to do that, but he managed it, widening his eyes at Maddie and Sawyer. He gave Max a few pats, and the baby let out a giant burp. Cole burst out laughing. "I did it!" Cole said. "Champion burper," he added. He looked at Maddie. "Now what do I do?"

"You can hold him upright or along your arm, a little of both, so he's not always one way. He'll let you know when he wants to be shifted. Babies love to squirm or cry with displeasure."

Cole smiled. "He seems pretty happy right now."

"Sure does," Maddie agreed.

Cole glanced around the living room, his gaze stopping on the double bassinets, the baby swings, the baskets of baby paraphernalia. "There are some events at the rodeo I'm thinking of signing up for," he said. "It would bring in a good amount of money."

"Except you don't want to do anything that would risk injury," Sawyer pointed out. "Because of the physical nature of your job, you need to be in top shape. And you've got these two to consider."

"Bronc-riding prize is a good one," Cole said. "And I'm pretty good."

"Takes one time to get injured," Sawyer said, his tone sharp.

"Says the guy who risks his life every day for a living," Cole said.

Sawyer brought Shane up to his chest and patted his back. "I'm not anyone's dad."

"You're someone's husband," Cole said, glaring at Sawyer.

A red hot pool of anger swirled in Sawyer's belly. He got up and walked with Shane over to the window, looking out. *Whatever you want to snap back at him, don't. Just shut up. He'll be gone in five minutes anyway.*

And back tomorrow for dinner.

Sawyer let out a breath.

"Cole, can I ask you something personal?" Maddie said.

What was this? He turned around, his gaze on his wife.

"I guess," Cole said.

"I'm curious about the names you chose for your sons. Max and Shane. Did you name them after anyone?"

Sawyer walked back over to the sofa and sat down. He was curious about that too. Maybe it was just a co-incidence that the initials matched his and Maddie's.

"Yeah, I did," Cole said. "The two best people I know." He didn't look at Sawyer or Maddie and seemed kind of embarrassed, which told Cole the initials were no coincidence. "I named them for you and Sawyer," he added, looking over at his brother for a moment.

All the ire that had been in Sawyer's stomach a few moments ago dissipated, and something like compassion took its place. Something else, too, that Sawyer couldn't quite put his finger on. He'd never get a handle on his brother—who he was, really, what he was made of.

No one is all this or all that, he reminded himself. But it made it easier to box up Cole if he were.

"That's beautiful," Maddie said. "Thank you. We're very touched, both of us."

"You touched, Sawyer?" Cole asked with a bit of the glare still in his expression.

"I thought it was nice," Sawyer said. "Meaningful. That's a better word."

Cole looked at him and nodded. "Good." He stood up slowly. "Well, I should get back. I said I'd do some extra chores in the barn at night for overtime." He gestured toward Maddie as though he wanted to hand the baby over, and Maddie took Max. Cole headed toward the door as if he couldn't wait to get the hell out of there.

It was a lot, he'd give his brother that. Sawyer well remembered the first night the twins had been here, and he hadn't exactly known what he was doing himself.

Maddie and Sawyer, babies in their arms, followed Cole to the door. He opened the closet and got his jacket and scarf, shrugging them on.

"See you tomorrow at seven for dinner," Cole said, then took another look at Shane and Max and hurried out.

A moment later, Sawyer could hear the annoying muffler roaring to life. "At least he'll be able to get that fixed now," he said.

"Sawyer Wolfe, is that all you have to say?" Maddie snapped, one eyebrow up high.

"There's a whole history between me and Cole you don't remember," he said, then regretted it instantly. That wasn't exactly her fault. *Cripes.*

"What matters is right now and the future," she pointed out.

He nodded slowly. She was right—to a point. The whole picture mattered, just as it mattered within their marriage.

He just had no idea what was going to happen. And it was killing him.

Chapter Eleven

They'd both made themselves scarce the rest of the evening, Sawyer in his study, stewing—or at least that was what Maddie thought he was doing—and Maddie organizing her closet, then cleaning the bathroom, then remaking the already made bed.

Finally, she'd exhausted herself. She'd already been wiped out mentally from Cole's unexpected visit, and now she was physically zonked too. She slipped into bed, pulled up the comforter under her neck and stared at the ceiling, wondering if Sawyer would be coming up anytime soon. Probably more like after 1:00 a.m. when he figured she'd be asleep.

Forget that noise, she thought, a little adrenaline racing as she got out of bed, stuffed her feet into her furry slippers and went downstairs to find her husband.

She stopped dead in her tracks in the doorway of his

study. He was sitting in his desk chair, back toward the door, flipping through photos on his computer—of himself and Cole. One filled the screen of him and Cole as young adults, making cannonballs into a lake or river.

Sawyer could be hardheaded, but the man wasn't hard-hearted. His brother meant a lot to him, problems and all, and instead of focusing on the bad times, he was clearly immersing himself in the good ones.

"Hey," she said softly, the ire completely out of her.

He turned around. "Hi. I was just going back in time, I guess."

"You two had some really nice moments, from the looks of the photos."

"Few and far between," he said. "But yeah. Like this one."

She walked over and put her hands on the chair back, peering at the photo. "Did I take that?"

"Yup. The water was cold so you didn't want to go in, but Cole and I dared each other. And of course we couldn't just dive in."

She smiled. "You okay?"

He gave something of a shrug, and she leaned closer to massage his shoulders. "Oh, that feels good. Thank you."

She kept massaging, loving the feel of his strong shoulders and thinking about the other night when they'd been so drawn to each other that they'd made love against their better judgment.

"I can't see Cole as a full-time father," he said, letting his head drop back. "Can you?"

"With time, maybe. He does seem very far from that. But necessity is the mother of invention, isn't that what they say?"

"For some people. For others, people like Cole, necessity means taking off to avoid responsibility."

She felt a knot in his left shoulder and kneaded a bit on that spot. "But he does seem to be trying, at least. He put care into finding this job, something he's passionate about, too, and one that comes with room and board. He's working, trying to build something for himself—and very likely, the twins."

"That build is going to be a while, though. He's not taking the twins for a long time, Maddie. In fact, I'd say years. Maybe never."

She stopped massaging and turned his chair around to face her. "And how do you feel about that?"

"I'd rather those boys I've come to care very deeply about are with people who will raise them with everything they need."

"And what's that?" she asked.

"Devotion. Commitment. Responsibility. We're a solid family in a solid home."

Except a week ago we were on the verge of separating.

She glanced at the photo, then back at Sawyer. "I think he wants to turn his life around and become a dad. That's the sense I got. But you're right that I don't have the full picture. I don't remember how he's behaved in the past. What you said about stealing from us? Taking my grandmother's bracelet? That's pretty bad." She could only imagine how that had hurt Sawyer, what it had cost him to harden himself the way he had after— Cole had finally crossed a line for Sawyer.

He nodded. "It's possible that having children, being

a father got to him. But wanting to change and changing are very different things."

"Let's go up to bed," she said, reaching out her hand. "I was exhausted before I came down, and now I might fall asleep on the floor in here right now."

She was so glad she had come down after him instead of wondering and worrying by herself in bed or pulling the covers over her head. Now they'd talked and she felt better and was sure he did too.

He smiled and stood and wrapped her in a hug. He smelled delicious. She could stay like this all night—and would, if he'd carry her and she could sleep in his arms.

Upstairs, she got back into bed, and when he emerged from the bathroom in a T-shirt and sweats, he looked so incredibly sexy.

"Think I was too hard on him?" he asked.

"I don't know. A little. Or maybe not. Maybe he needs someone being tough on him. Someone he knows cares. You heard what he said. We're the best people he knows." She smiled, recalling the reverence in Cole's voice as he'd said it.

Sawyer got into bed beside her, his gaze on the ceiling, hands behind his head. "He says stuff like that, and for half a second, it wipes away all the bad. I forget the theft, the lies. And then he turns around and ruins it five minutes later."

"He did okay tonight. I thought he was sincere."

He turned onto his side, propping his head on his elbow. "Seemed so. I don't know. I can't see him taking the twins anytime soon."

"You sound kind of glad about that," she said, facing him. "Are you?"

"They belong with us, Maddie. He's not remotely prepared to care for them. Not now or the immediate future."

"People *can* change."

"I didn't," he blurted out and then froze for a second as he seemed to realize he wasn't doing himself any favors.

He hadn't changed his position in seven years of marriage. He didn't want children. But he seemed comfortable with the idea of permanently keeping the twins.

Why?

She stared at him, feeling her eyes narrowing to slits as a thought occurred to her.

"You're comfortable keeping the twins because they're your nephews," she said. "Yes. That's it, isn't it? They're not your children. There'll always be that line there. So you're able to deal. Oh, and I get to be the 'mom' I've always wanted to be."

He tensed, moving onto his back and staring at the ceiling again, his hands folded over his chest.

She sat up. "Do I have that right?"

She knew she did.

"It's complicated, Maddie. I don't have all the answers right now. And everything is very new."

"Now you sound like Cole. Not okay for him but okay for you?"

He grabbed his pillow and walked out of the room.

Maddie turned onto her side and stared at her Woodstock alarm clock.

She wondered how many nights they'd slept in separate rooms. Those memories hadn't come back yet. But now she had a fresh one.

If you have to be stubborn at your own expense, that's bad enough, Sawyer remembered April MacLeod saying a time or two over the years. *But being stubborn at others' expense and taking them down with you? No good.*

He'd heard his mother-in-law's raspy voice in his head as he lay on the sofa in the living room, the throw barely big enough to cover up to his chest, Moose on the floor beside him. It had gotten him off the couch and back up the stairs not ten minutes after stomping down. Maddie didn't deserve this kind of treatment, him stalking off with his pillow because she was being too honest for him.

When he'd gotten into bed next to her and spooned against her, wondering if she'd shift away from him, he'd been relieved when she'd taken his hand and held it tightly.

"We love each other and we'll figure it all out," he'd whispered, then mentally kicked himself for saying something he's said at least twenty times the past year. Even if Maddie couldn't remember any of those times, she also deserved better than platitudes, but right then he'd been unable to come up with answers to her earlier questions.

Was she right? He was okay with raising the twins—and he *was* okay with that—because they *weren't* his children? He'd wanted to say, *If I'm raising them, they're mine. Just like they're yours*, but he knew what Maddie had meant, even if he couldn't articulate the difference. Did the word *nephews* make it possible for Sawyer to create an emotional distance between the twins and himself?

The morning didn't bring clarity either. Maddie was out of the room when he woke up, the bright sun barely blocked by the curtains. He listened for the sound of her voice downstairs, talking to the twins as he always did, but there was silence.

He got out of bed and went downstairs and looked around. No Maddie. No twins. He headed into the kitchen, where he was sure he'd find a note leaning in front of the coffee maker—he drank a lot of coffee these days—and there it was.

Took the twins out early for breakfast with my parents and then to hang out at MacLeod's for a little while. Might do some Christmas shopping after. I'll text you. PS. I let Moose out and fed him. —M

Moose now stared at him forlornly, missing her too. Sawyer had been hoping they'd spend the day together. To try to make up for yesterday, for the way they'd argued and his immature stomp off downstairs, though he had rectified that, and she'd welcomed him back with one squeeze of her hand. Maybe he should let her have a little space from him, since that was what she seemed to want this morning. They could meet up for Christmas shopping, since he wanted to buy for the family he'd "adopted" for Christmas, getting everything on their list and a whole lot more, plus start looking around at bicycles for Jake. Tonight, before the dinner with Cole, he'd volunteer at the community center and surreptitiously find out what kind of bike he wanted and what color.

He poured himself a cup of the coffee Maddie had

thoughtfully made, the silence in the house bugging him. It was too quiet. He used to like the quiet, grateful that Moose wasn't much of a barker unless he was alerting. But since two tiny humans had come into his life, his and Maddie's lives, their cries and shrieks had come to sound like music to him. He liked caring for them, figuring out their needs and meeting them. There was something satisfying about it.

Because of what Maddie had theorized—and it was just that, a theory—about being able to handle the thought of taking on the twins permanently because he had the buffer of uncle?

Maybe.

He didn't really want to think about that, so he took the stairs two at a time, showered, dressed in his uniform and drove to the PD. He conquered the mound of paperwork in his inbox, went out on a call with his rookie, Mobley, and strategized on a difficult case with sergeant Theo Stark.

He glanced at Theo's desk, the attached four photo frames containing pictures of his quadruplet toddlers, Tyler, Henry, Ethan and Olivia. Last Christmas, Theo had shocked everyone by the fact that he wasn't dead, after all. Supposedly killed in an explosion on the job, he'd faked his death to protect his wife, who'd been threatened by the mobster he'd been after. Theo had had no idea his wife had been pregnant with quads— and when he finally came back, they were barely a year old. The man Sawyer had known then had lived and breathed his job, taking the most dangerous cases, but he'd given all that up to devote himself more fully to his family. Sawyer hadn't been the chief back then;

he'd been promoted when the former chief had retired soon after, so he didn't know all the personal details. But Theo had gone from a guy he'd call a real lone wolf to a family man. And Sawyer wanted to know how. He and Theo were around the same age, and he'd always sensed a kindred spirit in the guy.

"Did you always want a big family, Stark?" Sawyer asked, his gaze on the photos.

Theo laughed. "I didn't want a family at all. But one was waiting for me when I finally came home. I had no idea how great it is."

"Kids?"

"The whole thing. A family. My wife—Allie. The quads. Sunday dinner with her family. Toddler classes. Nap time. Bath time. Story time. Colds and skinned knees. Sibling rivalry. I love it all. End of the day, I can't wait to get home to all that."

Sawyer raised an eyebrow. "What changed for you?"

"I guess I was hanging on to some baggage like a lot of people do. The quads forced my hand in letting go. My wife helped too." He smiled. "I was an idiot for a long time. I'm glad I'm not anymore."

Huh. He glanced at the photos again. He recalled hearing that the quads had been named for Theo—each one taking an initial. Tyler, Henry, Ethan, Olivia. That had choked up quite a few of them when they'd first learned Allie Stark was expecting quads and was going to name them after the "fallen" officer. He thought about Cole filling out the birth certificate application and deciding to name the babies after him and Maddie. He knew that meant a lot, but now that he really thought about it, he got kind of choked up himself.

"Things going okay with watching your brother's newborns?" Theo asked. "I'm full of tips if you need any."

"Thanks. I have to say, things are going better than I thought. You just do what needs to be done, and sometimes it's that easy."

Theo nodded. "Exactly. And plus, those little sneaks steal your heart without you even realizing it. One day, you just realize you're completely controlled by your devotion to people who weigh less than thirty pounds."

Sawyer laughed. "Or in my case, less than fifteen pounds combined."

"Happens that fast," Theo said with a smile. His phone rang, so Sawyer headed back to his desk.

His own phone pinged with a text. Jenna invited Maddie and the twins over, so she was skipping shopping today and would see him at home later.

He frowned. He wanted to be with her right now. Wanted to see the twins, hold them.

She pinged back a second later.

Oh, you know what I was thinking? Wouldn't it be nice if you talked to Cole about volunteering at the community center with you? You could spend some time with him, and he could spend some time around kids. Win-win.

Except that Sawyer and Cole couldn't seem to be in each other's company for more than ten minutes without biting each other's heads off. And Cole—volunteering? He couldn't see it.

He glanced at the time. Four thirty. He needed to be

at the community center at five for his shift. He thought about Jake Russtower, and how Sawyer had told him they had a lot in common. He also thought about Jake asking him one day if he and his own half brother were close, and Sawyer having to say no, that they barely spoke, let alone got along.

Maybe if he and Cole volunteered together, it would say something to Jake, show him something. And maybe he and Cole would have something else in common besides a rocky history.

Score a zillion for Maddie.

He pulled out his phone and texted Cole with the info.

Interested? he added.

I guess, Cole texted back. Predictably. He always guessed.

Jeez, lighten up on him, will ya? he heard Maddie say inside his head.

Which made him smile. What he would do without Maddie he really didn't know. Didn't want to know.

Okay, I can be there by 5:15, Cole wrote back.

See you then, Sawyer texted and put his phone back into his pocket.

So they'd volunteer together, then Cole would come home with him for dinner. That was a long stretch of time. Without Maddie to run interference.

Chapter Twelve

"Want to shoot some hoops?" Sawyer asked as he walked over to where Jake sat on the bleachers—alone again. The boy wore a gray hoodie and dark jeans, his mop of reddish-brown hair falling into his eyes.

"No." Jake stared straight ahead.

Sawyer sat down beside him. "Something on your mind?"

Jake shrugged. Sawyer knew that classic move well. It said, *Yes, but talking about it is hard for me.*

"I'm not great at basketball, but I've been told I'm a good listener." He kept his gaze straight ahead instead of crowding the boy by looking at him.

Jake frowned and crossed his arms over his chest. "My dad said we'd go ice fishing—just the two of us. He promised that we would the first weekend of Christmas break. And now we're not going."

"He tell you why?"

"Because of 'the baby,'" he said in a singsong voice. "The baby, everything's about 'the baby.' Of course Amy doesn't want to take care of the brat by herself, so now my dad said we can't go."

Jake looked equal parts angry and hurt.

"I understand why you're upset," Sawyer said. "Yeah, having a new baby kind of takes over for a little while. I know because I'm watching my brother's newborns for a bit. My life is definitely not my own."

Jake chewed his bottom lip and glanced at him. "Well, I'm sure if you wanted to take your kid ice fishing like you promised, your wife wouldn't make you cancel on him."

"I don't have any kids of my own, actually."

"So forget it," Jake said, rolling his eyes. "You don't even know what I'm talking about."

"What *are* we talking about?" a voice asked.

Sawyer turned around to find Cole standing there, dressed in jeans and his leather jacket. He nodded at Cole.

"Jake, this is my brother, Cole. I was telling you about him the other day. He's five years younger than I am."

"We have the same father, different mothers," Cole said. "Except Sawyer's the only one who got the father."

Sawyer was about to shoot Cole a look that said, *Really? That's appropriate?* But Cole's comment did serve the purpose of perking Jake right up.

"Why?" Jake asked, sitting up straighter and tilting his head.

Cole put a foot up on the bleacher and stretched his

calf muscle, then repeated with the other leg. "Our dad didn't want a second kid. One was enough. Sawyer broke the mold, I guess."

Sawyer shook his head. He was hardly the favorite. "Yeah right. Dad barely paid attention to me."

"You still grew up with him," Cole said.

"So, your dad stuck with the older kid and ignored the new one," Jake said, his dark eyes lighting up. "Interesting. Maybe there's hope for me."

"Oh, thanks," Cole said with a lazy grin. "So are we gonna stand around talking about unpleasant crud or are we going to shoot the ball?"

Jake grinned back and got up and stole the ball, dribbling it to the hoop and shooting. He missed. Cole stole it and shot—scored.

"Can you teach me how to shoot like that?" Jake asked, chasing down the ball and bouncing it to Cole.

"Just keep working on your shot," Cole said. "Find your best spot. Shoot it hard—mean it. And pop that baby in," he added, dribbling to the hoop and demonstrating all he'd said. Of course the ball went right in. "Also helps to be six inches taller."

Jake laughed. "Good point. My dad's really tall, so I think I will be too."

Sawyer stole the ball, shot—and missed.

"So what's my brother's excuse?" Cole joked. "He's six-two."

Jake loved that. "Burn!" he said, holding up his palm for a high five to Cole, which Cole delighted in receiving.

"Ha, ha," Sawyer said. "Everyone knows I'm a baseball guy."

"Uh, they do?" Cole asked, winking at Jake, who laughed again. Cole grabbed the ball and shot again and scored. "Look, Jake, if you want some one-on-one with your dad, just the two of you, I suggest you plan a sneak attack. Works in basketball, will work at home."

"I've already talked to my dad about it. All I got back was the usual whatever about 'the baby.'"

"No—the sneak attack isn't on your dad," Cole said. "He's not in control. It's the *stepmother* you need in your court." He bounced the ball for emphasis. "What you want to do is get her to see things your way. Then she makes your case for you and you get what you want."

Now that had Jake's total attention. He moved closer to Cole. "What do I say to her?"

"You say, Daphne, or whatever her name is—"

"It's Amy."

"You say, Amy, I really miss my dad. I know he has a whole new family and everything, but I don't get to spend any time with him one-on-one anymore, and maybe we can schedule something every week just me and him. Like every Monday, from five to six, he comes here and shoots hoops with me."

Jake rolled his eyes again. "Like she'd say yes. Right."

"Maybe she will," Cole said. "Especially when she knows what's in it for her."

"What could possibly be in it for her?" Jake asked.

Cole shook his bangs out of his eyes. "Two things. One, she gets to feel like she's bringing father and son closer together. Two, you'll get off her back. And a happier Jake means a happier house. Tell her you know you've been moping around and you think spending just an hour one-on-one with your dad here would really change things for you."

Jake considered that, biting his lip on a slow nod. "They do say I sulk a lot. She might go for it."

Cole dribbled the ball, turning and bouncing the ball between his legs. "I bet she will. Ask her when you get home tonight."

Jake stole the ball. "I will," he said, shooting and scoring a three-pointer. "Yeah! My first three-pointer! The crowd goes wild!"

Cole put his hands around his mouth and made a whooshing sound.

They spent the next half hour taking turns shooting. Sawyer had no idea Cole was so good at basketball—or with kids. He made a huge impression on Jake. It also helped that he was younger than Sawyer and looked it, with his mop of hair and "whatever" attitude, which appealed to Cole. Right now, Cole was telling Jake he was a cowboy, and he had the kid rapt as he talked about the border collie who worked the ranch as an honorary cowboy, keeping the herd in line.

Cole really had a way with Jake and could do wonders here at the center.

"I went here after school every day when I was a kid," Cole said. "At first I hated it, but then I never wanted to leave. It's a good program. You come every day?"

"Yup."

"How do you get here?" Cole asked. "Bike? Biking will build up your leg muscles for fast shifts on the court."

"I walk. My bike's too small now, and my dad said

they can't replace it right now unless he can find a used one. So my dad picks me up from here. Of course 'the baby' and my stepmother are usually waiting in the car, so he can never shoot hoops with me."

"I can definitely say my dad never picked me up from anywhere, ever," Cole said. "You know, I once had the best mountain bike. Huge tires, bright orange color, water-bottle holder, back rack. That bike was the best."

Sawyer stared at Cole, thinking about the comment about their dad. There was usually bitterness in Cole's voice when he talked about Hank Wolfe. But just then, he seemed more focused on Jake—and indirectly pointing out that getting picked up by your dad was pretty cool.

"That's what I would want if I could get a bike," Jake said. "A mountain bike. Either orange or silver."

Bingo. Sawyer had been planning to get some intel from Jake about the bike he'd listed as his sole Christmas want on the Holiday Happymakers form. Thanks to Cole, he got it.

"Maybe Santa will bring you a new bike," Cole said. "You never know."

"Yeah, sure. My dad can't afford it right now since 'the baby' gets everything. I wrote one of those wish lists for the Happy Holidaymakers tree or whatever it's called but since there's no such thing as Santa, I know I'm not getting anything. My dad and Amy will probably buy me a pair of pajamas."

"I hated getting clothes as gifts as a kid," Cole agreed.

"Right?" Jake said with a knowing nod.

"Jake, time go to," Vince Russtower called from by the side door.

Cole glanced over at Vince, seemingly sizing him up. "Remember, sneak attack," he said, fist-bumping Jake.

Jake grabbed his jacket and backpack with a grin and ran over to his dad.

"Wow," Sawyer said. "You really have a way with kids. That was amazing."

Cole shrugged. "Whenever I see a sulking kid, I think of myself, I guess, and get all empathetic."

"Well, I think you made a big impression on Jake. And your advice about talking to his stepmother about needing a little time alone with his dad was a great idea."

"It should work too," Cole said. "It did on my mom, and she hated our dad. I'd tell her I was the way I was because I never got to spend any time with my dad, and she'd sigh and call him up and try to get him to make plans with me. Not that our dad ever did."

"He just wasn't a good person, Cole. It had nothing to do with you or me. He was just…limited."

Cole shrugged and scooped up the ball from where Jake had left it, scoring a three-pointer. "I hate talking about this stuff. Is it time for dinner?"

Sawyer smiled. "No, but let's go wow some other kid with your basketball skills."

Now it was Cole who smiled.

Huh. Maddie had been right again. Volunteering together had done wonders for him and Cole in just thirty minutes of throwing a ball around the makeshift court.

"Jake has it better than he knows," Cole said. "But everything's relative, isn't it? I can't imagine Dad even picking *you* up from after-school care."

"He wouldn't have. I can tell you stories about walking miles in the snow—and mean it."

Cole grinned, then his smile faded. "You still grew up with him, though. You had a dad."

"And you had a mother. I didn't."

"Not the same thing," Cole said.

"We each had one parent," Sawyer reminded him. "How is it not the same?"

"You've said that a million times. And I've told you why a million times. You got the dad, I got no dad. We didn't have the same mom. There's no equivalency."

Sawyer thought there was, but he understood what Cole meant. They shared a dad and Sawyer had lived with him, and Cole saw him maybe five times before he graduated from high school.

"Hey, look, it's another me from elementary school," Cole said, then jogged up to the boy. He said something, and then a second later, the kid who'd been sitting alone was on the court, dribbling toward the hoop.

"You should come here as often as you can," Sawyer told his brother. "This is your thing."

Cole chased down the ball for the boy and bounced it back to him. "I did okay with Jake. I might have the answers to this little dude's issues too."

Sawyer smiled. "Talk to the director about setting up a volunteer schedule. Even twice a week would mean a lot to this place."

Cole nodded. "You think that's okay, though?"

"I think what's okay?"

Cole snagged the errant basketball with his foot and bounced it back to the boy, who was now practicing dribbling. "Making time for coming here when…" He trailed off, biting his lip and looking at the floor.

Sawyer tilted his head, not sure what his brother meant, where he was going with this.

"Because of the twins, I mean," Cole said. "I'm gonna volunteer with kids twice a week when I don't even take care of my own?" There was a sheen in his eyes, and he turned away.

Oh, hell. "Hey," Sawyer said, putting an arm around Cole's shoulder. "It's all about building a life that allows for fatherhood. The job at the ranch. Coming here. Working on who you are in positive ways. How you were with Jake, how you got this other kid up and playing? That says a lot about the kind of father you can be, Cole."

"You think I could be a decent dad?" He looked away again, biting his lip.

"Of course I think you could be. You just have to show up. And by that I mean you have to make a commitment in your head, in here," he said, bumping Cole's chest, "that your sons come first. Once you do that, everything else falls into place."

"Dinnertime yet?" Cole asked again. "I think I'm all talked out."

Sawyer smiled. "Actually, yes."

"Hey, wait," Cole said. "I just realized I'll be going from conversations I don't want to have here to conversations I don't want to have at your house."

"But the twins are there, right? That's why you have to deal."

Cole bit his lip again. "Still doesn't feel real. They don't feel like mine, Sawyer. Is that weird?"

"I don't know. They feel like *mine*. Is that weird?"

Sawyer froze. They did feel like his. Which was

the opposite of what Maddie had been talking about.
Shane and Max didn't feel like nephews. They felt like
his *children*.

For a moment he couldn't move, couldn't breathe,
couldn't think.

"You okay?" Cole asked. "'Cause you don't look it."

Sawyer wasn't sure *what* he was.

"And those four red ones with the big silver bows
are for you, Max," Maddie said, pointing at the brightly
wrapped gifts under the tree. "And Shane, those four
silver ones with the red bows are yours. What could
they be? I know—and you're both going to love everything, but you can't open them until Christmas. No
peeking either."

Both babies were staring at the twinkling, beautiful tree from their carriers beside her. She was sitting
cross-legged in front of the tree, rearranging the stacks
of gifts that had grown today. She might have gone a little overboard in MacLeod's, where she insisted on paying and finally relented to an employee discount when
her mother wouldn't hear of a MacLeod paying retail.
She'd gotten clothing and books and little stuffed animals for the boys, and then she'd done some shopping
for her family in the wonderful shops on Main Street,
buying her mom a pretty necklace and new fuzzy slippers she'd hinted she wanted, and for her sister a book
on baby's first year and a gift certificate to the Wedlock
Creek Day Spa for a massage and mani-pedi. She'd gotten her dad the Irish fisherman sweater he'd been cov-
eting from the L.L.Bean catalog, and she bought a big
rawhide chew for Moose. For Cole she'd purchased a

rugged watch with a cowboy on a horse on the center dial that she thought he'd like. All that was left on her list was Sawyer, and she was having a hard time coming up with a special gift for him. Luckily she still had a few days till Christmas Eve.

"Want to hear something crazy, boys?" she asked, turning to the babies. "I don't actually know if we open our gifts on Christmas Eve or on Christmas morning. No memory of that whatsoever. I'll have to ask Sawyer what our tradition is."

She heard his key in the lock and stood up, a baby carrier in each hand. Sawyer came in with Cole behind him, and unless it was her wishful imagination, both men looked relaxed and happy.

"Wow, something smells amazing," Cole said, sniffing the air. "What's for dinner?"

Maddie tried to keep the frown off her face. She'd expected Cole to rush over to the twins, marvel at their very being, ask how their day was. But Cole's first thought had been about how good the house smelled.

Was she being judgmental? Maybe. She slid a glance over at Sawyer, who was hanging up his and Cole's jackets. If he'd noticed, too, he didn't show it.

This is all new to Cole. Being here with the twins. Time with his brother. She'd been telling Sawyer to ease up; now she'd have to apply that to herself.

"I had a craving for pasta Bolognese and garlic bread," she said. She had to admit the house did smell delicious.

"I always have a craving for that," Cole said with a smile. He looked at the twins and gave a quick smile. "And here I thought babies cried all the time." He seemed fidgety and then sat down on the sofa. "They look so content."

Aw, he's just nervous, she realized. *These are his sons, and he doesn't feel connected to them because they've been here. This has to be really hard for him.*

She brought the carriers over to the sofa and put them down, taking out Max. "This little guy was asking when you'd be over. He kept saying, 'Is it dinnertime yet?'"

Cole smiled and held out his arms. Maddie carefully transferred him. "When will they actually start talking? Six months?"

"More like around eighteen months—there's a big range. According to my mom, I said only five words until my second birthday, then I never shut up."

"Was one of those words *cake*?" Cole asked. "You're a cake fiend."

Cake… Maddie froze as a memory overtook her.

She was in the kitchen, but it was dark, and she'd opened the refrigerator to sneak a piece of the chocolate cake with incredible mocha icing from her birthday celebration earlier in the evening. She heard someone coming down the stairs quietly, as if trying not wake the house—either Sawyer or Cole, since he'd asked to crash for a couple of days.

Moose was beside her, clearly hoping for a small bit of cake, which he was not going to get, and he hadn't alerted, so she assumed it was Sawyer, though Cole had paid him a lot of attention earlier, throwing ball after ball in the yard, so Moose likely thought of him as a family member now, despite Cole having not visited in a long time.

When Cole had heard it was her birthday, he'd run out before dinner and come back with two wrapped gifts in a Wedlock Creek Books shopping bag—a biography of Eleanor Roosevelt and a pretty blank journal with a matching fancy pen. She was so touched, and she'd written in the journal before turning in for the night earlier, about how glad she was that Cole was there and how she hoped this was the start of a new beginning for him and Sawyer.

She'd been about to open the fridge for her midnight snack of a sliver—okay, fine, a big slice—of cake—when she heard a clinking sound coming from the living room.

Curious, she headed into the living room, the moonlight from the filmy living room curtains guiding her way. She was surprised to see Cole fully dressed, duffel over his shoulder. He stopped short of the living room doorway as he saw her standing there and his eyes widened.

"Sorry to surprise you—I had a cake craving." She glanced at his bag. "Don't tell me you're leaving?"

"Uh, yeah, I have to. I, uh, start a new job in the morning. I didn't want to jinx it by talking about it. You know how it is when you start a new job... You want to sleep in your own bed, have your stuff right there."

Was he lying? She couldn't tell. Sometimes she thought she knew Cole, and then sometimes she didn't.

"Well, I'm so happy you visited, Cole. It means a lot to Sawyer. Even if it doesn't show, trust me."

He seemed uncomfortable, shifting his feet. "It was good to see you, Maddie. I'm glad you liked your gifts." He started walking to the door.

"Let me go wake up Sawyer. He'll want to say good-bye."

"Nah, we have our systems," he said. "We're not goodbye types, you know?"

She smiled and hugged him. "You come back soon. And I want to hear all about the new job. Text me, okay?"

He gave her a quick smile, then rushed to the door. "Tell Sawyer sorry for me, okay?" She assumed he meant about leaving in the middle of the night without saying anything. Then he was out the door. The beater car roared to life and he peeled away.

Sawyer had come down immediately at the sound of the muffler. "Where's Cole going at one fifteen in the morning?"

"He said he had to leave, something about a new job starting tomorrow and wanting to sleep in his own bed. He said you two weren't much for goodbyes, and to tell you he was sorry."

"Sorry for what?"

Maddie shrugged. "Leaving when we thought he was going to stay another night?"

Sawyer's expression changed then. He went into the kitchen and turned on the light, then pulled off the top of the ceramic cookie jar in the shape of a bear on the counter. There weren't actually any cookies inside; it was where they kept their house cash.

She frowned. "Oh, Sawyer, really?" Why did he always think the worst of Cole?

He peered in and pulled out two twenties and a ten-dollar bill. "How nice of him to leave us fifty bucks. Should I be impressed he didn't steal it all? There was over five hundred dollars in this, Maddie."

Her shoulders slumped, and she shook her head, tears coming to her eyes. "Sawyer, when I was in here before—I came down craving more birthday cake—I heard someone come downstairs and then a clinking sound in the living room. Then I went in and Cole looked startled and uncomfortable. Did he take something else?"

"Dammit." Sawyer stalked into the living room and turned on the lights, looking around.

"Oh no," she said, her gaze on the beautiful handmade wooden box with her name carved into it that her father had made for her several birthdays ago. "I keep my grandmother's bracelet in there." The beautiful diamond tennis bracelet her nana had given her in hospice, two days before she passed. Tears stung Maddie's eyes, and she knew it was gone before Sawyer even rushed over to open the box.

"Just some silver earrings in here," he said, shaking his head. The look on Sawyer's face was one she rarely saw. Red-hot anger.

Tears fell down her cheeks and she made her way over to the sofa and cried. Sawyer sat beside her, taking her in his arms. Things had been so tense between her and her husband the past few months, and letting herself be held by him felt so good.

"He's not welcome here anymore, Maddie," Sawyer said. "No matter what. Final straw."

She nodded against his chest, crying, holding on to him.

"Maddie?" Sawyer said. "You look like you're a million miles away."

She started, realizing she'd been so lost in the memory that she'd disappeared for a while. She was standing in the same living room—just several months later. With Sawyer, staring at her with concern.

And Cole, whom she could never quite read.

"Sorry," she said. "Just thinking about something." She picked up Shane from his carrier and stroked his soft little cheek.

As she looked over at Cole, a cold snap ran up her spine. She went from trusting him to not trusting him, just like that. She thought Sawyer had been too hard on Cole? She'd been too hard on Sawyer.

Suddenly she understood why one of Sawyer's favorite phrases was *It's complicated*. It sure was.

"Cole impressed the hell out of me at the community center," Sawyer said. "Heck, I mean," he added with a smile as he took Shane from Maddie and gave him a kiss on his downy head. *Let it go. If Sawyer is able to, just let it go.* Hadn't she been the one to say it's about now and the future?

Now and the future. She wondered just what was going to happen in the coming days. Or weeks. Or even months. Would Cole take back his sons?

And would Maddie say yes to her husband's offer of ten children because of the bargain he'd made when he'd been sitting by her hospital bedside, scared to death he'd lose her?

What she would give for a crystal ball for Christmas. One that actually worked.

Ugh, maybe scratch that, she thought. If she'd learned one thing from having lost her memory, it was that it was sometimes a good thing not to know too much. A blessing in disguise.

And anyway, things between the Wolfe brothers seemed to change on a dime. Right now, they were in a good place. Did she really want to know if that was about to change?

Chapter Thirteen

"Whoa," Cole said, standing suddenly and scrunching up his face. "I think someone just went to the bathroom." He held his arms out as far as they would reach. "Maddie, can you take him?"

"Actually," she said with a smile, "why don't you change his diaper? No time like now to learn how."

"Uh, no, thanks," Cole said, giving his head a little shake to move his mop of wavy brown hair from his eyes. He gave Maddie an imploring look. *Please take him—now.*

What? Did he just say no thanks about changing his son's diaper?

"Cole, it's one of the basics of parenthood," Maddie pointed out. "Changing diapers."

"I just haven't done it before. And to be honest, I don't want to." He grinned. "I mean, who would?"

Sawyer raised an eyebrow. "Cole, no one wants to change a dirty diaper. But you just do it. Like Maddie said, it's parenthood 101."

"Jeez, okay, fine," Cole said. "Kind of embarrassing to do it in front of people, though. Am I right?"

Sawyer gave a little roll of his eyes as he handed Shane to Maddie. "Let's go in the bathroom. There's a changing station. I'll show you the ropes."

"Great," Cole said so unenthusiastically that Maddie laughed.

Not that it was funny—at all. Cole would have to grow up. Then again, maybe they were just watching that in action. That was what family was. Taking the lumps with the great times. "Right, little guy?" she asked Max, nuzzling his cheek.

Five minutes later, Sawyer and Cole emerged from the bathroom, a triumphant look on Cole's face, Shane in his arms.

"That wasn't so bad," Cole said. "I mean, it was gross, but I got through it."

Maddie smiled. *Just wait till someone projectile vomits on you*, she thought. That had happened to her at MacLeod's one day—and when it wasn't your baby hurling all over you, it wasn't quite the same. It was much, much worse.

Wait a minute! She realized she'd just remembered that about MacLeod's. Not that she wanted to remember it. But it was another memory, a little one connected to something that had just happened as if she'd just plucked it right out of her head the way anyone accessed their thoughts. A jumble of memories followed, and she wasn't sure if it was the same time frame or not. She shook her head to clear it. Her memory was definitely on its way back.

"Should we feed them before we eat dinner?" Cole asked. "I like doing that. It's kind of fun."

Maddie smiled. "Actually, they ate right before you came. I tried to wait, but, oh boy, was Shane screeching his cute little head off to let me know they were starving."

"Oh, you know what?" Cole said, looking at his watch. "MacLeod's closes in fifteen minutes, right? I called this morning to order something for them, and your mom told me it would be ready tonight by closing. I got something personalized. I'd like to go pick it up and bring them back wearing what I got them. Your mom can help me change them into it."

Maddie caught Sawyer's hesitation, but then he said, "I'll have to install their car seats in your car. And don't speed."

"Bruh, I'm driving four blocks, and I'll park right out front."

Maddie glanced out the window. No snow today, so the roads were clear. How much trouble could he get into four blocks there, four blocks back? *Wait—don't answer that*, she told herself. "It was sweet of you to order them something. I can't wait to see what it is."

"Come on," Sawyer said. "I'll show you how to properly install the seats."

Maddie didn't love the idea of Cole driving them anywhere, even four blocks, but they needed to let him spend some time with the babies on his own. "I'll put them in their winter suits while you do that. You can lay Shane down in the bassinet till you're ready for the twins."

As the brothers walked into the foyer and put on their jackets, Cole said, "Maddie, I'm not ruining your spaghetti Bolognese, am I? I should be back in twenty minutes, tops."

"No problem," she said. It needs a good twenty minutes more. "And I wasn't going to put in the garlic bread for fifteen minutes anyway."

She took their fleece buntings from the closet and got the boys into them as Sawyer headed out with Cole. Then Maddie watched from the window as they installed the rear-facing car seats. She couldn't hear Sawyer giving Cole a lecture about the seats, but she was sure he was. They came back in, each taking a baby, and went back out. Maddie followed them and stayed on the porch, feeling a bit like her heart was about to be driven away. Sawyer joined her on the porch and put his arm around her.

"See you in twenty," Cole said as he opened the driver's door. "Get your phones ready to take pics."

"Oh, wait, take their bag," Sawyer said. "Just in case. The bag always goes where they go. Just has some diapers, bottles, formula—basics if you're stuck in traffic, that kind of thing." Sawyer collected the stroller bag and handed it to Cole.

"Traffic on Main Street?" Cole said on a laugh, putting the bag in the front seat. "That's my bro, always prepared," he added to Maddie with a roll of his eyes.

That's a good thing, Cole.

They watched the noisy black car drive very slowly up to Main Street.

Sawyer smiled. "I could actually ticket him for going *that* slow."

"Makes me feel better to see him inching down the street." She turned to Sawyer and squeezed his hand, then went inside, Sawyer following. "By the way, I remembered the theft. When Cole mentioned the word *cake* before, the entire incident unlocked in my head. Happy birthday, me."

"Yeah, I didn't want to mention that added zinger when I brought it up. But it made it a lot worse for me."

"You had a good day with him. I'm glad."

"Me too. And…" He trailed off as if suddenly shy about something, and Sawyer Wolfe wasn't typically reticent with what was on his mind.

"And what?" she asked, slipping her arms around his neck.

He looked at her, putting his hands on either side of her face. He kissed her, and she felt her knees wobble. With love. With desire. With everything that had come before and everything that was to come. She loved this man.

"And I felt something shift in me, Maddie. Just a little. But something happened tonight at the community center, watching Cole with Jake, the way the two of us were talking, really talking. I felt something give way, loosen up."

Wait—was he saying what she thought he was saying? Was he ready to start a family—and not because of the bargain?

As if he could read her mind, he added, "I'm not saying I'm completely over the hump. But something feels a little different inside."

She squeezed him into a hug and held him tight, resting her head on his chest and hopefully saying more than she could manage right now. He had to know how much that meant to her—even to the Maddie she was with one-eighth of her memories. She'd take that *little different inside*. It was very likely more than Maddie-with-*all*-her-memories had ever gotten from Sawyer. It was a beautiful start.

We're on our way, she thought.

"I'll go make the garlic bread," he said, and she could tell he was feeling vulnerable and needed some space with what he felt, what he'd admitted, the newness of it all.

She glanced at the clock. "Yeah, timing seems right. He should be back in ten minutes."

As Sawyer went into the kitchen, she missed him immediately. She missed the twins too. Felt strange to be in the house with Sawyer yet without Max and Shane.

Maddie spent those ten minutes appreciating the delicious aroma of garlic bread baking in the oven and having absolutely nothing to do but anticipate eating it and the Bolognese. She didn't have to be on red alert for a crying baby or diaper duty or feed a little being. She stretched out on the couch and put her feet up on the coffee table. She'd absolutely loved being a mom to the twins this past week, but it was also nice to do nothing at all.

"I stirred the sauce," Sawyer said as he came into the room. He looked up at the big wall clock. "Garlic bread's on warm right now, but if he's not back in five minutes, we'll have to gobble it up ourselves to save it."

Maddie smiled. "I'm sure he'll be back any minute."

Except he wasn't. Not five minutes later. Or ten.

He should have been back twenty minutes ago.

Sawyer grabbed his phone. He called the store. "April, it's Sawyer. Has my brother been in?" Maddie watched him listen. "Oh, good. Yeah, that does sound very cute. Great. Thanks." He clicked his phone off. "Your mom said Cole came in with the twins and she helped him change them into their new personalized pajamas, their names across the front. He left about five minutes ago."

So why wasn't he back? Now it was five minutes after that. Then ten minutes. It was a forty-second drive from their house to MacLeod's.

Sawyer was staring at his phone. "I just texted him. No response."

Maddie grabbed her own phone and called him. "He's not picking up. Because he's driving? Maybe his car doesn't have Bluetooth?"

"It does."

Maddie's stomach twisted. "Why isn't he back?" She heard the wobble in her voice.

He grabbed his phone again and pressed in a number. "Hey, Mobley. Do me a favor and look around for a small black Chevy, muffler on the fritz." He read off the license plate. "My brother was supposed to be back a half hour ago, and I'm worried he may have gotten into an accident. Any calls come in?"

"Nope, not in the past hour. Although I did see— and hear—a very noisy little black Chevy pass me on Main Street twenty minutes ago. It was headed toward the service road, not your house, though."

A chill ran up Sawyer's spine.

"Should I go looking for him?" Mobley asked.

"I've got it. Thanks, though," he said. He pocketed his phone, his expression grim.

"What's going on?" Maddie asked.

He closed his eyes for a second. "My rookie saw Cole driving south on Main Street twenty minutes ago. Headed out of town."

"What? Why?" The panic in her voice scared her even more than she was already.

"I'm going after him," he said, grabbing his leather jacket.

"I'm coming. It's not like there are babies here requiring me to stay."

She thought she felt a chill before?

What the hell, Cole? Sawyer thought as he headed to the Johannsen ranch, which was about fifteen minutes from town. The ranch—Cole's home now—seemed the likeliest place to start to look for his brother and the twins.

"He'll be there, right?" Maddie asked, worry in her blue eyes.

"I can't imagine where else he could go."

Maddie nodded. "He'll be there. Why didn't he just come back to our house? Why'd he take off?"

"We're going to have to get that answer from Cole. I just don't know."

They drove the rest of the way in silence, Maddie staring grimly out the window, Sawyer holding the steering wheel a little too tightly. Finally, they approached the sign for the Johannsen ranch and drove up the quarter-mile dirt road until a weathered gray farmhouse and two barns came into view. There was no sign of the little black car.

The border collie Cole had been telling Jake about at the community center came running toward the car to greet them. "Hey, boy," he said, giving the dog a pat as he got out. "Have you seen my brother?"

"Dog doesn't talk, so you'd better ask me," a grizzled voice said.

Abe Johannsen came off the porch and down the three steps. Sawyer had known Abe a long time; he was a fixture in town, particularly at Dee's Diner every morning at six for breakfast. His son, Joe, ran the ranch with a cowboy or two over the years, and now that cowboy was Cole. "Chief. You say you're looking for your brother?"

Sawyer met him near the base of the steps. "Nice to see you, Abe. Yes, I'm looking for Cole. Works for you, right?" Unless Cole was lying about that.

"Sure does. Hard worker too. He impressed Joe the past two days, and Joe's a tough one to impress. Of course, we only gave him the job because we knew he was your brother."

Okay by him. And he was relieved to hear Cole was working out here. Joe was a serious dude, married to an equally serious wife named Lauren, so Cole had to be bringing his A game to impress them. Their own kids, twins, had graduated from high school the year before and had enlisted in the army, if Sawyer remembered correctly.

"Glad to hear it," Sawyer said. "Is he here?"

Abe nodded. "Heard that mess of a car pull in about forty minutes ago. Over dinner Lauren said she might just have to front Cole a car so she doesn't have to listen to that muffler. If you drive down that way two minutes, you'll come to his cabin. Oh, and say hello to Maddie for me." He gave a wave toward the car, and Maddie waved back, though she likely didn't remember Abe.

Sawyer said he would and thanked him and got back into the car, where Maddie was waiting. He reiterated what Abe had said, and the relief on her face was something to behold. He drove the two minutes and saw Cole's car, then the cabin, small, rustic and dark brown. The evergreen out front was encircled with white lights, and he wondered if Cole had done that or if Abe had.

Sawyer and Maddie walked up the two porch steps to the landing. A small wreath was hanging on the front door. Another nice touch. Sawyer knocked, then found himself holding his breath.

No answer.

Sawyer knocked again. "I know you're in there, Cole."

Footsteps sounded, and the door opened. Cole stood there, looking a bit shell-shocked. As if he couldn't believe what he'd done and was now just realizing it. Good. Sawyer and Maddie would take the twins and go home.

"It's really cold out," Maddie said to Cole. "Can we come in?"

"Oh, uh, sure." Cole opened the door wide.

The twins were in the car seats at the edge of a big oval braided rug in the main room, one asleep, the other fighting sleep and losing. Sawyer caught Shane's eyes close and stay closed.

"I have everything under control, as you see," Cole

said. "So if you were worried about my sons, they're fine."

My sons. Had Cole actually used that phrasing before?

"So last we heard, you were going to MacLeod's and would be back in twenty minutes," Sawyer prompted.

Cole bit his lip. "I took them to MacLeod's and it was a madhouse—really crowded. All these women were coming up to me and the twins and saying how adorable they were and asking their names and saying how proud I must be, and I was like, I am proud. I didn't really think about that before. I *am* proud to be their dad."

Where the hell was this going? Nowhere good.

He's their father, he reminded himself, so many emotions slamming into him he couldn't tell them apart.

Maddie moved over to the tan sofa and sat down. She patted the seat beside her, and Sawyer sat too. He knew his wife, and she was telling him not to be combative. "You should definitely be proud, Cole."

He gave her something of a smile and sat in the chair across from the sofa. "Maddie, your mom helped me change them into their new pajamas with their names, and when I saw the twins wearing them, something just connected inside me. I can't fully explain it. It's like all synapses finally fired or something."

Sawyer could explain it. It was what he'd felt at the community center when he and Cole and Jake were together. The shift inside him—something big and previously unmovable had budged. Just a little for him, but it had. Now Cole had experienced that same thing.

Which meant what, exactly?

"Maddie and I are happy to raise the twins," Sawyer

said. "I just want you to know that before we go any further here. We love these boys like they're our own. If you're not up to being a father, full speed ahead, full commitment, we'll take them home right now."

Cole glared at him. "If you want a baby so bad, Sawyer, have one."

Sawyer felt the blood rush from his face. He glanced at Maddie, who had a million emotions on her face. "This isn't about me. It's about you and the twins."

"Stop calling them the twins and start calling them my sons. That's what they are. Mine. Shane and Max are my sons and they should be with me. I should be raising them."

"You should be raising them if you're in a position to do that," Sawyer said.

"I'll make it my position," Cole snapped. "I've been thinking about this. A lot. Yeah, I've got a lot to learn. But I'll learn it. Just like I learned to change a diaper tonight. I'm not abandoning my kids the way my dad abandoned me."

Ah. There it was. What this was really about. Sawyer had no doubt that Cole wanted to raise his children—because he knew what was it was like to be cast aside. But Sawyer did doubt that Cole had the necessary tools right now for the job.

"Cole, I understand what you're saying," Maddie said. "And you should be commended. You *are* their father. But I also hear what Sawyer's saying—for one, you work full-time."

Cole crossed his arms over his chest. "So do a lot of other working parents. You've heard of nannies?"

"On your salary?" Sawyer asked.

"I'll make do. I'll figure something out. There are day cares too. I think they're supposed to be less expensive." He turned to Maddie. "Don't even think about saying you'll be the nanny for free, because I won't take advantage of you like that. I've done enough of that already."

That surprised Sawyer. He stared at Cole, once again unsure what the hell to make of this. Part of what Cole was saying was right. Yes, he should raise his kids. Yes, single working parents managed every day.

But the part that was wrong had to do with Cole—and who he was right now. Could he surprise Sawyer and become a decent parent? Maybe with a question mark? If he really tried? But Sawyer was going to be very honest with himself and say not in the near future.

"So you plan to be a full-time father," Sawyer said. "Do you really understand how much your life is going to change? Starting right now, Cole."

Cole lifted his chin. "Yes, I do."

Sawyer looked at Maddie, who seemed to be trying to hide the same worry as he was. This felt too fast, too impulsive on Cole's part. But it wasn't like Sawyer could pick up the twins and leave with them and say, *That's all nice to hear, but we'll take them home. Come visit anytime.*

As his brother had pointed out, Cole was the father here. Not Sawyer.

Sawyer stared at the twins, both asleep, so peaceful, so beautiful. He wanted to rush over and scoop them up and run. But they weren't his. And he couldn't.

He cleared his throat, his chest all tight. "Well, then. We're fifteen minutes away if you ever need help, Cole.

We're both here for you and the twins. You know that, right?"

Cole's expression softened. "Yeah, I know. I've got this. And they're easy babies. You said so yourselves."

Maddie slid a glance at him. Cole had no idea. But there was only one way for him to find out.

It's like you want him to fail, Sawyer thought, shame creeping in. That wasn't fair to Cole. Or the twins.

"Since I gave you their bag," Sawyer said, "you have what they need for the night. But stop by in the morning or your lunch break and you can pick up some of their other things. The bassinets, their favorite lullaby player, clothes."

"I'll do that," Cole said.

Maddie looked like she might burst into tears. He needed to get her out of here, but the thought of leaving Shane and Max here was almost unbearable.

"Make sure to wash their bottles out well. And the nipples too," she said. "And use ointment if you see redness or chafing during diaper changes."

Cole grimaced. "I will. I bought a book on twins' first year from MacLeod's. Actually, your mom wouldn't let me pay. For their personalized pajamas either."

"Yeah, my mom's like that," she said. "You're family."

Surprise lit Cole's eyes, and he gave her a smile.

A cry came from behind them, and Maddie popped up, then sat back down. They were off-duty from here on in.

"Well, fatherhood calls," Cole said, standing and turning toward his sons.

Sawyer sure hoped so. For the sake of two newborns Sawyer loved very much.

He and Maddie stood and inched toward the door, both of them watching Cole pick up Max and cradle him against his chest. So far, so good.

But getting himself to actually walk out the door of this little cabin and leave his heart in those carriers was another story.

"I'll be fine," Cole said. "Really. I'm a grown-up."

Sawyer nodded. "Well, like I said, you need anything, we're here for you."

"Anything," Maddie said. "Text or call anytime, day or night."

"Honestly, you two can go now," Cole said, impatience in his tone. "I think Max wants to hear the book I got him today."

Maddie linked arms with Sawyer, almost hanging on him as if she needed the help physically walking out the door. But they did leave.

When they got outside, the door closing behind him, Maddie staggered a bit, almost like she had too much to drink. But she'd barely had a half cup of eggnog a couple hours ago.

"Maddie?"

She didn't say anything.

"Maddie?" he repeated.

She hung on to him harder, as though her knees would buckle if she didn't.

She was not okay. At all. He was upset about the twins, too, but Maddie was clearly taking it even harder. Although as he looked at her, she seemed *physically* ill right now.

"Help me to the car," she barely managed to say.

He opened her door and got her inside, then closed the door and ran around to the driver's side, sliding in.

Then all hell broke loose.

Chapter Fourteen

Maddie couldn't stop shaking. But when she looked at her hands, they weren't even trembling. Or were they?

She closed her eyes, dimly aware of Sawyer calling her name.

"I'm going to call 911," he said, reaching for his phone.

"You hate pickles," she said, wonder on her face. "Your father broke his ankle, and one of his many fiancées broke up with him because he'd need too much help. MacLeod's did even better this year than last year, and that's saying something."

He stared at her, his jaw dropping open slightly. "Maddie? Your memory is completely back?"

Tears filled her eyes and she nodded five times. "I remember! I remember! Oh God, Sawyer, it's all back!"

He let out one hell of a deep breath. "You scared me to death." He wrapped his arms around her best he could with a console between them. "My Maddie is back."

He had no doubt the stress of leaving Max and Shane in that little cabin with Cole had shocked her system.

"I'm back!" she said, laughing and crying at the same time. "I know my life again! What you've been through this week, Sawyer. Wow."

"I'm not the one who got into a car accident and lost my memory," he reminded her.

"I was in blissful ignorance, though. You, on the other hand, faced just about every one of your deepest fears. Head-on. And came out stronger."

He stared at her. "What are you talking about?"

"How impossible are you—*still*?" she said, her eyes twinkling. "The babies. Your brother. All of it."

But his expression told her he didn't feel stronger. That, in fact, he might be feeling the opposite. And his least favorite adjective when it came to himself: *powerless*.

She reached for his hand. "Sawyer, I know that leaving the twins with Cole feels wrong. No matter what he professes or wants to believe about himself. But we have to give him a chance. For one, we don't have a choice. For another, we need to have faith."

"You *are* back," he said, putting his hands on either side of her face and kissing her. Gently. Then more passionately.

"I have so much to say, too much. But all I want to say is that I love you."

"I love you, too, Maddie. You know that, right? Above everything else?"

She nodded. "I know."

The sound of a baby crying—Shane, if she wasn't mistaken—pierced the quiet of the ranch, and they both turned toward the cabin, where Cole paced back and forth, an infant in his arms.

"Maybe we can just live in the car, in this clearing," he said, eyeing the windows, "so we can keep watch."

She smiled. "Well, at least we know he's doing what he's supposed to. I think we can leave feeling okay about this. Let's give him a chance," she repeated. "And go home."

If you want a baby so bad, Sawyer, have one.

If she ever lost her memory again, she had no doubt in her mind that she'd never forget the look on Sawyer's face as Cole had said that.

Sawyer had seemed shocked, but she knew him too well. He'd been *surprised.* He'd said something had shifted inside him while he'd been volunteering at the community center and Cole had joined them, that the immovable had budged. And the surprise on his face told her that something had budged just a little more.

She felt more hopeful than she ever had.

In the morning, Sawyer expected a "we're fine, stop worrying text" from Cole, but none came. Which of course likely meant they were fine. But he couldn't stop worrying. Although, granted, it was barely seven.

But didn't cowboy Cole get up with the cows and chickens? Would he be working today? Who'd watch the twins? Grizzled old Abe? That wouldn't be happening. Joe or Lauren? Maybe. But he couldn't see it.

The twins were alone in the cabin. Screaming. Hungry. Wet. They'd be all alone all day.

Sawyer started pacing in his study, trying to tell himself that was not the case. But it could be. Cole wasn't exactly full of common sense. Maybe he thought he could leave the twins for a few hours and that they'd nap the whole time.

Where was the roll of Tums? He rummaged through his desk drawer in need of antacids, popped two and dropped down onto his desk chair. Moose eyed him and came over, putting his chin on Sawyer's thigh.

"Good dog," Sawyer said, petting his majestic head.

He heard footsteps upstairs—Maddie was awake. When they'd gotten home last night, she'd called Dr. Addison's service to leave a message reporting that her memory had returned, and the doctor had called her back almost immediately. She'd told Maddie to expect to be tired that night and not to fight it, that she needed a very good night's rest.

"See, it's almost a good thing Shane and Max aren't here to wake me up three times during the night," she'd said—gently.

If you want a baby so bad, Sawyer, have one.

All night, as Maddie slept beside him, he kept replaying that over and over in his head.

But instead of *Okay, I think I will* as his answer, he just felt mired in quicksand. Because he'd left his heart in that cabin and every old bad feeling about being unable to do what he wanted, what he needed, came rushing over him.

He couldn't control his father and make him act the way he should.

He couldn't control Cole and make him act the way he should.

Cripes. It was exactly how Maddie must feel about him. *I can't control Sawyer and make him act the way he should.*

He froze. *That* was what he was doing to his beloved wife?

He closed his eyes and leaned his head back, then snapped to attention. He couldn't sit here and get sucked down into that quicksand anymore. He needed to act. He needed to know the twins weren't alone in the cabin, crying their eyes out with full diapers. And hungry.

He took the stairs two at a time and found Maddie emerging from the shower, her pretty long brown hair damp past her shoulders. He was full of vinegar, but for a moment, everything faded, and all he saw was her— his beautiful wife. His *everything.*

"I thought I'd bring some stuff for the twins over to the cabin," he said. "Want to come?"

"You're so transparent, Sawyer Wolfe," she said. "You want to check on Max and Shane. You're envisioning them all alone, aren't you?"

"Guilty. And unfortunately, it's not so far-fetched."

Her smiled faded. "No, I guess not. But I'm sure they're fine. He's either taken the day off or he asked someone to stay with them."

"Eighty-seven-year-old Abe?" Sawyer said, raising an eyebrow.

"Abe is sharp as a tack," she pointed out. "He finishes the crossword puzzle in Dee's Diner every morning before anyone else at the counter. Dee told me that herself. Maybe he skipped this morning at the diner to babysit."

"Sharp and 'wants to babysit' are worlds apart, Maddie."

She laughed. "Let's go load the SUV."

Turned out that Max and Shane had not been crying and hungry and all alone in the cabin. Joe and Lauren had offered to babysit the twins in their house for a few days until Cole could line up a nanny. They also gave him a raise. The Johannsens had both sung Cole's praises—that he was twice the worker their last hand was, that he was exceptionally strong for a lanky guy and that he was polite, particularly to the people coming to the ranch to drop off this or that.

Sawyer and Maddie had been invited into the farmhouse and to say hello to their nephews. Joe and Lauren were actually thrilled to have the little guests for a few days. Joe had played peekaboo at least ten times with the twins, and Lauren had gone from the super-serious person he'd remembered to listening to an impressive bout of baby talk and watching her cuddle each baby.

Boy, did Sawyer feel better.

"I'm so glad you suggested bringing things over," Maddie said as they drove back toward town. "I feel so much better now. This just might work out."

"You know, it just might. Cole can be capable of good surprises too. I often forget that."

Because when it mattered, Cole had taken care of business. He'd gotten a solid job with room and board. He'd found trustworthy people—his bosses—to watch the twins while he worked. He had likely put out feelers for a nanny. Especially because he could now afford to pay for said nanny.

Maybe Sawyer would go over in the next couple of days and he and Cole could look at the cabin with an eye toward sectioning off a nursery with a room divider. Maddie was the interior decorator among them, and she'd do wonders with the place to turn it from cowboy cabin to cozy family home.

"I need to ask you something," Maddie said as he turned onto Main Street. He parked in the public lot near the chapel, since they planned on doing their final shopping for their Holiday Happymakers recipients.

"I'm listening," he said, turning to face her.

"I wasn't going to push with this. But given all that's happened, Sawyer, I do want to know where things stand. Are we having ten children? Or are we starting with one—maybe two at the same time, since twins do run in the family, and we did marry at this chapel with its legend of the multiples."

He knew what she was asking—if he was ready to be a father. And not because of the bargain he'd made. But because he wanted to be.

He reached into his pocket for the roll of Tums, but then realized he'd hurt Maddie's feelings if he ate one, let alone the entire roll, which he needed right now. He wasn't really ready for this question. But it had been the question for their entire lives, not just during their marriage. Not just this past difficult year.

Sawyer looked up at the chapel, just in time to see Champ, the beagle mascot, grab half a bagel slathered in cream cheese off the sidewalk that a man had accidentally dropped. He smiled to himself, glad he could smile right now. *That's the way, Champ. Go for the stuff that people drop instead of stealing.*

He'd have to talk to Annie Potterowski again about Champ being out loose on chapel grounds. Had he not told her to keep Champ on a short leash?

Yeah, keep thinking about the beagle right now instead of the important question your wife just asked you.

"Sawyer?"

He cleared his throat. "I just feel so up in the air right now. About Cole. Things seem okay, but it's been one day."

"We need to let Cole be. And please stop making excuses, Sawyer Wolfe. I want to know if your feelings have changed about starting a family."

He turned toward her. "I promised you ten kids if that's how many you want, Mads. So yes, let's start a family." Should he feel joyful that he was saying yes and giving her what she wanted? All he felt was that he was being pulled down further into the quicksand.

If you want a baby so bad, Sawyer, have one.

Why was this so hard for him? He loved Shane and Max. Loved caring for them, having them in his house. So why was he still so...scared? That was the word for it. Not a word the chief of police would ever want applied to him.

Her face fell, and she stared straight ahead. "So nothing has changed. You bargained for my life, the universe came through and now you're making good on your end of the deal. Great. I get the family I want with a husband who really doesn't want his own children." She opened the door and got out, hurrying toward the sidewalk.

No, no, no. This was not happening. Again. Panic clawed at him, and he got out of the SUV and chased after her, but she was gone. It was now just past nine and the shops were all open and bustling with last-minute shoppers the day before Christmas Eve. He peered into a few store windows, but he didn't see her.

He pulled out his phone and texted her. Maddie, let's talk. Please.

Not right now, she texted back.

His heart so heavy he was surprised he didn't drop to the ground, Sawyer went into the grocery store and ordered a ham for his Holiday Happymakers family's wish list, then bought a $250 gift card to the store. He stopped in MacLeod's, hoping to see Maddie, but she wasn't there, and April and Jenna were both very busy with customers. He bought pajamas for the baby as the mother on the form had requested, then stopped at the toy store for the toddler's yellow dump truck, then stopped into the gift shop for the wool socks for the dad with the Wedlock Creek logo on it. He bought ten pairs of those. He added another gift card, dropped it all in a red holiday bag and brought it over to the community center.

A woman behind the desk had a big smile on her face as he handed over the bag and the ticket from his envelope, explaining about the ham. She said she'd call the family today and let them know they could pick up their ham anytime today and she'd deliver their bag of gifts herself.

Now it was time to go buy Jake's bike. There was one bike shop in town, a big store at the far end of Main Street, and the place did amazing business given all the kids in town—and the multiples. Sawyer looked around the crowded shop, and there it was. The bike of Jake Russtower's nine-year-old dreams.

A silver mountain bike with orange stripes. He had the salesclerk add a water-bottle holder and a rack for

Jake's backpack. He also bought a silver helmet. He was about to bring both over to the community center, then wondered if Cole would be volunteering tonight. How could he, though? He could bring the twins, and Sawyer could watch them while Cole volunteered. He thought about Jake being disappointed if his new superhero didn't show up, and he texted Cole.

Volunteering with me tonight at the community center? I know Jake will want to see you, so I'd be happy to hang with the twins on the bleachers for even just a half hour while you connect with Jake. Oh, and I got his bike and a cool helmet. Maybe I'll give it to him there.

Cole texted back.

I'll take you up on that offer to watch the twins while I volunteer. Oh, and you should give the bike to his dad and let his dad give Jake the bike for Christmas.

Sawyer sat back in his SUV, stunned.

Yes, that was *exactly* what he should do. Whether Vince Russtower deserved that or not—*Jake* did.

You're absolutely right, Cole. I owe you one. Didn't even think of that.

See, I'm not so bad—all the time.

Tears stung Sawyer's eyes, and he blinked them back hard. Hadn't he just said that Cole was full of surprises? He sure as hell was.

Sawyer shook his head to get hold of himself and figured he'd do an online search for Vince Russtower's number. He could probably get it from Reed Barelli's registration list from the baby-rearing class he'd taught. He was about to drive toward the PD when he saw Vince Russtower standing on Main Street. He was alone, looking in the window of Wedlock Creek Toys. That was a lucky break. But then again, it seemed the entire town was out this morning.

He approached Vince, who seemed to be looking at a remote-control helicopter in the window. Only $39.99! Holiday special! the little sign beside it said. "Hey, Vince."

The guy turned, his chin lifting as he regarded Sawyer. "My son Jake never stops talking about you and your brother."

"All good things, I hope," Sawyer said.

"A little hero worship." Vince turned back toward the helicopter. "He used to make me feel like I was his hero, but since I got married and had the baby, we haven't had as much time for each other."

"Maybe you could hang with Jake at the center even just one night a week, show up an hour early to pick him up."

"I'm actually going to be doing that every Monday and Friday from now on," he said. "Amy—my wife—suggested that. She said Jake talked to her about wanting to spend more time with me."

Whoa. Score another gold point for Cole—and Jake for following through.

"Dammit, I wish I had the money for that copter," Vince said, staring at it. "Jake would love that. But we're on a really tight budget. I got him a book he wanted and some temporary tattoos I know he'll love." The disappointment on Vince's face was heartbreaking.

"Did you know that Jake filled out a gift request on the Holiday Happymakers tree? He asked for a bike. And I happened to get the request. Bike's in my car. Helmet too."

Vince's eyes widened. "Wow. You bought him a bike?"

"My brother and I think it would mean more if it came from you—if it's *your* Christmas present to him. You be Santa."

Vince stared at him. "Why would you do that for me?" He looked down at the ground, and Sawyer knew what he was thinking: *Why would you do that for me when I stole from the multiples class—a class I got a free pass to because I had only one baby and made a stink about discrimination against single kids?*

Sawyer smiled inwardly about that. Detective Barelli had had a soft spot for Russtower since he knew him from summer camp or something like that. Sawyer hadn't been that generous or gracious. And he'd always believed Russtower had stolen the bottles and blanket. But right now, everything seemed to be about second chances. Vince seemed different to Sawyer, though it had barely been six months since that incident. The guy seemed more grounded.

"Because it's Christmas," Sawyer said. "And because you pick up Jake at the center every night and sling his backpack over your shoulder. You're there for him, Vince. Maybe not as much as he'd like, but you do have a new baby. You give him that bike. It *is* from you." Sawyer extended his hand, and Vince shook it.

"I don't know what else to say but thank you. I won't ever forget this."

A few minutes later, the bike and helmet were in Vince Russtower's car.

And something else had been transferred—to no one. Something big and heavy. Something that had been pulling him in and under.

He let out a deep breath and walked along Main Street, thinking about what he could get Maddie. It had to be something very special, like she was.

An hour later, all he had was a gold heart locket on a delicate chain that he knew she'd love. The locket opened, and she could put tiny photos of her nephews on one side and photos of her sister's babies when they arrived in February. The locket was nice, but it wasn't enough.

He walked up and down the sidewalk on both sides of Main Street, peering into stores, looking through racks and displays. And the more he tried to think of the perfect gift for his wife, the more he realized something else, something he rushed back home to tell her.

Maddie put on the Woodstock earrings Sawyer had given her for her Christmas when they were sixteen. They were incredibly goofy, but the tiny yellow Woodstocks were wearing a green-and-red Christmas sweater, and they'd always made her smile.

She needed to smile.

She'd spent the past few hours at home—thinking. And realizing that the greatest gift she could give Sawyer was to let him be who he was. To her, he was a born father, daddy of the year. But for all his reasons, he didn't want to be.

What Maddie had finally realized was that she loved Sawyer Wolfe totally and fully and always had, and Sawyer Wolfe had never wanted kids. He'd known this, stated this, never veered from this his entire life. She'd been telling herself this for seven years, but she'd never *accepted* it.

She would be one hell of an aunt. To Shane and Max. To her sister's twins. She'd babysit a lot. She'd resume volunteering with the newborns at the hospital in Brewer. And she'd do all that without bitterness, without resentment. Because what she wanted more than anything, what she'd always wanted more than anything, was Sawyer. She understood that now in a way she hadn't before.

She wouldn't be a mom. But her life would be full and rich and happy regardless.

Okay, fine, it would take more than one morning to fully accept that she was letting go of a dream. But she was at peace with her decision.

She heard Sawyer's key in the door, a sound she wanted to hear for the rest of her life. Her husband coming home.

"I have something for you," he said, holding up a shopping bag from MacLeod's. "Luckily the store was so crowded that your mom and sister didn't even see me. I was able to buy this at the register with a sales-clerk who didn't recognize me."

She tilted her head. "Why would it be a secret?"

"Because the first person I want to know about it is you."

"What is it?"

"Oh, wait, before I forget, let me put your Christmas present under the tree," he said, taking a small package from his pocket and walking into the living room. He knelt down and put the little gift on top of one of the twins' presents.

She followed him to the tree. "So this—from MacLeod's—isn't my Christmas present?" she asked.

"Nope. It's more an everyday present." He reached into the bag and pulled out a large wrapped box and handed it to her.

She gave it a little shake. "What could you possibly have gotten me from MacLeod's Multiples Emporium?"

Moose watching from his dog bed by the fireplace, she ripped open the paper, then took off the top of the box.

A drapey off-white fuzzy sweater bedazzled with Mommy to Be across the chest.

She stared at it, then looked at Sawyer. "I'm confused."

"It's a maternity sweater. When I brought it to the counter to pay, the salesclerk said she bought her sister one, and it still fits her even though she's nine months now."

"I repeat—I'm confused," Maddie said.

He took her face in his hands and looked straight into her eyes. "I've been scared, Maddie. I didn't realize *that* was the word for what was keeping me blocked about children until this morning. I always thought it was something else. A lot of something else. But it's just pure *fear*."

Hope stirred in Maddie's heart. She looked at the sweater in her hands, and tears filled her eyes. "Are you saying…"

"I'm saying I'm sorry I denied you your dream of being a mom for so long. I'm sorry I've let you down. I want to start a family, Maddie. Right now. And I don't want ten children. I just want one to start. Twins would be just fine."

She put the sweater onto the console table and threw her arm around him. "I was going to tell you that I'm okay with not having kids. That all I've ever truly wanted was you."

"I want to be a father. I think I'm actually meant to be a father. And we already both know you're meant to be a mother."

Sawyer's phone pinged. Text from Cole.

We're invited for Christmas, right?

Sawyer held up the phone to Maddie, then texted back.

You three had better come. We might have gone overboard on gifts for our nephews.

Feel free to keep doing that for the rest of their lives. Good news—I hired a nanny. We went to high school together—I had a huge crush on her. Her dad's a cop for the WCPD—Mike Bauer. You probably met Bea a million times.

Sawyer envisioned a petite, talkative redhead in her twenties with big green eyes. A little girl had gotten separated from her parents at the multiples fair last summer, and Mike Bauer's daughter had been dropping something off for her dad and comforted the girl until her parents' came, drawing pictures with her.

Sawyer texted: Sounds great. Invite her to stop by Christmas Eve.

I already did, he texted back with a laughing emoji.

Sawyer smiled and pocketed his phone. "This is going to be our best Christmas ever," he said to his wife.

Maddie kissed him. "Yup. Let's go start that family right now."

He picked her up and carried her up the stairs, Christmas wishes they hadn't even known they had all coming true.

* * * * *

MILLS & BOON

Coming next month

SNOWBOUND WITH THE HEIR
Sophie Pembroke

'Tori, sweetheart.' Jasper whispered the words against her hair, kissing her head softly as her cries lessened. 'Wake up, love.'

And she did.

Lifting her head, she blinked up at him, tears still glistening in the half-light. 'I was dreaming…' She shuddered at the memory.

'About Tyler?' he asked gently. She nodded. 'Would it help to talk about it?'

This time, she shook her head, her hair whipping around in defiance. 'I just want to forget.' She looked up at him again, and there were no tears this time. Just a new fierceness to replace the armour she'd lost. Her body shifted, and suddenly every inch of her seemed to be pressed up against him, tempting and hot and everything he'd never even dreamed of.

That was a lie. He'd dreamed about it. Often. Especially since the night they'd spent together.

But he'd never imagined it could actually happen again, not here and now.

She raised her mouth, pressing it firmly to his, her tongue sweeping out across his lower lip, and his whole body shuddered with want and desire as he kissed her back. The kiss was deep and desperate and everything he remembered about their other night together. When she pulled back, just far enough to kiss her way along his jawline, Jasper could barely remember his own name.

'Help me forget?' she murmured against his ear.

And suddenly the heat faded.

Not completely, of course. The lust she'd inspired was still coursing through his blood, and certain parts of his anatomy were absolutely on board with her plan—right now, preferably.

But his brain, that frustrating, overthinking part of him—the part that had come up with a dream of a frozen river and this woman's hand in his—had other ideas.

'Tori…' He pulled away, as far as he could without falling out of the narrow single bed. 'Tori, not like this.'

God, he wanted her. But he wanted her to want him, too. Not just forgetfulness, not just oblivion. He'd had enough of that sort of relationship himself, when he'd first moved away from Flaxstone. The kind of sex that just blocked out the world for a time, that helped him pass out and sleep without dreaming of the life he'd thought he'd had and the lies that had lurked behind it.

He didn't want that with Tori. Not this time.

Continue reading
SNOWBOUND WITH THE HEIR
Sophie Pembroke

Available next month
www.millsandboon.co.uk

COMING SOON!

We really hope you enjoyed reading this book. If you're looking for more romance, be sure to head to the shops when new books are available on

Thursday 14th November

To see which titles are coming soon, please visit

millsandboon.co.uk/nextmonth

MILLS & BOON
MEDICAL
Pulse-Racing Passion

Set your pulse racing with dedicated, delectable doctors in the high-pressure world of medicine, where emotions run high and passion, comfort and love are the best medicine.

MILLS & BOON

THE HEART OF ROMANCE

A ROMANCE FOR EVERY KIND OF READER

MODERN

Prepare to be swept off your feet by sophisticated, sexy and seductive heroes, in some of the world's most glamourous and romantic locations, where power and passion collide.
8 stories per month.

HISTORICAL

Escape with historical heroes from time gone by. Whether your passion is for wicked Regency Rakes, muscled Vikings or rugged Highlanders, awaken the romance of the past.
6 stories per month.

MEDICAL

Set your pulse racing with dedicated, delectable doctors in the high-pressure world of medicine, where emotions run high and passion, comfort and love are the best medicine.
6 stories per month.

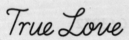

Celebrate true love with tender stories of heartfelt romance, from the rush of falling in love to the joy a new baby can bring, and a focus on the emotional heart of a relationship.
8 stories per month.

Indulge in secrets and scandal, intense drama and plenty of sizzli hot action with powerful and passionate heroes who have it all: wealth, status, good looks…everything but the right woman.
6 stories per month.

HEROES

Experience all the excitement of a gripping thriller, with an inten romance at its heart. Resourceful, true-to-life women and strong, fearless men face danger and desire - a killer combination!
8 stories per month.

DARE

Sensual love stories featuring smart, sassy heroines you'd want as best friend, and compelling intense heroes who are worthy of the
4 stories per month.

To see which titles are coming soon, please visit

millsandboon.co.uk/nextmonth

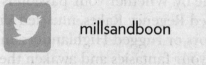

MILLS & BOON

HISTORICAL

Awaken the romance of the past

Escape with historical heroes from time gone by. Whether your passion is for wicked Regency Rakes, muscled Viking warriors or rugged Highlanders, indulge your fantasies and awaken the romance of the past.